THE COPPER BARD

A Dark Fantasy Adventure

THE SPLINTERED LAND
BOOK IV

RICHARD PARRY

The Copper Bard

The ancients don't want to stay dead. **Evanne will make them.**

Born with melodies in her veins and shadows in her blood, **she is a half-Vhemin bard who never wanted a war**. But when the ancient mountain fortress **Heaven's Gate erupts in fire and ruin**, chaos engulfs her home of Imshir. A cult has awakened something **that should have stayed buried**, and now it wants everything she loves **burned to ash**.

In the devastation's wake, **her parents are dead, her allies turn against her, and enemies from a far-off land ruled by the Raven Queen hunt her.** The only person more lost than she is **Tarragon— a fairy warrior who wants every last Vhemin dead.**

Evanne seeks justice. Tarragon seeks vengeance. But neither of them will get what they want unless they stop the true mastermind behind **Heaven's Gate's destruction**. If they fail, the land will **fall into ruin, and two realms will burn.**

Trust is a luxury she can't afford. Survival is a song she may not live to finish.

You're Awesome

You could have picked any book, but you chose this one. That means a lot.

Your support keeps independent authors like me forging ahead, writing the stories we love (and hopefully, the ones you love too). Whether you're here for the characters, the worldbuilding, or just a little escapism, thank you for being part of this journey.

You. Kick. Ass.

Roll for Narrative

WHERE WORLDBUILDING AND OVERTHINKING COLLIDE

Love stories that linger in your brain long after The End? Ever wonder why some books hit like a natural 20 and others critically fail their way into the 1-star abyss?

Join *Roll for Narrative*, my hub for sci-fi and fantasy lovers. I explore storytelling like a rogue casing a dungeon, review movies, books, and games, and dish out writing tips like a chaotic-good bard with a grudge against bad prose. No spam, just good stuff.

Join the quest:
https://rollfornarrative.parrydox.com

For my Rae, always.

Prologue

E vanne leaned closer. Her fingers hovered over the strings, lavender eyes curious. "You want to know what happened ... before?" A hint of an uncertain smile is thrown your way before she brushes back rust locks. "Okay. Here's a little something I wrote about the Saviour of Ravenswall." Another smile, but this one turns wistful. Her violet eyes catch some of that firelight between you. "Aunt Geneve? I know her. She's ... family. Let me tell you how it was."

Notes drop from the strings, clear and clean.

In the realm of Ravenswall, a tale unfolds,
Of a knight named Geneve, both brave and bold.
With a destiny entwined in fate's embrace,
She pursued a sorcerer, in a treacherous chase.

Geneve, a Tresward Knight, pure and true,
In service to gods, her loyalty she'd prove.

But her past, a mystery, before age five,
A lost memory, she struggled to revive.

WITH HER MENTOR ISRAEL AND FRIEND VERTILINE NEAR,
They embarked on a quest, shedding no tear.
Hunting Meriwether, the rogue sorcerer's name,
A destiny foretold, love and fame.

AS THEY JOURNEYED, MERIWETHER TRIED TO FLEE,
But his escape was denied by fate's decree.
Separated from comrades, they pressed on together,
Hunted by brutish Vhemin, in all kinds of weather.

IN THE WILD LANDS, THEY MET ARMITAGE, A VHEMIN ROGUE,
And ventured forth, united in their hope.
Through untamed wilderness, they dared to roam,
Until they reached the plague lands, a desolate home.

IN THE PLAGUE LANDS, A TEMPLE THEY DID FIND,
Where a dragon named Ormeon was confined.
Enslaved by Meriwether's father, cruel and unkind,
The dragon wreaked havoc, no solace to mankind.

GENEVE AND MERIWETHER, A FORMIDABLE PAIR,
Worked to free the dragon from despair.
With Israel and Vertiline, they fought for the Ravenswall's grace,
Against rogue Knight Champion Nicolette's embrace.

IN BATTLE, ISRAEL MET HIS TRAGIC END,
And Geneve's memory, a lost friend.

She learned the truth, her heart aching,
Israel, her father, a bond unbreaking.

AFTER THE BATTLE, ASSASSINS CAME WITH STEALTH,
From the Vide order, seeking the Queen's health.
Tracking them to Meriwether's father's reign,
The Lord du Reeves, they faced disdain.

CHAINING ORMEON WITH SPELLS, AN ANCIENT MIGHT,
Du Reeves led a Vhemin army, ready to fight.
Awakening Artifices, machines of old,
Their quest for power, a story told.

GENEVE FACED ORMEON, A BATTLE DIRE,
But spared the dragon from the fire.
Joining their cause, Ormeon's wings unfurled,
And Vertiline gained a metal hand, gifted from the ancient world.

TO THE NORTH, THEY JOURNEYED, MERIWETHER'S HOME,
Where his father had vanished, seeking to roam.
On this journey, Sight of Day's son was slain,
A loss that left hearts heavy with pain.

YET SIGHT OF DAY AND ARMITAGE, ONCE ENEMIES,
Became friends and brothers, their hearts at ease.
Across the seas, to Tebrani they sailed,
In the great city Imshir, a tale unveiled.

IN THE HEART OF IMSHIR, DEMONS HELD SWAY,
Possessing the people, leading them astray.

Awakening Heaven's Gate, a temple of old,
Meriwether called upon Feybrind, warriors bold.

DEMONS POSSESSED THE PEOPLE, IN A WICKED DANCE,
But Geneve, Meriwether, and their friends took a chance.
Facing Wincuf, the demon lord of night,
They battled with all their might.

IN THE FINAL BATTLE, GENEVE LOST HER ARM AND LEG,
But with golden magical light, Meriwether would beg,
He fashioned new limbs, a sacrifice made,
As he fell into the demon realm's shade.

HERESY AND DOOM FOLLOWED MERIWETHER'S SOUL,
But the gods answered, making the darkness their goal.
Cophine, Ikmae, and Khiton, standing tall,
Defeated the demons, banished them all.

GENEVE AND ORMEON, THEIR LOVE AND MIGHT,
Followed Meriwether, through the endless night.
The gate closed behind them, their fate unknown,
Leaving their friends in Imshir to mourn.

VERTILINE, ARMITAGE, AND SIGHT OF DAY,
Stood vigil in the ruins, where they lay.
Hoping for the return of their cherished friends,
For Geneve was the Saviour of Ravenswall, at a cost that never ends.

Damn Lies

The miracle arrived in the usual way.

The world didn't notice. Not immediately, and not before it was too late.

Sixteen summers passed in Imshir. The long days grew fat and heavy as the people who came to test themselves against the Platinum Warrior decided to settle down instead. This wasn't because they failed against her; it was because Vertiline was completely uninterested in cutting down imbeciles.

Imshir welcomed all who came. How could it not? Its streets were haunted and empty. It's no wonder, then, that the miracle favoured death. They called her Evanne, and this is her story.

THE MARKET'S CACOPHONY MADE EVANNE'S TEETH VIBRATE, AND the mélange of scents made her want to sneeze. Colourful tents and stalls stretched as far as she could see, each one offering wares that ranged from the mundane to the apparently magical. *I haven't seen any real magic here, except when Meefe outran the guard for selling 'lucky coins'.*

Towering over the crowd atop its hill was the school's tower, its disapproving shadow falling over Evanne. She ignored it, because the tower was just stone. What was inside it? Another matter entirely.

"I need twelve copper barons, and you need your strings fixed." Old Merle's voice carried above the market's hubbub. He fixed Evanne with a steely gaze, gnarled hand of iron on the neck of her instrument. If you called him wizened to his face, you'd get a punching, because despite washing out at the school, his right cross was epic.

"I need my strings fixed because I broke them—"

"I know. Beating someone's head in." Old Merle's sigh was one for the ages, almost loud enough to echo through the market and be heard across the seas in Or'sen. His stall was a treasure trove of musical wonders, strings of all kinds suspended like shimmering vines in the breeze. "Did your father put you up to it?"

Evanne looked at her hands. Bigger than they should be, and weaker too. Her shirt was pulled down below her elbows so the scales weren't so visible. "Dad is—"

"He's gone soft in the head, is what—"

"Let me finish!" Evanne glared. "Just because you're the only one with lute strings for a thousand klicks in any direction doesn't mean you can be a total dick."

That sat between them for a spell, just like Evanne's damaged lute. Or was it her damaged pride? Hitch touched icy fingers against her elbow. "It kind of does. Basic supply and demand economics. Merle—"

"You shut up," Evanne said.

"You what now?" Old Merle looked to the empty air at Evanne's elbow. "Is that boy troubling you again? Tell him to find someone else to haunt. No place for the likes of him around you."

"He said you could charge what you liked because you're the only one with strings. He took your side."

"I didn't—"

"Well, that's different then." Old Merle stroked his beard, trying to look upset and pleased at the same time. "How many did you say you beat down with the lute?"

Evanne sighed, putting a little Trick into it. "Here's the tale of it."

"The truth?"

"Would you like it?"

Old Merle snorted. "Would I get it even if I wanted it?"

Evanne let her fingers rest on the lute strings. Hitch hovered at her elbow, his not-quite-there face soft in the candlelight. Fui gave her a nod from his place behind the bar. He knew they'd come to listen to the Girl With Two Souls play. It was a nicer name than others she'd been given.

Fui's was a haven for the mysterious and the lost. The walls sported tapestries he claimed were gathered during the fall of Ravenswall, but Evanne didn't think battlefields went big on tapestry. It didn't matter; the tapestries worked with torches to lend a smoky tone to the air and soul alike.

The tune she struck up was merry. It suited the rich, thick air like a good whiskey might suit the throat. A crowd of regulars were littered about. These people came to Imshir from all parts of the world and preferred to leave their past in the past. Some even from far off Or'sen, paler than the local stock, all those strong arms put to better use these days than wielding swords.

The door slammed wide, six newcomers—

"Six? Even the Platinum Warrior would have trouble with that." Old Merle squinted. "Truth, now."

Evanne snorted. "She wouldn't. At six she wouldn't even break a sweat." This with a little pride, and perhaps some regret. The Storm lived in the Platinum Warrior, but not in her daughter.

"Sweat or no, you're barely competent with a lute. I can't see you—"

"Aye, *aye*. Get your hand off it, Merle." Evanne bunched her shoulders, then let out a breath. "Three it is."

THE DOOR SLAMMED WIDE, THREE NEWCOMERS CHASED IN BY HOT DESERT wind. They were cloaked in tattered, darkened robes, lending an unfriendly aura of dark foreboding. Their presence sent shivers through the room, like a sudden gust of icy wind. They wore hooded masks, concealing their faces in a veil of enigma. The tavern's regulars exchanged knowing glances, recognising that these newcomers were no ordinary travellers.

The sun had dipped from the sky but the sands outside Imshir remembered its heat well enough. Two men, one woman, all tough and gnarled in the way a hundred-year oak was. They'd come to test steel against the Platinum Warrior. See if the Storm still answered her call, or argue with the Sway that sometimes worked, other times behaved like a worn-out old nag.

Evanne didn't recognise them, but she knew their type. She fingered the brim of her hat, tugging it lower, hiding her face. She was a monster, and monsters weren't welcome in the light. That she had the voice of angels didn't matter. People didn't give her a chance to speak before they raised a blade or fist.

Hitch breathed on her neck. "It will be okay."

"Easy for you to say. You're already dead."

"Today isn't your day." He seemed confident, but the dead always did about her.

Fui gave her a little side-eye, because he wasn't paying her to talk to the air. Everyone knew the dead had nothing to say to the living, so most thought her borderline mad. Evanne wasn't mad, though. Uncle Day asked her once what she thought she was, and she'd said cursed. *He'd mock-laughed at her, despite the poetic ring her voice gave the word.*

Evanne strummed, hunching closer to the shadows beside the big hearth. It wouldn't be lit for a time yet, so it was good she didn't feel the cold like her father. All seemed well as she played, the crowd murmuring, until Fui's girl Kabili brought her mead. It was good, and took the rasp from her voice. But as she drank, her face caught light, and the three newcomers chose that moment to look over to see why the music stopped.

It might've been because they wanted to check out Kabili. Evanne had done her share of that already. They were close enough in age, but no one would want to tousle in the hay with a monster. Whatever the reason, they saw Evanne, and her face. The hard line of her jaw, the teeth that weren't quite right, and the lavender snake eyes.

Then it was shouting, and hands on weapons, and before Evanne knew it she was surrounded by six—

"THREE," CORRECTED OLD MERLE.

"Three gods, or—"

"Three people beset you," Old Merle said.

"Of course," Evanne sighed. "No room for creative license?"

"None."

EVANNE WAS SURROUNDED BY THE THREE NEW TO IMSHIR'S WONDERS AND terrors. The woman stood back a pace or two, leaving room for her steel if it came to that. Her companions weren't so patient, one hauling Evanne from her stool. "A ... Vhemin?" His tone was confused.

Hitch shrugged. "Always they go there first."

"I'm not Vhemin," Evanne said. "I'm not anything, really. You should put me down." Because for all she was half of one world and half of another, blood warm and cold, consorting with the living and the dead, she was still a sixteen-year-old young woman and weighed as much. A bushel lighter or heavier, depending on whether you used the human or Vhemin scales.

"I'll put you down when you're dead," the man hissed. Evanne didn't think his breath started out great, and the ale hadn't improved it.

"Take her outside," the other man snarled. "We'll show these Vhemin scum what attacking our homes brings. Justice!"

Fui hollered from behind the bar, but no one seemed to care. Kabili was gone, the door to the yard slamming in her wake. Gone to get aid, or just to flee. Help wouldn't arrive in time. Evanne looked to Hitch. "You said today wasn't my day!"

"Who you talking to?" The man with his hand bunched in her shirt looked at the empty air beside the hearth.

"I didn't say you would get a free ride," the ghost said. "Work a little."

Evanne kicked the man in the shins. She had no leverage, but he startled well enough. She grabbed his shirt in turn, then slammed the lute into his head. It was a sloppy blow, and if the Storm could love a half-breed like her it wouldn't have answered her call at the abortive attempt. It bought her a little more time, the man flinching, so she kneed him in the balls with enthusiasm.

He let her go, sucking air while trying to throw up, and Evanne grabbed the lute's neck with both hands, stepped to the left to avoid the chair his friend swung at her, and clobbered the man in the face.

The lute gave up at that point, pieces of delicate wood hitting the floor, strings broken. The woman drew steel, lamplight orange carried on the blade, snarled, and ... stopped. Evanne's scattergun was pointed at the woman's face.

The moment held. The woman looked at her companions, then the scattergun. "But ... that's a holy weapon."

"And I'm a holy person," Evanne nodded. "Now get out."

OLD MERLE STROKED HIS BEARD. "YOU GOT YOUR MOTHER'S scattergun?"

"And if I did?" Evanne felt the jut of her chin, but liked the look well enough.

The shopkeeper trailed his fingers over Evanne's lute. "And you've repaired the lute well enough since just last night! That Feybrind of yours—"

"He's not mine. Uncle Day is—"

"Peace!" Old Merle raised his hands in surrender. "Was but a trick of the lips. There's no owning here, and never will be, despite what might be fashionable in Or'sen." It was difficult to tell with the beard but Evanne thought Old Merle might have the hint of a smile about him. "We also haven't discussed how this is my problem. Why this lute, magnificently repaired, needs new strings that *I* must pay for."

"Ah. That's the best part of the story." Evanne hitched her hip next to the counter top. "The story alone is worth a regal."

"A regal!" The old man burst out laughing, then wiped a crinkled eye. "Let's hear it then."

Evanne raced after the thugs. The air outside was trending cooler now, and there was no Kabili in sight to heat up her thoughts. She could see the faint heat footprints left by her assailants. They were warm to her half-Vhemin eyes. She'd have satisfaction before the night was out, and damn her human weakness.

A crash from ahead. She slowed her roll, hand going to her holster. The lute hung from her other arm, neck clenched in her fingers, ready to strike. She heard muted whispers, wishing for a moment some half of her was Feybrind, so's to get the cat people's hearing.

That's Old Merle's shop. *Now what would six assailants—*

"Blessed Cophine," said Merle. "It's back to six? And when did the lute get repaired?"

"You said it yourself. Couldn't have gone down that way. Now hush." Evanne grinned her pointed teeth. "We're getting to the finale."

Perhaps three people could make noise enough for six. Evanne sneaked closer, scattergun drawn, wearing shadows as her armour. She arrived at the broken door leading to Old Merle's storage room. Evanne had no idea why three down and out hoodlums would want to hide among sealing wax and drum skins but there was no accounting for taste.

She poked her head around the jamb. Inside: the three stooges, working with a hooded lantern. The man she'd kneed in the groin looked uncomfortable as he rooted about, but the other two were in fine form. The woman held up her prize: a small box with a metal clasp. "I have it!"

Evanne squinted. She'd not seen the box before, but that wasn't surprising. Old Merle was miserly with access to his storeroom—

"'WARE," SAID OLD MERLE. "DANGEROUS GROUND."

OLD MERLE HAD NO OCCASION TO OFFER HER ACCESS TO THE ROOM, EVEN *when she'd offered to help him store the heaviest boxes inside. He wasn't here, but she was, and it was time to stop the thieves once and for all. She stood, stepped into the doorway, and shouted, "Drop it!"*

Three sets of eyes moved to her. The woman did not, in point of fact, drop the box. The thieves as one marked her drawn scattergun. The man she'd kneed in the best place ever spat. "You've only two rounds in that weapon. There are three of us, monster."

"Hard for one to carry two coffins though." Evanne considered the man, sniffed, then showed her pointed teeth. Some might call it a smile, and the darkness would keep the lie well enough. "You can go. If you like, that is."

"I can what?"

"Go. Out." She stepped aside. "That way you won't be shot and I can kill the other two and be done."

"What kind of freak show are you?" hissed the woman. "Clyde is my brother true."

"I'm out," said Clyde, who stepped past Evanne with a protective hand in front of his nethers. Evanne heard the beating of his feet as he tried to distance himself from his mistakes.

"Fuck," offered the other man.

"Not you, not ever," Evanne countered. "Now Clyde's gone, who wants it?"

The woman hurled the box at Evanne, then rushed her, sword savaging the night as it hungered from its scabbard. Evanne fired, but the box collided with the scattergun, and she hit nothing but air. The lantern's light would've night-blinded a human but her Vhemin eyes saw true. She crouched, the woman's swing missing her neck and overbalancing her assailant. Evanne straightened with gusto, putting her shoulder into the woman. As the air left her Evanne hit her upside the jaw with her lute.

Down, and out, just in time for the man to come at her with a wicked-looking knife. Evanne heard tales of Vide assassins with similar weapons: the blade black as night, sharp as sin. Where a two-baron thug would get a blade like that was anyone's guess, but the question could wait. She pivoted about the thrust, her lute clutched close. Evanne heard the cry as strings died against the steel's edge. She snarled, all bared fangs and lavender snake eyes, then head butted the man.

Her father would've been proud. The man dropped like a two-baron doxy at the wharfs with a new ship in port. And she still had one round in her gun. She holstered it, fingered broken strings, then fetched the box. "Ah," she breathed. "Now what's inside you then?"

OLD MERLE LEANED FORWARD. "A BOX, YOU SAY?"

"A box," Evanne confirmed. She swung her satchel in front of her, rummaged inside, and drew forth the box. "Here you go. Metal clasp. Sorry about the chipping on the corner. I think the scattergun caught it and—"

"Fuck me," Old Merle said. "You found my wife's old keep chest."

"Not you either, not ever," Evanne said. "The story is worth a regal, and the box two. But all I want is new strings for my lute."

The shopkeeper leaned close, beckoning her with a weathered hand. She leaned in, companionable-like, and tried on a conspiratorial smile. Old Merle stayed quiet for a spell, long enough she wondered if he'd had a stroke, then he said, "Did you break into my storeroom trying to find strings?"

"I'm shocked and offended by the allegation." Evanne kept her smile up, but it felt a heavier lift. "That's a libellous thing to say."

"It's not libel if it's true."

Hitch drifted through the counter top. "He's not wrong."

"Strings, Merle. Can I have them or not?"

The moment held, then the old man showed teeth that could've been in better condition. "You were right, Evanne. It was a regal-worthy story. For this chest, here are your strings." She snatched them as he put them down. "Break into my storeroom again and I'll have you flayed."

"Fair," Evanne admitted. "Good day, sir."

He barked a laugh. "Good day, m'lady. Try not to get killed by someone less understanding before dinner."

Chapter One

Tarragon Greyflight wanted to die. The thing stopping her was being in a very small cage, a very long way below ground, without her sword. She was a fairy and had been here for seven or eight hundred years. Keeping count was *hard* without the sun. The cage was in a prison that doubled as a laboratory, a dark space that brimmed with forgotten experiments and decaying machinery. The walls were still strong, which was part of the problem, but a little moss found root about a hundred years past and lingered still.

Helio died six months earlier. He'd been in the cage beside her, always quick with a joke, but his feeding tube stopped working. His glimmer died, and took Tarragon's will to live with it. The view didn't help; the floor was a mishmash of grime and crumbling tiles, with scattered debris from centuries-old equipment strewn about. Broken glass vials and beakers lay in jagged piles, their contents long since evaporated or turned to a sticky residue.

The two of them lived here—*if you could call it living*—since they'd been captured. Itikari sent them on a mission, and somewhere along that mission someone captured her in a net, and then: surprise! Small cage for all eternity. It sucked. Sucked! And when Helio left with his jokes, leaving a crumpled, desiccated pile in the bottom of his cage, Tarragon was left with no one to talk to.

No one to remind her of why life was worth living.

"I wish I had my sword," she said to no one in particular, but mostly to the dead woman lolling at a table three meters away. The woman had died slightly less than seven hundred years ago, because she'd been shot in the head. She had been nice enough for a sociopath, all smiles when there was no need for needles, and might have let Tarragon and Helio free.

Her name was Meredith or Mazretha, or perhaps Mawisroh. It didn't matter much, not now and not before, because she was a scientist who worked for Vehement Systems, and Vehement were the sworn enemies of Itikari. Tarragon was a spy for Itikari, and that meant she and Mefothah—*who names their baby Mefothah, anyway?*—could never be friends.

But even an enemy would be good about now, because Tarragon hadn't spoken to anyone in six months, and for seven hundred years before that, no one but Helio.

The monster who'd shot Minah—*that's it! Her name was Minah!*—had been a smaller-than-usual brute. He'd looked at the fairies, his gun, sniffed, and walked away. When Helio asked *what about us* the thug had sighed, and said, *they don't pay me enough to kill the pretty things*. And like that, he'd left them, and no one had been here since.

She rattled the bars of her cage. They were good steel, built in a way that a tiny person like Tarragon couldn't open. With enough of a run up she might use her glimmer to melt through, but the cage was only about two humans' hand spans across. If she had a sword, it'd be different.

"I'm sorry you died, Minah." The woman didn't answer of course. Her skin was long gone, the skeleton beneath a misery of off white. The lab coat remained, untouched by time, clean as if newly spun. Minah had worn glasses, an interesting affectation from a time when such things were fixable, and those glasses had slipped from her sloughing face about a hundred years into Tarragon's imprisonment to lie on the edge of the table.

The table was a bit more average than the rest. It was made of actual wood, which meant it was having a rough time of things about now. A few longhorn borers had made their way in here and spent a lovely time in the table until some long-dormant system had sprayed the room with poison. It'd made Tarragon sneeze—Helio hadn't minded it—and then the borers were dead too.

Tarragon eyed the glasses. The arms looked like they could hold an edge if you had time to carve such. They could be, in a certain light, swords. If only they were two metres closer. Ah, well. It was time for lunch anyway.

She ambled to her feeding tube, giving it a kick. It spat out a small blob of paste which tasted like peanut butter, in a good enough way, but peanut butter for seven hundred years was getting old. Tarragon munched without much interest, then stopped chewing as a thought hit her.

Borer. Table. Glasses. Feeding tube.

She wished she was a Builder like the rest of her kind. She'd not been good with metal things. Sure, better than the Bigs, but the same could be said about rock apes. Helio sucked too, which is why they were Itikari spies and not Builders. But: the feeding tube. The table! And the glasses.

She kicked the tube, got more not-quite-peanut-butter, and hurled it through the bars of the cage. It flew, trailing some of her glitterdust, to *splat* on the table.

The table didn't seem to care.

Tarragon went to work with great industry. She threw hunk after miniature hunk of paste on the table. After a puff of dust, she knew she was onto a good thing. Seven tiny heartbeats later, the table gave up its seven-hundred-year vigil, slumping in a brown eddy of wood dust.

The glasses fell. Bounced. Tumbled toward the cage.

Tarragon hurled herself toward the bars, wings aglow, arm outstretched. The cold steel against her face smelled of old metal and ill remembered hate. Her fingers clutched nothing, grasping for something, *anything*, and then: she had them.

The glasses were in her hand. Tarragon breathed for a moment, hand trembling, the glasses over a fall to the floor, then very slowly pulled them back to her. It took a bit of doing and a lot of swearing, but she got the glasses into the cage. The lenses got scratched, but she didn't need those, and Minah wouldn't care.

Tarragon flicked a wing, motes of emberbright tumbling to the floor, before slicing the arms of the glasses free. A little elbow grease, and yes, more swearing, and she had two oddly shaped plastic swords with a heart of what was probably iron.

"Here we go, Minah. Time to go." Tarragon fluttered, struck a pose, then swung with all her minute might. She gave as much of her ember as she dared to her weapons, the let's-call-them-blades glimmering with fairy might, and managed to cut through the bars of the cage in two strikes. The swords didn't like this much, sloughing apart, but their work was done.

Tarragon spent a moment or two catching her breath, because ember made her live, and she'd used most of what she had. Then she burst free of the cage and flitted to hover before Minah. The dead woman had a rectangle of plastic above her breast pocket. Tarragon stole it, then headed for the door that hadn't opened in seven hundred years.

She was free.

Chapter Two

Evanne spent time with the dead. It was what she did every morning.

She and Hitch slouched by a low stone wall that had seen better days, away from the market proper. This path was a backstreet of a backstreet, useful to know if you were the kind of person with sticky fingers and low means. It fed into a ruined square which used to be the market, before Evanne was born, and before Mama and Papa saved the world.

Living up to that legacy is a chore. The dead don't want anything from me. So, Evanne hung out with them.

For their part, the dead didn't mind. The dead didn't do much of anything except pretend to live lives they lost long ago. There, a farrier, putting shoes on a horse. Except there was no horse, not even the ghost of one. Just the farrier, a little fatter and shorter than most she'd seen, wrestling with a beast that was long gone.

Across the market, a hawker trying to sell... She squinted. "Cabbages? Flowers? What's he on about?"

"Rutabagas," Hitch suggested.

"I see." Evanne nodded. "Yes, there's no one buying, because everyone hates rutabaga. It makes sense."

"You could ask him," her ghostly companion wisped. "Try just one more. For luck."

She glared at Hitch, but couldn't tell if he glared back, which spoiled the effect. He was mostly translucent, faded and tattered at the edges like an old cloak, and let the daylight through. She didn't know what his face looked like. "They never talk. The dead have nothing to say to the living."

"Except me."

"Except you," Evanne allowed with a growl. "He's been trying to sell rutabagas forever. You'd think he'd get the idea by now."

"It's only sixteen years." Hitch walked with her toward the maybe-rutabaga seller. Or, at least she thought it was walking. He didn't have legs, not all the way down, just wafting along as if a good breeze could take him. But the weather didn't move Hitch any more than her glare. "That's when they all died. When Imshir fell, right before you were born."

She shored up beside the rutabaga hawker. "Hey! No one's buying today." She waved her arm in front of the ghost's face as he earnestly entreated someone who wasn't there anymore to buy something. It was a shame no one was left to buy. The man looked so earnest. "*I'd* buy a rutabaga from this man." Evanne rummaged in her satchel for a small notebook, and a little longer for the pencil she could never find. *If your eyes show belief, then the other person will want the same thing*, she wrote. "And I wasn't born straight away. You make it sound like Mama and Papa had a scattergun wedding."

Ignoring the remark, Hitch looked over her shoulder. "What are you writing? More Tricks?"

"Piss off," Evanne suggested, snapping the book closed. "I can give you directions, if you need them." She pointed with her pencil toward the destroyed castle at the top of the big hill overlooking the city. "Up there, maybe."

Her companion gave a shrug, drifting through the hawker as he did so. The hawker didn't seem to mind. He had nothing to say to the dead either, it seemed. "It's a long way."

Evanne tossed her Tricks notebook into the bag, slapped the flap closed, and ground out a glare. "Best you get started then."

"I'd get so lonely without the warm blanket of your sarcasm," Hitch said. "I'll stay. You need company while you restring that lute you broke robbing Old Merle last night."

"I did no such thing!" Evanne's voice rose, and she wound it back down. "I interrupted the robbers myself. You were there!"

"Hmm," said Hitch, which didn't sound like agreement. "Make sure you don't drink too deeply from your own Tricks."

The hawker stilled for a moment, then swung his ghostly gaze north. All the ghosts in the market did the same thing, a ripple spreading through them like rings in a pond. Toward the broken tower, then they yearned forward a stumble step at a time.

"Great," Hitch said. "The fucking cat."

"Uncle Day!" Evanne squealed. She broke into a run, and damn how tired she'd be at the end. Her body was as broken as her soul, but she couldn't stop her heart from wanting to see the Feybrind.

DAMN THESE LEGS. SHE STAGGERED UP THE HILL TOWARD THE school's tower, breath rasping un-Vheminlike in her chest. The lute banged against her bag, unsettling her balance, and making a difficult job harder. At least there weren't people here. The noise of the market fell behind, taking the musky smell with it. Warm wind touched her, ruffling rust locks, plastering them to her face.

Hitch ghosted by her side. "You could just walk. He'll still be there if you don't run."

"Spoken like someone with no flair for the dramatic." Evanne wheezed around a corner, hand outstretched, the pale human skin of her forearms disappearing into her shirt. Her hand left a sweat print against the old stone in a way her Vhemin scales couldn't.

"Spoken like someone who doesn't like cats," Hitch argued.

"I don't know why I keep you around." Evanne braced her hands on knees, sucking like a bellows.

"Because you can't get rid of me. Believe me, if I could leave I would have. You're slower than a wet April. Put some back into it."

Hitch bobbed encouragingly, voice turning sonorous. "You can do it. I believe in you."

"Eat a big bowl of dicks." Evanne spared Hitch another glance, then lurched on. Her breath came in fits and starts, heart hammering its uneven rhythm, but she kept going. She scampered through the Craftsman's District, ignoring the allure of Whitetower Ward in favour of the school's keep.

Ghosts she left behind. She might be slow, the unkind calling her feeble, but she at least had a pulse. The ghosts didn't like leaving where they'd anchored in death, or life, or whatever made them do what they did. But they always came for Sight of Day.

She burst through the shattered keep gate, winding up the hill toward the broken palace. It'd gone to seed since Imshir fell, but since the city was in the middle of a desert nature had not laid claim to it again. It was just busted old rocks and bad memories.

At the steps leading to the keep's main doors: a Feybrind. He sprawled on the steps, basking in the summer sun, eyes closed. His horse nosed the ground in a way that implied it was used to disappointment. She ignored the fat saddlebags, putting on a last burst of speed. "Uncle Day!"

The Feybrind opened a glorious golden eye, stretched, and stood just in time for her to cannon into him. Evanne wrapped him in a hug, panting into the cinnamon sweet smell of his fur. The cat put a hand on the back of her head, stroked her hair, then slipped free. His hands moved, Handspeak clear and slow for those without the People's speed and grace. *{You need to work on your approach. You are not stealthy at all.}*

Evanne snorted, ignoring the tell-tale twinge in her stomach at the closeness of the Feybrind. It'd always been there. Her father said he had it too, maybe worse, but said it'd been a small price to pay for *a friend worth all the Vhemin in the world.* "It's been *ages.*"

{It's been four months. I've had longer naps.} The cat half smiled, ignoring her breathlessness as if her feebleness was what everyone was like. *{Are you well? Have you managed to lose that peskersome ghost?}*

Hitch sighed. "Tell him—"

"The peskersome ghost ... *lingers,*" Evanne said. "Once, a long time ago, Imshir had an outbreak of yellow fever. It swept from Crimsonfair to Whitetower. They barricaded the streets, waiting for people to die. And they died! A lot. But the plague spread from Imshir to the surrounding lands. People died of yellow fever for years. They called it the Twenty-Year Plague. I think Hitch is my own personal Twenty-Year Plague."

"I resemble that remark," the ghost said.

Sigh of Day's wonderful golden eyes roamed. *{He's here, isn't he?}*

"Like syphilis, he never really leaves."

{I see.} The cat's eyes grew sad for a moment as he gazed down at Imshir. *{And the rest?}*

Evanne turned toward the city. The legion of ghostly forms stagger-stepped up the hill toward them, looking through her and toward the Feybrind. "Aye. They're coming."

{I wish I could tell them...} The cat's hands stilled. *{It doesn't matter.}*

"They know." Evanne clasped the Feybrind's hands in her own. "They know you're sorry. They come to thank you."

The keep held all the secrets. Evanne wasn't supposed to go in there, which was a fight her parents lost before she was five years old. The Platinum Warrior, wise to the ways of battle, set her sights on a new challenge: educating her daughter about the perils of demons. *Don't touch, hot* was the basic lesson, and Evanne was fine with that. Demons seemed to suck the joy out of just about everything, almost broke the world—*twice!*—and she lived on the edge of a city literally killed by their last invasion attempt.

She *wanted* to touch, though. The inside of Imshir's dilapidated keep-turned-school was a wonder. The walls held carvings depicting ancient battles between people, Vhemin, Feybrind, and devices too devilish to understand. A scrabbling climbing grass like ivy's buck-toothed cousin tried to scale the walls but couldn't really stick the landing. The doors they passed were heavy, still standing after years of existence.

The air was cooler here, thicker, *closer*. It smelled like nothing else, and Evanne wondered if that was dead demon musk, or something brought on by the Sway. Mama didn't use the Sway often.

Much of the wreckage of the battle *slightly* before her birth had been cleared up. No broken chandeliers littered their path. No broken benches or corpses littered the way. But no one had spared time in here dicking about putting on a fresh lick of paint, because it felt like things lived in the walls. Watched, and waited.

Mama said it kept her sharp. For Evanne? Yeah, it was all *don't touch, hot.*

So, to the keep they went, but she kept her hands (mostly) to herself. Sight of Day strolled at her side, golden eyes everywhere without seeming to be, hand a careful close distance from his sword.

Evanne cleared her throat. "They're all dead. Your sword. You won't need it."

{You tend to need a weapon when you least want to hold it.} The Feybrind relaxed a micron despite his words, Handspeak flowing like visual music. *{How is the village?}*

"It is full of petty people."

{Who did you try stealing from this time?}

"The cat's not stupid," Hitch allowed.

"I hope you both have a horrible accident." Evanne swept her rust locks aside. She liked it shoulder length, but it didn't always agree. Her mother's platinum tresses seemed to yearn for the ground. Her father's short hair didn't need cutting. She was lost somewhere in the middle ground of not quite long enough, not quite short enough. Not platinum, not dark as rock. *Muddy*, perhaps, with a heavy lacing of saffron. "Anyway, the settlement is *fine.*"

{Fine never means that.} The Feybrind paused at an intersection. Crumbling mortar salted the ground around a massive stone block that lay in the middle. *{The keep is dying, too.}*

"We had another five come to test their luck and steel against 'the Platinum Warrior'." Evanne gave a few air quotes for good measure. "So, we now have five new students."

Sight of Day half smiled at that. *{It seems the deluge is slowing. Good. News is getting out that she can't be beaten.}*

Evanne snorted. "She can be beaten. I beat her!"

{*One time! And you cheated.*}

"'There is no cheating in war'," Evanne quoted. "Who said that?"

The cat's tail lashed. {*I forget.*}

"That's right! It was *you*." She dimpled impishly at him because she knew he claimed to hate it but didn't really, pointed teeth peeking out, before leading Sight of Day past the fallen stone. The sound of steel on stone came, faint as a lark on the wind. "We're almost there."

A short walk took them closer to the sound of violence. A double door waited, closed, perhaps even sullen. Evanne shouldered it aside to take in a room about twenty meters a side, complete with pillars and high-set windows. Also, there were ten people trying to murder her mother.

The Platinum Warrior stood in the middle of the room. She didn't even have the grace to breathe hard. Vertiline held a crooked stick like a sword, her posture achingly perfect. Five people were already on the ground, one out for the count, the other four clutching various parts of their anatomy and groaning. Their metal weapons lay on the pavers, not having made a nick in the stick Vertiline held.

A woman with jet hair and a good eye shadow game turned at Evanne's entrance. Vertiline stepped forward three steps and tapped her on the back of the head with her stick. The stick glowed as she swung, hit with a *crack*, and the raccoon-faced woman dropped like a bad rhyme. "Sloppy." Vertiline's voice was cool, calm, almost ... *bored*. "Never lose your focus."

Two rushed her, and she just ... wasn't there anymore, sidestepping like she was made of air. Evanne had little skill with a blade, but she loved watching her mother play at war. She was just so damn beautiful at it. *Unlike me*, a voice in her mind said. Evanne gritted her not-quite-shark-teeth. *But I make better music.*

A door at the far end opened, a brute the size of four ordinary men striding through. Armitage wore knee-length shorts but no shirt. His muscled torso didn't wear time like most men's despite the creases holding counsel with his eyes. Vhemin didn't wrinkle like people, but snakes still aged. Evanne looked at the pale scales over his shoulder and most of his chest. An old injury. She knew it still pained him. He admitted it in the quiet of their home, but let none of it show here.

Vertiline turned, a smile warm as the sun touching her lips. No longer *bored*, but *radiant*. His voice was comforting, like warm sand beneath your feet. "You fuckers still haven't dropped her?"

Vertiline's smile dimmed somewhat at that. Four of the Platinum Warrior's opponents took that moment to rush her from behind. She swept to the side, stick blazing like a falling star, breaking a leg, arm, sword, and shield, leaving four more on the ground. Vertiline pointed her stick at Armitage. "Ho, monster. I expected you to be on my side."

"Eh," Armitage said. "Cat?"

{Brother.} Sight of Day slipped across the floor, giving a cautious berth to Vertiline's opponents. He made Armitage, slipped inside the big Vhemin's arms, and embraced him.

"Take five." Vertiline lowered her stick as Armitage disentangled from fur, heading toward her. Evanne's father grabbed her mother, kissing her deep and long.

A man with an ugly scar on his forearm took that moment to rush Vertiline's back. Armitage swung her aside with the same ease an ox would move an ant, wound up, and punched the man so hard his legs and head reversed heights. "The boss said 'take five.' She didn't mean five more beatings. Fuck off."

Vertiline brushed platinum hair back. "Love. You say the sweetest things."

{He's barely literate. This is not poetry.}

Evanne held by the door. No matter how often her mother said she was welcome here, she didn't feel at home in the world of steel. That place was for the Platinum Warrior, not Evanne the Half-Made.

Sight of Day stood next to a fallen student. *{What of these?}*

"Cartessa will be along." Vertiline tossed her makeshift weapon to the ground. The golden glow left it as it dropped, an ordinary stick again, not a weapon of the gods. "She needs to practice Sway."

Armitage grunted. "Who needs a beer?"

"It's eleven in the morning!" Vertiline linked an arm with his.

"I'm sure there's a point there, but I can't work it out." Armitage dragged Vertiline along, collecting Evanne in his other arm as they reached the door. "C'mon, kid."

Her father was big, sure. Gruff, to a certainty. Strong like the core of the world. She leaned into his cool embrace, feeling warmed by it despite his cold blood. Evanne smiled up at him, because although she was tall for a human woman, she was nothing on her father's massive size. "I'll take a beer."

Vertiline frowned across her father's chest at her. "You will—"

"Fine by me," Armitage rumbled, hefting them both along. "Beer all around."

"I don't know why I bother." The Platinum Warrior rolled her eyes, but smiled all the same.

"It's because beer is so good," Evanne offered. "And it's an excuse for an early lunch."

"We should go to Crimsonfair Farthing." Vertiline's long legs kept her at the front, hair flowing like a wave. Evanne thought she was beautiful. Always had, and always wanted to look like her. Long-legged, blonde, strong and lean, and perfect. Not a ... *half.*

{I wish you wouldn't call it that.} Uncle Day strode backward so they could see his Handspeak, making it look easy like he did with anything and everything. *{We don't know what they called it.}*

"We kinda do," Armitage argued, hefting their picnic basket. It gave a happy *clink* as bottles within huddled closer. "There are books." He waved his hand, as if *books* were like *diseases.*

"The books are in Tebrani," Evanne said. "They are so unemotional. 'This is the farrier's district' is not as poetic as Crimsonfair Farthing." She tried not to look at the bundle Sight of Day carried. It looked like, *maybe,* an axe, except the Feybrind carried it as if it weighed nothing at all. He'd tied it with a bright silk bow.

"It's less honest," Hitch offered. "The people of Imshir wanted a farrier's district, not a Crimsonfair Farthing."

"Well, they're dead, so they don't get a vote." Evanne looked down before raising a fist. "Hear me, ghosts! If you speak, I will listen!"

{The dead have nothing to say to the living.}

"Aye, aye." Evanne waved the cat's comment off. "And yet, they follow." The cluster of shades about them would have been cloying if she hadn't been used to it. *I grew up with the dead as companions.* "And yet they love you."

Vertiline sighed. "I wish I could make them ... stop. The world is saved, and yet the dead linger with their tasks not yet done."

"Fuck 'em," suggested Armitage.

"Not today, not ever," Evanne said. She ducked a good-natured cuff from her father and dodged an eye roll from her mother. "What's in the package?"

Sight of Day glanced down at the ribbon-bound bundle. *{A surprise.}*

"For me?"

{Who it's for is part of the surprise.}

They found an old broken down taverna by the waterfront. Her mother said it used to smell bad by the docks in the first days they kept vigil, but without people or fishing boats the sea reclaimed all, leaving a salty freshness. The rest of Imshir's folk didn't come into the old, dead city proper. The Platinum Warrior hadn't forbidden it, because her mother had no time for rules or ruling. But people didn't come here. Maybe it was the ghosts. While Evanne was the only one who could see them, people claimed a chill at odds with the hot desert air when the dead clustered close.

Her father's picnic basket yielded rich booty: home brewed beer for all, good crusty bread, salted pork, desert stone fruits, and a half wheel of soft cheese in a grease paper wrap. Uncle Day sliced pork while Evanne stole a plum. They four ate in companionable silence, broken by Evanne's beery burp.

"Keep it classy." Vertiline didn't sound like her heart was in it. Her gaze rested on the water, or perhaps the horizon far beyond.

Armitage shifted his weight. "You're just jealous you can't compete with Vhemin majesty."

{That was not majestic.}

The Platinum Warrior put her bottle down, then reached across the table and took Sight of Day's hands in hers. "Dear heart. Why have you come?"

The Feybrind held still for a moment, then freed his hands. *{To* *bring a gift.}* He lifted the bundle from beneath the table, handing it to Evanne. *{For you.}*

She took it, eyes wide. It was the work of a moment to free the silken cords and lift the paper. As she opened the present, she smelled sandalwood and a hint of fresh lacquer. Red-stained wood glinted under the sun. Evanne lifted her prize free, holding it up to the noonday light.

"Very nice," Armitage growled. "What is it?"

"Can't you tell, Papa?" Evanne held it to her chest. "It is love. It is distance and time brought close. It's the nearest city, holding your furthest heart. It is myth and rhyme. Rhythm and hope."

The big man looked at what she held, then to Evanne, and finally to Vertiline. "Did you understand that?"

{It is an instrument of the ancients,} Uncle Day said. *{I found it below the earth. I believe it is called a,}* and here he spelled the word letter by letter, *{guitar.}*

Vertiline looked at Evanne's guitar, then Uncle Day. "A what?"

"It's a lute with six strings, Mama."

"I thought it was love. Distance and time." She brushed back hair. "Hearts and hope."

"I *knew* you were listening." Evanne brushed the strings with human-enough fingers. The guitar didn't sound like a lute. Richer, perhaps, or sadder, as if it remembered the ancient dead, but was too polite to make a fuss.

Vertiline looked to Sight of Day. "You've been hunting again?"

The cat spread his hands. *{As you've been holding vigil, I've been seeking. It is what we do, the three of us. For our honoured friends.}*

"That's not why you're here," Armitage said. "We know Red and the runt went away. The dragon too." He scratched at the seam of his scar, Vhemin-strong fingers rasping at scale. "It's what we said we'd do. Tilly, to mind the gate. Me, to mind the people. And you, to hunt. Until the end of time, when the seas dry up, or some such."

"I will hold," Vertiline whispered. She shook herself. "But you are not hunting. You are here. And while your company warms my bitter, twisted heart in a way the sun can't, I am suspicious."

{I'm not a thief! Look to the fruits of your loins.}

"What did you steal this time?" Armitage growled.

Evanne bridled. "I think we're getting off track. This isn't about *me*. It's about Uncle Day and why he's not doing whatever the desert asks of him."

Her father gave her a flat stare before turning back to the Feybrind. "She's got a point. The thievery will keep."

"Hey! I didn't—"

"What I want to know is whether trouble's on your heels." Her father sipped beer, then leaned back. His chair gave an ominous *creak*. "About time I had an honest fight. All these new Supplicants are a waste of good air."

Vertiline leaned forward. "Rebuilding the Tresward isn't easy—"

"That shouldn't be your job, either." Armitage shrugged. "I didn't say your fancy school was a problem. It's nice to have a hobby."

"A *hobby?*" Vertiline's voice rose at least two octaves.

{*I found a place,*} Sight of Day said. {*I found a place of devils, and they are waking up.*}

Chapter Three

The problem with Bigs was their general obliviousness to anyone or anything configured differently. Take Tarragon, for instance: fun-sized. Some might say small, but only once. But she had wings, which meant she could fly. Fly through ancient corridors, or flit up stairs.

What she couldn't do was open an elevator shaft that hadn't worked in centuries. If the Bigs had put in a handy tube she could zip into, the story would be different. Or, left the stairwell unlocked. But no! The imbeciles figured anyone in here would also be Big, and thus have access to human- or Vehement Systems Architecture-sized strength.

Tarragon needed to get out, and while she'd escaped her prison, it left her flying about a subterranean facility that hadn't seen a broom, much less people, in almost a millennia. Which sucked, because there was a lot of dust, and also no one to help her get above ground to the sun. It felt suspiciously like a *larger* prison. Variation was nice, but seeing the sky would be better.

She found tools easily enough. Lots of tools! They were all for Bigs, though. She couldn't lift a hammer, let alone heft a pry bar. This last she found in the hands of a desiccated monster who might have been the same one she'd spoken to eight hundred years ago. But with the face looking all ruined like that, it was hard to tell. Tarragon flitted closer, looking into long-empty eye sockets. "It's not that you all look the same. That's racist! I just can't tell with what's left if you're ... well. *The* guy."

The dead monster didn't say anything, which Tarragon took as a good sign. She wasn't up to beating up a zombie monster. Not without her sword.

The corpse was next to a stairwell, pry bar inserted between the jamb and the door. He hadn't made it far, perhaps because the middle of his chest was missing. There was dusty brown stuff that might have once been his insides all over the door. A small hole in the monster's forehead gave the real cause of death. Tarragon knew a Vehement Systems Architecture with a sucking chest wound would, eventually, just walk it off. It's why it sucked to fight them, and why Itikari were losing this damn war. When she got up top, she'd return to the front lines, get another sword, and kill a few more monsters.

She just needed to get out. That's *all*.

If only she had a power cell. Or a Build Engine. One of those would be handy about now! But Vehement Systems didn't have Build Engines. They didn't have fairies, or dragons, or the Fey Branded. They had humans, Personates, Artifices, and their foot soldier monsters they called Vehement Systems Architectures. Which was dumb, because they weren't anything like a trellis or cantilevered arch.

"Power cells," Tarragon said. "Those might be a thing." Because while Vehement Systems didn't have Build Engines or cool fun-sized Builders to go with them, everyone needed batteries.

She did a one-eighty in the air, heading back the way she'd come. Ignoring the cafeteria—nothing edible would have come from it eight hundred years ago, let alone today—she found the lab where she'd done jail time. Tarragon ignored Minah's body, moving to her workstation. It was a ruin of metal and plastic, but within the guts of the dead machine she found her prize: a power cell. It didn't look in good condition, which was perfect.

After a few minutes kicking wires and swearing at build tolerances an apprentice would be ashamed of, she emerged with the cell. She buzzed past Minah, struggling a little with the load of the ancient battery, then headed into the corridor.

She almost dropped the power cell in surprise. At one end of the corridor was still the dead Architecture and the prize of the door. The other end? A person.

Maybe. It didn't seem likely. *Best try for the polite approach.* She put a little fairy light into her voice. "Hello!"

The person didn't respond, instead choosing to shuffle-step closer. He drew a firearm from a holster, pointing it at Tarragon. Nothing much happened, because if the elevators were out the guns were probably busted too, but it showed the fairy *intent. That person wants to kill me. Time to go.*

She turned wing and fled, heading toward the dead Architecture. No time to do this pretty, because while the person at the end of the corridor didn't have a working gun, his presence and actions told her two things. He was probably not all the way human, being dead and reanimated and all that, and he'd already tried to kill her. Given enough time, he might turn *try* into purposeful murder.

"I wish no one worked out how to bring the dead back," she told the Architecture as she fussed with his pry bar. "The dead don't like it! It's why dead soldiers suck for anything except guarding eight hundred year old mausoleums."

The monster didn't say anything. *Winning.*

Tarragon spared a glance at her foe. He'd made surprisingly good ground, now half-way toward her and picking up speed. It looked like his shuffle-step gait was turning into a shambling run, or some kind of controlled fall that running postponed for a while. She positioned her power cell beside the pry bar, then put her shoulder under it. She heaved.

Nothing but swearing. Tarragon glanced back again. The undead shambler was almost on her. She gave a small scream, squatted, and put some curry unto her lift. The pry bar *screeched*, then rose. The let's-call-it-a-zombie got its hand on her at that moment, pulling her away from the pry bar. The bar, previously stuck in the door, continued to be stuck.

The zombie hefted her toward its face. It only had one eye left, but the usual number of components in its head, like teeth, to keep it let's-call-it-living. It opened wide, about to chow down on Tarragon.

Squeak. Creak. Then, *clink* as the bar slipped down. The metal hit the power cell's contacts, shorting in a brilliant sapphire-white arc. The *bang* was concussive, more a feeling than anything Tarragon's ears could process. The base of the door fragmented, the frame split, and a piece of molten pry bar sheared through the zombie's arm holding Tarragon.

The arm and Tarragon both hit the ground. She kicked ancient rotted fingers aside, blind, flitted in a panic into what felt like a wall, and lay on the ground, stunned.

My eyes, she thought. *I should have closed my eyes. Rookie mistake.*

Her sight came back soon enough, because Itikari made her better than human normal. The zombie was sitting on its ass about five meters back, most of the front of it char black, but it struggled to rise. What held it down was the missing arm. It kept trying to use both arms, but one was on the floor by Tarragon and thus not useful anymore.

She stood, dusted herself off, and ducked through the crack in the door. She found herself in an ancient stairwell. Dark yawned below, and also above. Tarragon jumped for sky, then flew straight into a wall. Her wings were damaged, either from the power cell discharge or the zombie. They'd heal well enough, but it was going to be a long, slow climb.

Scritching came from the door. Tarragon spun, froze, then sprinted for the stairs. She was going to make it a long, *fast* climb.

GETTING ABOVE GROUND TOOK A LONG TIME. THE ANCIENT STAIRS were almost as tall each step as she was, meaning she scuffed her elbows and knees while climbing, her wings useless for anything but the merest hint of lift.

The old stone wasn't smooth, either. Grit and muck got all over her. She smelled like her prison: musty, dusty, and dry. Tarragon didn't have a timepiece handy, and since she'd left her feeding tube behind—calibrated to deliver three squares a day—she didn't have a good handle on what twenty-four hours felt like anymore. When she made it topside, it was night-time. Darkness was a good enough cover for a Big, but Tarragon's glimmer would give her away. She'd best find cover.

But: four thousand steps took a long time to get up, and she put that on her ledger for *someone will pay for that*. Once she found the war front, she'd do her part, no problem. Time for a small breather first, though, befitting a small spy.

The air, though: clean and sweet. Better than air had a right to be, and if she was a judge, better than she remembered. Perhaps someone had Built new air scrubbing technology, or the Three's Wardens had worked their Sway on the world, so Itikari's legions didn't die in droves from black lung. That might be too much to hope for, though. The Wardens didn't bend the knee or take orders. They talked to gods, and if Tarragon did the same she wouldn't have much time for front line soldiers either, no matter which side they were on.

The exit to the Vehement Systems bunker was shattered, and whatever cracked that walnut looked to have happened ages past. The doorway was a ruin, overgrown by a blackberry thicket. It explained why no one had come to rescue Tarragon. Not that she'd expected it, mind. She was a lost soldier, neither here nor there in the battle that spanned the world.

Her wings felt better, so she fluttered through the blackberries, settling on an ornery branch studded with old thorns. The flight wasn't easy, and she veered to the left a lot. She helped herself to a blackberry, breaking the fruit in both hands. The juice stained her arms, and was the best thing she'd had in her life. She did a good job of gorging herself on its friends, almost making herself sick after eating what felt like a hundred of them.

She slicked back her hair with a juice-stained hand, beaming. "Whatever was in that feeding tube sucked compared to this." She took one last berry for the road and began her trek to the front. It'd been a mere twenty klicks away when she'd been captured. Her insertion behind enemy lines had been easy, the exit less so. Her intelligence wouldn't be worth a damn anymore, but she could still use a sword like it counted.

Tarragon hop-fluttered to a rutted track. She took stock, touching the rude dirt of the roadway. "You weren't here last time I passed this way. Maintenance budgets are down, I guess?" She paused at a grinding groan from where she'd come from.

Had that zombie made it out as well? That was a problem she still couldn't solve. Least ways not with a broken wing and no sword. Her best bet was speed, finding friends, or finding enemies. It wouldn't matter, because the animated dead weren't well loved by either side. This one didn't wear a uniform, so Vehement Systems would cut it down just as well as Itikari forces.

She eyed her blackberry, then tossed it aside with a sigh to mark the ages. She headed toward the coast, because there used to be a settlement there. It was an average collection of cousin-lovers and goat herders when she'd been captured, part of the Tebrani empire but not well established. Instep? Inbred? *Imshir.* That's it. A tiny place of maybe ten houses and a latrine. If it still existed it would hold help. If not help, someone would have a bent pin she could use as a sword. At that point, the zombie and her would have a more equitable conversation.

Tarragon put on her best flight speed. It wasn't great, barely a Big's jog, because she kept listing left and hitting the ground, so she augmented her airtime with bursts of running. Tarragon hated running, because it made her sweaty and breathe hard, and neither of those was a good look for a spy. In training, her commander had said, *If you fuck up, make it look like you meant to do it. And always—Tarragon Greyflight! I'm talking to you here!—make sure you look good doing it.*

The bad road wasn't the worst part of the surrounding land. Aside from the blackberries, everything here was dead. The best the ground could produce was scrubby green-brown weeds. They poked through the sand, scree, and rock verging the roadside. This used to be the fertile lands that fed armies of both sides. A breadbasket nation, but ... there was nothing left. *Which side scorched the earth?*

She eyed sky, then did a double-take. "Cophine's summertime hat, where are the *moons?*" Because the sky was empty of them. She couldn't see Cophine's luminance, or Ikmae's grey shadow. Khiton was totally gone, but he sometimes did that anyway, hiding behind Ikmae. As far as gods of war went, Tarragon felt he was on the average side, but there weren't a lot of other options.

Her heart gave a small flutter that couldn't *possibly* be fear. She picked up speed, heading up a small rise. If she was right, just beyond was the cesspit Imshir, and someone there would have answers.

She crested the rise, and came to a hard stop. Her glimmer faded in a moment of shock. Below was a desert plain, where jagged fangs of rock jutted from the ground. Perhaps it was the earth's memory of a battle that broke the planet's spirit. Beyond ten klicks of ruinous, poisoned terrain stood a mighty walled city. It could only be Imshir, the east shoulder cozied to the waves, the west abutting desert. To the south, Heaven's Gate still stood, but the mountain fortress was still and silent. No World Engines burned with the fires of industry. The warning lights were silent.

Imshir was … *wrong.* It was *silent.* For all it could have held tens of thousands, perhaps hundreds, it was … empty. No, wait: *there.* Tarragon squinted. Near the western wall was a keep that had the amateurish look of Big construction. Beside it, huddling close as if afraid, was a small collection of lean-tos and houses. Fires burned in the night.

Fires. Burning.

Tarragon swallowed. "Did we lose?" She looked to the sky again. "Cophine? Tell me we didn't lose. The world was too important!"

Cophine didn't answer. She, like all the Bigs, was gone.

Tarragon held back a tiny sob. There *had* to be survivors. People who knew what happened.

People who would pay for the fall of the Itikari.

Chapter Four

Night in the desert was Evanne's favourite time. Her Vhemin-human body didn't always know how to deal with hot and cold, but she could put on a wrap to keep warm. It was hard to take her skin off in the sun. She couldn't sweat all over, which was both awesome and troublesome, but led to her love of the night.

She was by the docks. The wharfs had seen better days. Not many ships came to Imshir anymore. Not since there was no one to trade with except the Platinum Warrior's school. Most traders came by rutted track through the desert. It was more of a known quantity for Tebrani folk. She sniffed. "It feels like it's been a long time between pilgrims."

"You hate pilgrims," Hitch argued. "You really hate them."

"That's because they're so needy." Evanne sighed. "I like what they bring, though."

"Beer?"

"Ideas."

"Ah." The ghost gave the memory of a lopsided smile. "You mean Tricks."

"You say potato, I say Tricks." Evanne used her Vhemin-given eyes to scan around the piers. Not a hint of heat anywhere. Her father could see people's blood heat for klicks in the dark. Her range was limited, but still beat the pants off a human. "Why does no one come here?"

"The company."

"I hope you had a horrible death." Evanne drew her shawl tighter. "Maybe in an accident involving horses and a mill."

"Perhaps it's how I lost my legs. And arms." Hitch shrugged. "Or maybe we just can't see them because I'm a ghost."

"Perhaps one day you'll remember more than a sense of sarcasm." Evanne turned to the sea. She closed her eyes, breathing in the world. No gulls gave their cries at this time. Just the gentle shush of the sea eternally washing the shore. "There is so much here, Hitch. The school has books and history. The city has much just sitting there for the taking. Why does no one come?"

The ghost was silent for a while. "This city is cursed. No, hear me out. It had a tyrant demon king. Before, when the world was whole, it was scorched by one side or the other. All the long years in the middle were just arguing the finer points."

"You remember that?" Evanne spared the ghost a glance.

"I feel it's ... *right*." The wind blew through him like a sigh. "I died, Evanne. I died a long time ago. I think I died badly. And I've been walking the world ever since to find someone to put it right."

"Sucks you found me." She looked away. *No one would need the help of the Half-Made. I can't even run for more than ten steps without breathing hard.* The ghost said nothing, and she gave him a little side-eye. "Right?"

He almost reached for her, then seemed to remember he had no arms below the elbow. "Wait. What's that?"

"Don't change the subject. We're having a moment."

"The moment can wait." The ghost took a few cautious steps over the waves. "Yeah. There's a boat."

Evanne rubbed her eyes, then peered across the cold black of the sea. Sure enough, a glimmer of light bobbed a few klicks out. "It's a ship."

"What I said."

"You said 'boat'. This is a ship. Whole different thing." Evanne straightened. "Does it seem odd that we spoke of pilgrims not five minutes past, and here they are?"

"You don't like coincidences?"

"I don't like the world listening to me. *I'm* the one with Tricks. Not the universe." She scratched her chin. "Well, let's go get someone."

"Your mother hates pilgrims."

"Then we'll get Papa." Evanne headed off at a good saunter. If she couldn't run, she'd turn walking into an art form.

BY THE TIME SHE WRANGLED ARMITAGE AWAY FROM HIS CUPS AND back to the docks, the ship was a lot bigger. It was bedecked in rigging fitting royalty, except it wasn't big enough for the Raven Queen's flagship. It was like the queen's ship had a baby, and sent that to Imshir. Snapping pennants still bedecked the masts. Sailors in uniform strutted, making fast or leaning to, or whatever sailors did.

Armitage spat into the waves. "It's a funny-looking boat."

"Ship," Evanne corrected, although her heart wasn't in it. "Like it's not big enough for the job at hand."

"Oh, it's big enough all right." Armitage pointed to a man standing on the bow. "I know that fucker." His finger moved a micron to the left. "I know her, too."

Evanne peered through the gloom, wanting the human part of her eyes to work a little harder. There *was* something familiar about the couple on the prow. Almost like an old married couple, tired of their time together but too used to it to fix things for good. "Is that ... Uncle Heser?"

"'Uncle Heser' is a queen's man." Armitage frowned. "Perhaps we shouldn't tell your mother about the other."

"Aunt Barret?"

Armitage winced. "Just so."

The ship took its sweet time mooring at Imshir's broken docks. Perhaps a contributing factor was the state of the piers, rotted fangs of wood doing little to hold the ship in place. Evanne read *Light Treader* in gold leaf on the side as she pulled close. A gangplank landed with a boom and a clank, and an honour guard tramped down.

Evanne counted ten men and women wearing serious-looking black armour. She leaned close to her father. "Do they know there's no one here to fight?"

"I reckon not." Armitage rolled his shoulders, then tramped toward the guard. "Which of you fuckers is the rude one?"

The guard glanced amongst themselves. A man with a beard tinged the grey of old ash stepped forward. "Rude?"

"Must be you. The guy in charge." Armitage hitched his belt. "See, this ain't the queen's dock. It's not the queen's city. The polite thing is to ask if you can dock here."

"We have a treaty," the man stammered.

"A treaty doesn't mean shit on the sands," Armitage growled. "Blood gets spilled."

"We're ... on the docks," the officer said.

"Stop playing with the lad." Aunt Barret ambled down the gangplank, in her full Vhemin warlord attire. Armour. Axes. A robe, of all things, and Evanne didn't remember her ever holding much stock in those. Her gravelly Vhemin voice rough as new cut stone. "He doesn't know which way is up most days, especially Thursdays."

"Ma'am." The officer's face switched to an impassive mask. Evanne marvelled at the Trick, pulling out her notebook to jot it down.

"I ain't playing," Armitage said.

"Sure you are," the Vhemin warlord said. "You're playing for time, so you can work out what's going on. You're playing for fun, because watching humans squirm is *funny*. You're playing for position because your daughter is here." Her leathery face broke open in a shark-toothed grin. "How are you, love?"

"Good, Aunty." Evanne gave her best sharp-fanged leer back. It wasn't authentic Vhemin, but it was the thought that counted. "Did you bring me anything?"

Hitch gave her a sideways glance. "What is it with you and presents?"

"I brought you an idiot," Barret said. "Heser! Get on down here."

Heser the Cheg sauntered down the gangplank. He looked a little more world-worn than Evanne remembered him, but the Queensguard was made of rock, steel, and honour. World-worn but not worn out, not even close. *Another Trick to remember*. He squared his shoulders. "It's Heser the Cheg, you senile harpy."

"Been saving that for a rainy day, have you?" Barret let a little Vhemin into her voice. "Eh. It's not bad. I'll give you a point."

"Much obliged." Heser the Cheg approached Armitage. "We come on a matter of urgency."

"But without the queen," Evanne's father rumbled.

"Perhaps there is somewhere we could talk." Heser the Cheg eyed Evanne. "The queen requests—"

"She can't have my daughter." Armitage crossed his arms. "If that's what you came for, best get on your boat and fuck off right back to Or'sen."

"Uh," Heser the Cheg said.

"Don't be a fool," Barret barked. "We're here for the beer. Now where is it?"

THE BAR WAS WHAT HER FATHER CALLED *AMATEURISH* BUT ONE OF the only ones Evanne knew. The settlement on the outskirts of Imshir grew around the wreckage of a dead city because no one wanted to live inside its walls. Evanne was the only one who could see the ghosts, or admitted to it, but no one else managed to stay in there with them for long.

Some had tried. A few went mad. All left within six months of living in one of the abandoned houses within the city.

So: the bar was outside the city proper. It nestled against the western wall of Imshir, allowing a clear view to the north and south. The bar smelled of good beer and spice. Mutton was roasting somewhere, and it set her stomach growling worse than Aunt Barret. A blaze set in a brick fireplace pushed the night cool of Imshir's desert away. People talked jovially, ale and wine raising the volume, but not roughly, or angrily. The people here knew how to get along. Perhaps because there were so few of them.

Heaven's Gate still glowered at them from the south though, the big mountain silent and still. Evanne had heard about the time it birthed a small Feybrind army, but since the fighting stopped no one had been able to get inside it again.

I imagine Feybrind still in there. It's kinder than thinking there are none left.

"A penny for your thoughts," Hitch said.

"You mean a copper baron," Evanne said, somewhat absently. She craned to look over the shoulders and heads of various patrons to where her father stood at the bar. It wasn't hard to see him, but Heser the Cheg and Aunt Barret were shorter, and thus obscured by hard-drinking sorts.

"I ... sure." Hitch slung himself into the seat opposite her. He had no forearms, but he still leaned forward like they existed and held up his weight. "A copper baron seems worth one of your bright ideas."

"You're no real judge of quality. You've been dead for hundreds of years. My ideas are worth at least a regal, if not a solar." Evanne didn't know how long Hitch had been dead, but he sometimes spoke in a way that suggested he might have lived before the world broke.

"As you say, but I've no regals and not a solar neither." Hitch edged forward, perhaps shifting from forearms to prop non-existent elbows on the table. She couldn't make out his face, not really. Just lighter glowing spots where his eyes would be, or the soft line of what might've been a hard jaw. Could have just as easily been a soft jaw, but she liked her imagination to give him the benefit of the doubt. "What do you think they meant when they said the queen wanted you?"

"They didn't."

"It was implied."

"Fair enough." Evanne eyeballed a woman eyeballing her from a table not two metres distant. She had the look of the desert about her, dark skin and hard seams about her eyes holding little humour left after the water had been sucked out of her. "Problem?"

The woman considered the question, giving it a fair three or four seconds. "Do you know," and here she leaned forward, as if sharing a secret, "you are talking to yourself?"

"I'm talking to Hitch," Evanne said. "You're new?"

"I'm definitely not new. I've broken thirty five summers against my shoulders. The sun has chased me to ground more times than I can count." A sniff. "But I'm new here. To Imshir."

"Ah." Evanne shook her head. "This isn't Imshir. Or, we call it Little Imshir. To respect and honour, but not to steal. You see?"

A nod, slow as chewing dried meat. "The name tells me naught of why you speak to illusions brought by water madness on the sands. Who is Hitch?"

Evanne glanced to the bar once more, hoping for a more rapid arrival of her beer. "He is my inspiration."

"Sounds like madness," Hitch offered. "You should've led with 'spirit guide'."

"The day you guide me is the day I lead with that," Evanne countered. She turned to the woman. "I'm Evanne. They call me the Half-Made."

"Shahla. I'm a trader from north of the sands." Shahla looked into her cup. "That's not true. I'm a trader—"

"You're a trader from the world," Evanne said. "You've crossed the desert made of sand, and the other made of salt water. You live by coin, but fairly made, a goatskin swapped for wine cask, or silks for leather. You heard, even as far away as your route normally wanders, of the Platinum Warrior and the school she's building. You felt it a thing that couldn't be believed, this new Tresward, when nothing remained of the old except empty bastions and tarnished Smithsteel. So, here you sit, drinking beer as good as any, in Little Imshir, wondering why the Half-Made talks to herself, and perhaps questioning why you came."

Shahla grunted. "Close enough. You got one thing wrong, though."

"Aye?"

Shahla tossed back her drink, then stood. "I don't question why I came. I question why it took me so long to get here. A good night to you both." The weathered woman nodded close enough to where Hitch sat, then ambled away.

"Courtesy," Hitch marvelled. "She remembered I was here."

"More like, she knew who my mother is, and feared offence."

Armitage, Aunt Barret, and Heser the Cheg arrived at the table. Papa sat on Hitch which made the ghost growl, but Armitage never seemed to notice or care. He pushed a beer cup in her direction. "Don't tell your mother."

"She says the same thing about you." Evanne gave a tiny imp's glance over her cup.

The taverna door banged open, and the Platinum Warrior entered with Uncle Day on her heels. She made it to the table, eyed Evanne's cup, then Armitage. "Husband. We must talk."

"She's old enough to drink! We even agreed—"

"Priorities. Where's mine?" She raised an arch eyebrow, looking down at Armitage. Evanne marvelled at the Trick, but didn't write it down. She'd noted this one in her book in what felt eons past.

With a growl, Armitage stood and headed to the bar. Vertiline took his seat, then stared at Barret and Heser. "Sight of Day brings alarming news."

"The cat talks too much," Barret grumbled.

{I am mute. I don't talk at all.}

"Figure of speech."

{Again, with the speaking.}

The old Vhemin sighed. "Not tonight, Tilly. Tonight, we drink. We toast! We renew our bonds of friendship, so if blood is spilled, it isn't ours. Tomorrow, I will speak with you about your daughter. It's not what you think. I don't think it's what any of us think."

Vertiline put her hands on the table. "I will drink to friendship. Always and forever you are my family."

"And the rest?"

"The rest can wait for tomorrow." Vertiline shrugged. "Try not to get too drunk. I need to see if you remembered what I taught you last time."

HANGOVERS DIDN'T HAPPEN TO EVANNE, OR APPARENTLY TO THE Platinum Warrior.

Dawn broke over Imshir like a fire-touched blanket. All the residue of heaven lay across the cold sands. Evanne watched it all from her perch on the side of the broken keep. While she might not have the endurance of her father, or the grace of her mother, she had the drinking fortitude of both combined.

Last night the bottle couldn't touch her, and she watched in a kind of horrified fascination as Aunt Barret drunk herself to the floor, passing out atop Heser the Cheg whose constitution checked out after the seventh round. Her father finished at closing time, or closing time arrived when he finished, because no one closed the bar while he was still drinking, but there was one that Evanne hadn't seen leave, nor marked as fallen. *Mama.*

Vertiline was out on the sands, where it was still ice cold from the night. The sands were uneven as sands were, but Vertiline moved as if she was on the smoothest flooring. Evanne could see the flash of a blade as dawn kissed glass, and the answering golden glow of the Storm as she swept through one of the twenty-one hundred patterns. Evanne didn't know their names, because who had time for that anyway, and her lack of stamina meant she started to wheeze about step ten or so into the most basic.

But she never got tired of watching. Even at this distance, with her mother reduced to ant-like proportions, Evanne held her breath with the world, waiting for the next step.

"She's really something," Hitch offered. "I couldn't do that sober, and look at her go."

"Why did she take a horse?" Evanne sniffed her jerkin, somewhat alarmed at the beeriness of it. "She never takes a horse."

"Perhaps you should take a horse and find out."

"Horses hate me."

"Horses don't know you well enough to hate you. It's just the Vhemin blood in your veins." Hitch stood over a fifty-metre drop, standing on air, looking transparent as always.

"Papa said he had a bear." Evanne looked at the drop. "Maybe I should get a bear."

She felt Hitch wince. "Maybe you should try mastering something easier, like a rideable rabbit."

"You've no sense of adventure." Evanne reached for the coil of rope curled up like a sleeping python. "Hullo. She's coming back. Is she cutting her morning routine short?"

"Seems unlikely."

Evanne hitched the rope to a weathered gargoyle, then threw the rest over the side. She grabbed on, slithering down, the rope hissing against her gloves. Good calfskin they were, a present from Old Merle from the time she'd lied about saving his sheep. Only half her skin was Vhemin scaled, and her hands were merely soft human, unsuitable for anything much at all.

The ground approached as was its habit, and she slowed her descent like the pro she was. *I bet Mama is heading to the Gate.* So, she set her feet on the cobbles and wandered that way herself.

The gate wasn't *actually* a gate. As near as Evanne knew, it had never been a gate. The room looked like giants used it as a playpen. All that remained in the centre was a scorched ring of stones. A giant crack ran through the middle of the floor, the edges blackened by an ancient fire. Her mother came here each day, her father each night, and neither wanted to tell her about why the stone had melted or the room broke.

Sure, sure: they'd talked of dragon rider Geneve, and the Holomancer Meriwether. Geneve's dragon Ormeon, and the sacred blade Requiem she used to save the world. Evanne captured the Tricks they used when talking of their lost, even though it near broke her heart to listen. She wanted to meet Geneve, because the Knight Champion sounded like her kind of girl, or the one Evanne wanted to be. Tough like a Vhemin. Soulful like a human. Heart strong like the best of both.

But of the battle? Her parents said little at all.

The room was different today. A sandalwood trunk sat perhaps five meters away from the charred ring. Evanne hadn't seen the trunk before, and she'd broken into almost everyone's room here. It was a puzzle she was itching to unwrap, but first: honouring the dead.

Evanne approached the 'Gate', but avoided the centre. She didn't like the ring, despite how it might open a path for the lost to be found.

It made her sick to walk over it, but like her ghosts, no one else felt it at all.

Also, her ghosts never walked over the gate. Even Hitch wouldn't enter, and he didn't have legs that reached the ground. None of this stopped Evanne walking right to the edge of the scorched stone, her toes against the circle of smudged ... writing? Letters of some kind anyway. Too blurred by time and hate to make out. And there she stood, just as she did every day as the sun was highest, because while her parents held their vigil, they couldn't see ghosts.

And Evanne very much thought Geneve, Meriwether, and Ormeon were dead.

While it wasn't midday yet, now was as good as any. Evanne cleared her throat. "Hello. I'm sorry you had to leave. If you need someone to talk to when you get back, well." She scuffed her toe on the ground. "I know the dead have nothing to say to the living, but just in case, know I can see you. Hear you, if you want to speak, and tell your story, Tricks and all. I can do that for you."

"They might not be dead," Hitch said. "They might be fighting a demon army, just like—"

"I know, Hitch." Evanne turned from the old circle and eyed the trunk. "What do you suppose is in there?"

"Only one way to find out." Hitch drifted to the chest, leaning close. "Looks like someone built this thing to last."

Evanne joined him, removed her gloves, and crouched to lay human hands against it. The wood was rough, but stained well enough. Sandalwood scent rose to meet her. The lock looked big and serious, so she'd need big serious tools. She felt about in her satchel, bringing a set of jeweller's tools into the light. "Let's see if we can encourage cooperation."

"I admire how you come to a mausoleum prepared with thieve's tools."

"These are jeweller's instruments, spectre. And we're not stealing. Just a bit of ... legerdemain." Evanne squinted. "This might take a moment."

Hitch made a noise that sounded like *hmmm*, but with a little more sarcasm than thoughtfulness. She ignored him, inserting a pick alongside bent wire. The innards of the lock were big, and a little more complicated than the usual fare found even on merchant wagons. After fussing for a few moments, she was rewarded with a happy *click* and the clasp popped open.

Evanne let out a breath she didn't know she was holding, then lifted the lid. She glimpsed shining steel before a scrabble of loose stone made her jump up with a guilty start, the lid slamming closed.

Vertiline arrived through a gap in the broken wall, easing over crumbling stone like a dancer over smooth floor. She held her scabbarded blade in one hand, her metal hand out for balance. Evanne hadn't met anyone else with a metal hand, but her mother wore this one like she'd been born with it. The Platinum Warrior strolled to her, stopping near the chest. "I see you found your present."

"My ... you what now?" Evanne blinked, then looked to the chest, the popped lock, and back to her mother. "A chamber of horrors doesn't seem like a good place for a present."

Vertiline looked to the scuffs Evanne left on the gritty stone, tracks that led into the centre of the Gate, perhaps imagining Evanne talking to the dead as she often did. Then gazed back at Evanne and smiled, soft like the dawn outside, and pulled her into a hug. "You are gentler than I deserve."

Evanne breathed in her mother's scent, something like flowers and dawn rain, then disentangled herself. "I'm not gentle." She bared not-quite-shark-teeth. "I'm Vhemin tough."

"I see." Vertiline stroked her hair. "Perhaps I should have said sensitive. No, don't let that mouth run away before it knows where the goal lines are set. All who come here see char and broken stone. Only you are reluctant to step into the gate because of what you feel. But you do it anyway. You have her heart, and for that I am blessed." A cloud crossed the morning sun of her mother's face for a moment. "A blessing I do not deserve. But enough! Evanne, attend."

"I'm attending. I've been attending while you saluted the sun or whatever you did on the sands. Why so far? Why out there?" Evanne toed the chest. "And what's in here?"

Vertiline touched the chest with a gentle hand, then sat on it. "How old do you think I am?"

"Blah blah Tresward blah," Evanne said. "You've told me stories. You don't age while the Light touches you. You look thirty hungover, maybe a little younger after a good sleep."

Vertiline frowned. "Hungover? I do not—"

"And where I'm going with that is that you've looked the same age my entire life. I know I'm only sixteen summers."

"Fifteen."

"Sixteen soon enough." Evanne sniffed.

"Well, Miss Almost Sixteen, I am almost seventy years old. The Light holds my body at the point it first touched me. The Tresward don't get to die of old age." She sighed. "I was never any good at this. Israel..." She trailed off, looking over Evanne's shoulder, eyes unfocused.

Evanne turned, but there was nothing there, not even a ghost. She'd never seen Israel walk the empty streets of Imshir. She was *sure* she'd have known him, if not from her mother's stories, then from her father's. He'd told her once, *I've never known one so tall and straight. Stick up his ass, but he loved his daughter true.* "He's not there."

"I know, dear heart. He ... left." Vertiline ran a hand through ever-straight hair. "Aunt Barret and Heser the Cheg have come to take you away. No, keep your lips closed a moment longer. There are things that must be said. They will not have you. But." She pursed her lips. "The world does not bow to my Sway. The Three walk the land as people now, and no longer govern. Perhaps they never did."

"Moons I've never seen and lands I don't care about. What's in the box?"

A wry smile. "Aye, we'll get to that. I think Barret will say there's a new danger. Heser will tell a tale of a crypt none can enter but the dead."

"You've talked to him?"

"No. But it's what makes sense because you see both worlds. And thus, the gift." She stood, then opened the chest. Within, gleaming steel, so bright it was almost white. "This is my armour. It is perhaps twenty kilos. You are strong enough for it. The Vhemin within you can bear the weight of the world when the rest fails. It was made by a dear friend, a small angry man named Kytto. It is Tresward Smithsteel and will never get dirty or rust. It will look like this until the end of days."

Evanne looked at the armour, breastplate atop the rest, a burnished sun embossed on the chest plate. She knelt, fingers touching the Smithsteel. She could *feel* its age, the promises kept, the klicks walked, the *time* it held the line. Evanne closed her eyes, breathing in sandalwood and oil. "I've never seen you wear it."

"I've never needed to." Vertiline lifted the breastplate free. "Not for a long time. We settled accounts, but debts have a habit of dying badly. If we are attacked—"

"Who's going to attack us?"

"Find the armour. Put it on." Vertiline put the breastplate aside, then pulled out half a gauntlet. It'd been shorn through, the break blurred like the metal had melted. She touched it with her own metal fingers. "It will protect you against most things. I will protect you from the rest."

"I don't know how to put it on."

"Then ask your spectre. He has seen enough to know the way of war." Vertiline eyed the air where Hitch stood. "Right?"

"I can help," Hitch admitted. "I know war."

"He said he can help, but..." Evanne trailed off. "What of the school?"

"Sensitive, as I said. Or, gifted." Vertiline turned away a moment. "All supplicants came to test steel against mine. The bargain was simple: one bought, and if they fail to mark my skin they must serve. All train in the old ways, but ... Evanne, my sweet. I am a warrior, and the last of my kind. You know I am no teacher. I fear they will be insufficient."

"Don't tell them that. They'll freak." Evanne lifted a shiny greave from the box. "I don't know if this will fit."

"It will fit. I am taller than you, a little slimmer perhaps. Do not expect a glove. Expect it to keep you *alive*." Vertiline turned away. "When the fighting starts, I want you to run. Do you hear me?"

"Mama, I—"

Vertiline turned, blue eyes hard, but also wet. "Do you *hear* me?"

Evanne took a step back. For right *there* was the Platinum Warrior.

A woman who could bend the world through Sway and had not lost a fight in sixteen years. Stronger than the gods, and more faithful. And she was so very scared, not for herself, or Imshir, or for the school. Evanne saw the Trick, plain as the scales that covered part of her body. Vertiline was afraid for *Evanne*. "Mama, I hear you."

"Then promise you will run."

Evanne looked to Hitch. The ghost eased back. "Don't look at me. I'm the dead guy here."

"I will get the armour, and then I will run." Evanne looked at the chest, the gleaming Smithsteel at odds with the weight in her heart. "I promise."

"Good girl." Then the Platinum Warrior was gone, and it was just Vertiline, her mother, the one who sang her songs slightly off key to ease her to sleep. "I pray I am wrong. I pray no evil comes here. But no one has answered my prayers for sixteen years."

Chapter Five

Daytime was full of Bigs walking around doing confusing things. *Is that what shoeing a horse looks like? And why is that woman pulling a bucket out of ... by the Three, she's drawing water from a well.* Daytime sneaking wasn't a thing: it wouldn't have worked for her because while Bigs were close to blind and deaf at all times, they weren't complete nonces and she was sure to be spotted. Especially since she'd be trying not to gawk at the various peculiar things they did. So, she tried to sneak into the settlement as dusk gathered close.

She didn't see any air cars, and no dragons flew the skies. There weren't any Artifices. Personates were absent—*thank the merciful Three*—but Three's Wardens were also missing in action. Although never numerous, she saw none of their kind anywhere. Last time she'd been to Imshir it was smaller, but still had a garrison of the Wardens.

Her gimpy wing was still giving her stick, so she ambled across the dunes as best she could. The collection of sticks and tarps that made a settlement near Imshir's wall looked a good target. This time of day a few people still plied trade but were working on closing up for the day. It was a perfect time for someone small and nimble to sneak in.

Tarragon was getting hungry, which put her stomach at the top of the priority queue. She spied a stall—quite rustic as these things went —with spitted meat and flatbread. It was past a shack displaying silks, beyond one offering spices. She could smell the deliciousness from her vantage by a crumbled piece of masonry. *I've no money, but I'm a spy! Piece of cake.*

It took her all the time dusk took to change clothes into proper night to reach the stall, as she had to avoid people, horses, and wagons, none of which noticed her, which was a mixed blessing. The food stall remained open. The stall was minded by a middle-aged woman with a game leg, which was surprising as that kind of thing could be fixed at any corner clinic. *Couldn't it?*

The seller was doing a brisk trade, but only humans bought here. She saw none of the Fey Branded, and thankfully none of Vehement System's Architectures. She wasn't sure if she could take one in her current state, but after eight hundred years below ground she was itching to try.

When the bad thing happened, it did so all at once. The first part arrived when someone slammed a pot over her. The outside world vanished, replaced by the dusty interior of ... let's call it *artisanally-made* pottery. She could see rough fingerprints preserved for all time by the firing process on her makeshift prison's walls. The base of the pot, which was currently the ceiling, had a small hole in it. Her glimmer flared, and she shook her fist at the hole. "Hey!"

An eye appeared at the hole. Human enough, brown, the slight yellowing of sclera suggesting a life of hard liquor or cigarillos, but curiously without anger. What Tarragon saw was curiosity. A man's voice, rough like the rain, came to her well enough through the hole. "Hey yourself."

"I was on my way to dinner. What's the meaning of this?"

The eye blinked. "I didn't think fairies were real. I mean, I heard stories, but—"

"So you thought you'd imprison the first one you met?" Tarragon bared tiny teeth. "Didn't anyone tell you the way to a woman's heart is with kind words and a gentle manner? Imprisonment should never be your first go-to. Or even your second, come to think of it. Actually, imprisoning a woman shouldn't be on the list at all."

"These are difficult times." The man cleared his throat. "You could be a spy."

"I *am* a spy, you half-wit. The thing you want to consider is who's spy I am." Tarragon scuffed sand. "I'm Tarragon, by the way."

"Merle. Some people," and this was said with a hint of resignation, as if Merle were thinking of someone in particular, "call me Old Merle, but Merle will do just fine."

"Now we're introduced, will you let me out? Or do I have to break the very walls of this prison into dust?"

A pause. "It's a pot."

"I'm not sure what your point is." The pot lifted, and Tarragon breathed that oh-so-clean air again. She thought of glaring at Old Merle—the man *was* weathered like an old tree, with an impressive beard to boot—but a tiny tingle of happiness stopped her. "Thank you."

"I'm sorry for putting a pot on you."

"It's okay." Tarragon glimmered. "You could buy a girl dinner to make up for it."

Old Merle laughed. "Aye, that's the right approach. Your wing doesn't look good."

"I had an accident."

"Perhaps you could tell me of it while we eat." He bent, holding out his hand, and after a moment's consideration Tarragon climbed aboard. Old Merle lifted her to his shoulder, and she stepped on, enjoying the view. "What do you fancy?"

"I've been eating nutrient paste for eight hundred years. Honestly, dry bread and water would be fine."

Old Merle chuckled, and she could feel his mirth through her feet. "We can do a little better. Probably see to your wing, too. I'm no expert on fairies, but I've done some animal husbandry."

Tarragon puffed up, glitterdust falling onto Old Merle's shoulders, then let her breath out before leaning close to his ear. "You haven't seen anyone like me in a long time, have you?"

"I reckon not. Been alive forty years—"

"You look eighty!"

Teeth gritted, Old Merle steamed on. "Been alive a long time, but never seen one of the wee folk." He stamped toward the food stall Tarragon had targeted. "After we eat, perhaps I can introduce you to someone."

"I don't need a match maker. I need a sword. Perhaps four centimetres long. If you can find me a Build Engine, I can make one myself."

Old Merle waved to the food seller as he approached, then shored up at the counter. The woman glanced at him, then did a double-take at Tarragon, and switched her expression from *bored* to *astonished*. Old Merle leaned forward. "You got a problem? It's like you've never seen a fairy before."

The proprietor opened and closed her mouth. "I haven't, Merle, and that's a fact."

"Well, now you have. I'll take two flatbread with hummus and," he *hmm'd*, "whatever meat is fresh."

"It's all fresh."

"Never sell to a seller, and never lie to a liar," Old Merle said, placing a few coins on the table between them.

Tarragon watched the woman sweep them away as if by magic. "What were those?"

"Seven copper barons." Old Merle tapped his foot.

"Was it … *money?*" Tarragon was aghast. "What *happened* here?"

"Let's talk over dinner," Old Merle suggested. "I think this conversation is going to get more confusing and I'd like to have some food in me before we start."

THEY ATE AT OLD MERLE'S SHOP, WHICH CONTAINED A COLLECTION of bric-a-brac the likes of which Tarragon had never seen. The closest thing she could come up with was *antiques store*, except she didn't think anything here was an antique. Most things had been made, and badly so, by human hands. She spied one or two very precious items barred away behind the counter that had the gentle beauty of what the Fey Branded could make. A lantern with intricate filigree, and a sword that bent the meagre light about its blade. Sweet, and perfect, like their best smiths would conjure.

There was nothing here fairy-made. Nothing that took a power cell could be seen.

Old Merle spun a story while they ate at a desk piled with ledgers. A lamp that smelled of smoke and oil pooled light at her feet. Tarragon put her back against an ink well, marvelling at the rich smell of it. *How do you make ink? I don't think even the best Builders would know how. What happened here?* Merle spoke of kingdoms and war, of people and places she'd not heard of. Tebrani was still Tebrani, but ruled by a tyrant before the Saviour of Ravenswall and the Platinum Warrior saved them. Ravenswall turned out to be in Or'sen, which wasn't a place she'd ever heard of, but it sounded like an aborted attempt at saying Forsaken quite quickly. She'd called the front on the far shores Forsaken Lands. Perhaps the name stuck.

Old Merle said Tebrani was a desert, and Or'sen a garden, which was completely the wrong way around. Of the Three's Wardens, there was no sign, but Old Merle mentioned Tresward, Feybrind, and Vhemin, all of which sounded like the word hopscotch that could turn Forsaken into Or'sen. He didn't mention Itikari or Vehement Systems, not once.

She wolfed at least her body weight in food while he spoke, then let Merle eat the rest of her flatbread. She pestered him with questions like *where is the cloud city* and *is the front far*, to which he looked as confused as she felt.

I'm not just confused. I'm ... feeling ill.

After he ate, he donned a tiny monocle and set the lamp to burn brighter while he looked at her wing. "Hmm," he said, after a moment's inspection. "Your wing looks like it would be at home on a child's toy."

"I am *not* a toy."

"Peace, tiny person." Old Merle removed the monocle, then pushed himself away from the desk. He moved to the back of his store, a barge in a sea of silt. After rummaging about he returned with a small plane. "Here. Like this."

Tarragon eyed it suspiciously. The plane wasn't powered, because of *course* nothing in this Three-forsaken land used a power cell anymore. It wasn't a plane, not really, more of a glider, fixed wings and not even a rubber band for power. She sniffed. "This *thing* and I are nothing alike."

"Hmm," he said again, but louder this time. He popped the monocle back in, then dissected one of the glider's wings. He pulled out a tiny spar and a small length of thread. He placed the spar against her wing and bound it in place with the thread. "Try that."

She gave an experimental flutter. "It's not bad."

"Not bad?"

"I mean, it'll probably hold, but I won't be able to use my Strike Force or—"

"Are you planning to kill someone here?" Old Merle bent, bringing his massive face closer to her tiny one. "I don't know what a Strike Force is, but Imshir is a city with enough dead lining its streets. We are peaceful, fairy."

Tarragon crossed her arms. "That's what they all say."

"I really must introduce you to Ev—" A shrill cry broke across whoever Old Merle felt she should be introduced to. Tarragon knew the flavour of that sound. Fear, overlaid with a healthy salting of denial, all from a woman's throat unused to such endeavours.

Then, silence. She and Old Merle looked at the door to his shop. Then Tarragon gave him a glance. "Do you have a sword?"

"Not a small one."

"It's not small, it's perfectly sized for... Oh, never *mind*." She buzzed from the table, glimmerdust sparkling as she rose. "Thank you for the help. I'll go fix whatever that," she jerked a thumb at the door, "was."

Old Merle smoothed his shirt. "No. Thank *you*."

"What for? You bought me dinner and fixed my wing." Tarragon looked at her feet, because even hovering she felt abashed. *I need to regain some control of this Big. They have too much attitude as it is.* "To be fair, it *was* after you tried to imprison me."

"Aye, and that's fair. The thanks is for letting me see something truly wonderful again. You." He extended a giant finger to bop her nose, gentle in all the ways that mattered. "Now go. Go! I will find a bigger sword and join you in a moment."

Tarragon flitted around his head, her gimpy wing holding well enough but with that buzz. It threatened to set her teeth on edge. "As you wish." Then she sped for the door, jinked, and passed into the night through an open shutter.

Free, *and* full of good food. Now, to kill something that deserved it.

THERE WERE A LOT OF BIGS RUNNING AROUND AND GETTING underfoot, which was more or less their standard mode of operation. Tarragon grabbed a little sky, getting above the roofline of the shanty-town outside Imshir. A little more air beneath her let her see that while Bigs ran into each other, they did so more or less away from the part of the settlement she'd entered through.

"I don't like coincidences," she said to the stars, who said nothing back.

Tarragon set off, eyes peeled for anything she could use as a weapon. Heck, she could use a needle if there was one, but around here it looked like no one knew how to make anything sharp and fun-sized.

She reached the edge of the settlement, which was now blessedly free of Bigs, except for one. The Big looked familiar in a bad way: it was the undead guardian she'd escaped from yesterday. *No, be honest: I freed it.* She gritted her teeth. It was a problem that wouldn't keep. Descending, she put a little cayenne into her flight path, the buzz from her wings getting louder, her glimmer brightening. She felt the heat within, the starlight that gave her form burning ever brighter, and then...

A Vehement Systems Architecture. Or, as Merle called them: a Vhemin! She saw the monster, one of the largest she'd ever seen, and perhaps older than any other. If he was a human she'd have said he was mid forties, but she wasn't great at measuring the age of the enemy. The monster lumbered at the undead guardian, a mattock held in both hands, ready for business.

Undead horror or living horror? The choice was simple. The

undead was a *situational* horror, but the Vhemin was the *enemy*. And he was here, at the front! Time to get to work.

She tilted her descent, angling toward the monster. The buzz must have alerted him, because he turned snake eyes in her direction, stumbled, and that's what caused her to miss slamming into him with her glimmerfire. Tarragon went right past, wings beating the air for purchase, glimmer raining hot starfire on the dusty sand below.

The Vhemin tripped and hit the dirt, mattock tumbling free. She cruised around for another pass, sizing the creature up. *Definitely the biggest one I've seen. Overexcited pituitary gland, perhaps.* The undead creature had noticed them and changed course, but was headed for her, not the monster, which cinched it. They were in league, and the Vhemin had to die. She squinting, coming down for another slam.

"A fucking fairy," the monster grated, voice deep like an anvil in conversation. "Say, do you know—"

Whatever Tarragon might have known was lost as she impacted the Vhemin right in the torso, centre mass. Before she hit, she noted how this monster had deep scarring across his chest, like he was a gingerbread man and someone had eaten his shoulder, but—because their horrible kind were difficult to kill—had grown back. Then, *boom*, she set the monster on fire.

She bounced off, hitting the ground, her new wing brace popping free. Tarragon was stunned, bumped her coccyx, and felt sick. The undead horror's eyes widened, perhaps with delight, but more likely some memory from beyond the grave, and it lumbered toward her.

The Vhemin roared, slapping his massive chest with both hands, trying to beat the flames out. The zombie wandered right past him, lurching toward Tarragon, hand outstretched.

A sound like heaven's air raid siren went off. The air shook, the sound so loud Tarragon's teeth vibrated. The zombie paused, looking behind Tarragon. She took the moment to scramble back like a crab, then risked a glance at Heaven's Gate.

The mountain fortress's top opened, just like it should when presented with an undead enemy, but not just *one* undead. Old stone and trees sloughed away from the slopes, the details lost in the gloom, but backlit by a ruddy red that came from within the edifice. "Oh," Tarragon said. "We're fucked."

The darkness turned red-white as the mountain fortress woke, and Tarragon went night blind for a moment. She heard a young woman's voice, tight with fear and anger. "Papa!"

And then someone slammed a storm lantern atop her, and Tarragon was in prison. *Again.*

Chapter Six

Screaming isn't good.

Evanne was on her feet before her brain had a chance to get in the way. She'd been mid-Trick with Cleo, who was pretty but vacant, and hanging on Evanne's every word about that one time she'd killed a lion. They were facing each other, elbows on a table, faces almost close enough for magic to happen, the half-told story right there between them. A half carafe of rice wine sat, mostly empty, and two glasses besides.

Evanne had come to this little table with her carafe and a single glass, no clear idea of what she meant to do, but with her mother's words ringing a gong in her mind. *No one has answered my prayers for sixteen years.* And they'd just spoken of how Evanne wasn't yet sixteen, so that made Mama's last answered prayers before Evanne's birth. The intent was clear. Her mother had wished for something else, and been gifted with the Half-Made.

I bit my cheek so hard it bled. At least the Vhemin in me didn't sit by. It's healed now.

Stealing wine from the school's stores was easy enough, and then stealing some more took a *little* work because she was sloshing a degree to starboard by then. By the third bottle she'd thought a carafe at a time was how things were best done, and Cleo had arrived along with a second glass, a kind of Trick by itself, and they'd sat together while the sun slunk low, tail between its legs.

A light touch. Laughter. And Cleo hadn't stared at her Half-Made teeth, her traitorous lavender-yet-Vhemin eyes, just stroked a finger along the cool skin of Evanne's forearm, and they laughed some more.

But then a woman's panicked cry went up, and even Cleo's doe eyes registered minor alarm. Evanne realised it was night time, the sun well gone, along with most people.

So: the feet. Hitch ghosted near. "Sounds like you need to get the armour?"

"What?" Evanne took a stumbling step toward the screaming, brain still at the bench with Cleo. "We've got to help!"

"You're drunk. You're also angry. And—"

"I'm *not* angry!"

"Furious, then." The ghost waved a translucent blue arm. "But just this morning, you promised your mother if dark times came, a ruckus on the heels of the dogs of war, all of that, you would get the armour, *her* armour, put it on, and run." He looked down, the soft lines of his face clearly staring at her feet. "You are running, of a fashion, but in the wrong direction."

"But the screaming." Evanne blinked, the world listing a little to port this time. "I feel I should do something."

Hitch heaved a sigh. "I only care because I'm the one who gets blamed every time you do some damn fool thing. Which," he raised an arm, "is *all* the time. All! The! Time! You do something stupid as regularly as a clock hits the hour."

Evanne bridled, then noticed the now empty table. "You've made Cleo leave."

"No, the screaming made her leave. She did what a sensible young person would, which is run in the opposite direction from danger. Your mother runs a school. There are Tresward there."

At mention of Vertiline, Evanne bit her lip. "Aye. Aye, the *school*. The *students*. The mighty *Tresward*. All worth more than the Half-Made."

Hitch backed up like she'd slapped him. "The Half-What?"

She pushed through his ghostly form, storming toward the scream-ing, which had been joined by more screaming. Evanne felt her weak human heart struggle, pounding in her chest, a kind of sick lurching rhythm that no one could dance to. Oh, the Three had made her strong enough, her limbs lean and muscled, but they'd lashed that heavy wagon to such a feeble donkey. She couldn't *run*. Hell, Evanne couldn't even *jog*. Which was *why* the school was more important to her mother. All those healthy bodies who could complete a pattern before their breath gave out.

Evanne used that strength to stamp toward the ruckus, pushing people aside who ran around doing nothing useful. She tasted the rice wine on her breath, the hard edge of it, the keenness of the liquor urging her heart to do *better*. Evanne gritted not-quite-shark-teeth, baring them at the night, her not-quite-Vhemin-enough eyes giving her enough to chart a course with. Blooms of blood heat overlaid the cooling canvass of tents, and she felt a hunger gnaw her.

"I'm going to eat someone's heart," she promised the night, knowing she lied, but it's what she was best at. Tricks, always more Tricks, to shore up the feebleness inside her.

Old Merle bounced off her, an old rusty sword in one hand. His aged eyes were wild, but he didn't run *away*. He was headed in the same direction. *Good. Except...* Evanne grabbed his arm. "Merle. Merle!" She clicked fingers before his eyes. "You must get away. No, give me that before you hurt yourself." She took his sword, leaning on a Trick she'd taken from a guard. "Danger comes. The shadows have fangs and they hunt human flesh. I'm safe, because I'm not," and she paused for effect, the rice wine fumes spoiling it some, "all the *way* human."

"But there's a fair—"

"Go!" She slapped him on the thigh with his own sword. "Cleo is back that way. Others, too."

He nodded, tight and sure, because that's what they did out here on the edge of the hungry sands. They looked after each other, and Evanne had the sword. Old Merle? He had a calm voice and a good heart. A face no one would run from. He was better to help those with fear aplenty.

Whirling, Evanne broke into a stagger-step run. People thinned out, then were gone. And, finally, she was through.

"Oh, my." Before her was a scene her rice-wined head made little sense of. A dead man lurched toward a glittering ember on the ground. Her father slapped at flames that chewed at his skin. Evanne made the human part of her eyes focus, the glittering heat on the ground turning into a fairy. The tiny person burned, and it didn't take Uncle Day's fancy maths to work out who set fire to her father. Evanne grabbed a metal storm lantern from a stall hook, bent the top open with Vhemin strength, and slapped it over the fairy.

Then the dead man was on her. He'd ignored her father, perhaps because Armitage was on fire. When she wasted time imprisoning the fairy it got to her, and reached rotting fingers for her throat.

Evanne hollered, set her weight low, and shoulder barged the creature. The dead man bounced away, arms pinwheeling but slow enough it looked absurd, then slumped to the ground like rotted straw. She stabbed her sword into the ground, tore canvas from a stall, and smothered her father with it. "Papa!"

A sound like the end of times broke the sky open. Red light cascaded over Evanne, pushing the Vhemin heat-vision into hues of firelight, but everywhere at once. Her skin felt warm, then hot, right before the dead man exploded into a shower of burning, ancient rot.

Right before the dead man died in a way no one could kiss and make better, Evanne saw the red heat coalesce into a single, hard line that reached from behind her and right into the heart of the monster. She whirled, then whimpered, dropping to hug her knees.

The mountain is alive!

Heaven's Gate, the friendly giant that always stood at their backs, had split open. A single, monstrous red eye larger than Imshir's ancient keep glared at the night from the top slopes. The vermillion gaze of that single orb moved, searching, *hunting* for something.

It fixed on Evanne, and she felt very small. Smaller than the fairy, and perhaps of less worth than dust. Then it moved on, the red light finding her father. He'd managed to gain his feet, arm smouldering char but not immediately on fire, before red cascaded over him like a blanket.

Hitch shouted, "Evanne, *no!*" But she wasn't listening. Evanne screamed, her foolish feet moving by themselves again, and she was in front of Armitage before she could do anything. She grabbed Papa, holding him close, the smell of burned meat about her, crispness against her skin as his burned arm touched her, held her.

Waited for the end with her.

She felt the red hate against her back, the impossible weight of Heaven's Gate on her shoulders, then... silence. She opened her eyes, the night world fading back to cooler tones of night. Where the dead man had stood rotted meat still burned, the sand beneath him melted to clear glass, a trough of wispy smoke marking where he'd been.

"Let me out!" the fairy squealed.

Evanne ignored her, tilting her face to her father's. He smoothed her hair, then rubbed a tear from her cheek. He bared proper Vhemin shark teeth. "That was fucken dumb."

She snorted a laugh, then choked on tears. "What was that, Papa?"

"No real idea. It ain't done, though."

Evanne glanced behind her. The red eye was still there, but it had moved to the west, gazing out across the vast desert. That ancient, terrible sound broke the heavens, and a red lance of hate spat across the desert. An easy ten klicks away out there on the sands came a gout of fire. It bloomed tall as ten houses atop each other, reaching a long, curling finger toward the stars. "That's ... that's Clink's camp."

"Can't be." She felt her father's rumble in his chest.

The mountain turned its face, another lance of doom striking father out in the desert. More fire, but the tremble of the earth still touched Evanne's soles. "And that has to be where Rust holds sway."

"Clink," Armitage growled. "Rust. Two Vhemin who aren't assholes. What do the ancients want with my kin?"

"Our kin," Vertiline announced, sweeping from behind a line of tents. "Husband."

"Wench."

A smile, quickly gone as the Platinum Warrior faced her daughter. "And here you are, without armour, and an ancient terror on the loose. I thought we'd talked of this."

"But, the mountain!" Evanne blurted. She pointed to the storm lantern. "And a fairy, too."

"Let me out! LET ME OUT!"

"You should let the fairy out," Vertiline said. "There aren't many Builders left."

"If she's a Builder my aunt was a goat." Armitage simmered. "Actually, it's tricky to know. Vhemin don't keep great records. My aunt could've been a goat, I guess."

Evanne stalked to the storm lantern, grabbed the discarded lid, and quick as fancy talk whipped it back on, fairy still inside. She held it up to her eyeline. "Hey." She shook the lantern. "Hey! Why'd you attack Papa?"

"All Vehement Systems Architectures must die." The fairy leaned close to the glass, eyes widening. Evanne saw familiar disgust, so she shook the lantern again because she was bored with that. "What are you?"

The mountain groaned again, another pillar of fire growing in the night. Evanne bared not-quite-shark-teeth. "Someone who's hungry."

"Someone who's not sober, either. I can smell ... is that *rice* wine? It's coming through the vents. Could you," the fairy flicked her fingers, "stand back a pace or three?"

Vertiline faced the mountain. "I must deal with this."

"Eh." Armitage sniffed. "It'll probably solve itself if we stand here arguing long enough."

"It hunts our family, and I will not abide." Vertiline bound her hair into a quick tail. "Will you get our daughter inside? If it's not too much trouble in between you failing to best a fairy, and fight a single of the forgotten dead."

Armitage rubbed his chin. "The little fucker caught me flat-footed. I was distracted. I was—"

"We knew it would happen." Vertiline's face smoothed a shade, and she took three quick steps to Armitage, hand on his jaw. "Can you get her inside? She is all that is precious."

"Papa? What did you know would happen?" Evanne looked at them both. *All that's precious? That's a weird way of referring to an unanswered prayer.*

"I'll do it." Armitage pushed Vertiline away, but gently, almost regretfully. "Come back to me."

"Always." Vertiline broke free, then hurried to Evanne. She held her at arm's length. "Let me see you, now."

"What for? I'm the same as I was yesterday."

"Because tomorrow may never come." Blue eyes, but wide, afraid, then Vertiline pulled her close. "Listen to your father. Get the armour! Promise me."

"But." Evanne swallowed, then nodded. "He would have died."

"And next time, you might. It is the bargain he and I made. We are nothing, but for you." Vertiline kissed Evanne's cheek, then she was gone, long legs striding into the night, sword at waist, her eyes now focused on an ancient mountain.

Because only the Platinum Warrior could think to fight a mountain. Evanne gave the fairy one last shake, then turned to Armitage with a brittle smile, half monstrous, half afraid. "Where to?"

THEY STAGGERED THROUGH SANDY STREETS EMPTY OF THE USUAL smiling faces. *At least Old Merle got people away.* Evanne kept glancing at the mountain, the red eye seeking, *always* seeking. It glanced their way every so often, but Armitage kept his bulk hunkered down. Keeping to cover, behind low stone walls, or shacks in a pinch. Imshir's empty streets gave them no trouble. The eye kept glancing at them, hazing her blood heat vision to red, but stuttered and stumbled on. Almost like it couldn't believe what it saw.

Evanne looked at the pale human skin on her forearms. *Is it ... confused?* It wouldn't be alone. Evanne felt confused most days of the week ending in Y.

Her storm lantern glittered. "Hey! Monster!"

Evanne held the fairy up to her head height. "Quiet, you."

"I've never seen a Vhemin with lavender eyes before." The fairy crossed her arms, wings aflutter. "What did you Bigs do?"

Evanne rolled her very not-quite-Vhemin eyes. "We didn't set people on *fire*, that's for sure."

"Quit gassing," Armitage growled. "You can play with your food later."

"I'm not going to eat the fairy, Papa." Evanne lowered the lantern. "Well, not all at once, anyway."

"Hey!" The lantern rattled as the fairy tried to pry it open.

Evanne felt her weak heart thudding in her chest. *There's a lot going on. I need to sit ... but not yet.* "We need to find Aunt Barret."

Armitage glanced at her, snake eyes softening the barest of degrees. "Aye, we do." He sniffed. "She'll be in the barracks, if she's smart."

"So, the pub, then." Evanne squared her shoulders, facing Imshir. The pub was snuggled against the walls, as if against a protective older sibling. Then she stopped at what she saw. All Imshir's dead, no longer shoeing horses or selling rutabagas. All *here*, and on the move. "Oh."

Armitage glanced back at her tone. "Oh?"

She pointed. "All the dead are here. They never go outside the walls."

Hitch slipped on silent feet to her side. "They're looking at Heaven's Gate."

Ghosts lined the ramparts, some floating down the side, a gleaming, glimmering tide heading toward the mountain.

"That's something you don't see every day," the fairy said.

Evanne raised the lantern. "You can see them? No one can see the dead."

"Of *course* I can see them." A tiny eye roll, and Evanne grudgingly admitted despite the size, it would rival her best efforts. "I'm a *fairy*. What's more interesting is *you* can see them. Bigs can't. Doesn't work that way."

Evanne raised an eyebrow, then lowered her lantern. *It'll keep. We need to keep the living safe.* They made time as best they could, arriving at the small tavern. The old merchant woman leaned against a railing outside, admiring the mountain, a mug in her hand. She absently raised a toast as Evanne passed.

Inside: furore. Evanne swept rust hair from her face, looking for those most important. There was Old Merle, bellowing for calm, and adding none of his own. Friendly faces, a few students from Mama's school, and the odd visitor. But—*yes, praise the Three*—Barret sulked near a back wall, Heser the Cheg by her side. A quick glance showed Uncle Day not far off, golden eyes everywhere, his usual half-smile absent.

The fairy rattled her cage, tiny voice piping up. "A Fey Branded! Hello, cat! Over here!"

Uncle Day's gaze found Evanne, half-smile settling on his face for a moment, then he saw her lantern. The smile left. He held his hands higher so she could see his words as her father bulled his way across the throng. *{You found a Builder. I don't think they like being used as light sources.}*

Armitage beckoned for Aunt Barret and Uncle Heser to join them. "Here's what I know. The mountain's pitched a shit fit. It's killing Vhemin. And we—"

"Of course it's killing ... wait. Did you say Vhemin?" The lantern shook in Evanne's grip, so she raised it, the fairy now at their height. "You're Vehement Systems Architectures."

{Where have you been?}

"Can you get me out? The Fey Branded are Itikari's faithful servants."

Uncle Day took a step back, eyes hard. *{I think I see. Let me catch you up.}* He snapped his fingers as the fairy glanced at Aunt Barret. *{Eyes on me. The People are slaves no more. We know no,}* he spelled out the unfamiliar letters, *{Itikari. There are humans, some very confused—}*

"Watch it," Uncle Heser said, tone ominous. Evanne liked the Trick, but there wasn't time to write it down.

{And some wonderful. Those you call Vehement are Vhemin. Like the humans, they're confused.}

"Watch it, cat," Papa growled.

{There are no more gods. The demons are gone. It cost more than we could pay, but the ledger is clear.}

The fairy looked at her hands, forming the unfamiliar Handspeak for *Vhemin*. She glanced at Uncle Day. "I understand now." She gave a tiny nod. "You're all bonkers."

Uncle Day sighed, then looked to Armitage. *{What news, brother?}*

Armitage glared, seemingly at everyone at once. "The mountain's killing Vhemin. Got sand in its eye, looks like. Tilly's headed up the slopes to ... have a conversation. We've got to keep the Vhemin inside, which is a boggle, because we always love a good scrap."

Heser the Cheg's frown deepened. "Vertiline went ... *alone?*"

"She's good at this shit. She'll be fine." Armitage's tone held bluster, but Evanne heard the Trick of it.

Uncle Day put a fur soft hand on Armitage's shoulder. *{You are a terrible liar.}*

"She *will* be fine."

{That's not the lie.}

Evanne bit her lip. "We should go see."

THE RAMPARTS WERE DEFENSIBLE, HAVING BEEN DESIGNED BY A MAD demon king to thwart all pretenders to his stolen throne. It made them a perfect vantage for watching the eye of the mountain, while not being watched back. Evanne leaned against a wall, the night breeze still hot enough to whisper kind words on her cool skin. *I don't run as ... hot as Mama. Warmer than Papa, though.* Her hair tickled her neck. "If it wasn't for the mountain killing everyone, it'd be a nice night."

Armitage, who hunkered below the wall line with Aunt Barret, glared. "Which means it's not a nice night."

{It can still be a nice night.} Sight of Day stood on the wall, catlike grace immune to falling-induced terror. *{Don't be such a downer.}*

Hitch leaned on the wall as much as a ghost could. "I wish I could tell if the night was nice. It's just ... night, I guess. Less bright than the day."

Evanne leaned toward him, for all the good it would do. "Let me tell you of it then. The stars above watch, as they always have, but they don't judge. The wind is kind, a gentle presence, where even those in threadbare rags can find comfort in its embrace." She closed her eyes, breathing deep. "The desert blooms with hidden life. Flowers afraid of the scorching sun are open, looking for moons that are no longer there. Up here, it's quiet. The people of Imshir shout below, but up on the wall their voices are muted, like a distant waterfall. Heaven's Gate rages, but not at us. There is an odd kind of peace, because we wait for an end, but don't know what it is." Silence put hands on her shoulders, and she opened her eyes. "What?"

"I guess the night isn't all bad," Armitage admitted.

{Might even be nice, if imminent death wasn't on the horizon.}

"We're out of beer," Aunt Barret grumbled, shaking an empty bottle.

Heser the Cheg, slouched next to her, offered her his. "Don't take it all."

"And there goes the neighbourhood," Hitch murmured.

From the fairy, nothing at all. Evanne lifted her prison to the rampart wall. The tiny person fluttered, but her face said *reflecting* rather than *brooding*. They waited for the Platinum Warrior to do her thing.

When it happened, the start was easy to mark: a threefold strike of lightning hammered the side of Heaven's Gate. That mighty sound rang again, almost as if the mountain groaned, and that terrible red gaze swung down the slopes. Evanne held her breath, and the night breeze held it with her. The heat lance razed down the slopes.

Lightning blasted back. Evanne pointed. "There! Mama!"

They couldn't see Vertiline. She was a mote fighting a titan, but her efforts were easy to see. The Storm walked as her ally, the night sky splitting open as the Three's power answered her call. Evanne imagined her mother's perfect steps, a blade of glass holding warm yellow Light, as the mountain tried to strike her from its slopes.

"She's winning," Armitage's voice was tight.

"Hush," Aunt Barret whispered, but she too looked on in wonder.

"Eight hundred years, but this remains. Thank the Three." The fairy glimmered a little brighter.

The mountain and Vertiline fought, and step by painful step, the path of her lightning walked up the slopes. *She's getting closer to the eye. She's almost at the top.*

Heaven's Gate's eye shimmered, then swivelled to the west. The merciless lance struck again, not at Vertiline, but ... *itself.* The details were hard to see at this distance, but the gouges on the mountain's hide were clear. The lance razed rocky slopes, destroyed scree, and immolated what shrubs still shrouded the slopes. Evanne stumbled as the ground shook, the parapet before her cracking, rock and dust spilling hundreds of metres to the ground below.

The mountain broke open. Ruddy red molten light gaped, followed by a spume of yellow-red melted rock. Crooked claws of magma surged forth, rending their way across the slopes. Lightning blasted once more, then... nothing.

"Mama?" Evanne gripped the parapet, fingers bruising against stone.

"Fuck this," Armitage said. "Wait here."

{You will die.}

"And so I'll die. But I don't think so. Look how the eye slips, like a drunkard's gaze." Papa turned to Uncle Day. "Will you guard my cub?"

{Why do you ask questions you already know the answer to?} The cat looked away. *{I am faster than you.}*

"Not for long enough. And that's a long fucken way." Armitage hauled Evanne close, his embrace tight. "Kid, here's the deal. Tilly needs me. I'm not saying she needs me more or less than you, just that I can help her, and you don't need help right now."

"I can come with you—"

"You can stay the fuck here and do what the fuck you're told." Armitage held her away. "This one time, Evanne. *One* time, please, for me. Will you wait?"

She looked away. "But..." *But he said 'please'. Papa never says please. He doesn't have to.* "What can I do?"

His yellow snake eyes softened. "Live, stupid." He let her go, turning to Barret. "You got a ship?"

"Go," she said. "I know the way of war better than you. The mountain burns, and your mate has fallen."

Armitage nodded, touched Sight of Day's cheek, then he was gone. Evanne blinked, tears pricking her eyes. "What just happened?"

Uncle Day stepped before her. *{Hear me. The mountain is dying, but it will kill us in its throes. We will go to the docks and board the queen's ship. It is not a promise of your service to the Raven Queen,}* he glanced golden eyes at

Barret, *{but a necessity of our survival. When it is safe, we will come back. Until we are away, it would be amazing if you didn't do something stupid. Can you handle that?}*

"I don't think she can," Hitch said, but the joke was stillborn.

Evanne sniffed. "But what just happened?"

"The end," Aunt Barret growled, creaking to her feet.

"No." The fairy glimmered brighter. "That was just the beginning."

THEY MADE THE DOCKS IN A MAD DASH, TAKING NOTHING BUT WHAT they carried, but snaring people as they passed. Lava crept across the desert, and Evanne felt terror in her weak, crippled heart. For her mother, the best swordswoman in the world, and her father, who was Vhemin-tough but cracking with age. Evanne was sick with the feeling, choking on it, and whimpered when she thought no one was listening.

"At least you're sobering up," Hitch whispered.

The queen's ship was ready for them, smartly dressed navy officers waiting their pleasure. Lines were cast off after they boarded with refugees in tow. Evanne spied Old Merle, who gave her arm a squeeze as she passed.

The *Light Treader* weighed anchor, seeking the open sea, as the mountain behind them roared out its agony. Evanne closed her eyes, turning her face away. *Please be okay,* she thought. *Please. Please. Please.*

Chapter Seven

When Tarragon was imprisoned—*again*—she was annoyed mostly with herself, once the seething red rage passed. *Some spy I am. I got put in a box by a kid.*

Her swinging cage wasn't all bad. Storm lanterns weren't made for comfort, sure, but this one had shutters she could encourage open a handspan or two to let the delicious night air in. It smelled of hyacinth and raspberry, which she felt out here in the desert was more likely a sign of a brain tumour than anything else, but she would enjoy it while it lasted.

Speaking of the kid, the might-be-Vhemin held her carefully enough. Tarragon had both time and opportunity to examine her as they walked. *Or, she's walking. I'm swaying.* The skin of her forearms wasn't scaled like the rest of her kind, smooth human skin the colour of cut copper overlaying an impressive musculature. You would *not* want to arm-wrestle this one, no ma'am. Her gaoler wasn't as tall as most Vhemin, but sported longer hair, tarnished to old rust by the sun. Tarragon glimpsed a scattering of scales rising from her shirt to meet human skin at jaw and nape. And those beautiful, almost luminescent lavender snake eyes caught at—

"What are you staring at?" the kid asked. She lifted Tarragon to eye height, giving her a squint, which marred the impressiveness of her eyes a shade. "Something on my face?"

Tarragon fluttered, broken wing be damned. "Yeah. Your nose."

"Snappy comeback," the ghost said, in his ghostly way. Tarragon thought he held himself in a military way, like a soldier she might have met eight hundred years gone. No uniform adorned his pale blue form, so she couldn't tell which side he was on when he died.

The sound of boots on planks stole the conversation away. They were at the docks, hurrying toward a ship that wanted the freedom of the sea. Tarragon spied her name on the hull, painted by a careful hand: *Light Treader.*

The might-be-Vhemin carried her to the stern, perhaps to get out of the way, or perhaps to see the mountain rage. Tarragon felt warmth in her heart at Heaven's Gate lashing out. This was the *front*, Three dammit, and there were far too many Vhemin walking and *breathing* for her liking. Tarragon didn't know why the mountain slept, or what woke it, but it would peel the enemy forces from the skin of the earth as they didn't have their vile Artifices for protection.

"We make better stuff," she huffed.

"What?" The girl's voice was rough in all the right ways to catch the ear and draw the eye.

Tarragon shook herself, glimmerdust trickling to the lantern's floor. *That's the vile hellspawn of the enemy. Except it ...* she *looks different.* "Itikari. You know, your *enemy.*"

A blink. "There are no Itikari here. Wait. Is that a person, or a group of people? Itikaris? Itikari? It—"

"It's a combine," Tarragon supplied. "Made of people."

"Like you?"

"Maybe." Tarragon huffed. "My CO should be here somewhere, but—"

"CO?"

"Commanding officer." Tarragon tried a small lie. "I'm a soldier."

A blank stare, then the might-be-Vhemin guffawed. She threw her head back, laughter knocking back the horror of the night. "Please," she gasped, wiping an eye. "I thought I was the most pitiful creature to ever draw breath. A bung heart and not enough blood to be one thing or another, but I stand corrected. Lo! A soldier the size of a sandwich."

Tarragon shook one of the shutters. "Let me out of here and I'll show you what kind of soldier I am!"

The ghost leaned closer. "A small one?"

Tarragon felt the red fury return. She hissed, "At least I'm still alive."

"Eh." The ghost shrugged. It was difficult to make him out, what with his lower legs and forearms faded from memory, and his face a smudge, but he might have been handsome. *Might*, if he wasn't allied with a horde of demons. "Fair."

...Fair? The fuck? "What kind of Vehement Systems troops *are* you people?"

"We're not troops," the ghost said, but there was a catch of something in his voice, like he wasn't quite sure. "I'm Hitch. This is Evanne. We live here." He glanced at the shore as it pulled away. "Or, we did."

"You don't live anywhere," Evanne said. "You need to be alive to live somewhere."

"Endure, then." Hitch shrugged. "Do you have a name, oh mighty soldier, or should we call you Sandwich?"

Tarragon pursed her lips. Perhaps if she could get on their good side, they'd let their guard down and she could be free..? It was basic spy craft, too common to be worth much, but any port in a storm. "Tarragon Greyflight." She eyed the coastline as it eased into the distance. The mountain's eye shifted, listless. *The targeting matrix crashed. I always said they were glitchy.* Lava glowered its way to the sea. If everything about the shore didn't promise a horrible way to die, it might be quite pretty.

A clomp of boots on deck pulled at the frayed strings of Tarragon's attention. She fluttered about, taking in the ancient-beyond-reason Vhemin matriarch that seemed to have a problem with everything. "I need to talk to the lantern."

"Sandwich," Evanne said. "We're calling her Sandwich."

"Great. I need to talk to Sandwich." Barret didn't wait for permission, just stamped right on up to the storm lantern, which wobbled on the railing in a truly terrifying way. "What did you do?"

"I, uh." Tarragon looked at Evanne, hoping for a shred of support, and then realised the depths of ice in those lavender eyes offered none. *I guess I did try to incinerate her father.* "Nothing, really."

"'Really'," the matriarch rumbled. "'Really' is a term we use to mean many things. In this situation, did you do nothing, or a little bit of something?"

Tarragon huffed. "I escaped your vile clutches."

"What's this about, Aunt Barret?" Evanne glanced to the shoreline. "You don't think the fairy—"

"I don't know what to think," 'Aunt' Barret said. "I think the mountain is having a shit fit, and I didn't start anything, and just this one time neither did your father. The only person who's new on the scene is the one you put in a storm lantern, and Sandwich—"

"It's Tarragon!"

"Sandwich isn't big. I'm pretty sure I could take her in a fair fight," Barret paused to reach into her mouth, yanked, and pulled free a bloody hunk of shark tooth before flinging it over the railing, "but you can never be too sure. Which is why I'm asking." She glared baleful snake eyes. *My, but she's impressive.* Tarragon looked past the weathered-by-time facade, spotting the warrior behind it. Not an agent-soldier like Tarragon, someone who'd flunked out of Builder School and became a spy because that's how things worked. But maybe someone who'd lived on a planet that tried to kill her her entire life and still made it through to an advanced age. *Watch her. Old she might be, but she probably* could *take me in a fair fight.*

Tarragon sidled up to the shutters of her prison. "What's your story?"

Barret looked at her bloody fingers then wiped them sort-of-clean on her jerkin. "No story, fairy. No time for the telling of 'em, really. Got a job to do and not a lot of time to do it." She turned to creak away.

Tarragon hammered the shutters. *I need information. Nothing is what it used to be.* "Wait! Look, I know this is a confusing time. I'm confused. The mountain, she's confused too. But, I guess. I know I'm going to hell on a full scholarship, but what's your deal?"

Barret chewed that over. "What's a scholarship?"

"It's a thing where someone pays for—"

"Is it important?" Barret glared at the coastline, but she seemed to glare at everything, so Tarragon didn't read much into it.

"No, but—"

"Save it. Plenty of time for words once the killing's done."

"Aunt Barret?" Evanne took a cautious step to the weathered Vhemin. "What killing?"

Barret wiped blood from her lip. "Time will tell."

TARRAGON FUMED ON HER RAILING PRISON OUTLOOK. THE COAST drew farther away, but not with any real urgency, because this boat used *sails*, for pity's sake. Tarragon hadn't heard an engine since she'd popped topside, and while that was pleasant enough, it also meant everything happened slower.

"Look." Hitch's ghostly arm drew a line to the mountain.

Evanne joined them at the railing. The maybe-Vhemin's fingers gripped the railing so tight, Tarragon saw her fingers bleached by the strength of her grip. Tarragon couldn't be sure, but she thought she heard the young woman whispering, *Please, please, please,* over and over.

Tarragon stopped staring at Evanne, who was worth staring at a lot more—*if only she wasn't the enemy!*—and directed her attention to the shore. Heaven's Gate's eye was lurching about as ancient systems tried to do something useful. It couldn't seem to look low enough to spot the interlopers on its slopes anymore, so it looked out to sea. *Oh, my. Its gaze isn't steady.* The mountain's eye looked unfocused, three-days-drunk, and if there was an Artifice on approach, even a small one, the fortress would be done in.

But ... were there were more Artifices? The terrible machines of the enemy were absent.

"That has to be your father," Hitch said. "I mean, it was ready to die before, and now it's doing ... something. It hunted him before. Maybe it seeks him still."

"Uh." Evanne bit her lip, those delicate fangs drawing blood. "What if—"

"Peace, Evanne. I shouldn't have said anything." Hitch stepped through the railing to stand over the sea so he could face her. "There are many what ifs. What if we die? That's not so bad. Look at me."

She laughed, then strangled it quickly. "Hitch, I'm so worried."

"The problem with idols is when they fall." The ghost looked past the maybe-Vhemin, and his voice was far away, struggling with a memory.

Heaven's Gate was good at choosing moments. The slurred glare of the eye spat hate, a red lance hitting desert sand, but unable to score a hit on whatever assaulted the slopes. "Yes," Evanne hissed.

"Uh," Hitch said. "Yes?"

"Yes." She swept her hair back. "It fights, because enemies still live. Mama and Papa are still alive."

"Got it." Hitch glanced over his shoulder. "So what's that all about then?"

The eye spat hot death a couple more times, then paused as gouts of molten sand and rock fell back to earth. It reoriented, the beam coming on hot and strong, and focused at the ground at the mountain's feet. The sound, even out on the waves, was immense, a smothering blanket of rage.

Tarragon glimmered to get Evanne's attention. She couldn't be heard, so ... Handspeak. *{Let me out.}*

{It's nice to want things.} Evanne turned back to the spectacle. A spume of molten rock fountained into the sky. From here it was pretty enough, but near the impact site the air would be on fire. Nothing would survive for klicks.

The mountain's rage continued, the eye focused on the ground, and then, all at once, Tarragon realised what it was doing. She flared, drawing two sets of eyes. *{We must flee. We must put on all speed to get away.}*

{We are.} Evanne flung an arm to the open sea. *{It's literally what we're doing.}*

And then, it was too late. The earth by Imshir cracked, so loud Tarragon stopped being able to hear anything at all. The sea shuddered, the gentle rolling ocean trembling before shaking in fear. *Earthquake*, Tarragon thought. *We're screwed.*

The mountain had dug a furrow in the ground, hunting for the tender seam where the earth cozied up to itself. It'd gone full rogue, the guiding intelligence no doubt mad after eight hundred godless years, and it decided to suicide.

Imshir's delicate houses shook, then shuddered into rubble. Rock dust rose, a cloud obscuring the stars on the horizon. And still, the mountain carved into the earth. The *Light Treader* listed as a massive swell lifted the boat. Tarragon looked to see, and her glimmer faded for a moment. The swells coming in would be the start of a tsunami of the ages.

The captain of the *Light Treader*, nobody's fool, pointed the ship into the swells. The air pressure changed, and Tarragon's ears popped, despite still not working well. A gust tickled her hair, then a gale slammed her jail. The lantern was swept from the railing, and she fell.

Then, didn't. Above, Evanne's strong arm caught the lantern, lavender snake-eyes like charmed jewels.

The ship rolled, then went belly up. Water.

More water. Darkness. She glimmered, glimpsing spars and ropes, bodies, outstretched hands. Barrels and sails. Evanne's panicked eyes, still holding the lantern. Not letting her go. Hitch trying to get their attention, useless as the dead always were.

A glimmer, brighter than hers, as tectonic plates deep in the ocean sundered, lambent glow and orange fire. The water boiled, cloudy, but so angry and red.

I'm drowning! Tarragon rattled storm shutters, the ocean trying to crush her glimmer. And then she was gone, sucked deep, into the hateful below.

Chapter Eight

Salt.

Salt fucking *everywhere*.

Evanne dragged her hand through sand, spat more sand, then curled over and threw up. This wasn't just salt, it was water *and* salt, and tasted like yesterday's bad life choices. She croaked, spat again, and wiped grimy fingers across her eyes.

Everything hurts.

She was on a beach, but not an idyllic location for a picnic. There were jagged black rocks rent through the sand. They reached tall, jagged fingers out to the ocean. Her eyes followed the stones into the sea, where she spotted the remains of what was probably the *Light Treader* marooned on a spire of ebon fang. It was hard to tell because the ship was a good klick off easy, in a different, crumpled shape to when Evanne had been onboard, and her vision was blurry.

My head hurts. Evanne touched her forehead, fingers coming back bloody. The sand beneath her was awash with red sticky, ebbing to a delicate pink where the tide had left her for dead before receding. *My lip is cut.* She tried to touch her lip with the other hand and almost passed out again from the pain. She held her traitor arm away from her body. *There's a spike of rusted metal through my arm. That's ... unexpected.*

She wanted to throw up, but stood instead. *I am Vhemin!* Staggering, she ignored the spike through her arm, because it would hurt to pull it out. It wasn't bleeding too bad but if she yanked it free it would start pissing like one of the fountains in Ravenswall Mama told her about. Her heart pounded with the strain, feeble, valiant, pathetic. The weakest part of her, the human, brittle inside.

The beach went on as beaches tended to. There was an unfamiliar hill to the north, little more than a mound of rubble. She blinked. *That can't be Heaven's Gate. There's ... nothing left.*

She spotted a man in a Queensguard uniform, waved, then lowered her hand as she realised what he stood next to. *That's his body. The man is dead, and that is his ghost.* She covered her mouth with the non-agony hand, then staggered away from the waterline. Black shapes floated in the water. The dead outnumbered the living a hundred to one, because she was the only one still breathing.

"Hitch?" Her voice was broken, jagged like old glass. "Are you there?"

The spectre drifted free of a wisp of ocean spray. "I'm here, Evanne. But are you?" He floated about her. "You look like shit. Did you know there's a hunk of steel in your arm?"

"I'd noticed." She steadied herself. "I need to find Uncle Day. Aunt Barret. Uncle Heser." Evanne swallowed. "Mama. Papa."

"Maybe pick one, start with that, and work your way up the list." He shrugged. "No need to get disappointed all at once."

Evanne rounded on him. "This is not the time!"

Hitch spread his maybe-hands, indistinct but unapologetic. "Evanne. *Evie.* Listen."

"Don't call me Evie."

"Evie, everyone is dead. It is better to hear it now, than spend an hour, day, or week waiting for another slice against your heart." Hitch looked away. "I remember that much, at least."

She felt something in her crack. "I ... I'm sorry. It's—"

"No, I'm sorry." He drifted on the breeze. "It's been a big day. I'm ... unused to so many new faces." He gestured at the ghostly Queensguard.

"Let's get a fire going." Half-made she was, weak and human in parts, but a little of Mama's warm blood had kept her from dying in the frozen seas. She shivered, the cold-blooded part yearning for rest. "If they see the fire, they'll come."

Hitch said nothing. There wasn't anything to say.

IT HADN'T TAKEN LONG TO FIND A TINDERBOX AMONG THE FLOTSAM. It was well-sealed, a little battered, but oiled leather inside kept the flint and tinder dry. She found a case of what looked like rum, all but one bottle smashed, but one would do well enough. Sailcloth was easy enough, fallen spars likewise, and working one-handed she managed—with only a little swearing—to get a makeshift pavilion up, and a fire going near it. Being one-handed was the hardest part. That, and swooning with pain.

Food. Alcohol. Fire. She gnawed salted pork, no better or worse off from its dip in the ocean. She'd used driftwood to start the blaze, and had hunks of the *Light Treader* drying upwind of the fire.

Uncle Day was the first to find her, and when he arrived she ran to him, unable to hold in a sob. He dropped the brace of rabbits, pulling her close. He didn't even have the decency to look like he'd been in the drink, his brown coat smooth and glossy. Perfect, like all Feybrind. His fur-soft hand stroked her hair. She ignored the twist of bile in her stomach, that traitorous Vhemin part of her, and breathed in the cinnamon smell of him. "You're alive."

He held her at arm's length, golden eyes soft and warm, then pressed his fingertips together. *{We are small but select few.}* Sight of Day's eyes widened, and he jabbed a hand past her shoulder in the universal *what's that?* gesture.

She spun, then almost passed out as her arm screamed raw pain. Evanne staggered back, Sight of Day's hand on her elbow, supporting her. She spat bile. "Ow!"

He held up the spike that'd been lodged in her arm, red dripping to the thirsty sand, then tossed it aside. *{I don't know if you'd noticed that.*

Vhemin are,} his hands closed as he hunted for the right word, *{peculiar. Let me bandage that.}*

"It's fine. No, don't touch me. Do something useful, like skin those rabbits."

The Feybrind half-smiled. *{You'll thank me in the morning.}*

"Not likely." She returned to her brooding perch by the fire, but she couldn't stay angry for long. She'd found Sight of Day.

AUNT BARRET ARRIVED NEXT, DRAGGING AN UNCONSCIOUS HESER the Cheg. She tossed the queen's man against a log, then snared a half-cooked rabbit from a spit above the fire.

{They're not done yet.}

"What's your point, cat?" Barret chewed, bones crunching, then looked to Evanne. "You're not dead." She spat a tooth into the fire. "What happened to your arm?"

"There was a shipwreck. Did you notice it?"

"Ha hah." Aunt Barret didn't even sound a little amused. Her face softened as she looked at Uncle Heser. "He's going to need more than a hug." Her eyes moved to Evanne's arm. "So are you."

Evanne hugged her arm, hiding it with her other one. *I'm not a real Vhemin. It'll heal, but not as fast as them.* "I'll be fine. Playing the lute before you know it."

{That reminds me.} Sight of Day pointed south. *{I think your guitar is that way. We should pick it up.}*

"You didn't bring it with you?" Barret sighed.

{It was a guitar or food.}

"Fair call." The Vhemin matriarch looked into the fire.

"I'm going to go for a walk. Maybe get the guitar." Evanne tried not to hunch. "I'll be back soon."

"Whatever."

{I will come with you.}

"I'll be fine." Evanne looked into Sight of Day's golden eyes. "I just need..." She trailed off, unsure.

{Me too.} The cat half-smiled. *{Scream and run about in circles if you get into trouble. We'll come running.}*

Evanne grinned, unexpected, always warm in her heart when the Feybrind was near. It was the human part, not the traitorous sickness in her stomach from the Vhemin, and she cherished it. She trudged away from their small camp, eye out for survivors, but carrying no hope in her heart. There were too many ghosts for survival to be a common trait.

She'd moved perhaps seven hundred metres from the camp, found a dune, scaled it, and drifted down the other side. Evanne glanced to her left, where Hitch lingered. "You've been quiet."

"I've been thinking. It's different. Quiet means sulking, which is what you do. Thinking is what I do." The shade drifted on, ignoring her scowl. "What we want to know is what woke the mountain."

"The fairy?"

"You're not that dense." Hitch paused. "Well, maybe you are—"

"At least I've got a body to be dense with." Evanne sighed. "No, that's not a good one. I want a do-over."

"Because you admitted to being dense?"

"I've got a head injury."

"You're making this too easy." Hitch seemed to smirk, as much as anyone with no face could. "If the stories keep faith, Knight Champion Geneve went into the mountain with the sorcerer—"

"Geneve didn't go into the mountain. It was just the holomancer." Evanne bit her lip. "They came out with a fairy and a host of Feybrind."

"Aye, I listened to the story at your mother's knee, too. I had to, because I'm stuck with you. You're like a, a," he gestured to the wreck, "useless anchor."

"Anchors don't walk about. Anchors aren't smarter than you."

"Smarter, aye?"

"Aye." Evanne looked to the ruined Heaven's Gate. "I remembered the important parts of the story. The dragon went in."

"Ormeon the Redeemer."

"The very same." Evanne pointed to the waterline. "Looks like my guitar."

"Well, Miss I Know the Important Parts of the Story, tell me what woke the mountain's fury." Hitch looked over the ocean. "It's been here a long time. A fairy came out before, so one appearing isn't what did it. There have been Vhemin aplenty for as long as there's been sand."

"You think someone did something?"

"Vague but on the right track." Hitch stuck not-hands in invisible pockets. "Heaven's Gate was a fortress. It had undead guardians and magic mirrors. The lich king of a fallen order held court, his phylactery in residence. It was not meant to *accidentally* do anything. It was a weapon of the ancients, meant to hold this line."

"What line?" Evanne glanced across the sand. "There's nothing here. There never has been."

"Not 'never'. Do you remember what Sandwich said? That the enemy was here, and she thought you," and this earned Evanne a little side-eye, "were one of them. Vehement Systems."

"The Vhemin." Evanne nodded, but slowly, because her brain was sluggish. "They built a fortress to stop them going any farther. Their god emperor held court and made his last stand. The gods watched above, armies dying below."

"Something like that." Hitch sounded uncertain. "I remember *something*—"

"You might be the one with a head injury." Evanne scrubbed at salt-laden hair.

"Maybe." Hitch shrugged. "Thing is, no one builds a fortress that's easy to accidentally turn on. It's not like a lantern. It's a castle with might enough to challenge the heavens. So—"

"So, some*one* turned it on." Evanne pursed her lips. "Who?"

"Bad people, is my guess."

Evanne felt a little queasiness stir in her gut. "We've had enough of devils and such. Come on. Let's get the guitar."

They walked to the water, sand firming under Evanne's feet as it got wetter. She dragged the guitar case from the teasing surf, brushed it off, and opened it. Inside, the guitar was as it'd been when Uncle Day gave it to her: gleaming polished wood, strings, and the hint of sandalwood.

Movement at the dune line caught her eye, but when she focused she couldn't see anything. "Did you see that?"

"See what?"

"Up there." Evanne snapped the case's clasps shut, then headed toward the dunes. "Might be survivors."

"Might be 'devils and such'."

"Hah." Evanne's head was clearing, the wound on her arm throbbing less, and the sun had dried her clothes. She couldn't see her camp, but a trickle of smoke still ebbed toward the sky from where it lay. She scaled the dune, a hail dying on her lips.

"Curious," Hitch whispered.

A hundred metres off, two Feybrind stood by a basket that glowed, which meant a fairy was *probably* within. A third Feybrind jogged toward them, casting a glance back at Evanne before putting more curry in her stride.

Evanne jogged, heart lurching in her chest, to get near the Feybrind. "Ho, cats." She was met with eyes of hard glass. Agate, amber, emerald, all stones, no warmth anywhere. She tried for half a smile, trying to keep her not-quite-shark's-teeth hidden. "If that's a fairy, she's with me."

Hitch glanced between those hard Feybrind stares. "You shouldn't say the fairy's with you. Something's not right here."

Evanne glanced at him, then back to the cats, who wouldn't be able to see the spectre. *Try a different approach.* "Sorry. Sometimes I talk to myself. I'm Evanne."

She waited, but got no introductions. The Feybrind who'd run from the dune line looked to her companions, Handspeak flashing faster than Evanne could understand. She caught *Traitor* and *Enemy* and *Prisoner*, which all seemed roughly right until one near the basket unlimbered his bow and loosed an arrow at Evanne faster than thought.

But not *quite* faster than her reactions, which dragged her sullen body to the left. The arrow kissed her cheek. "Ow!" She dropped her guitar, hands up, and spoke quickly, words falling over each other. "My mother is the Platinum Warrior. She has the Tresward school at Imshir. We're friends of the People—"

And that was all she got out before the first woman was on her, agate eyes hate-filled stones, furred hands curled to claws.

Evanne managed a scream before those hands found her throat. Feybrind were fast, so very *fast*, and she found herself on her back, hands in guard, trying to breathe. She scrambled, hand finding wood, and she wrenched the guitar case into the Feybrind once, twice, and on the third hit furred fingers loosened enough so she could get some air in.

She felt her face turn into a snarl, because today had been *difficult*, and she'd almost *died*, and so *fuck* this cat. Evanne fought like her father taught her, not the delicate patterns she had no talent for, but the rough and ready sluggery of his line. Her Vhemin-strong fist caught the Feybrind in the head, and even at such a poor angle the grunt behind it knocked the cat aside.

Evanne scrambled for height, took an arrow in her arm, screamed, turned, and ran like the dogs of war were behind her, because these were *Feybrind*, and they were good, and kind, and she couldn't beat them, couldn't even *fight* them with her heart, couldn't get away fast enough, or—

An arrow took her in the leg, and she fell. Hitch beckoned her. "Evanne, get up. It's barely a flesh wound. Get up. Seriously. Get *up*, get *up, getupgetup*—"

A hand on her jerkin hauled Evanne upright, and she felt the razor bite of a blade in her back. She screamed again, and then the hand left her, and she fell. She heard arrows, three, five, nine, and then nothing at all.

"They should've gone for the head." A shadow, all bulk and grim misery above a leathery hand. The hand? That was soft enough. *Aunt Barret.* "Are you okay?"

Evanne sobbed. "I've been ... there was ... but they're *Feybrind!*"

"Aye. He needed a distraction, so at least I served a purpose." There was pain in the matriarch's voice, the aged Vhemin settling beside her. Evanne rolled, careful of the arrow in her leg, to face the woman. Barret had eight arrows in her chest, one in her arm, but didn't look more than tired. Evanne looked to the Feybrind, and saw Uncle Day standing above three of his own who would never stand again, eyes eternal and sad, as he slicked blood from his blade. "Aye, child. They were Feybrind, and they went for you. And because of that, they are nothing anymore."

"Something's not right," Hitch said.

"No," Evanne said. "Something's really wrong." She dragged herself to Barret's side, leaning against the old woman, and shook while she cried. Barret curled an arm around her, and held peace enough for two.

Chapter Nine

When the probably-Vhemin woman had stormed over the hill, Tarragon had been ready to die. It was because the Itikari Fey Branded were about to kill her, which wasn't an expected outcome of meeting one.

She'd woken covered in sand, wings bedraggled, no sparkle left, and trudged her slow way up the beach. Tarragon ate a small crab because it threatened her and she was hungry, but the meat had no flavour. All the way up the sand she'd wondered, *Why did the mountain attack itself?*

Because that's what it had done. Unable to kill whatever it had tried to square away, it'd turned its own lower slopes and the surrounding lands to magma. The resulting catastrophe was assured, because Itikari built things *right*, not like those simpletons at Vehement Systems. *She* was an Itikari product, much like a Build Engine or a Star Drive. Or the Fey Branded, those clever felines who did all they were Commanded.

Bemused, she'd been caught unawares by one of the Fey Branded, who'd waited in the long grass at the top of the dunes. The Fey Branded woman had put her in a basket, and if Tarragon had glimmer left she'd have burned her way out, but it wasn't going to be that kind of day.

The cats argued about her, their clever fingers moving whippet-quick, whisper-quiet, and always angry. Tarragon was confused, because the cats were never angry. Or, almost never. They did as they were told, and they did it well, and if they didn't, they were Commanded to, and then they went about whatever business was demanded. These seemed *feral*, a wildness and spirit to them she hadn't seen before.

They were all armed, their weapons and clothes as beautiful as expected of the Itikari's finest crafters. But *rustic*, as if they were working with hand tools, a needle and thread, or shears. *This world doesn't make sense. I went away, and everything changed.*

She caught *prisoner* and *enemy* and *monsters* in the cats' Handspeak, which Tarragon could get on board with, assuming they were talking about Vhemin and not fairies. But they also said *mission* and *human* which was weird. The rest of their conversation was hard to make out, because the basket was well-made with only small gaps between the reeds.

One cat ran away to the dunes. The other two arrived at a decision, put Tarragon down, and seemed ready to stab her until she stopped moving. Then the maybe-Vhemin woman had arrived and said the most curious thing.

She's with me.

Which wasn't true, because they were *enemies*, by the Three, and enemies weren't together, no matter how good they looked. The Fey Branded attacked Evanne, which didn't go well for anyone, but Tarragon was impressed with how Evanne fought. She was young, not of the Three's Wardens, but accorded herself without pissing her breeches, and did the sensible thing of running away when faced with overwhelming odds. Because no single Vehement Systems Architecture could take on a Fey Branded. The Itikari made their servants too well for that.

What really surprised Tarragon was when the other Fey Branded she'd met at Imshir, all beautiful golden eyes turned hard as the sun, killed the other two. He did it while the old matriarch who'd called Tarragon a sandwich killed the last one. Which didn't make sense either, because the matriarch was ready for the knacker's yard, and should've had lost against a Fey Branded, but Tarragon watched it through her basket, breath held, while her wings shivered in fear.

What surprised Tarragon the most was how the Fey Branded with the golden eyes had killed his kind without being Commanded. She'd never seen them fight without Command, because it's not what they'd been made for, no matter how good they were at it.

"Fucking ferals, all of them," she said to no one in particular.

"How long?" The ghost sat beside her, forearms over knees, hands and feet missing, which was strange because ghosts were usually fully assembled, no matter how they died.

"You what?"

Hitch leaned closer. "How long have you been out of the world?"

"Um." She counted on her fingers, lips moving soundlessly. "Eight hundred and thirty-two years."

"Shit's changed." Hitch's tone was flat. "Someone's going to let you out of this basket soon. Here is what you need to know. No living side won the war. It was demons. And they didn't win, either. Everyone lost. No, don't interrupt, and don't shake your wings at me either. I don't *care*. I care about her," his not-arm stabbed at a sobbing Evanne, "and you're going to make her life hard unless we have this conversation."

Tarragon's lower lip trembled, so she bit it. "What conversation?"

"Eight hundred and thirty-two years of history in twenty-five seconds." Hitch looked away. "I don't remember much at all. Most of me's faded away, do you see? But I can recognise the pure. Evanne is. Her heart, I mean. She loves to laugh. Tells stories. Her voice is the purest thing I've heard when song comes to her lips. She doesn't hate those who can run like the wind. She hates herself. So you *will* be kind to her."

Tarragon nodded. "She's ... Vehement Systems Architecture?"

"No." The ghost sighed. "She is half-human, half-Vhemin."

"Impossible." *But it explains why she's, like, hot.*

"And yet." Hitch looked at the sky, a couple fluffy clouds drifting on the wind. "Demons worked both sides, turning the world into a ball of hate. They imprisoned the Three, and we helped them do it."

"But—"

"Not finished," he said. "The end of the war was an end for all. The world broke, and almost everyone died. The Itikari fell. Vehement Systems crumbled. All the other works of humans faded. Nothing was left. The Architectures became clans of roaming monsters. Vhemin. The Fey Branded moved to the edges of the world, and are the Feybrind. We remain." He paused. "I mean, living humans. I'm not much of anything anymore."

"What about fairies?"

"There are none." Hitch wasn't unkind. "The Kingdom is no more, leastways not as I know. A fairy helped them fight the demon king, but fell. Vertiline spoke of one Builder Geneve knew before the fight at Imshir, but she'd never met him."

"What were their names?"

"Yasmine Glittercone fell in the final fight. Sunbeam Jinglewood, earlier."

"I know ... knew Yasmin." Tarragon's brow furrowed. "She was clever. But a traitor."

"Hmm." Hitch stood. "You might want to rethink your perspective. I said I recognise the pure, and I see it in you too. You could be of great help, or you could just be a sandwich."

"Are you threatening me?"

He laughed. "I'm dead, fairy. I can't hurt anyone. Not ever again."

TARRAGON WAITED, ALTHOUGH NOT PATIENTLY. SHE WASN'T BUILT for it, in the same way she wasn't built to ride a horse. Her glimmer returned in fits and starts. Not enough to burn through the basket, but enough to warm her a little.

While she waited, she watched the enemy. The Vhemin matriarch screamed only once as the Feybrind pulled arrows from her, but she didn't hit the cat. Evanne yelled as the shaft was removed from her leg, but Tarragon thought it more performance than reality.

"Why is she pretending her leg hurts?"

"Because it gives her something else to think about," Hitch said.

"Her mother and father are probably dead. Everyone she knows is buried under magma or salt water. This merry band is all that remains of her family."

"Hmm." Tarragon wanted to argue about how Fey Branded and Vehement Systems Architectures couldn't be *friends* let alone *family*, but she wasn't so sure anymore. "They trained me, you know."

"To Build things?"

"I wasn't good at that, so I became a spy." Tarragon turned her back on the field triage station, leaning against the walls of her cell. "I'm a good spy, or I was. But I meant, they taught me about what was possible. About how cats and scaled can't be friends. It makes them sick."

"To borrow from you: hmm."

"We made them that way. So we'd be sure, you know? Who was on our side." Tarragon ran a tiny hand through her hair and was rewarded with a sprinkling of glimmerdust. "They made the monsters from humans, sharks, and crocodiles. Did you know that?"

"They also made them from tribe, heart, and duty." Hitch pulled his knees closer. "We made them to die so we wouldn't have to, and they're almost all that's left."

"Humans made things well enough, before they had Builders." Tarragon shrugged. "The Fey Branded are made from humans and three strains of large feline. It's why they smell of cinnamon." She sighed. "I miss the way things were."

"All the killing and the dying?"

"I'm not sure that's stopped." Tarragon paced her cell. The basket was big enough for a workout, if she was inclined. She wasn't. "I miss ice cream."

"I miss being alive. You need to get some perspective."

"Like how the Fey Branded and the Vehement Systems Architectures call each other kin?" Tarragon shook her head. "I can't understand it."

"Perhaps it is because there are no more Architectures or Branded. They are Feybrind or Vhemin. They own their names, because the ones we gave them weren't fit." Hitch stood. "They're coming over to talk. Be nice."

Tarragon turned, smoothing her hair. "Were you Itikari?"

"I don't think so." Hitch put not-hands in pockets that turned to dust an age past. "I think I was with the other guys."

The basket was whipped from above her, and she blinked in the sudden light. The ochre sun was heading toward its bed, perhaps marking four in the afternoon. Above her, three faces, but not unkind. The matriarch looked angry, but that felt like a default setting. Sight of Day was sad, in an elegant way. Most wouldn't mark it, but Itikari knew their own. Evanne crouched, her face pale, worn by the chisel of the day. "Tarragon."

Tarragon inclined her chin, giving her wings a flutter. *Be cool. Just because she's got eyes I could get lost in doesn't mean she won't kill me.* She tried to look down her nose, but the height difference made it difficult. "Evanne."

"You are from the same tribe as the Feybrind?" Evanne kept her eyes on Tarragon, but the fairy sensed it was because she didn't want to look at the cooling bodies of three dead cats.

"Tribe? Oh, I get you. Yes, we are Itikari. Itikari made Fey Branded first. Then us, the Builders, and finally the dragons. I don't suppose you've seen a dragon?" Tarragon didn't hold out much hope.

"I have never seen a dragon, but I have felt the weight of her regard on everything we still hold dear." Evanne held out her hand, and Tarragon cautiously climbed aboard. The maybe-Vhemin stood, holding Tarragon at her eye height. "Ormeon was her name, and I live because she doesn't."

"You owe the enemy?"

"They are not the enemy!" Evanne's teeth flashed, and Tarragon was reminded just how dangerous the Vhemin could be. All anger, and so hard to kill. "*Your* war is over!"

"Then why do three Feybrind lie dead?" Tarragon swept a tiny arm, an angry slash to the corpses behind her.

"I don't know." Evanne looked away. *Interesting. She is sad that those who tried to kill her lie dead.* "Why were they going to kill you?"

"I admit, that's weird." Tarragon gave a small jump, but her bung wing wouldn't let her get any sky. She landed on Evanne's hand in a shower of sparkle. "We're on the same side."

"But what if we're not?" Evanne frowned. "Uncle Day has a theory."

{*It's more of a group effort.*} The Feybrind stared at the flattened edifice of the mountain. {*The People are scattered. We don't have time for kings, or...*} He trailed off, hands still for a moment, eyes seeing something in the trail of years past. {*We don't have time for such things. We have our forests and our ice vales. We make what is needed. We bring it to those who need it. But we diminish. Always, we are at the edges of the world. There is no place left for us to stand.*}

"The Fey Branded weren't made for war." Tarragon pursed her lips. "You're ... *cats.*"

{*We are children of the world like any other.*} Sight of Day shrugged. {*I believe there may be a rogue faction. It lines up with whispers from Or'sen.*}

"It's why we're here," Barret snarled. "Ravenswall continues, but Chancery to the east was lost. Our lords are missing, and our armies are," she growled, looking for the word, "*lost.* It's not that they've died. They just aren't there anymore."

"Vhemin troops?"

"Mostly," Barret admitted, "but there are humans among them too. The cats serve as spies only, because there aren't enough left to do the dying."

"So, you're saying there's a rogue faction of," Tarragon waved a hand, "people out there who are making mountains destroy settlements, and also causing armies to vanish as if the ground swallowed them whole?" She pursed her lips. "Feet like those don't tread without a sound."

{*They do if they are Feybrind.*}

"Uh," Tarragon said. "But the cats and fairies are on the *same side.*"

Sight of Day looked at the fallen. {*Are we?*}

Evanne put Tarragon down, then hurried to the Feybrind. They sized each other up, the human playing at being a Vhemin, and the cat with the metal-hard eyes. Then she grabbed him, squeezing him tight, and pressed her face into his chest. Her words were muffled, but Tarragon got them well enough. "We are. You and me. We're on the same side."

Sight of Day's face softened, and he put a furred hand on Evanne's head, smoothing her hair, holding her close. After a moment, they disentangled. *{I forgot for a moment.}* He looked at the crumbled mountain. *{There's a lot on my mind.}*

"We need to see what happened," Evanne said. "We need to find if Mama and…" Her lip trembled, and Tarragon marvelled at the steel that seemed to grow inside her as she bit it. "We need to *see*."

"Great, more fucking walking," Barret said. "Well, let's eat something and get some rest first."

"We should go now," Evanne said.

"Says the one who wasn't shot, to the one who was."

"Uh." Evanne looked at her feet. "Thanks for that."

"Eh." Barret stood, swayed as if in a breeze, then charted a course for the dunes. "I'm going to see if any beer washed ashore."

Chapter Ten

Night is when the magic happens.

Evanne felt the kiss of the sea breeze, feeling a little more normal after she'd eaten, napped, and then spent time alone waiting for the stars to come out. She tuned her guitar, playing for the dunes, waiting for the sun to fail and the stars to reign.

"That sounds nice," Hitch offered. "I haven't heard a guitar in a while."

"Oh, you remember this?" Evanne gave him a little side-eye. "You don't remember who you were, where you worked, or how you died, but you remember guitar music?"

"Only the good stuff," the ghost said. "I think I used to play, a little." He held his arms out, then stared at where his hands should be. "Or maybe I didn't. You'd need hands for that."

"Hands are overrated." Evanne teased the strings, the instrument sad enough for two. "They get you into all manner of trouble."

"They get *you* into trouble. Most people use them for more useful things."

"There's nothing more useful than borrowing things or playing songs." Evanne glanced at Hitch. "You sure you used to play?"

"No."

"Let's see. Come here." She beckoned him closer. "Sit with me."

"It feels weird."

"Don't be a baby." Evanne glanced at the stars. "Everything feels weird, Hitch. The whole world. Mama and Papa are gone. My friends are dead. Cleo ... Ah." She stroked the guitar. "I feel like there are so many things that could've been, that never will be."

"The world has been like that since forever." The ghost stood, stretched, then drifted to her. He settled within her, the odd blue smudge creeping out where he didn't align with her frame perfectly. Hitch held his arms within hers. "Like this?"

"Like that," she agreed. "What would you like me to play?"

She felt his hesitation, his struggle with memory, and then she saw it, clear as glass, bright as day. A chord, welcomed by a series of single notes onstage. She bent her head, fingering the fretboard, callused fingertips kissing strings, Vhemin fingernails as picks. The guitar eased its music across the sand, vying with the dune crickets.

Evanne played for her mother and father. She played for Cleo, and for Old Merle. The guitar remembered Imshir with her, a melody given her through an age of time by a ghost's memory. She felt Hitch playing *with* her, his not fingers next to hers, his sad smile mimicked in hers.

IN A LAND WHERE SHADOWS LINGER LONG,
In a kingdom lost to time's cruel song,
We gather here, hearts heavy, heads bowed low,
To bid farewell to souls we used to know.

OH, IT WHISPERS THROUGH THE TREES,
A sombre dirge, carried on the breeze,
In this forgotten kingdom, tears we send,
To say goodbye, to mourn, as we transcend.

ONCE A RULER, NOW A HUMBLE GUEST,
In a world where sorrow never takes its rest,

We'll remember the tales of days of old,
As we weave our stories into threads of gold.

OH, IT WHISPERS THROUGH THE TREES,
A sombre dirge, carried on the breeze,
In this forgotten kingdom, tears we send,
To say goodbye, to mourn, as we transcend.

THE CASTLE WALLS MAY CRUMBLE AND DECAY,
But the memories we keep will never fade away,
In this land where legends quietly blend,
We'll carry your spirits, dear friends.

STARDUST ABOVE, ALL SHIMMER AND GLEAM,
In the tapestry of time, we find our dream,
Though we part ways, the bond remains unbroken,
In the words unuttered and love unspoken.

OH, IT WHISPERS THROUGH THE TREES,
A sombre dirge, carried on the breeze,
In this forgotten kingdom, tears we send,
To say goodbye, to mourn, as we transcend.

IN THE ECHOES OF THIS MOURNFUL SONG,
We find the strength to carry on,
Though we part ways with heavy hearts, my friends,
In this forgotten kingdom, this is not the end.

HESER THE CHEG CAME FIRST. THE QUEENSGUARD CAPTAIN CAME on unsteady legs, eyes wide with wonder. Evanne could see the blood heat of him, the bright coursing surging that said *I live*. Barret came next, the matriarch slow and deliberate, ear cocked, face holding an expression Evanne had never seen before: a kind of soulful surprise. Sight of Day arrived on the wind, tail calm, golden eyes reflecting the stars.

Last came Tarragon, the fairy's glimmer marking her progress through the long dune grasses. She hop-flitted near to Evanne, her wing still not flight ready.

Evanne finished Hitch's song, then touched her cheek, feeling the wetness. "Hitch, that was wonderful. What's it called?"

"I don't remember." The ghost sounded strangled with frustration.

"Where did you learn that?" Tarragon's face went from hard to sad. "You shouldn't know that song."

"Hitch showed me." Evanne sighed. "What's it called?"

"It is *The End*. It was written by a woman almost nine hundred years ago. It is the funeral song of the Vehement..." She wound down. "It's a funeral song. That's all."

"Balls," Barret said. "Put your toys away, Evanne. It's time to see what's left of your home."

Evanne put the instrument back in its case, then snapped it closed. The clasps gave a comforting *thunk*, a promise that what was inside would be right there when she needed it.

IT DIDN'T HAPPEN AS FAST AS ALL THAT. THERE WAS A LOT OF walking, and not a lot of singing or happy dances. They'd washed ashore leagues distant, and even walking at night was thirsty work in the desert. Evanne found water in the supplies, and they were squared away for food, but it didn't make the toll on her feet any less.

They walked single file, Heser the Cheg at the rear, Barret at the front, and Evanne with Sight of Day in the middle. Hitch wandered off aways, his glimmer of pale blue like a lost star on earth. Tarragon rode on Sight of Day's shoulder, because she *trusted the cats, and not you vile monsters*, despite *the cats* being the only ones who wanted her dead.

No accounting for taste. It didn't bother Evanne, because the fairy was punchy, and there was only so much of that you could take from a sandwich-sized person. She eyed Aunt Barret, the old Vhemin trudging along, not complaining, and thought, *I'm barely sixteen and I'm complaining. Aunt Barret is ancient but doesn't complain.* She jogged to Barret. "Aunt Barret—"

"It's just Barret, kid. I'm not your aunt."

Evanne snorted. "And Uncle Heser isn't my uncle. But you are in my heart, and there is no better word." She touched her chest, remembering the Trick of it.

Barret gave her a sidelong glare. "Does that shit work on people?"

"Usually," Evanne admitted.

"Well, fuck off with it. It's not going to help here." But the matriarch gave a smile slightly less ghostly than Hitch.

"How do you do it?" Evanne felt her heart beat faster, limping a faster rhythm, unable to keep time with the music of her soul. "My mother and father are ... they're not here. We got shipwrecked. A mountain exploded! We're walking through the night, and unless I've missed something you haven't slept, *and* you were shot."

"How do I do what?"

"Keep going," Evanne husked. "It seems very hard."

Barret trudged along, and was silent so long Evanne thought she'd dozed off on her feet. When she spoke, her voice was stone chips on slate. "Did you know I'm younger than your father?"

Evanne looked away. "So I was told."

"Well, I'm telling you too. The ancients had armour that made us Vhemin *strong*, Evanne. We became mighty. Weapons of god-forged steel that could bear the brunt of the Tresward's Storm. I wore the blue-runed armour and felt like one of the Three. But it made us sickly. Weak, in the end. Weaker than the rest."

"It aged you."

"It fucked me off, is what it did." Barret eyed the ruined mountain ahead. A ruddy glow smudged the sky, reflected from smouldering ruins, a promise of the earth's molten might burning still. "And there are still people out there," she jabbed a gnarled finger in an easterly direction, "who want to do it all again. I'm not going to *die* for them, kid. I ain't done killing. Not yet. Maybe not for a while yet. So, I walk. I get shot. I do what the Raven Queen wants, because she and I see eye to eye. No, don't interrupt. Yes, we have snake eyes and shark teeth. Our skin is scaled. But we're all done bleeding for some*one* else. Now we're bleeding for some*thing*. The Raven gets it. I get it. And so I keep *going*."

Evanne looked back at the rest of their group. "I'm glad you're here." She left no Trick in the words.

"I'm not. I can't sleep properly and it takes two days to work up a decent shit after eating meat."

Evanne snorted. "I think we should ... wait. What's that?" She cast her arm toward the dark desert sands.

Barret swung about, squinting into the gloom. "I see nothing."

{I saw it. A glint, perhaps of a lantern.} Sight of Day's eyes narrowed. *{Furred and scaled each see the night differently. There is only one of us who sees as both do.}*

Hitch appeared at Evanne's elbow. "I feel it too." He hugged himself. "There's someone out there."

"Well, this just became a party." Barret beckoned. "Heser! Get up here and start being useful."

THEY APPROACHED WHERE EVANNE SAW THE LIGHT. HER HALF-Vhemin eyes hunted for heat, but got nothing back. The human part of her vision strained in the dark, unable to see well with only starlight's guidance.

Sight of Day held a muffled Tarragon close. He'd swaddled the fairy in his cloak, barely a glimmer to be seen. Evanne feared the fairy would give them away if she thought those on the sands more friends than the 'foes' she rode with, but hoped even a failed Builder would remember who tried to kill her.

Uncle Heser led their group, a gnarled branch in his hands. "This would be easier with good steel."

"This would be easier if we weren't here at all," Barret growled. "Try to be professional."

The Queensguard gave her a flat stare. "All I'm saying is, we should—"

Out of the darkness, a swarm of claw and blade. The sand erupted, Feybrind bursting from burrows. Evanne had a hot second to admire how they hid their body heat from the Vhemin and their presence from Sight of Day, and then the cats were upon them.

We won't survive this. The thought hit her like Storm Light, a hard pillar of knowledge from the Three above. And then she thought, *Ah. So it is.* There wasn't time to explain, and her mouth wanted to bite, not talk.

Evanne dropped her shoulder and charged, ignoring Heser's, "Wait!" She remembered the hands at her throat, the arrows in Aunt Barret, and the tall standing over the tiny as the Feybrind threatened Tarragon. She snarled, all sharp-enough teeth, hair flying, and impacted a cat trying to tackle Uncle Day.

The enemy cat went flying, but Evanne didn't follow. She saw Sight of Day's golden eyes widen as she reached beneath his cloak, yanking Tarragon free. She held the fairy aloft, ignoring the *what are you doing, you great oaf, put me down!* and tore the swaddling free.

The fairy's indignant brilliance glared across the sand, glimmerdusk raining. Evanne's human eyes were blinded, as were the Feybrind's, but her Vhemin eyes saw heat. She heard Barret's roar of approval, answered with her own, and punched the Feybrind she'd shoulder-barged in the side of the head.

An arrow skimmed past, and she clamped her jaws shut. *They might be night-blind for a second or two, but they can still hear fine.* Evanne tossed Tarragon aloft, hoping the fairy's wing was good enough to keep her above harm's way, then waded in.

Uncle Heser, cudgel swinging, human eyes useless, but body more than willing.

Barret, holding a Feybrind above her head with one arm. A snarl, spite and hate, ancient-wrought.

Evanne, hands around another's throat. Her stomach, sick. Her heart, pounding. A cut on her cheek, a claw or blade, who even *cared.*

That sickness in her stomach, oh but it was *sweet*, it was sauce for a hunger she didn't know she had.

The night blazed, golden-white. *"STOP!"*

Evanne cringed away from the light, hiding her face. She heard sand hiss, the scamper of feet. Silence. She blinked away tears, her Vhemin's heat vision glaring hot vermillion, her human eyes seeing nothing but brilliance.

Tarragon fluttered down, one wing still tatty, brilliance fading. Her light faded, revealing furrowed sand. Three shallow pits where the Feybrind waited for them. Blood in a smear, whose Evanne didn't know. The fairy landed, then swayed. "You can't kill them."

Barret spat, then worked her jaw. "Why not?"

"Because..." Tarragon fell to one knee, her glimmer almost gone, but her voice wailing. "Because they're *cats*."

SAND WHISPERED AS A WICKED WIND PICKED UP, CARRYING something rotten on the breeze from the sea. Evanne wondered if it was people that festered in the ocean. If there'd been enough time for her friends to decay into fish food and brine.

She carried Tarragon in a small sling by her heart. The fairy was out cold. The glimmerfire she'd used to hold back the night took everything out of her. *Spent.* Evanne didn't know why she was the one carrying the spare snacks, but Uncle Day had half-smiled, touched her cheek, and said, *{Sometimes it's not about you.}*

They found the Feybrind's camp only a short hop away. It was a crude affair by human standards, barely serviceable for Vhemin scavengers, and a travesty for the cats.

Uncle Heser lifted a tattered blanket. "I've seen better on a penny beggar."

"They have their priorities right." Barret lifted a beautiful sword from its shroud of oilcloth. "They're here on killing business."

Evanne found herself by Sight of Day. She held her hands still for a moment, wondering what to say, then, *{Are you okay?}*

He sighed. *{No.}*

She nodded. *{Neither am I. Maybe we can be not okay together.}*

The Feybrind half-smiled at that. *{You are one of the marvels of creation.}*

{I'm just confused,} Evanne admitted. Then, because the Feybrind's Handspeak wasn't *right* for this, she said, "I ... felt hungry. Before."

He turned, smoothing her hair. *{I know.}*

"I don't want to feel hungry." Evanne looked away from his kindness in those wonderful eyes. "I want to go home."

She felt a touch on her chin, and he turned her face toward him. *{You are home. With me.}* He looked to his feet for a moment. *{You are my kin, cub of my brother. I will always be here.}*

Evanne felt her eyes well, blinked, and took a deep breath. "I know. I know! But ... what if *I'm* not ... here?"

{Where would you go? It is a very small world.}

"I mean—"

{I think all of us must find our place to stand. For some, made of half wonder and half glory, it is difficult.} The Feybrind smoothed her hair again. *{But I will stand with you.}*

"We don't deserve you." She sniffed.

{I know.}

She laughed, then headed toward Uncle Heser. "Did you find anything?"

"A few coins. A handful of paper. Blank, of course." Heser the Cheg held some sheafs out to her.

Evanne took them, held them to her nose, and breathed. *Cinnamon.* "Why do cats have blank paper?"

"Why does anyone have paper?" the Queensguard replied. "I've no use for poets."

"Good talk." Evanne shuffled further on, her eyes picking out stray heat in the sand. An eddy of remembered heat. She walked on, steps cautious for more hidden people lurking in the sand. Gods, but she was tired. She glanced back at Barret, wondering how someone who looked over two hundred could be walking around with more enthusiasm than Evanne. *Get a grip. Bite down. Harden up. All that.* Evanne tried a sharp-toothed grin, teeth glinting their Trick at the night. *Good enough*.

The sands farther from the camp were peaceful. It wasn't that the *sands* weren't noisy, the wind still being a twat about it, but Evanne wanted time alone with her thoughts. Up was down, and there wasn't any going back. She'd, what, almost killed a Feybrind today, and she'd *wanted* to. *Oh but Papa, you didn't tell me—*

"What's that?" Hitch pointed to the east.

Evanne turned like a horse with a jerked bridle. "You what?"

"Yes, I know you're moping. I get it. I want to mope too. That song was ... intense." Hitch held his left arm up as if remembering a fret board. "I *knew* it, Evanne, and while we played, I knew *you*. No, don't interrupt. I have been with you every step of your life."

"In a non-creepy way."

"Totally," the ghost agreed. "Don't let it bother you that I watch you when you're sleeping."

"You're such a dick."

"But despite seeing you, and thinking I knew you, I never did. Not until now. That moment we played—"

"I played."

"*We* played." He waited her out, and when she nodded, drifted a few paces off. "I missed your Papa and your Mama. Like they were *mine*. Birthed me, cared for my hurts, and Khiton have mercy, but I want them back." Hitch sounded like he was gritting his teeth, but it was hard to tell. "I want to mope. But I want you to live more than that, and over there is a thing you need to get eyes on before it eats your face."

Evanne wiped her face, but there were no tears. *None left, maybe.* "Okay, we'll look at your patch of sand."

"It's not just sand, it's—"

"I get you." Evanne straightened her jerkin, then rubbed at her collar where the salt made it stiff. Where the scales ran up the back of her neck the collar wasn't doing much, but the side of her throat where she had her human frailty the skin was rubbing raw. "Monsters?" She sniffed. "I'm gonna teach them what a monster is." She stalked off toward the danger, still wearing a fever-bright smile.

"It wasn't your fault." Hitch drifted at her left.

"I almost killed one, Hitch." She glared at him, anger making her voice hard, but she wasn't sure who she was angry at.

"Aye. Aye, I was there. But ... do you see? It's the way you were made."

"All the weaknesses of a human, except this super-important one," she snarled. "The Half-Made. The Poorly-Made. The Wickedly-Made. The—"

"Are we moping again?"

She barked a laugh. "You're all right, Hitch. You're all right."

"Focus, child of two people." The ghost swept an arm at a mound. "Your doom."

The mound was small, perhaps the size of a starved pony, or a big dog. Evanne's eyes hunted for heat and found a glimmer. *They ... left someone here?* The ember anger of blood, hidden beneath a shroud. She stalked closer, right hand hooked into claws, left out, and tore the shroud clear. "Behold, the Doom of Evanne. An unconscious woman." She lowered her arm.

"I was hoping for something a little more dramatic," the spectre admitted. "This has the feel of an anticlimax." He looked about. "Still. Seems odd, doesn't it? A woman out in the desert all alone, a stumble from an enemy camp."

"Might not be her enemy."

"Then why's she out here?"

Evanne ignored the ghost, squatting beside the woman. She was in that delicate vale between thirty and fuck-knows, because her skin was smooth, and her black tresses were untouched by silver. Evanne turned her face to the wan starlight. *Full lips. Made to smile, but she spends a lot of time frowning.* Salt and sand crusted her eyelashes, eyebrows, and hair, which suggested a shipwreck survivor like Evanne. Except Evanne had never seen this woman before in her life. Someone on the crew? A person belowdecks?

Aside from the oh-so-pretty face, the woman had a nasty gash on her forehead. It was crusted over, and would need cleaning before her blood coiled on itself. Evanne lifted the shroud, shaking the sand out.

It was a cloak, maybe red, maybe just a trendy not-quite-black. Only sunlight and a good wash would tell. "This looks expensive."

"You're very perceptive."

Growling, Evanne hefted the unconscious woman and slung her over her shoulders. "She weighs nothing at all. Like she's eaten naught but starlight her entire life."

"Then she's probably fragile. Be gentle."

Evanne offered the ghost another growl, then headed back for camp. By the time she'd arrived, the rest of the party had the air of people wanting to move on. Evanne called out as she got closer, because she didn't want to be shot. "I'm coming back in. Get a fire on."

Sight of Day reached her first, his golden eyes soft and concerned. {Who is that?}

"No clue. But she's been hit in the head and needs to eat a pie." Evanne eased her burden to the sands, leaning the woman against a log. "There."

The cat took a step back as he got a clear view of the woman's face, and she heard Barret mutter, *Another damn one.* But it was Uncle Heser who crouched beside her. The Queensguard's hands were gentle as he turned the unconscious woman's face toward him. "Where did you find her?"

"Out there." Evanne waved a hand toward the general darkness. "You know her?"

"The whole world knows her, child." Heser the Cheg beckoned to Barret to join them.

"I ain't your servant."

"Barret!" He barked.

The old Vhemin grumbled a bit more, but as she leaned closer, she sucked in air. "Is that—"

"It is."

"I'll get a fire on. It can't be helped." Barret glared at the night as if daring lurking Feybrind to return. "This confounds things, human."

"Aye, monster." Heser worried his canteen out, moistening a cloth and dabbing the woman's face.

"Who is she?" Evanne looked between them.

"It'd like to know, too." Tarragon sparkled closer, bringing her light to bear on the woman's face.

Uncle Heser sagged a little, then rubbed his face. "This is someone who was at sea on the *Gallant*. A warship made to end all wars. Three times the size of the *Light Treader*, and built to stop dissent. Her voice has been silenced. All is lost."

"The what?" Evanne said.

Sight of Day pulled Evanne to her feet. Brushed her off and smoothed her hair again. There was no half-smile about him this time, though. *{This is Morgan, the Raven Queen of Or'sen.}*

Chapter Eleven

T he ... *queen? Since when did we have a queen?*
Tarragon flitted about, still feeling weak but able to hit sky for short stretches. The beautiful maybe-Vhemin young woman was looking as shocked as Tarragon felt. *Maybe she didn't know they had a queen either.*

The fairy cleared her throat. "A queen?"

"You were expecting a king?" The wider, balder man with the weird name Tarragon wasn't bothering to remember glared at her. "All know the Raven Queen is the best Or'sen has seen since—"

"This isn't about emancipation." Tarragon huffed. "Girl power. Rock on. Kick the balls! All that." She punched the air. "What happened to the head of the Itikari? His Council and all they ruled?"

Lots of blank stares. A blink or two. The grumpy matriarch adjusted her belt. "The who?"

"Mama said there was a lich," Evanne mused. "Eternally alive, but not. A kingdom buried beneath the mountain. Guardians of undeath, rotted but unable to sleep."

"Sounds like the guy," Tarragon agreed. "He's in charge."

More blank stares, then on cue all of them laughed, except the cat who did so silently. {*Little Light, the dead rule nothing but ashes.*}

"Well, shit. That explains why," Tarragon pointed at Heaven's Gate, "the mountain blew its stack. We've got to get the Council operational again." The blank stares were getting irritating, so she added, "If we go to the mountain we can find people who know what happened."

"Oh," Evanne said, brushing rust-copper hair aside. "We were going there anyway, but so we can find those who live."

"More monsters?"

{You've much to learn, Little Light.} Sight of Day offered her his arm, and she alighted on it then scampered to his shoulder. *{There are few monsters left, and none of them have fangs.}*

That didn't sound right, but Tarragon let it ride. Once she had the Itikari Council kicking again, things would *change* around here.

THEY'D TRUDGED ALL NIGHT, AND MOST OF THE DAY.

The ruins of Heaven's Gate snarled ruddy light while the sky was dark, and wheezed acrid yellow-black smoke as dawn came. The mountain's ruins were small, slumped, but in the magical way of distance, became big all at once. The ground at the mountain's base was mostly loose shale. Nothing grew here, and so the party walked on.

Tarragon wanted to go around the mountain's base, because climbing an active volcano was for suckers, but Evanne would hear none of it. She'd stalked off, palm out when Tarragon tried to protest. It was a childish motion, but, Tarragon admitted, surprisingly effective.

The Vhemin was one of the hated enemy, and the maybe-Vhemin was probably making up numbers on the team. The walking human was a human, which meant *fickle* or *ornery*. The Feybrind was the odd one out and should've been with her. If she'd had her sword, they could have made short work of the other three, except the maybe-Vhemin was damn hot, and Tarragon hadn't had much action in eight hundred years.

The human, speaking of being human, carried the *other*, unconscious human. She was frail, boots to haircut, with a physique only sustainable by the very rich. Or, a desk job, but there didn't seem to be many desk jobs going these days. *I don't even know why I'm with these losers.*

That's not it. She cleared her throat, careful not to be too loud from her perch on the cat's shoulder. Their ears were very sensitive. "I'm confused."

{*You're scared. That's not the same thing.*}

She stamped her foot. "Whatever you want to call it, this isn't right. Can you get me a sword?"

{*So you can kill my friends?*}

"So I can be useful." Tarragon used her wings for balance as the cat's weight shifted. "And maybe kill the bad guys. Once I work out who they are."

{*You've worked out not all is what it was.*} The cat sighed, his shoulders lifting like an ocean swell. {*Well, baby steps, I guess.*}

"Sword?"

Sight of Day clambered over rock. Tarragon could feel the heat still coming off from the mountain's fury. {*I will make you a sword. Once we find my brother and sister of heart, and see what can be done for anyone still in Imshir.*}

"Huh." Tarragon took off, hovering before the cat. *My wings are getting much better.* "You're not worried I'll run off? Kill your buddies? I'm looking for the catch."

{*There is no catch.*} The Feybrind turned those wonderful golden eyes to the horizon. {*If you run off, you weren't meant to be here.*}

"Uncle!" Evanne's voice was hoarse.

Sight of Day sped past Tarragon like she was a land-bound sow, the breeze of his passing tugging her wings. She buzzed after, her gammy wing giving nothing but agitation, then stopped as she saw the valley below. "Well, that's a change. Not a good one."

They'd climbed high enough to get a view of Imshir. Evanne had crested a rise, foot on a rock, those beautiful lavender snake eyes as far away as the sky. Below, a jagged trench at least two klicks wide ran from the sea and through the city. Imshir was more a ruin than before, stones scattered, water and sludge peppered within. And 'within' was arbitrary, because Tarragon could see no more walls. Small fires burned in taller buildings out of the ocean's reach, perhaps set alight by the mountain's might.

Tarragon watched Evanne's eyes track from the city down, down, *oh no don't look*, down to the base of the mountain. Flames licked at the very stone of the hillside. Magma ran like blood from a giant. Heat shimmered the air where nothing could live. No birds flew. Not even an insect buzzed.

"Bugger me," Barret suggested.

"Mama," Evanne choked. "Papa." And then she was gone, running where she could, scrabbling where she couldn't.

Sight of Day was on her heels, and for a moment Tarragon thought the Feybrind would stop her, pull her back from that terrible heat, but the cat was looking with her, hunting, praying.

The ridiculously-named human turned to Tarragon. "Will you help? Now is not the time for sides or wars. People bleed below. Do you see?"

"People like those?" Tarragon pointed to movement through the heat shimmer. She squinted. It looked like a group of humans carrying farming implements. "Perhaps they're coming to help dig."

"We're not that lucky," Barret growled. She slipped over the edge of the mountain, heading down to help Evanne.

"Come," the human said. "Ride with me."

"I can fly!"

"So I see." He patted his shoulder, somewhat awkward with his burden of unconscious queen, and she alighted. "I'm Heser the Cheg."

"I know." She bit her lip. "But I forgot."

"Sure." She felt the strength of the man, built like Vhemin but encased in skin rather than scale. Relentless, even though he'd walked as they had while carrying another. A fire in this one, no doubt, and perhaps worth remembering his name for. "Let us see what the next few hours hold, Tarragon. Stick with me. I'll keep you safe."

"But ... you don't know if you can trust me!"

"No." Heser the Cheg shook his head as he descended. "But I know you're small, and alone. I was like that once. I think it'd have been nice if someone bigger stood between me and the lash."

Tarragon held onto his ear. "What kind of man are you?"

"The ordinary kind."

I don't think so, Heser the Cheg. I don't think anyone's ordinary. Not anymore.

THE TRIP DOWN THE MOUNTAIN WAS QUICK FOR TWO REASONS. Evanne's enthusiasm for helping her parents lent the young woman's steps speed even Tarragon was jealous of. The maybe-Vhemin staggered, gasping, and the fairy wondered what was wrong with her. Marvellous musculature, but no gas in the tank. The mountain wasn't very large, but the could-be-a-Vhemin stagger-stepped after just short bursts of speed.

Tarragon kept casting nervous glances over her shoulder, afraid the ruined Heaven's Gate would rise and kill them all. But there wasn't anything left of the darn thing. It was such a ruin nothing recognisable as a system of war poked above ground. She spied the odd strut, bent like a dowager's hump from the tremendous heat. She spared an idle thought for what must have happened to the controlling intelligence. Had it died in glory or agony?

Only the Three would know, and they were gone like so much else.

Queen Morgan jounced along in Heser the Cheg's arms. The man must have been pushing fifty summers but he carried his charge like she was weightless. He didn't even have the decency to reach an arm out for balance, as if he challenged the mountain to try unsettling him. The woman's face was deathly pale, but Tarragon knew that was fashionable in some circles. Hard to tell if she was dying or just a heavy hand with the foundation.

No, she's dying. Look, her lips are the wrong shade of blue.

They reached the base of the mountain as dusk settled. Like the other Itikari installations, Heaven's Gate didn't settle into foothills or other nonsense; the hill stopped where ground began. A few loose stones, a little shale, and then they were back on familiar sand. The people coming toward them were a raggedy lot and Tarragon couldn't help but label them as *serf* or *peasant*.

They had farming implements, but Tarragon felt something was wrong. The odd lantern did nothing to dispel the gloom that gathered at their feet.

Hitch glimmered into being. Took one look at the crowd, and said, "Evanne, get out of here."

Evanne ignored him, and half-jogged to the villagers, then slowed. "Friends. Have you come to help?" Her voice was uncertain, and Tarragon winced.

Merle stepped forward, which made Tarragon smile. The old man looked more bedraggled than before, but a good ship sinking would do that. He held a shovel, but in a somewhat more thoughtful manner than his fellows. "We came to see what was left. What might need killing."

"Demons," a woman behind him agreed.

"Evanne," Hitch hissed. "Now. Go!"

Evanne laughed, but the spectre might have rattled her. To Tarragon's ear it rang of forced merriment. "There are no demons, Merle. Not anymore."

"And yet, the mountain's dead. Been here since before time and memory."

"Not quite." Tarragon waved from her Heser perch. "It was made by Itikari about eight hundred and fifty years ago."

"Witchcraft," came a muttered voice from the back of the crowd.

Heser the Cheg grumbled. "Might not be a good time for a history lesson."

"Nonsense." Tarragon steamed on. "There was some sorcery used in its construction, but this is mostly a Builder product." She felt pride in her words, for all she'd failed her exams.

She could feel Heser's wince in the cant of his shoulders. "You just confirmed what they feared."

Old Merle held his arm up. "Friends. Friends! We've long known Heaven's Gate was a miracle of the ancients. The battle with the demon horde was won because a group of Feybrind came from within."

Evanne took a step back. "If you didn't come to help dig, why did you bring a shovel?"

"Question's a good one." Barret stamped forward, stabbing a finger at a short man with a mattock. "You. Yeah, *you*. No, don't hide behind your friend. Why are you here?"

The short man looked concerned to be singled out, but then he found a reserve of courage, his chin jutting. "The school is gone. We must do what needs doing."

"Aye?" Evanne cocked her head. "And what's that?"

No response, other than shifting feet, the odd murmur. Tarragon didn't understand humans very well, but she knew enough about them to know none individually were as dumb as a group. "Are you going to do something stupid?"

Old Merle gave her a glance. "I'll be happy to dig."

"You'll do no such thing, Merle. She's the cause of it!" A woman who looked to be no more than a teenager stepped forward. Her clothes were ripped, a red stain on her pants marking an injury from the shipwreck. She was pretty enough, Tarragon thought, except for the sneer on her face. She held a rake in one hand, but her other stabbed accusation at Evanne.

"Cleo?" Evanne took another step back. "What do you mean?"

"Nothing's right anymore!" Cleo looked to start something she couldn't finish, all attitude and fire, but Merle's arm across her chest held her back. "*Your* parents woke the mountain. *Your* blood kindled its fire. Our homes are a ruin. The blame's at your feet."

Tarragon leaned close to Heser's ear, keeping her voice low. "Did people get stupider in the last eight hundred years?"

"You've got a demon, too. We all see her." Cleo glared at Tarragon. "Oh, yes she glimmers oh so prettily—"

"Thank you," Tarragon said.

"But she's a vile creature. The attack started when she arrived. You were at the heart of the fire, Evanne. You survived. How did you survive?" Cleo pushed past Merle's restraining arm. "My family are dead, but you're standing without a scratch!"

"Fuck." Barret gave a weary headshake.

Evanne took another step back. "But ... Cleo. We had *wine*." She sounded so confused, Tarragon felt something in her chest.

Cleo screamed, raising her rake, but Merle grabbed the handle. Old he might've been, but it looked no harder for him than taking candy from a baby. He kept his voice low. "There'll be none of that."

A rock hit Evanne in the forehead, and she stumbled back with a cry, hand going to her scalp, coming back red and sticky. Another whizzed past her head.

Old Merle faced the crowd, arms wide. "No! Stop!" Hitch was at the old man's side, taking a step forward, then back. Able to see what was coming sure as Tarragon could. Powerless, because he was already dead, just a memory held together by scraps of loss and loneliness.

Tarragon wanted a sword. She *needed* a sword. If she had a blade, this would've been over by now. She wanted to leap to the sky but knew her wing wasn't up for it. Heser moved like a bull, but not at the crowd. The Queensguard was running away, and for a moment Tarragon wanted to wheel her mount around and go toward the fight.

Then she saw those blue lips, and that alabaster skin, and knew the man was right. Queen or not, one didn't take casualties back into the fight.

She turned to see their retreat. The Feybrind with the golden eyes had a blade out, standing at Evanne's side. The maybe-Vhemin sobbed, hand still to her bleeding head. The Vhemin matriarch waded toward the crowd, took a stone for the face, and ignored it. A man hit her with a shovel, so she grabbed his head in both hands, *squeezing*. Tarragon felt sick as he screamed, horror meeting pain before the noise stopped as his skull burst like a dropped gourd.

Barret let the body drop, then staggered as someone stabbed her with a spade. It was a sloppy strike but the blood flew nonetheless. Sight of Day slapped aside a stone meant for Evanne with a casual sweep of his blade, then took three sure steps to Barret and drew her back.

Merle still had his arms wide, shouting for order, for *something*, but no one listened. He turned to Evanne. "Run, girl. Run!" And then took the metal tines of a rake in his back. He hollered, stumbling to his knees.

The rake was held by Cleo. Barret roared forward, snatching the rake. "You forget what fighting Vhemin is like!" She hit Cleo with the rake so hard the haft snapped, and the young woman fell senseless. Evanne screamed, maybe *no*, or maybe just a wail.

Another implement gouged the matriarch. Sight of Day fought beside her, the cat taking a glancing blow from a shovel, but making it look like he meant to. *He will fall. They are fast and true but not meant for long fights.*

Old Merle staggered upright, unsteady, but his voice was strong. "*Stop!*"

And, just for a moment, everyone did. He walked to stand between the crowd and Sight of Day. "You get her out of here."

Tarragon didn't understand what he meant, but Sight of Day nodded, then went to Evanne, pulling her away. Barret snarled, blood leaking, but shark teeth bared. Tarragon had fought enough Vhemin to know she hadn't much left, though. A slight slump of those massive shoulders. She couldn't fight this crowd, or not for long. So, the Vhemin retreated with the cat. After Tarragon and Heser. All because Tarragon didn't have a *sword*.

Evanne stopped. "Merle!" Her voice was a sob. "I didn't stop thieves. I lied."

"I know, child." He didn't look at her. "Get along, now."

Hitch waited with Merle. Tarragon knew the old man couldn't see the ghost, but it was the one thing the spectre could give. *So he doesn't die alone. Not really.* Someone swung at the grizzled shopkeeper, and Evanne screamed, and then Sight of Day had her over his shoulder like a bawling sack, and Heser ran, and Barret stumbled too, as the remains of a village murdered a kind old man at the base of Itikari sin.

Chapter Twelve

Evanne felt sick. Her stomach roiled with it, bile chewing her throat. She couldn't stop sobbing as Sight of Day sprinted from the horde of villagers.

My family.

Hitch sped along beside them, his ghostly form angled forward as a pale concession to their speed. "There was nothing you could do!"

"I could've fought!"

Sight of Day gave her a shake, the best he could do with his hands occupied by holding her. The cat slowed, his endurance burning out like a flash-flood's vengeance, and he put her down. They were in a place still within sight of Imshir and Heaven's Gate both. There was a stubby tree nearby, but the Feybrind didn't lean against it. Cat-perfect, even in exhaustion. *{Can you run?}*

She swallowed. "Not well." She glanced over his shoulder. "Where is Barret?"

The Feybrind snapped his fingers in front of her face. *{She is coming. She is hurt but will be very upset if her sacrifice meant you get hurt too.}*

Evanne felt the sickness in her roil, surge, fight for freedom. Words wanted to come out, Vhemin-strong, hateful. She didn't have the strength to stop them. "We should kill them!"

{Perhaps we can do that from a safe distance.} Uncle Day pointed with his chin past her shoulder. She turned and spied Uncle Heser's retreating form, the glimmer glow of fairy light marking his path. *{The dumb human has the right idea.}*

Evanne swallowed, bent over, and threw up. Snot and tears, bitter bile. "I'm going back for Old Merle."

Sight of Day rolled his eyes, but she could see the heaving of his chest. Hitch drifted to her. "Evanne. Listen. We will not survive. I didn't spend eight hundred years waiting for you to lose you now!"

Waiting for me? It'd keep. "But—"

He stepped into her, like he had when they played. She shivered at the touch of his soul, fingers in her mind rather than beside hers on a fretboard. Her heart hammered, chest heaving, and she saw—

"*I need to get out there.*" *Hitch strained at the hands holding him.* "*She's going to die.*"

Marcus stood before him. Perfect, haughty. "*If you go, you die.*"

"*Then I'll die.*"

Evanne shuddered. "What was that?"

"I don't remember!" The ghost snapped. "But we'll never find out if we stand here."

Evanne looked back. Aunt Barret stagger-ran toward them, the old Vhemin on the raggedy edge. She was cut, bleeding, and so *angry*. Evanne felt the monster in her chest get angry too, want to join her and make a stand, because Vhemin didn't run, they didn't *quit*, they fought, and here was a fight worth—

"It's not worth it," Hitch said. "Hear me. You will join Barret in a last stand. She is injured and you're—"

"Inexperienced?"

Sight of Day looked to the air where Hitch might've stood if he hadn't been ... *within* her. {*Are you talking to the ghost or have you gone quite mad?*}

"I was going to say unarmed." Hitch drifted free a moment. "The cat will fight better than you both for perhaps a minute, but he is tired. His hundreds-years life will end in a moment because you won't fucking *run*."

"*He* could run," she snapped.

"I thought you were the smart one," Hitch said. "In a moment Barret will be here. She is made entirely of the stuff that makes you stupid. No, don't interrupt. All her race are. Strong, and brave. But not indestructible. That's a Trick you haven't learned."

"Go for the head," Evanne whispered.

"Right," the ghost nodded. "But there are Tricks you know. Words to say, and the way they're spoken. They can shake the world. You must tell her to run."

"She's already running!"

"She is running *to* something. Making her run *from* something will be much harder."

Evanne bit her lip, stomach clenched, that sick-sweet wanting her to *fight*. She glanced at the mountain, and thought of Papa, and what he would do.

But what would Mama do? The Platinum Warrior, so perfect, so deadly. So unlike Evanne, the Half-Made. Vertiline would do whatever it took to save those she loved. "She built a school in the desert because she waits to help Geneve."

Sight of Day glanced between her and where he thought Hitch was. {*Of course. You don't think the Platinum Warrior likes sand?*}

But the monster in her bared its teeth. She glared at Hitch. "What would you know?"

"Enough. I'm dead, remember?" He turned to Barret, almost on them. "I will help you whatever you want to do. I am with you to the end, be it in five minutes or five hundred years. But you must decide."

"Fuck!" She screamed.

Sight of Day blinked. {*It's hardly the time.*}

"Uncle Day." She held his hands. "Barret will want to fight. She mustn't. She will die."

{We all will.} He folded her hands in his.

"I'm not ready for you to die." She swept hair from her face, spat to clear her mouth, then beckoned Hitch. "It is time."

Barret slowed as she approached, then bent to put hands on knees, breathing hard. "I need a fucken minute, then we can raze these inbreds from the earth."

Evanne felt Hitch drift into her, his heart in hers. It steadied her, the hammering, limping surge of her own broken one calming. "We aren't staying."

"Did the hit on your head knock the sense from you? We're not leaving an enemy at our backs. We're—"

"Leaving." Evanne felt for the Trick of it, the words that would make this champion quit the field. "Hail, Barret. I see behind you a trail of unbroken compromise." Hitch leaned into her words, the cool gravebreath misting from between her teeth into the warm desert air. "We are heading toward our real enemy. Not this rabble. They're unworthy of you. *Beneath* you. Lesser than, do you see?" She pointed to the dwindling speck of Heser and Tarragon, the Queensguard still carrying his royal charge to safety. "He runs toward tomorrow's victory. A shared burden. The clan, for all." She was close to babbling, uncertain of the right words, but sure of the sound of them. "If we stand here, we will beat a few worthless peasants into their graves. And none would blame us, justice served, and served well. But we would miss out on the prize. Axing those who stole your years from you. Bringing doom to those who broke our ship, and harmed your liege. I see it in your eyes. You owe the Raven Queen, not for rank or title, nor control of her armies. She gave you hearth and home. A *new* clan. Do you forsake her for death by some fucking *serfs?*"

Barret's eyes flashed, and for a moment Evanne thought the old woman would hit her. Shark teeth bared. Sight of Day's tail was quite still, the Feybrind motionless, unwilling to be the stone dropped in this particular pond. Then Barret laughed. "You little cunt."

Evanne shared her grin. "Let's be on, then."

"I'll be coming back for these assholes," Barret promised. "Once we're done."

"Aye, and I with you." She offered Barret her hand, and for a slice of time it wasn't *Evanne* and *Aunt Barret*, but *Evanne the Half-Made* and *Warlord Barret*. They clasped, and Barret's grin widened. "They made you well, kid. They made you well." Then she loped off, old bones creaking, but too much will to let it slow her.

Hitch stepped from Evanne, and she stumbled, faint and hot, the cool of her words exchanged for heat inside. Sight of Day caught her, brushed her off, and steadied her. *{How did you do that?}*

Evanne gave a sickly smile. "It's just a Trick I learned, that's all."

It wasn't that the anger of the mob burned itself out; humans couldn't find them at night, so hiding in the desert was simple enough. Evanne just had to keep her teeth clenched so she wouldn't scream, and the rest was easy.

Would I scream... or cry?

It was a fair question, and not one she had time to answer right now. They padded across the sands, night nipping their heels, well away from the ruddy human-shaped hues of heat that stalked farther toward the ruin of Imshir. The villagers figured them to head to Heaven's Gate, perhaps seeking sanctuary behind the skirts of the edifice they thought Evanne had woken. Then, they headed back to Imshir, still spread out, still seeking.

She lay beside Tarragon. The fairy had accompanied her to this vantage, the tiny person strangely quiet, hiding her glow within the folds of Evanne's cloak. She shared a little warmth, which Evanne didn't mind at all.

"Why do they head to the city?" Evanne crouched behind a huddle of desert grass. The dune beneath her was well cold, her blood sluggish with it, not enough human in her Vhemin to prop her up. She gritted her teeth, the fire of anger keeping her warm enough.

"Muppets," Tarragon suggested, her voice small, not really behind this slur of the ancients.

Muppets? Evanne gave her a little side-eye. "You what now?"

"She means they're simple," Hitch said. He stood in faded blue amid the grass, unafraid of spying eyes, because only fairies and the gods-touched could see him.

The fairy glimmered, but only a little, because Evanne's cloak wasn't a cure all for her light. "They think you're like them. Going where it's safe. Back to hearth and home."

"I'm never going back there," Evanne spat.

"Which leaves but one question," Hitch offered. "Where *are* we going?"

Evanne turned her back to the grasses, laying down so she could see the stars, but careful not to shake Tarragon. The little person sat, back to Evanne's shoulder, hidden, but ... *there.* "We need answers. Someone came here to destroy our home. I need to know why. I need vengeance."

"I need a hot meal," Tarragon said. "Could we start with that?"

Evanne sighed. "I guess we could. If we head west for a day's march we'll hit Clink's camp. Or, what's left of it. Find supplies and get our bearings."

"And a meal?"

"And a meal, Sandwich," Evanne smiled. At least, it felt like a smile. Same number of teeth in it, same stars watching from above. But it felt different. Hollow, like her lips were made of lies.

"If you call me that one more time, I will cut a bitch," the fairy swore.

Chapter Thirteen

Tarragon didn't know how the Bigs did it. Walked all day, in the blasting heat, sun like Khiton's hammer, all without water. They walked in the desert, sand, scree, and the odd animal skeleton marking their journey. *Tebrani used to be a garden nation. Crops for all. Rich, and green. What happened?*

Despite this being a shit place to make your home, the Bigs lived here. *Endured.* And walked, from danger, or to it. Like, the oddly-named Heser the Cheg didn't even have the courtesy to stumble with his ward, and he was just... *human.* Tarragon could understand the Vhemin Matriarch well enough, though. Their people were made for war, or *from* it, the dregs of ballistae and nuclear fire put into a human-shaped sausage, meat for the battlefield grinder.

And then, there was the cat. He carried her, steps ever sure, golden eyes alert, and somehow sad. She clambered from the hammock-like sling she cruised in at his chest, flitted up to his ear, and said, "Why did they try to kill one of their own?"

She got a golden glance. *{That's what you want to ask?}*

"I want to ask other things." Tarragon's eyes found Evanne's back, the might-be-Vhemin walking with her shoulders back, too much spite in her to let her spine bend even a little under the sun. *Maybe about her.*

How does the impossible union of Vhemin and human bring a beautiful marvel? Lavender eyes to marvel the gemstones of a Feybrind. But ... priorities. "I need to know so many things. Why does one human carry another who looks both inbred and useless? Why do we march toward Clink's camp of Vhemin, a people who were built to kill yours?" Against Tarragon's better judgement, she pointed to Evanne. "And what's her deal? How can she see ghosts? Why do they talk to her?" She felt her heart pick up the pace. "Why did the mountain kill itself? Why did the Feybrind attack me?"

Tarragon hadn't realised it but her voice rose to a wail at the end. It earned her a wince from the cat and a half glance from Evanne, but the matriarch didn't grace her with a glare, and Heser the Cheg trudged on, his inbred-yet-beautiful burden held close to his chest so the sun didn't mark her face.

{All these answers are linked.} Sight of Day shrugged, and she rode the swells. *{Why do you need a sword? Why can't you Build things? Where were you for eight hundred years?}*

"I was a prisoner."

{But no longer?} The cat gave her a half-smile. *{An interesting turn of events.}*

"I mean, I got away. Busted out. Broke the jail doors down and went on the lam."

{It took eight hundred years for you to do that?} Sight of Day shook his head. *{A miracle you could manage it so fast.}*

"Are you saying ... what, that I lucked out?"

"He's saying it's connected, fairy." Hitch drifted close. "That you escaped at just the right time."

"Ugh," she said. "This world sucks."

{I don't know.} The cat padded on, tail quiescent. *{It's got you in it. It can't be all bad.}*

CLINK'S CAMP WAS RUINED. SIMILAR TO THE BASE OF HEAVEN'S Gate, the heat weapon had cleaved great gouging marks into the earth's flesh. There were bits of Vhemin distributed throughout the surrounding area, along with what looked like pieces of horse, wagons, and buildings. They approached it anyway, the misery becoming clearer with each step.

It was hard to imagine what had been here. You could guess a few sticks still upright at a perimeter might have been a fence or wall of some kind. Larger piles of wreckage suggested barns, bars, or meeting houses. Scraps of fabric and kindling told a story of houses and tents sharing space with each other. *But I don't know. They don't Build like we do. Not anymore.* The smell of smoke drifted on the wind.

Tarragon whistled. "This camp is all fucked up with no place to go." She kept her voice quiet, so only the Feybrind would hear. She might be a spy, and these people might be the enemy, but she could feel their pain. "What can we do?"

{We help.} Sight of Day moved through the village, tail lashing.

Evanne trudged amidst the wreckage, eyes bright, but no tears. She bit her lip sometimes, fingers trailing on her guitar case, but said nothing at all while she looked for survivors. Barret turned over masonry or wall fragments looking for any clue someone might live, but stopped when she hefted aside a chunk of stone the size of a pony. Beneath was half a child. The old woman said, "Ah," then crouched, putting her head in weathered hands.

It was a Vhemin child. Tarragon left Sight of Day's shoulder, fluttering to the ground without face planting, and hopped to matriarch's side. The child was crushed, mostly just meat in the shape of a smaller person, but no legs. Tarragon looked to the north, picturing a blast from Heaven's Gate throwing this piece of rock here, collecting the child on the way, and, what? Ripping her... him? Was it a girl or a boy? Ripping them in half.

Is that what happened?

When Barret spoke, Tarragon realised they'd been staring at the corpse for minutes without moving. "The weapon. You made it?"

Tarragon glanced at the matriarch, but there was no malice there. There was ... *nothing* there. Empty eyes. "Itikari, yes. I didn't. I mean, I couldn't. I'm not a Builder." She bit her lip. "But if I knew how, I would have."

Barret nodded. "What made you hate us so, Little Light?" She stood, brushed her hands against her pants, and walked away.

Tarragon looked at the dead child, then at Barret's back. "I..."

She stuttered out. What was there to say?

THE HOT MEAL WAS WELCOME. EVANNE SCARED UP SUPPLIES, AND Sight of Day cooked. The cat was a master of the skillet, as were the rest of his race. He served up slivers of a lean meat like venison, but Tarragon knew it wasn't deer. There were no deer anywhere near here. Not anymore.

The Feybrind worked wonders with spices, a touch of paprika and garlic making Tarragon want more than her tiny share. She watched Evanne while she ate. The might-be-Vhemin chewed like a machine, slow and methodical, eyes on the fire, lavender inviting in reflected reds and yellows.

"We can't stay here," Heser the Cheg said. "We need weapons. Horses. A ship wouldn't be too much to ask, would it?"

"We can't go back to Or'sen," Barret snarled. "It's why we're here in the first place."

Sight of Day offered her another sliver of not-venison. The matriarch nodded her thanks, chewing. {I feel there is important data missing.}

"We came here with her," Barret used her meat as a pointer, gesturing to probably-not-a-real-Queen Morgan, "because Ravenswall is under siege. Assassins kill the Queensguard on silent feet. Our rank and file, filed to nubs. Missing patrols. The whole deal. The queen was in danger, so we..."

"We ran," Heser the Cheg said. "We ran at night, and we ran fast. No one knew where we went, and I find it surprising our fight reached here before we did."

"It's not just your fight." All of them startled at Evanne's words. Her eyes still held the fire, but her lips curled. "They didn't kill your city."

"I didn't mean it like that," Heser the Cheg said.

"I know, Uncle Heser." She turned those beautiful eyes to him, then back to the flames. "Mama said the queen couldn't have me. What did she mean?"

"There are crypts," the Queensguard said.

"That's cryptic," Tarragon said.

"Oh, well done," Hitch said. "We're playing word games while we eat dinner in a graveyard."

"Shut it, Spooky." Tarragon tore off a tiny piece of meat, chewing. "There are crypts everywhere. This world is ancient beyond measure. You can't stumble three klicks without hitting a shrine to fuckwittery. So, pretty please, with a cherry on top, can we get to the point?"

Evanne's eyes left the flames, found hers, and for a hesitant moment, smiled. It was a shy smile, if a maybe-Vhemin could be bashful. "Well said, Sandwich."

"When I get my sword—"

"There are crypts that can't be opened," Heser the Cheg said. "We go to them with magicians, just like Geneve and Meriwether did. But they don't open. And then, they do, for no reason. But they're empty, robbed, riches gone, or perhaps they were always gone." He stroked a hair from Morgan's forehead. "We are troubled, because it means someone is creeping about, stealing relics, probably killing our people, and we don't know how."

{You believe Evanne can open them?}

"I believe we're running out of things to try." Heser the Cheg shrugged. "But that's not why I'm here. I'm here because she would've died if we stayed."

The fire popped, startling Tarragon. "I don't know what kind of door wouldn't open to a mage's touch."

"I do," Hitch said.

Chapter Fourteen

"What do you mean, you know?" Evanne stalked between a ruined wagon and a stone wall slumped into a hunchback by heat. They'd left the firelight behind, the ghost trailing her like an errant puppy. Tarragon had followed them, but the rest remained by the fire. "You're ... *dead*, Hitch. You don't remember dick."

"I admit, it's hard." The ghost squatted atop the melted wall, elbows on knees. "Pieces come to me in fits and starts. The whole thing—"

"Spit it out," Evanne snarled. "These people are dead! That house there," she stabbed a finger at a hole in the ground, "was Cleaver's place. He made *toys*, Hitch. Big hands, you know? Made for holding the axe or sword, but he preferred the rasp after the chisel. The fucking mountain," her arm swung like a compass, "killed them all. And here come people from a far shore, with tales of magic doors and you are the one who suddenly remembers things?"

"Sometimes the dead need a reminder," Tarragon offered. "They don't—"

"And you can shut it too, Sparky." Evanne rounded on the fairy. "I bet you're *happy* the Vhemin are dead. The big enemy! I remember.

You came to us with the dead on your heels. The mountain woke. We should've killed you, but here we are, enjoying a night stroll."

The fairy's glimmer died, cut out like a candle doused with a bucket. "I didn't ... I couldn't—"

"And thus does the world roll on. Hitch, with his broken memory. A fairy who didn't, who *couldn't*. You know who *could*? You know who *did*?"

"Ah," sighed Hitch. "I was waiting for this."

"My *mother*," Evanne spat. "My *father*. They lie beneath a mountain of slag, and you only just *remembered* about doors that..." And just like that, her words ran out, her voice cracking like old clay. Her face was wet, though, not dry like it should be. Not hard as stone, ready to fight, ready to rend. Weak, the human frailty of her withering under the weight of need.

The fairy took a step back. "Maybe I should come back—"

"Stay," Hitch said. "Let me tell you part of a story. No, save your bile, Evanne. I have heard it before. I spoke the same anger, before the world broke last time." He looked to the sky. "The Three watched me, but no one helped. Except," he seemed to hunt for a word, then growled.

"You don't remember," Evanne hissed.

"Not yet. Not enough." He flowed from the rock, reaching for her. "Take my hand."

"Eat a bowl of cold cock."

He looked at his outstretched arm, the hand missing, then let it fall. "It will only take a moment. It's better if I show you."

Tarragon flitted closer, her glimmer barely a glow worm's. "How can you speak, spectre? How can you show her things? The dead have no words for the living."

Evanne glared at the fairy, then grabbed for Hitch. "Okay, asshole, show me—"

"I NEED TO GET OUT THERE." HITCH STRAINED AT THE HANDS HOLDING him. "She's going to die."

Marcus stood before him. Perfect, haughty. "If you go, you die."

"Then I'll die." Hitch stood, the weapon whining as it dug into him for what it needed. It took, then took some more ... and then he was strong. He shoved Muriel away, shoulder barged Marcus, and stepped through the gate.

Dawn's light. Hard, like the sky always was. Three moons, and the battlefield below. Hitch crouched, then jumped.

EVANNE STAGGERED, HITCH STUMBLING FREE. THE GHOST SHOOK HIS head. "Sorry. Not that one. That's ... not ready. There's another."

"So many dead," Evanne hissed. "I could see the carpet of them beneath the hill. Below, and you wanted to soar. How did you fly?"

"I don't remember." His voice was almost a wail. "But here is another tale." And he stepped into her again.

"YOU'RE SURE THIS WILL WORK?" THE VHEMIN'S VOICE WAS ROUGH, BUT Hitch knew how soft his touch could be. "You're sure you can keep the Itikari guessing while we steal it?"

"I'm sure of nothing." Hitch stamped about the narrow alley, his breath frosting in the winter air. Details were indistinct. The memory of garbage in a pile there. Or was that a person, in rags? The fragments slipped in and out, but he remembered the cold. The frigid air, and how it made the Vhemin slow. How the Vhemin came anyway.

The armour kept Hitch warm enough, but there was something about this place that took the very heart of him away. "I am Itikari. You are Vehement. But we can make this war stop."

"The armour won't answer to us."

"It will," Hitch promised. "But not today. We need the research team on it."

"So we lock the door, throw away the key?" The Vhemin touched his face,

scale rasping the stubble on Hitch's jaw. "Wait until the sickness takes you from me? What then?"

"I'm not going anywhere," *he lied.* "We work together. A door that needs your hand and mine. That's how it'll work."

A nod, but the hand fell. "The Itikari will kill you."

"Vehement will kill you."

That got him a shark-toothed smile. "Eh. They've got to go for the head."

EVANNE FELL TO HER KNEES AND THREW UP. HITCH WAS FADED, HIS blue almost gone, but his voice was strong enough. "Do you see?"

"You made the door?" She spat carrot—*always fucking carrot.* "I feel so bad."

"I don't feel amazing either, but ... at least I feel something. I've been dead for so long, Evanne. Hundreds of years waiting for just the right..."

"Time?"

"Person." He shrugged. "I think, anyway. I know that doesn't help. There's so much missing."

"What is going on?" Tarragon approached Evanne like a nervous torch, flickering with each step. "What did you see? Where did you go?"

"Was I gone long?" Evanne stood, heart limping like a discordant drum. "Hitch was ... Itikari."

"Or Vehement." The ghost sighed. "Both."

"Ah. That makes perfect sense, and explains why I think he's a dick." Tarragon avoided the puddle of sick then jumped, wings a-glimmer, and landed on Evanne's shoulder. Evanne had to admit her weight felt good there. Just as right as a day the correct length to get everything done. "He was a *spy*. Like me. I don't trust spies."

Evanne snorted. "Hitch? He's been my companion for as long as I remember. Always slightly blue, slightly see-through. Not a useful person—"

"Hey."

"But there all the same. I can't remember a time he wasn't there. Like I've got three parents, but one is dead."

Tarragon swung out, legs on Evanne's shoulder, holding onto a lock of her hair. Evanne was very close to her. *She is ... stunning. It's not just the light within her.* "What's your point?"

Evanne mentally shook herself. *Focus.* "What's he spying on?"

"Oh, sorry. I didn't mean he's spying on *you*. I mean he was a spy and then died. Doing spy stuff." Tarragon kept swinging. "Isn't it obvious?"

Evanne gave Hitch a long stare. "Are you a spy?"

"No." His head shake was the firmest motion she could remember him giving. "I don't remember what I was, but I wasn't trading in secrets for a higher power."

"Not all spies work for higher powers, ghostie." Tarragon glimmered as she hung out on Evanne's rust locks. It wasn't *quite* annoying, but Evanne found the light-becomes-dark out of the corner of her eye distracting. "Sometimes they do it because they think they should. Those ones often die, which makes a surprising amount of sense."

Evanne waited for Hitch to respond, but after the silence got to the awkward side of things, she cleared her throat. "Hitch, tell her. You're no spy. You'd have to be good at something to be a spy, right?"

"Not always. Look at the fairy." But the joke capsized, all hands lost. "I feel ... something's right in what she says. No, don't look smug, you little glowing twat. There was a thing I tried to do."

"What was it?"

"I don't know." He looked at the sky. "I died for it. I died badly, Evanne."

"And you locked a door behind you." She shivered. "And no one can unlock it."

"Oh, I know someone. Do you feel it?" He swept his arm out to the desert. "All these years. Time burdening a man with memory he wasn't supposed to carry. Waiting for you."

"No pressure, right?" She tried for a grin, and found it stuck for a moment.

"No pressure," he agreed. "I think ... I think when I failed, the world broke."

That sat between them, then the fairy coughed. "I know you're a dick, but you're not a super dick. What I'm saying is breaking the world was more than a one-man lift."

"Hmm." The ghost looked away.

Evanne turned that stone over in her mind. *Hitch, waiting for me. His lover, gone. Dead by the thousands, and he went to face his enemy anyway. And now, always with me.* "Fuck it."

The fairy gave her an appraising glance. "I thought you'd never ask."

"You what?" Evanne blinked. "Wait. How? No, never mind. Look, what I'm saying is, we need to find the door. See if I can open it."

Hitch glanced at her. "The door may not exist anymore. It's not even a door, I don't think. I think... I think it's something I *had*. I might not remember it right. There could be—"

"My family is dead," she said. "There is nothing for me here. If it's all the same, I'd like to travel away." She thought of Cleo. "Leave the memories behind and see what new ones I can make. There's a Trick to it I've yet to learn, and I need all the lies I can gather. *You'd* be helping *me*."

Tarragon flittered free, her wing holding true for a moment. "Certain death. Danger! Ancient ruins, and a legion of bodies? I'm in."

Evanne tried a laugh, and it lingered well enough. "Let's talk to the others. See what—"

A woman's scream cut her off. Evanne blinked, glanced at Tarragon, and then they dashed toward the sound.

Chapter Fifteen

All *these people are crazy.* Tarragon felt the thought arrive like a sharp tap to her forehead. Right on its heels was an unfriendly companion: *I'm crazy for being here with them.*

The maybe-Vhemin Evanne headed off at a dead sprint, but pulled up short after a few paces, hand to chest, eyes wide. Tarragon buzzed past her, wing still a little dicky but at least it held her weight now. She zipped through a broken window in a wall, under half a wheelbarrow, and around a boulder. She was heading to where the screaming came from. All was quiet now, which could be both good and bad news.

Tarragon had enough time to think, *And this is why I need a sword,* before she was hit from the side. Stunned, she fell from the sky, tumbled under a cart, and lay staring at the slice of ground-meets-night-sky she could see.

There was a new Feybrind in the camp. She had amber eyes flecked with gold, but there was nothing warm about them. She was near the probably-not-a-real-queen with a blade, the naked metal calling starlight to gleam on its edge. Tarragon looked to the right where another Feybrind stood with a stout stick, which was what had knocked her out of the sky.

A lot of people were shouting. The maybe-a-queen was no doubt the screamer, and she was awake, eyes hard, and despite holding naught but a broken hunk of stone, fear warred with anger on her face. It was the pinch around the eyes that said to Tarragon, *This bitch is about to do something stupid.*

Heser the Cheg came roaring from the darkness behind the stick-wielding cat, who simply sidestepped and clubbed him senseless. Sight of Day padded back from the darkness, bow in hand, but held his distance when he saw how close to the okay-so-probably-a-queen the amber-eyed cat was.

There were a lot of swishing tails.

"Get away from her." Barret trudged toward the fire. She dropped a horrible-looking creature to the sand, wiped her hands on her jerkin, and sniffed. "I won't ask a second time."

Tarragon gave a tiny groan which no one seemed to notice. The stick-wielder leaned his staff in the crook of his arm, then said, *{We are taking her with us.}*

Barret laughed. "You'll be lucky if you take your lives from here."

{Dead or alive, makes no difference.} The Feybrind had opal eyes, deep and cool.

"That's bollocks." Barret held up her hand but didn't look. "Evanne, come no closer."

Sure enough, Evanne made it to the edge of the firelight. Those pointed teeth were bared, but curiously she'd found no weapon. She carried her damn guitar, and despite seeming intelligent did the stupid thing of coming closer. "I want to tell you a story."

That was the point where everyone moved at the same time. The cat with the sword lunged for the queen, dodged the rock, and knocked her sideways with a punch to the jaw. She swept behind the queen, amber gold eyes glaring, and put her blade to Morgan's throat.

Sight of Day fired his bow, placing three shots at the Feybrind with the stick. This didn't seem to bother him, because he moved the stick *tock tock tock*, catching all three arrows with it. Barret charged, roaring, "Come here you opal-eyed fuck!"

And then it was more-or-less on.

Tarragon looked about for anything like a sword, feeling sick, pain shooting down her side. Barret and Stick Guy grappled, the cat's tail lashing, claws at the matriarch's throat, and the Vhemin looking like that bothered her not at all. Sight of Day dashed toward Morgan and the other cat, bow discarded, blade in hand, but held a wary distance, tail *swish, swishing.*

Evanne closed her eyes, set her fingers to the strings, and played. It was such a weird thing to do in the middle of a brawl that everyone, even Barret, paused. She played with her eyes closed, head cocked, and after five notes dropped to the silent sands, she sang.

The breath misted from her lips, cold as ice, rime forming on the guitar's neck. Tarragon couldn't have told anyone what song Evanne sang. There was little to grasp, but the music, oh *my.* Little notes flitted about Tarragon, setting her wings to flutter and her heart to race. Before she knew it the fairy stood, a tiny war cry on her lips, and she charged the cat with amber gold eyes.

In the heart of the darkest night,
    Where shadows dance and fears take flight,
    There stand souls so bold and true,
    Beacons of light in all they do.

Raise your voices, sing it loud,
    Strength and valour, we're endowed.
    Fearless hearts, we stand as one,
    Defying darkness we conquer all.

We'll conquer mountains, cross the sea,
    With hearts untamed and spirits free,
    With hearts of dragons and spirits free,
    We'll shape fate in bravery.

Tarragon didn't understand how so many words could come so fast, or how the song seemed to have feelings, or gave them. Bravery, strength, and fearlessness. The emotions landed as thunderclaps, the guitar speaking, Evanne's voice crying. Tarragon caught a glimpse of blue as Hitch's form edged out from the maybe-Vhemin's.

Tarragon felt her blood surge. Her head cleared, the malaise that dragged her wings and kept her grounded leaving in just a handful of heartbeats. She stood, wobbled, and coughed, speckling the back of her hand with glittergold blood. She looked at the rime forming on Evanne's guitar, felt the chill of it in her blood, and jumped into the air. She shot past Morgan's head and right for the stick-wielder, because she was going to have a piece of that fool.

She dodged an absent-minded swing from Barret. The Vhemin matriarch was losing the fight because no single Vhemin could take a Feybrind. It just wasn't in the range of possibilities their race had been dealt by the Three. No one would play a hand that bad, and yet Barret was, all for a human and another cat. If Tarragon had a few more cycles later on she'd unpick that. But for now, Barret was closest to dying, and Tarragon could fix that.

Bouncing past that swing, the fairy caught updraft, glided high, then swooped low. The *opal-eyed fuck* with the stick tried to beat her out of the sky, but she saw it coming, and put a little more curry into her wings. She buzzed low, hit the ground with a tiny *thump*, landing on one knee, fists clenched around soil. She held for a heartbeat, pulling the world to her. The opal-eyed fuck tried to dodge Barret's swing and stab down with his stick at the same time, and it was just this unbalancing Tarragon waited for.

She shot up, all glimmer and hot fire, and just as she reached the cat's head height, she landed a savage uppercut. She smelled burning fur as she bounced back, the cat stumbling, stick warding. Barret pressed the advantage, snarled, "Hold this," and slammed her fist into the Feybrind's gut.

The stick fell. The Feybrind didn't, all cat grace and poise, pivoting with the blow, knife-edged hand strike hitting Barret's neck. The Vhemin grunted, but didn't pause with another body blow, this time a wince-worthy rib shot. The cat accordioned, the air going out of him, and he landed face-first on the dirt.

Barret was about to wind in with a kick, but Tarragon wasn't having any of this. They might be mean cats, but they were still cats! There would be a reason to all this madness. *Brave, strong, fearless* still thrummed her blood, heart afire, and she grabbed sky, hovering at Barret's head height. "Hold!"

The Vhemin tried to wave her away as if she were a fly, but Tarragon had a few more skills than the average insect. "Buzz off, Sandwich."

"Hold, I say." Tarragon flitted close, her height right at Barret's left eye. "Your opponent is down. What about answers over death? Or is that too cerebral for your kind?"

She saw about thirty emotions play across the Vhemin's face, those snake eyes hard, but Tarragon didn't wait. There was another cat. She sped across the melee just in time to see Sight of Day take an uppercut of his own. He stepped aside, tail lashing, looking like he *meant* to be hit in the face, but it was best not to leave things like that to chance.

Tarragon buzzed between them, drawing amber gold eyes and plain gold alike. The enemy Feybrind tried to grab her, which would've worked except Sight of Day stabbed his rigid fingers into her exposed armpit. She staggered, and he stepped forward, put a foot behind her heel, and let gravity do what it did best.

The cat fell and found Sight of Day's sword at her throat. Tarragon didn't need to say *hold* to him, because he wasn't a warlike imbecile. She flitted between Barret and Sight of Day, unsure of what to do next, *brave strong fearless* still hitting her soul like a thunderstorm.

Evanne's song faltered, her fingers frozen on the guitar's neck. Then she sagged to one knee, Hitch left standing in her shadow, faint, just an imprint on the world, then he was gone. Her breath eased out again, ice misting the air, tiny crystals raining to the sands. She fell on her face, guitar in an outstretched hand, and she sighed. Where her breath hit the sands, it iced. Tarragon could see crystals on her eyelashes.

"Fuck me," Barret growled, eyes moving to the ruins, scanning for sorcerers. "What happened to her?"

It's not another enemy. It's a price to be paid. Tarragon felt it in her bones, zipping to Evanne's side. The maybe-Vhemin's lavender eyes were glassy, and Tarragon could *feel* the cold of her. She knew cold didn't radiate, hotter to the cooler and all that, but she was a Three-damned fool if it didn't feel like it. The air around Evanne was from the arctic, a ghost of winter plains and ice tundra.

She put a hand on Evanne's cheek. "You're so cold. Oh my." She leaned close, putting her body against Evanne's face, letting her glimmer warm through. She fluttered her wings, a tiny fan of heat, fighting the cold still coming from Evanne's mouth.

"So sleepy," Evanne said. "But you're warm." The maybe-Vhemin put her free fingers around Tarragon's legs.

"You're going to die of hypothermia. If you were really a Vhemin you'd be dead already. Are you a Vhemin?" Tarragon put hands on Evanne's fingers. The flesh was human enough here, no scales, but not warm enough to be human.

Barret lumbered close. "What's wrong with her?"

"She's freezing to death." Tarragon hiccupped. "She's going to die." *Hiccup.*

"Then we put her by the fire." The matriarch hauled Evanne up. A scampering of feet heralded the enemy Feybrind running, but that was a problem for later. Barret dragged Evanne by the front of her jerkin to the fire, then dropped her by the coals. "We need to build it up."

Tarragon shook her head, circling Barret's head. "There's no time. I can try something. I can try it just once. After I try it, I'll be helpless. Do you understand? Out for the count."

"So I could make you into dessert?"

Tarragon hiccupped again. "You could."

"Why are you hiccupping?"

"I'm scared." *Hic.*

"Huh." Barret crouched beside Evanne. "If you save her, I will—"

"Don't jinx it." *Hic.*

Barret scowled. "Always wanted to know what fairy tastes like. Maybe there'll be another time."

Hic. Tarragon ignored her, flitting to Evanne's side. "Evanne? Don't go to sleep. Eyes on me." That beautiful lavender gaze found Tarragon, and for a moment she wondered what would *really* happen if they were the same size. Could they go out for coffee? *Hic.* And what was she so scared of? *Hic.* "Well, here we go."

Letting her glimmer out could be done all at once, or gradually. The trick was how much, over how long. Fairies weren't very big, so they only had one or two good goes inside them before the tank ran empty. Tarragon flitted above Evanne's still form, gimpy wing buzzing, and let herself out.

It was like breathing out slowly, except a breath that lasted minutes, not seconds. Her glimmer brightened, the warmth inside her leaking out, a tiny sunbeam in the desert night. Her luminance eased the night back to a respectful distance. She saw Sight of Day's eyes gleam, and marked the tall shadows her light show made of the ruins. *If the Feybrind attack again, I'll be helpless.* But it was too late. She let her essence out, which brought the desert up to twenty degrees C, then an easy thirty. She passed a sweaty forty, ice dripping from Evanne, and when she made the air hit fifty Celcius even Barret took a step back. Evanne steamed under Tarragon's gleam, the ice banished, the air drying. The young woman breathed the heat in, cold out, chest working like a bellows.

A cluster of confused moths fluttered close, then veered from the heat. Tarragon held on as long as she could, then her strength gave out. She plopped to the sand beside Evanne. She wobbled, then sank to her knees. Those dream-worthy lavender eyes opened, and Evanne reached a finger to touch Tarragon. Gently, like she thought the fairy was spun glass. Then she said, "I knew you were nice."

Enough. Tarragon leaned against Evanne's chest and did what she really needed to do: she passed out.

Chapter Sixteen

Golden.

Evanne opened her eyes and saw gold. Warm, endless. The sickness in her stomach was usual, *welcome*, because she knew Uncle Day was there.

{You decided not to die. Well done.}

She tried to reply, came out with nothing but a croak, and tried again. Her voice was husky, the whisper of ancient sands. "Water."

She felt fur soft hands help her up. Sand plastered one side of her face, and she felt past hungry and all the way to empty. The Feybrind held a chipped cup to her lips, and she swallowed salty, brackish water. She was parched but that didn't make it taste sweet. The stories lied about that. It tasted like *life*. Behind Sight of Day were the coals of a morning cookfire. The day had marched on without her, the sun telling a tale of lost breakfasts and approaching lunches. "We made it?"

{Thanks to you.} Uncle Day refilled her cup from a jug beside him, then helped her drink again. *{For a hero, you spend a lot of time on your face though. Have you thought about improving your image?}*

She laughed, then coughed. "Everything hurts. I feel ... burned inside."

He watched her, eyes roaming, but gentle, always gentle. *{You almost died. I was therefore almost worried.}*

Evanne snorted. "I didn't know if I could. I wanted to help you all, but I only had enough for a little..." She struggled for words. "I felt like Hitch and I could make just one Trick. Get someone into the fight who could make a difference. So I looked for the fairy, and... wait. Where is Tarragon?"

{Like you, working on her image.} He clasped his fingers for a moment. *{No, no lies between us. She almost died, as you did. No, wait.}* Sight of Day put hands on her shoulders as she made to rise. *{The fairy will live. So will the Raven Queen and her ridiculous guardsman. Even the monster draws breath.}*

Evanne looked away, uncertain. "That's what I hoped would happen."

{I'm here to talk about you. Before he,} and Uncle Days hands trembled for a moment, *{before my brother left, he asked me to care for his cub. There are complicating factors.}*

"Complicating?" Evanne looked to the sands but saw no furred bodies. "You mean the Feybrind who turn claw and fang against us."

{I think it is unusual for the People to make war. It is especially unusual for them to attack me, because I am magnificent.} He offered her more water and let her hold the cup this time. *{We are few. We could do many things, but assassination and abduction have never been writ in vibrant colours on our souls. The People make things, heart of my heart. We don't destroy. Not us. It can't be us.}*

Evanne watched his hands still, saw the gentle slump of his shoulders, an internal release of a thing he held inside. "You have seen a new truth."

{Perhaps I've seen a truth that was always there. Perhaps we are not so different from our makers.} His half-smile held bitterness.

"And perhaps it's all bullshit." Evanne brushed rust locks aside, ignoring the sand flaking from her skin. "We've seen two of the People try to harm ours. They were poorly supplied. They could be acting alone. Renegades or crazy. Right?"

He gave her a long, sidelong glance. *{Two renegades who could sink the* *queen's ship? I know the People are workers of wonders, but that feels like a stretch.}*

"Maybe." Evanne didn't want to agree. "We need to get the others together. I've got a plan."

{Three's mercy, we're going to die.}

"That could happen." She looked past his shoulder. "But before then, I need a moment."

Sight of Day glanced to the sands beyond her. *{You shall have all the moments you need.}*

EVANNE WALKED PAST THE COOKFIRE, HER FOOTSTEPS SLOWING. THE shade beyond the coals was familiar, and for all that she hoped she wouldn't see him. *Not him. Never him.* She gave him a glance anyway, and he fell into step beside her.

As always, the ghost said nothing. They never had words for the living.

Her feet sank into sand, and for a moment she was grateful for the small task of locomotion. It stopped her having to say anything, but that's not what he needed. *Not why he's here.* She led him to the edge of Clink's village, stopping when they were past the destruction's verge. She stared out at the desert, the ghost watching with her.

"It's peaceful here." She felt the wind stir her hair. "I wish you could talk to me. Let me know what you want."

The ghost said nothing, but he walked on a few more paces, then turned to stare in Imshir's direction.

"Ah," Evanne said. "No, there's nothing left for you there. Me, neither." She felt the words building in her, the Trick of them, and let them come. "See, I thought for a long time it was my home. How long? Until two nights past, if we're honest." She looked at her feet. "I don't think I was honest enough with you in life. You deserved more from me."

The ghost eyed her, then shook his head.

"No? You want more lies?" Evanne laughed. "I've falsehoods

aplenty. Here's one. I was loved. Another? People welcomed me. I had a home. A place to be not ... *different*. Do you see me? These scales," she ran fingers up the back of her neck, "this skin?" She held her forearms up to him. "My heart is weak. I won't survive, but I don't think it matters. This world is unkind with people who dare to be different. But you? No, you weren't unkind. You were always so very nice to me."

She felt the tears on her face, the quiet trickle that wouldn't be denied. The ghost walked to her, transparent hand to her cheek. This close she could see the wounds of how he died, the mark on his face where the stick broke his jaw, the bruising of his neck where boot or fist left their memory. He touched her tears, then pulled his hand back.

"No, you can't feel them. I don't know why you can be seen and not heard, missed but not touched." She sighed. "I'm sorry this happened to you. I'm so sorry, Merle."

Old Merle stepped back, then offered her a wry smile. Turned his back and walked into the desert. Left, to go where dead men went.

"He died with purpose." Hitch's voice at her side, wistful, perhaps wondering if he had done the same.

She turned to the shade. "What did we do last night?"

"I don't know." He watched the sands, not looking at her. "I didn't know we could."

Evanne sniffed. "But we saved them."

"You almost died."

"You almost did, too."

"I'm already gone, Evanne." He gave her some side eye. "Three's mercy, but you don't cry pretty, do you?"

She choked out a laugh. "I wish I could go with him."

"Merle? No, you don't. You hate yourself for it, but you want to live. The blood of heroes thunders in your veins. Work still undone calls to you. All of that." He looked away. "Makes you wonder though, doesn't it?"

"Wonder what?"

"Where Vertiline and Armitage are. Why they haven't come to you, as all shades do."

Evanne wondered for a moment, half-hopeful, then tossed the thought to the sands. *They're not here because they have no unfinished busi-*

ness. They half-finished everything sixteen years ago. She turned on her heel and stalked back to the camp.

SHE COULD FEEL HER BLOOD COMING TO A SLOW BOIL AS HER TREAD led her back to the others. They were warming themselves by the rekindled campfire. A pot of something that smelled like coffee was slowly turning to sticky tar beside the flames. Heser and the queen held cups, but weren't drinking. Barret held a cup, and looked like she regretted that choice.

Sight of Day glanced her way. He had the wisdom of his people, no coffee cup in hand. *{Have you brooded sufficiently?}*

Evanne ignored him, doing a quick scan. Heser the Cheg brooded over his cup. Barret wore a grimace. Tarragon inspected the coffee pot but kept her distance. Queen Morgan held her cup like it was porcelain, the contents the finest around. *Ah. She's the one who thinks she's in charge. Let's start there.* She stabbed her finger at the queen. "Oi. You. Why did the Feybrind want you?"

"Your Majesty," Heser the Cheg said.

"You what?" Evanne blinked.

"You address her as your majesty. Or Queen Morgan."

Hitch chuckled. "For an uncle, he doesn't know you very well."

Evanne rolled her eyes, then faced the Raven Queen. "Was it because you're a sorcerer and can open ancient temples?"

Silence lapped at her feet in the wake of her words. Queen Morgan stood, brushed sand from her clothes, and fixed a steely eye on Evanne. "I am the Queen of Or'sen. I don't need any—"

"It's not about what you need." Evanne closed her eyes, rubbing her forehead. "Your Majesty. Queenie. Whatever. It's been a long day, and it's not even ten in the morning. The one before this one was average too. Unless I miss my guess, you've also had a lousy couple of turns under the stars. Like I said, it's not about what you need. It's about survival. Everyone I know is dead or wants me dead. A ghost dogs my heels—"

"Hey," Hitch said.

"And he won't shut up. But this time he's said something that's sent the rains away. The skies clear." Evanne looked up, hearing the Trick of her words. She had them, she could see it by the way their eyes fixed on her, and how they ignored the wind that tugged at hair and clothing alike. "He was a spy for one people or another. And he was stealing a weapon. Hid it beneath the earth, a mighty vault of wonders sealed until someone else could touch the door and open it."

"I never said—"

"Thing is," Evanne rolled on over the spectre, "I need a weapon. People are coming for me." She thought of the cats who attacked them, then Cleo. "Be they human or Feybrind, hands clutch for my throat. They killed my family."

"You seek justice?" Morgan's voice was steadier, but she raised an eyebrow.

Evanne saw the Trick of it, how she wore power better than any high born's gown, and almost smiled. "I seek survival. I won't complain if revenge comes with it." She threw her hand at the sands behind her. "I just said goodbye to one of the good ones. If there's a chance I can stop more falling, I'll take it." She raised her chin. "Or is justice reserved for humans? What of the monsters?"

The Raven Queen looked into her cup. "Are you sure you did not know the Saviour of Ravenswall and her beloved, my lord Meriwether du Reeves? You speak as they did."

{Her parents are from stock as noble.} Sight of Day sighed. *{They have kept watch these long years. Holding out, kindling a tiny shard of hope.}*

"It doesn't matter." Evanne gave the queen a sly, sidelong look. "You're good at dodging the hard questions, huh."

"I'm happy to speak of justice," the Raven Queen snapped.

"Oh, of blood blue and suchlike, I'll warrant you can talk without end. But not about the other power that burns in your veins. The power of the Three, to change the world, to break man and beast and cast the heavens into shade. You are a sorcerer true, are you not?" Evanne felt her chin jut, and let it all the same.

Morgan blinked. She spoke with a voice that rang with the bell of truth. "I am no sorcerer."

Evanne let her face widen into a smile. "We'll see about that."

Tarragon flitted up. "So. This weapon. Was it Itikari or Vehement?"

"Does it matter?" Evanne eyed the little fairy, her small yet perfect body, her immaculate hair. *Never had trouble in* her *life.*

"It might," Tarragon muttered.

Evanne felt her smile turn feral. "The Itikari made things that tried to kill you, Sandwich. But you know what? It doesn't matter. They're gone. *All* of them. Dust and ashes. They burned this world, left it—"

"Not all," Tarragon said.

"You what?"

"Not all." Tarragon pointed in the general direction of Imshir and Heaven's Gate. "The mountain remained. No, don't flash those gorgeous eyes at me. I see what you're doing, and it won't work! Here's the thing. The mountain can't just," she shook her hands, agitated, "*wake up.* Something wakes it. A person, usually a sorcerer, opens it. Itikari liked sorcerers." She glimmered. "*I* like sorcerers. But it doesn't matter. The mountain is ruled by a Council. The Council needs launch codes."

Evanne wondered where her smile had gone in the last ten seconds. "What's a lunch code? Why do the Council care about arguably the most forgettable meal of the day? Breakfast, I can get behind. A big dinner, perhaps roasted meat with—"

"Launch. *Launch.*" Tarragon dripped glitter dust in agitation. "The Council is eternal. Unemotional. They don't get het up or lose control at a pretty face."

The tiny light is taking the piss, Evanne decided. "So the Council decided to ... go full suicide, get non-emotional and destroy my home?"

Tarragon shook her head. Evanne could see the radiance in her, feel a little warmth on her face. "No, that's not it. Wait. I think I see what's going wrong here. Let's try another way." She pursed her lips. "The Council don't live there."

Evanne looked past the fairy to the desert sand beyond, then at the blank faces of her companions. Heser the Cheg looked the most lost, the Queensguard silently counting on his fingers. The Raven Queen stood apart, head bowed, thinking. Barret looked like she wanted to kill something, but it wasn't personal. Only Sight of Day showed curiosity. *{Where do they live, then?}*

"They used to share their code between all Itikari installations. It was a planetary defence—"

"Code?" Evanne felt lost.

Tarragon looked between her and Sight of Day. "Oh. Horses. Black-smiths." She crossed her arms, thinking. "Here it is. They're every-where. The Council exist at all Itikari places. The ones that still work, anyway. So—"

"What the fuck is going on?" Barret growled.

"They're killing my people," Morgan hissed. "That is what the fuck is going on."

{I found your guitar in a place across the sands that was opened like an ancient flower.} Sight of Day looked at his hands for a moment, as if willing different words to come from them. *{It was not there two summers back. I think they are killing everyone.}*

"Not everyone," Hitch said. "The cat lived."

Evanne gave him a sideways glance, then turned to Sight of Day. "Hitch said you walked out of the guitar place and didn't die."

That was about when everyone looked at Sight of Day. The cat raised one eyebrow. *{Perhaps these weapons have excellent taste?}*

"Kills everything except Feybrind," Tarragon murmured. "Look, I've got doubts. I have a lot of them! There is a bunch of strange stuff going on that I don't understand. No one's got a Manifest handy, do they? No? Okay, we'll have to take this one day at a time. Base princi-ples. Core engineering. All that." She did a tiny flip. "Here it is. I'm not sure any of this is relevant. Because of him." She stabbed a finger at Hitch.

The spectre followed the line of her arm to his chest, then looked back to the fairy. "Why me?"

"You were a spy. You had a weapon that was part Itikari, and part Vhemin. Tell me it isn't true." She *hmm'd*.

Hitch looked at Evanne, then bowed his head. "I ... don't remem-ber. No, spare your bitterness, Evanne. I don't have a failing memory because it vexes you. I can't remember because I have spent eight. Hundred. *Years*. Drifting, without a body. Your anger is nothing compared to mine. If I had a head, I'd hit it." He paced, the sands leaving no trace of his passage. "But I think she's right. I had a weapon for all. Or perhaps none. But it was made by Itikari, and changed by Vhemin. And I think it killed me."

Evanne bit her lip, wanting to reach out to Hitch, to touch him, or ... but no. He was dead and wouldn't feel her fingers no matter how much she wanted him to. "I'm sorry."

The spectre shrugged, then walked apart. Tarragon looked after him, then turned to Evanne. "I can help." She drifted a handspan to the left as she thought. "I want answers. I need to know why my side fell, and yours did too. I'd like to know who won. I'd really like to know where the chain of command is. But all that's irrelevant, because I know something that makes it all... unnecessary." She sighed a tiny sigh. "They left me, don't you see? I wasn't a very good spy. It's how I got caught. And so they left me for eight hundred years. No one misses me. No one at all. And I don't like that very much."

Evanne stared after the fairy, light dim as she drifted in the opposite direction from Hitch. Sight of Day watched her go. {*Those with tiny bodies don't have small souls. They are as fierce and brave as the rest, and deserving of the same things as any who walk or fly under the stars.*}

"Balls," Evanne whispered. Then, louder, "Well, I guess we're decided. Hitch, Tarragon, and I will go to find this weapon. What of the rest of you?"

Chapter Seventeen

I*t's only a matter of stealing a ship.* Tarragon clutched a miniature shawl close to hide her glimmer. *If only this was Itikari turf.* She hunched on Evanne's shoulder, one hand tangled in that wonderful hair. Evanne didn't smell like a person, or like a Vhemin either. This close she smelled like earth, warmed by the sun, just after spring bloom.

It was enough to make a fairy lose her focus.

They'd all come. The ridiculously-named man who stayed ridiculously close to the queen. The queen, who walked the earth as if she owned it, despite coming from a kingdom across the waves. The Matriarch, and the warrior poet cat who seemed sad a lot of the time. *And let's not forget the fairy, and ... whatever Evanne is. Difficult to forget her, because of how good she smells.*

"Well, I guess that's a four-horse town, not a three." Evanne yanked Tarragon's attention back to practical matters. Below them lay the outskirts of a small fishing village. Tebrani people wandered about doing whatever it was fisherfolk did. Tarragon didn't know how fishing worked but she'd never thought it included so many big wooden crates of dead fish, fish drying on racks, or fish smelling bad.

It was lucky she was near Evanne's scent, because it was far better than fish. "I only see three horses."

"No, there." Evanne pointed.

Tarragon saw the straggler. "That's a donkey."

"Still counts." Evanne set off toward the town. Her steps were sure, surer than Tarragon thought they should be, because the plan—such as it was—was to con someone into giving them a ship. Boats snuggled at the single wharf stretching into the salty ocean, but to Tarragon's eye they looked the sort of thing one boarded only if one wanted to drown.

They drew a few stares, but no one screamed and ran from the maybe-Vhemin or real Vhemin behind her. Heser the Cheg stayed close to the Raven Queen, but Sight of Day strolled ahead, eyes alert, but tail motionless enough. "Does no one fear for their lives?"

"Hmm?" Evanne glanced at Tarragon. "Oh, from Aunt Barret? No. Tebrani has enjoyed peace from Vhemin since I was born. Papa squared it away with the tribes, and, and..." She wound down like an old clock, steps slowing for a moment.

"It's okay," Tarragon said, knowing it wasn't. But she wanted it to be. "To miss him, I mean."

Evanne said nothing, eyes front, until they reached a ramshackle collection of wooden planks someone laughably thought was a tavern. Tarragon marvelled at the artistry of the crudely drawn grapes on a sign banging in the sea breeze. "They really went full-spec on that, didn't they?"

Evanne gave her a small smile, a hint of very sharp teeth behind it. "I don't think it needs a sign hereabouts. Everyone here knows the general store," she pointed at another, slightly smaller hovel, "the ship-wright," her arm swung to a dilapidated structure near the waterline, "the whore's house," the finger directed Tarragon to a shitty building but with new paint, "and the bar." Her arm finished its circle, pointing at the tavern.

"Been here before, then?"

"Just once." Evanne pushed the door of the tavern open. It creaked in a way that said *maintenance is optional*, then stuck. Evanne shouldered it aside, and Tarragon clung on to make sure she didn't fall free.

Inside, the light wasn't good. Tarragon whistled. "If this was an alley, it'd be the kind you'd get knifed in."

"The ale is rich enough." Evanne marched to the left, where a bar sagged out the remainder of its miserable life. A fat man stood behind it, not bothering with the pretence of polishing glassware. There was no glass, just wooden mugs in a rough stack, and no one here had the imagination to think they'd be clean.

Patrons in various states of drunkenness were scattered about the room. To Tarragon's eye, most were well gone, but a few still had a fighting chance of falling sideways rather than face first when they slumped into unconsciousness. "You ... drank here?"

"I did." Evanne swept her hair back as she made the bar and addressed the barkeep. "I need a ship."

The man gave her a slow once-over, then looked behind her. "What would a couple Vhemin, two humans, and a Feybrind want a ship for?" His voice was surprisingly light, as if he didn't need to shout too often to maintain order. *Maybe his ale really is rich enough.*

"Sailing," Evanne breezed. "We want to take swimming lessons in the deep waters off the coast."

The bartender laughed. "Well, have a care. The ground shook not long back. Big waves reached us here. Not sure what it's about, but it didn't sound good."

"It wasn't." Evanne's voice was still light but had a hard clipped edge. "Imshir is no more. Its people are mostly dead. The rest are scattered, leaderless."

The bartender chewed that over. "The school is gone too?"

"That too." Evanne leaned her guitar case against the bar. "We need a ship, and we need a captain who's not too drunk to sail."

"Curious word you're using. 'Ship'. Implies a host of potential I'm not sure you'll find here." He glared at an ale-soaked sop who looked to be rising. "Keep your knickers on, Telgo. I mean no disrespect to the *Seaspray*, but you haul fish who don't mind it leaks below the waterline."

Telgo, half upright, paused, checked his drink, and sat. Evanne sighed. "We're not fussy. Even a leaky boat would do."

"For swimming?"

"For the most epic of sea voyages. We seek Or'sen, the forgotten kingdom beyond the seas. Riches and fame await us! I will make my name as a singer, and my companions will keep order while I play."

The bartender laughed again. "Aye, I think you might. Well, don't talk to Telgo. He's been drunk for three days. Check the ship farthest from the beach. The ship is the *Salt Donkey*, and captain Jackal is fair enough."

"Jackal," Evanne mused. "Not a name that inspires confidence."

"It is what it is."

"Fair." Evanne pulled a small coin from her belt pouch, dropping it with a *tinkle* on the bar top. "Thank you."

"You don't need to pay for advice." The barkeep left the coin there.

"No, but I like to." Evanne flashed him a smile, one Tarragon wished she'd see more of, then led them to the door.

THE TRIP DOWN THE JETTY WASN'T ACTION-PACKED, AND TARRAGON was happy about that. There'd been too much 'action-packed' in the last few days. *I'm reaching overload. It's like my head's about to explode. After eight hundred years below ground, I'm not people-trained anymore, let alone ready for action.* She tugged Evanne's hair. "How do you people do it?"

"Hmm?" Evanne stopped her scanning of what could only be derelict hulks in her search for the *Salt Donkey*. "That one." She headed for the least ruinous ship, which was also the largest.

"Right at the end, like the barkeep promised." Tarragon leaned closer to Evanne's hair, gathering rust locks to her. "Everything seems very exciting. There are people trying to kill you all the time. And you've got no guns. You've got a guitar. That's it! A guitar against the world."

Evanne gave her a sly look. "I've got a fairy, too. Not many bards have one of the fey folk."

"Bard, huh?" Tarragon liked the sound of that.

"Bard." Evanne nodded. "I can't fight for shit, but I can lie with the best of them. And I'll do it for copper barons. No need for a regal.

Hell, I can lie for *free*." They pulled up at the *Salt Donkey's* hawsers, a rude gangplank leading across to the deck.

"Normally a gangplank goes up," Tarragon said. "Is this ship so leaky it's riding low?"

"Hmm," Evanne said, but with more feeling. "Fairy, we have a negotiation ahead of us. I'll do it like I do everything. With style, panache, and a salting of good luck. That's how I get through life with bad looks, worse teeth, and blood that's so impure even the vampires would spit it out. I've no clue how most people make life work, but that's my recipe." And with that, she put a foot on the gangplank.

A *snap-crack* of a whip came from behind them. Evanne whirled, Tarragon almost falling free, only her hold of rust locks keeping her moored on the maybe-Vhemin's shoulder. The rest of their party turned with the noise. *A loose whip isn't something a fairy wants at her back.*

A ship a berth down was the source of the ruckus. It was a shitty collection of spars and spit, aboard which stood three surly sailors. One wore a cap that might've been jaunty an eon ago, and he was the one with a whip. The whip was raised, his free hand on the halter of a goat. The goat's eyes were wild, a red lash mark already leaking blood. The goat didn't want to go up a gangplank that looked good for suicide missions only. Tarragon bared tiny teeth, readying to grab some sky and punch someone's face in.

The oddly-named Heser the Cheg was already moving. He stamped forward, leaving the Raven Queen safely behind him, and shouted, "Ho! I've not much use for a man who whips his own goat."

The man with the whip gave Heser the Cheg a glare, then very deliberately whipped the goat again. The animal screamed, tugging frantically at the halter. "Yeah, but it's my goat, innit? So best you shuffle on."

Heser the Cheg had a foot on the gangplank, at which point the remaining two sailors stepped in. One barred the way, the other fetching an ugly-looking boathook. The hooked end was covered in what might've been the dried remains of fish, and in Tarragon's opinion would be guaranteed to cause sepsis. Heser didn't slow, and Barret was moving on his heels. Sight of Day's tail lash, lashed, the cat fingering his bow. Hitch watched on, unable to touch the world. Evanne took a faltering step toward them, but none of that was what drew Tarragon's attention.

The Raven Queen's face had gone hard, lips pulled back in a snarl, fingers hooked into claws at her side. Tarragon felt the draw of power, but no fireballs flew. The low rumble of thunder sounded across the ocean, but no lightning struck. *Evanne was right. She has power, but what kind?*

The sailor barring the gangplank made for Heser the Cheg, lunging forward. The Queensguard took his lunge, grabbing outstretched arms, and then kicked the man between the legs. His boot hit so hard the man got a little air time, and then he tumbled from the ship to splash into the water.

Barret growled, "Got your back," crouching low, ready to step in and help, but there was no room on the gangplank. The man with the whip gave an ugly leer, then hit the goat again. Tarragon's eyes were on Morgan, the queen jerking as the animal took another blow, then another. It tried to scrabble back on the decking, bucking, and the whip came down again.

The man with the boathook came forward, the weapon coming in an overhead arc toward Heser the Cheg. The Queensguard caught the haft in one hand, a *slap* of sound followed by another rolling boom of thunder across the water.

Evanne took another step, shuddering, hand half outstretched toward Morgan. Tarragon could *feel* the eddy of power yearn between them, two magnets of opposite poles struggling to meet. The ocean reared, a wave breaking across the wharf. Sight of Day looked across the ocean, eyes widening, but Tarragon had no time for the sea. It wasn't going anywhere.

Heser wrestled the man with the boathook, the Queensguard's strength bearing the other man back. Barret was on the gangplank, snake eyes fixed on the man with the whip, who'd gone from confident to fearful. He let the goat go, turning to the ruckus, raising the whip again.

I should do something. But what? She still had no Three-damned sword. Her attention shifted to a movement in a box of dead fish.

It wasn't a rat. The dead fish were *moving*. A mad parody of vitality, dead eyes still lifeless, but bodies struggling for the freedom of the ocean. A shark's fin knifed water beside the jetty, another beside it, the animals of the ocean *called* here. Heser and his opponent staggered as something big hit the boat underneath. Thunder tolled, rolling on, striding across the waves and lapping like a new tide against the sandy shore.

Cold air seeped from Evanne's mouth, her lavender eyes glassy, hand still reaching for Morgan. The Raven Queen's face was hard as the sea spray broke about her, hair whipped by the wind. The wharf rocked, the ship beside it bucking, the sound of breaking wood booming above the thunder. Another shark cruised the seas, then another.

Tentacles rose above the ship's railing. Heser the Cheg saw them, dodged a blow from the whip, then took a step back. The sailor grinned in triumph, then screamed as he was dragged over the railing by coiling loops.

Barret lunged into the fight, barging the enemy captain. More wood splinters. The ship shuddered, sinking. Heser and Barret shared a look, then turned for the gangplank, their faces reading different versions of *let's get the fuck out of here*.

The wharf shuddered, and Evanne staggered. Tarragon shouted, but couldn't remember what, probably something useless like *wake up!* because the maybe-Vhemin's eyes were still locked on Morgan.

A voice boomed over the noise of a sinking ship. Evanne turned as a massive ship lumbered right through the *Salt Donkey*, breaking the smaller ship into fragments like it was a badly-made toy in the hands of an excited two-year-old. A bearded man was at the railing, hands clutched about rigging. "Ho, friends! You'd best come aboard, before the sea eats you whole."

Lightning slashed the sky behind him. Sight of Day's eyes were wide with shock, and he took a faltering step back. Tarragon trembled, dropping from Evanne's shoulder to prostrate herself on the deck, because she knew who this man was, and he was no man at all.

Evanne snapped out of her daze, and the thrashing dead fish settled. She scooped up Tarragon without a thought, tossing the fairy up onto the new ship. Tarragon tumbled through the air, wings stabilising as she flew, and she caught a glimpse of the ship's name in bold black on her hull: *Courage*.

She hovered, watching Evanne push Sight of Day toward the ship. He scampered forward, bounding aboard, hand down to help Morgan. The Raven Queen was back with them, eyes clear, and she glanced back at the sinking fishing vessel, but there was no helping anyone there, the water beneath churned to red foam. Even the goat was gone.

Heser and Barret helped each other from the water. The Vhemin had a torn-off shark fin in one hand, blood drooling from a ghastly grin. The Queensguard was wet but looked whole. They came for the ship, Sight of Day helping them up. Sailors came to the side, pushing the ship free with boathooks.

Last of all to board was Evanne. She gave a last glance at the ruined wharf, then tossed her guitar through the air, leaping with an outstretched arm toward Sight of Day. Tarragon loved how her hair streamed in the wind, and how the muscles in her arm bunched. And then the ship was moving, the stormy wind helping her across the ocean.

Tarragon landed on the deck before the captain, then fell to her knees again. She couldn't find words, not the right ones, and hid her face against the rough wood of the deck, stammering, "My lord."

The captain chuckled, a rich, warm sound. "That's enough of that. Get up. Introduce your friends, Builder."

Evanne crouched beside Tarragon. "Fairy. Who is this, and how do you know him?"

"How do *I* ... how could *you* not?" Tarragon looked between them.

"I admit, he seems familiar, but..." Evanne trailed off as she glanced up at the captain. "Who is he?"

"He is Lord of the Endless Dark. He is the end of the span of life. Evanne, this is one of the Three." Tarragon clutched at her hand. "This is Khiton."

Chapter Eighteen

An *overweight merchant captain is the most unlikely aspect of the Three I've heard of.* It wasn't that the fairy had gone all to pieces. The little light seemed high strung, and if Evanne knew one thing about the world, it was that feeding drama led to more drama. Evanne set her feet wide on the deck. The ship about her trembled, but in anger, not fear. The rigging above was of high quality, not a ripped or patched sail to see. It was a three-mast vessel, large, paint gleaming as if freshly applied. She tossed her rust locks, eyeballed the captain of the marvellous ship, and said, "That smells like bullshit."

He blinked, then guffawed, his hands holding his belly. "Aye, you were what we promised." He sobered, looking at those behind her. It gave Evanne an opportunity to take his measure. Dark-skinned like most Tebrani, burnt by the summer sun on the winter seas. His eyes twinkled, but behind that she thought she saw depth like the ocean below. His face was worn, carrying perhaps fifty summers. Less than a god might, and more than a merchant still at the helm should. His clothing was muted, but he wore no armour as the Lord of the Endless Dark was supposed to. And where were his sword and shield? *This* was no Khiton. This was at best a two-baron jackanapes who conned people with sweet lies.

I should know. I'm cut of the same cloth. She rewound the conversation. "What do you mean, you promised? Who promised, and to whom?"

But definitely-not-Khiton swung about, bellowing orders, and the ship surged from the docks. Evanne caught the splash of oars and the grinding of tortured wood as the *Courage* laboured free of the *Salt Donkey's* wreckage. She felt the wind kiss her cheek, so she turned to face it, and saw something that made her mouth hinge wide.

Uncle Day bowed. To the jackanapes. *{Hello, god. Where have you been?}*

"A promise is a promise," the definitely-not-a-god said. "I've not set foot on land for sixteen years, cat. You?"

{I've been trying not to die. Some days are harder than others.}

"This can't be happening," Evanne said. "You're not a god."

The jackanapes' smile didn't dim. "Perhaps we could swap stories over wine. Or ale, we've plenty of that, and a little rum too. Refreshments will arrive. I've candied dates and soft, smokey cheese from the north."

"Do you have anything that used to have a pulse?" Barret worked her shoulder with a wince.

Evanne took a step toward the matriarch. "Are you okay?"

That got her a glare. "I'm fine, kid. I just got in a punch-up because fucknuts there," she jabbed a finger at Heser the Cheg, "couldn't keep his ward under control."

"I am no one's ward." Morgan stood taller, eyes flashing.

"Spoken like a ward." Barret grinned shark teeth. "Let's eat."

This will take some unravelling. Evanne stood at the port railing, staring at nothing as the seas whisked by. The *Courage* wanted to skim and soar for all her merchant's bulk. Lanterns hung from the three masts and the rigging. While their light was warm enough, and banished the dark well enough, there was nothing fancy or godlike about them. Simple flame with oil cast simple light as the night cozied in.

She was alone. Hitch was about somewhere, but not making himself felt. *Probably poking about belowdecks.* It gave her plenty of time to brood, chin on hands, elbows on the railing, while the sea foamed below, and she dreamed of salt freedom. *It's better than thinking of what's behind me.*

The might-be-a-god called himself Mazin, for a reason no one could explain to Evanne's satisfaction. It rankled, because it was the same name Mama said Khiton used when he stole a human's skin. Mazin ran the *Courage* between Tebrani and Or'sen, selling good steel weapons and armour one way, wines and silks the other. Nothing about that was special. He didn't make magical weapons or illusory silks. It was all ... *ordinary*. Evanne had seen the hold after she'd put a couple tankards of ale away, and while Mazin's cargo was good steel, it was just forged the usual way: iron and coal. Nothing glimmered like the legendary Smithsteel armour her mother had given her. *And why does a god enter the freighting business? Don't they have better things to do?*

"Hello."

Evanne jumped, spinning, her gimpy heart lurching. It was Tarragon. "Oh. You scared me."

The fairy buzzed closer, a look of annoyance on her face as she glared at one of her wings. She landed on the railing. "It hasn't come right, you know. It will probably make a noise forever. Some spy I'll be without silent wings."

"Forever? How long do fairies live?" Evanne looked from the sea to Tarragon. The fairy glimmered, a rose-gold glow coming from somewhere inside her, dimmer than her usual radiance. She leaned back on the railing, close enough to Tarragon to feel the heat of her radiance. "Sorry. Maybe it was just a turn of phrase. I've got a lot on my mind."

"Yes. Your world ended two days ago. Your mother and father are missing. Your town is gone. Friends, lost, or turned against you." She ambled closer to Evanne's propped elbows, then leaned against them, staring out at the sea in the same direction. "We live as long as we want to."

"You decide to ... not?"

"Sometimes." The fairy shrugged, a tiny movement Evanne still felt through her sleeve. Tarragon was not just warm, she smelled faintly of fresh-baked bread. "Most of the time we've still got lots to do. Building things takes a lot of fairies, and..." She trailed off.

"And you've lost everyone, too." Evanne nodded. "I've never met one. Heard stories, of course. Mama knew a fairy named Yasmine. Just like she knew a merchant named Mazin."

"He's not a merchant."

"Walks like a duck," Evanne argued. "I've seen nothing godly about him except his girth."

"That's because you're not looking in quite the right way," Mazin rumbled from behind her.

Evanne whirled for the second time in as many minutes. Tarragon jumped aside with a small yelp. The merchant had slipped up on surprisingly quiet feet. Evanne felt her chin jut. "And how should I look?"

"With your eyes. The ones your mother and father gave you." He shrugged. "How are Tilly and Armitage?"

"Dead." The word dropped free before Evanne could stop it.

Mazin shook his head. "The world did not shake, Evanne. I have listened to it for many years and when a great person passes the planet's heart rings like a bell. Did you hear the gong of the heavens? No? Then they still live."

"What kind of merchant are you?" Evanne stared, wondering for a hot second if he *might* be a god.

"A prosperous one." Mazin joined her at the railing. "I know a Trick or two of my own. Yes, I know what you call them. No, I'm not going to tell you how I know, because you won't believe me. You think I'm a charlatan, a conjurer of lies, someone who takes the dreams of people and spins them into tawdry income. I've known many people at the end of their span and could tell many a tale. But that's not the promise I made."

"Huh," Evanne offered. "That's a lot to take in."

"There's a lot going on." Mazin glanced at the fairy. "Does she listen to you?"

"Sometimes." Tarragon had settled out of arm's reach from Evanne, sitting with her feet dangling over the railing. "We're still working out how to talk to each other. I thought she was my enemy."

"All your enemies are dead, Tarragon Greyflight." Mazin gusted a sigh. "You'll have to Build new ones."

"You're a weird merchant," the fairy offered.

"You're a weird fairy," he countered. "Look at you, with nothing to Build and no sword either. There are plenty in the hold below, but you haven't grown big enough for them yet."

Evanne bridled, feeling a surge of protectiveness. "Watch it, Tubby. No one makes jokes about her size except me."

"Stop helping," Tarragon urged. "Do *not* call the God of Endings, 'tubby'."

Mazin laughed, deep, rich, and without any hint he'd taken offence. "Oh, they made you well, Evanne. They made you perfectly."

"Who?" Evanne turned away, bitterness in her mouth. "The Half-Made?"

"Vertiline, the best swordswoman walking this world. Armitage, the courage of the best of men in a monster's body. Those two. Surely you know them?" Mazin joined her at the railing, looking at the sea.

"I don't ... know." Evanne bit her lip. "My mother said she didn't want me."

He gave her a glance. "Did she now? And how did she say that?"

Evanne pressed her lips together, remembering. "She said no one has answered her prayers for sixteen years. When I was born."

"Do you know what she prayed for, sixteen years ago?" Mazin stood, eyes bright, and for a moment Evanne could've sworn red burned in their hungry depths. "Vertiline sickened through her long months of pregnancy. The growing baby within her burned hot and froze with cold. Her blood grew sluggish. Your mother withered." He glanced at the ocean behind them, if looking for where she might be on dead Imshir's streets. "She asked us to let you live. Not her. Just you. And we said we could do it, for a price."

"What cost?" Evanne whispered, rubbing the human skin of her arms, feeling the weakness of it.

Mazin caught the movement. "Cophine said we needed someone to begin again. Ikmae wanted to bridge the old and new worlds. But me ... I hungered for someone to wield a black blade and cut the rot from the world."

"And you got *me*." Evanne laughed, a brittle sound. "Oh, you got suckered in that one."

Mazin gave a sly, merchantlike grin, as if he'd just about closed a good sale. "Your mother ... she is a fox in a henhouse. We," he put his hand on his broad chest, "are the hens in this parable. She said we could have what we wanted, but we had to give something up. Her, dying, but still fighting for more. The life leaving her, skin sallow, but her eyes ... they burned like stars. I will remember them until the day I meet my own end. She held my hand, and said I couldn't have you."

"She what?" Evanne looked to Tarragon. "She didn't even know me. And if she did..." She looked down at herself, imagining the scales meeting skin, her not-right Vhemin eyes, and feeling the rust locks that couldn't grow long enough.

Mazin sighed. "I forget when you are young you are also stupid. The last saviour was easier to talk to."

Evanne bridled. "I will knock your teeth in, old man."

"Better," he approved, posture not shifting a millimetre. "You shouldn't mope."

"I'm not ... okay, maybe I was," Evanne allowed. "I've got a lot to mope about. And I'm sixteen! It's my—"

"Fifteen."

"I'm almost sixteen," she gritted.

The god playing as a merchant smiled. "Your mother wanted just one thing: you. All you could be, the endless possibility of your life stretching down many long years ahead of you."

"What did you want?" Tarragon's voice was small at Evanne's elbow. "To make a thing that had never been, what was the price?"

"A new order," Mazin said. "We wanted the Tresward back. A school to lead all schools, not burdened by the sins of the past, fresh-faced and ready to go. A force for justice, if you'll allow an old man some poetic license. A group made from the people of Tebrani and Or'sen. Strong and incorruptible. Our price for you was a teacher: the best swordswoman in the world at the Tresward's head."

Evanne thought for one heartbeat, two, then brayed laughter, slapping her thighs. "Oh, you got suckered. A mountain blew up your school."

"Perhaps." He shrugged. "Is it the people that matter, or the world they change?"

"You're making exactly zero sense," Evanne said. "The school's gone. All the people in it, ash or rot. And I guess if you'd been there you might've helped. But gods seem to do little but sail the high seas and get preachy."

Mazin rumbled on as if she hadn't spoken. "We each promised to not set foot on Tebrani soil. To let Tilly run her school, her way. So, she could save the world one more time."

"The world was already saved," Evanne blurted. "It was saved sixteen years ago."

"Was it?" Mazin glanced at the fairy. "Why was the Builder a prisoner? And your ghost companion—what of him? He has paced from one sandy shore of Tebrani to the other, unable to rest. The queen of a foreign land comes to you, cap in hand—"

"That's one thing Morgan doesn't do. Beg." Evanne crossed her arms.

"Still looking at people the wrong way, I see." Mazin straightened. "I've said enough for now. You'll have questions aplenty, and I will answer. And when you're ready, you *will* save the world."

"Wait." Evanne looked at the seas, then back to the merchant. *The god.* "What did you want?"

"That's not the question you want to ask." He touched her chin, finger soft, and for a moment she felt the universe held its breath.

She felt a tear trickle down her cheek, and bit her lip. "What did *she* ... what did Mama really want? It can't have been the Half-made. The lost, the ill wrought, the—"

"Don't you see?" Mazin let his finger drop and turned away. "We got exactly what we wanted. All of us."

"W ELL, SHIT." E VANNE SIGHED.

Tarragon sidled back up to her arm, leaning against it again. "What is?"

"I think he's *actually* a god." Evanne bared her teeth.

The fairy laughed. "Of course he's a god. That's what I said. Sight of Day said it. Even the Raven Queen knows she's outmatched. But you? You—"

"I went in, Vhemin style."

"You went in like you left your brain in a jar at birth." Tarragon slid down Evanne's arm, sitting on the railing with her feet dangling over the edge again. "It wouldn't have needed to be a big jar, though."

"Can you swim?" Evanne felt the laughter in her voice despite the implied threat.

"Bitch, I can fly." The fairy gave a contented sigh. "I've never seen someone talk to a god like that before."

"Seen many people talk to gods?"

"Lots." She considered the sky, then returned to Evanne's shoulder. "They walked among us, before they were moons."

"And now they're cluttering up the streets again. Great." Evanne ran a hand through her hair, careful to not disturb Tarragon's perch this time. The fairy was warm, soft, and now smelled of gingerbread and allspice. *It's nice having her around. Even if she wanted me dead.*

"What are you going to do?"

Evanne pursed her lips. "What I said before. Go to Or'sen. Get Hitch's weapon. Maybe find Cleo. Punch her lights out." She blew out a lungful. "I hadn't thought beyond that."

"Have you thought about the queen's link to you? Back at the docks. You were ... vibing together. She is a mage, no mistake, but a weird one. It's probably because she's been dead already and you're a necromancer."

Evanne started upright, Tarragon dislodging again with a tiny squawk. "I am *not* a necromancer! They—"

"Commune with the dead?"

Evanne opened her mouth a time or two. "Well, I talk to Hitch. Some others. That's hardly communing—"

"What about the guitar, hmm?" She hovered over the sea below, dripping glitter dust. "You can play, but you... you *woke* me, Evanne. You got me up from near death to fight. That's a powerful magic. It didn't come from me, and it didn't come from the Raven Queen. It was all you."

"I'm ... just a good singer," Evanne said, hearing the lameness of it. "Wait. The queen's been dead before? How do you know?"

The fairy gave an eye-roll, then turned a barrel roll as if it wasn't enough. "Same way I knew Mazin was Khiton. It's writ on her face. It follows her in the stars."

"You see the Trick of it?"

Tarragon settled on the railing. "What's a Trick?"

"Like ... when you know how to say a thing to make another feel it. Or how to hold your face to make a person believe a lie. But you do it with your whole heart, even the broken part, and it works." Evanne rummaged in her satchel, and pulled out her notebook. "Here. I take notes."

She flipped the pages, Tarragon following along. After a few turns, Tarragon whistled. "You need therapy."

"Apparently. I'm a necromancer."

"No, you need killing because you're a necromancer. You need therapy because you're a sociopath."

Evanne grinned in the dark. "You say the nicest things."

Chapter Nineteen

The promised land wasn't what Tarragon expected. Her first warning was smoke on the horizon. As the *Courage* slipped through the waves, mean and quick for such a heavy ship, the clouds ahead marking landfall were tinged a sooty grey.

She was at the prow, enjoying the sea air and salt spray in equal measure, Evanne by her side. The maybe-Vhemin had been with her most days of their sailing. As Tarragon remembered the planet, the voyage by sea should've taken weeks, but after less than one, land was already in sight.

A *burning* land at that.

"Is it supposed to be on fire?" Tarragon pointed. "There. That smudge is smoke."

Evanne hunkered beside her, following Tarragon's arm. "It has that look, I'll allow."

Tarragon stole a glance at Evanne. Skin tanned darker by the week at sea. Rust locks stiff with salt, lavender snake eyes soft and deep. *Oh, my. I could fall into those eyes.* "Old tech."

Evanne gave her some side eye, flashing Tarragon another glimpse of that luminous stare. "You what?"

"Old technology. When we make ... *made* war, it was with hyper beams and starlight drives. Dragonfire and glitter dust. Nothing stayed about long enough to burn. Wood to ash, just like," she snapped her fingers, "that."

"I get it. The world sucks since you got back to it, and of all the things we should be good at, we're sucking worse at war." Evanne pursed her lips. "You know, there's hope to be found somewhere in there."

"People are probably burning alive."

"And there goes the hope." Evanne stood, crossing her arms. Since boarding the *Courage* Evanne had got rid of her ripped, cut, and blood-stained jerkin, opting for a sleeveless vest. It showed off her biceps, which were worth showing off. The maybe-Vhemin caught her staring and hugged herself. "Stop looking at me like that."

"Like what?"

"Like I'm a freak show." Evanne rubbed her arms, hands rasping from human-skinned forearms to Vhemin-scaled upper arms. "I know I'm made wrong."

Tarragon blinked. *It's always like this. Just as we're getting closer, I say or do something and she hears or sees something else.* "I didn't mean—"

"Land ho!" The bellow came from the crow's nest high above in the mid mast. A seagull squawked in counterpoint. "Land ho!"

Evanne glared at the man above. "Asleep on watch were you? We saw that hours ago from down here."

The sailor in the nest peered down at them. From so far above he seemed no larger than Tarragon. "And you said nothing?"

"You need *some* job security," Tarragon hollered back. "We can't make *everyone* on the ship look bad!" This rewarded her with a grin from Evanne, and something in Tarragon's chest relaxed. *She is quick to anger, and quick to forgive. It is the way of the short-lived.*

Sight of Day joined them, sauntering with easy Feybrind grace from the midships to the forecastle. *{This is not good. Last time I was in the Raven Queen's city it burned, but not like this.}* He frowned, staring at his hands as if blaming them for a misstep. *{I didn't set it on fire, in case anyone's asking.}*

"Of course. You were on the ship." Evanne arched her back. "Best I get my guitar. When we land we're not coming back for knickknacks or pretty things."

{I meant last time.}

"And yet you were there both times." Evanne strode off. "I don't believe in coincidences, Uncle. You should be more careful of which cities you burn."

Sight of Day glanced at Tarragon. *{I really didn't.}*

"I really don't care," the fairy said. "If the science of today is anything to go by it would be a breeding ground for cholera and syphilis anyway." She hopped into the air, gammy wing buzzing, and did a loop around the Feybrind's head. "Best press the reset button and start again."

{You use words I know, but put them together in a way that starves them of meaning.} The cat's tail swished. *{It is a peculiar and quite annoying trick.}*

LISTLESS, TARRAGON DRIFTED THE SHIP UNTIL SHE FOUND EVANNE. The maybe-Vhemin was at the rear part—*Stern? Is it a stern?*—wind chasing rust locks about her face. She was nose to nose with a god.

"I don't give a shit," Evanne bunched her fingers into a fist, "if you're Khiton or the ghost of my ancestors. I'm going ashore. When I get there, I'm going to take Hitch to his weapon. He, in turn, will give me the weapon and we will crucify every person who raised arms against us."

"It is dangerous." Khiton stood, arms crossed, face a thundercloud. "Hitch's temple lies in the blasted plague lands. The sands hold the kiss of death. If the sharks don't get you, the poisoned air will. The cities' ancient guardians are ready to repel invaders. You carry no Storm or Sway. You will die. This will break the promise."

Evanne jerked a thumb at her chest. "I'm *Vhemin*, you cretin. We don't die easy. Go for the head or don't go at all. And I've got a guitar." She patted the case slung behind her.

"You'll still die." Khiton's chin jutted. "I didn't make all the things come to bear only to have you—"

Evanne turned away from him, palm thrust behind her. "Death, destruction, and more death! We're going to stop the dying."

"With a weapon you don't understand and have never seen?"

"With whatever it takes," she spat. Those perfect lavender eyes found Tarragon, and she relaxed a micron. "Oh. Hello, fairy. We're going to certain death. Do you want to come?"

"I'm in," Tarragon confirmed. "Just one small insignificant detail needs massaging."

"My shoulders *are* knotty," Evanne confirmed. "What news?"

"There is a god behind you." She glimmered. "He is the god of endings. Hearth and home. And let's not forget war. He could march up to that shitstorm," she gestured to the smoke on the horizon, "and make it all stop. Short trip, a glass of wine at the end, and home before bedtime."

Evanne turned to the god. "Well, Mazin? She makes a good point."

"I made a promise." The god shrugged, as if that explained all. "I won't set foot on land until Knight Champion Vertiline says I may. That was part of the bargain. Leave well enough alone."

"There are extenuating circumstances," Tarragon protested.

"All the lawyers are dead. I made sure of it." Mazin—*no, that's Khiton, keep it straight*—smiled.

"That feels overly convenient." Tarragon huffed.

"Would you break a vow? The stars die when gods don't hold true. And we've not enough starry lights in the dark sky." Mazin looked out to sea. "You are certain you won't stay aboard this ship until the hurricane clears?"

"My parents didn't raise a quitter." Evanne's brows furrowed. "I'm not sure what they raised, but it wasn't one of those."

"Then attend." The god straightened. "You are going to the heart of the plague lands. You will find a forgotten temple. Inside is all you seek, and more." He looked at his feet. "The things you find will leave your heart rent. You will have your weapon, but you will learn the truth."

"What's so bad about truth?" Evanne's frown deepened.

"Everything," Mazin sighed. "When you find the weapon, look for this mark." He drew a circle in the air, then stabbed a dot in the middle.

"An eye?" Evanne blinked. "Your mysterious sign is a human eye?"

"It's not an eye," Mazin grumbled. "It is the mark of—"

"I don't care," Evanne said. "An eye, a pancake with a single blackberry atop, what difference? I will seek your mark. What will I find near the mark?"

"A gift," Mazin said. "You will need it because the weapon isn't what you think. You will want it because you suck at fighting."

"Hey."

"It's true." The god shrugged. "You didn't study the twenty-one hundred steps. Your heart labours with the smallest of burdens. And—"

"My heart will be fine." Evanne glowered at the rapidly approaching burning city. "You going to dock?"

"No." The god grinned, all teeth. "No foot on land, remember?"

THE DOCKS CONTINUED TO APPROACH AT AN UNHEALTHY SPEED. THE *Courage* shouldered through the waves, great clouds of spume flung above the railing to splash against Tarragon. She shivered in delight, thrill tickling her stomach. She didn't know what Khiton was up to, but he was a god. *Gods have the best plans.*

The fairy was at the stern, Evanne with her, Barret and Sight of Day close at hand. Heser the Cheg and his queen stood apart, him placid like a deep lake, her angry, hands chopping the air as she whispered. Tarragon didn't think there was much worth listening to there, so she looked to the helmsman instead.

He was a weathered soul, skin dark like boot leather, hair bleached like sand. He was also under a lot of strain, because the god leaned close, hissing in his ear, arm pointed at the sea south of Ravenswall's wharfs. The helmsman, nobody's coward, wrestled the wheel like a titan turning a planet. The *Courage* slewed, waves thundering against her wooden skin, and hove southward.

Gods have the best plans ... but I don't understand this one.

Ravenswall was burning. Sure, sure, the parts of it that were made of stone were simply blackened: the main spire of the keep rising above the ruckus, skirts sooty, to look down in a disapproving manner on the Artist's Borough around it. But the rest of the Borough was a ruin, thatched roofs and wooden planks burning with frenzied flare.

The city beyond cried in panic, billowing plumes of blackness stretching skyward. Ravenswall was a lot bigger than Tarragon remembered ancient Imshir being, but it wasn't a patch on a proper modern city. *Or, is that ancient? It's hard to keep it all straight.*

As the *Courage* thundered through the chop, Tarragon spied something in the harbour's waters. She glimmered, pointing. "There!"

Evanne visored her eyes with a hand. "What am I looking at?"

"It's a transport gate. Or what's left of one. It didn't use to be under water." She *hmm'd*. "Most of this water didn't use to be here. It was a departure point. Back there," Tarragon pointed leagues in their wake, "was where the sea started. But here? Nothing like this." She felt sad, a soft, heavy feeling in her chest.

"Fairy? What is it?"

"It's nothing," she lied. "It's just ... I had a picnic here a long time ago."

The ship lurched, sails billowing as they found a new heading, then a *boom* as wind filled canvas. The *Courage* surged, now heading northward, right toward the docks.

"I don't understand," Tarragon said. "We're going to crash."

"Why are you surprised?" Evanne brushed rust locks aside. "Mazin may be a god, or a man, but he's all the way crazy."

"But ... gods have the best plans! This is not a good plan!" Tarragon glittered in distress. "The ship will break apart. The tolerances of this material—"

"What of us?" Evanne showed those wonderful, slightly pointed teeth. "Will we break apart?"

"Probably ... not?" Tarragon wasn't sure. "It's not my field, and I didn't pass my exams."

"Good enough." Evanne turned to their companions. "Ho! We're going to crash. It will be bad. Later, I will sing of it. For now, we need to get off this ship and over there." She cast a muscled arm toward the city's heart.

"Not quite." Hitch drifted free of the ship's rear mast. "We need to go past the city."

"Whatever." Evanne tossed her head. "In the city are horses."

"Horses don't like you," Hitch countered.

"And carts," the maybe-Vhemin gritted. "Which we can put horses in front of."

"If you think that's the best plan," the spectre agreed. "Just don't lose sight of the prize. It's not Ravenswall."

"Here's what we'll do." Queen Morgan swept past Heser the Cheg. "When we land, we'll gather the queensguard. Once we have a sizeable force, we'll—"

"Not even a little bit right," Evanne said. "I mean, if you want to play soldiers, go for gold. Now's as good a place as any to part ways. But we're leaving the city."

"I'll be taking Heser the Cheg and Barret," Morgan countered.

"Fair," Evanne conceded.

"And Sight of Day."

"Evanne," Tarragon said.

"No way," Evanne said, not changing her tone. "Not today, and not on the weekends either."

{I have some thoughts on the matter.}

"Evanne!" Tarragon glimmered to get the maybe-Vhemin's attention, but Evanne ignored her.

"How about a wager?" The queen raised an eyebrow.

"I prefer a competition," Evanne said. "Maybe arm wrestle?"

"Evanne!" Tarragon hollered, but the queen was on full noise at this point.

"Don't be absurd. A running race is the only way—"

The ship hit the docks with the thunder of splintering wood. It was a new enough sound for Tarragon, more used to the tearing of metal and the hiss of light beams. Wood groaned when it broke, as if it didn't want to give up all at once. The *Courage* shuddered against the broken span of the docks. The marvel of it was Mazin's—*no, that's Khiton!*—

crew didn't even blink, as if ramming into a new port was how things were done around here.

Evanne stumbled to one knee, stood, caught the queen, turned, steadied her guitar case, and jumped over the side. Tarragon blinked. *One second she was there, the next, gone.* She hovered an indecisive second, then sped in pursuit. The cat leaped after Evanne, golden eyes hard. Behind him, Barret roared a challenge, although to who Tarragon couldn't tell: the docks were deserted. *Which means whoever burned the city came from land, and all vessels we could use to evacuate are already gone.*

Evanne bounced from broken plank to roughened spar, then turned to the ship when on even ground. "Ho, Mazin!"

"Ho, Evanne!"

"Thanks for the ride," the maybe-Vhemin called, then turned and headed for a city on fire.

Chapter Twenty

I had no idea about any of this. Evanne strode off the docks, guitar jostling her back, smoke in her eyes. *Also, I have no idea where I'm going. Think fast.* The harbour district scribed a bloody crescent before the city proper. The castle, home of the Raven Queen, stood above all, wearing a cloak of ashen misery. Evanne heard screaming, and the sound of battle, but both were muted by distance. *Whatever happened here packed up and moved on.*

It left all the bodies, though.

There are more people laying here dead than I've known in my life. They were scattered, as numerous as reeds strewn on a floor. There, a man lay with surprised eyes staring skyward, no mark on his body indicating what killed him. To his left and right, the parts of a woman who'd been cut in half, the wound precise, almost impersonal. Four paces farther on, a child with a missing head. Beside him, a dog that barked no longer. Upon a cart, two teamsters clutched arrow shafts in their chests with dead hands, heads bowed.

No one looked like they'd suffered, taking time to bleed out their last on old stone near the water. Everyone here looked like they'd died fast, almost efficiently, damage inflicted to rend soul from flesh with the least fuss.

Evanne slowed, then crested to a halt. "Why?"

She jumped as a hand came down on her shoulder. Barret, the old matriarch's voice harder than Evanne had heard before. "No Vhemin did this."

Queen Morgan drew beside Evanne. "Your people know war."

"I ain't arguing that point." Barret pointed to a man nailed to a wall with his own sword. "There. We'd have taken the sword. Look at that one." Her arm swung to another with his throat slit in a surgical line, his white butcher's apron stained crimson. "We'd hack the head off. One blow or two, leave a raggedy stump, right? Whoever did this was ... productive. Like death's a factory, people in one end and sausages out the other."

{It makes you wonder.} Sight of Day padded past. *{I've never seen anything like this.}*

"I have." Evanne turned at the small voice near her ear. Hovering, Tarragon clutched her hands, small face bleak. "I've seen this one time before."

"What is it, fairy?"

Tarragon glanced at Sight of Day. "You were supposed to be craftsmen!"

{We are.} The cat sighed. *{We are the best at all we do.}*

"You're saying Feybrind did this?" Barret sulked for a moment. "Makes sense, I guess. The cat's not half bad in a fight."

{Thanks.}

"And that pretty blade of his is more scalpel than sword." She nodded. "But there are fuck*all* of you, and a lot of dead people here. Seems even with your steel and a strong tailwind you'd need more than a handful to do this."

"There's another story here." Evanne felt the truth of it, a Trick that felt monstrous and seductive. "We're at the docks. Imagine. A ship comes here, carrying Feybrind. Make it two ships if you like. The number's not important. The cats swarm from deck to dock, taking all on the blade or bow. Into the city, where they hunt larger prey." She put her hands on her hips. "But these people didn't run, no? A few, perhaps, but what if they had help?" Evanne tasted bitterness. "Like Cleo. A friendly face at the front, blades behind."

"Humans and Feybrind working together?" Barret chewed it over. "I guess. But why attack Ravenswall?"

"Duh." Tarragon flitted closer to the keep. "This is a transport station. There is a vault beneath the earth. It may still hold treasures. Someone woke Heaven's Gate. They raised the living dead where I was held prisoner. All over the land someone is pushing buttons that are marked 'do not push' and they are doing it to everyone."

"Everyone except Feybrind," Barret said. "No cats died here."

{Perhaps.} Sight of Day stood from his examination of a corpse. *{It could just be we've yet to see the worst of it.}*

THE WORST, AYE? Evanne marched up old stone steps leading from the docks to the city. They felt older than time under her feet, no Trick in it: just age, a lot of it, and a million feet. She could see where the stone had been replaced, the granite bleached a different shade by the passing sands in the hourglass. But even newer, lighter-coloured stones were smooth. *No, the worst is not what's seen, but what's unseen. Where are they all?* She cast about for the spectres of the dead, but only Hitch hovered nearby.

I have no idea how many people it would take to smooth stone to the texture of a baby's skin. She paused, then on a whim touched the steps. Gritty, sure, but an honest kind of dirt, no Trick or lie here either. There wasn't a slave's sweat soaking the stone, no beast of burden overworked and panicked. *This Morgan runs a city well enough, so perhaps I should be kinder to her.* She glanced at the Raven Queen, caught the upturned nose, and gritted sharp teeth. *Nah. Maybe we'll save that for tomorrow.* Regardless, it didn't explain the lack of ghosts. Even with a happy bunch of dead, there would be that *one guy* who was churlish because of his lot. Standing on the path to the heavens, but one foot anchored in the sewer of this world.

Tasks undone. Looking for someone to do 'em, too. She glanced at Hitch. The ghost stood, arms akimbo. *Yes, he has a task for me, and no mistake. He just can't remember what it is.*

"You going to take all day getting up these steps?" Hitch broke her reverie, looking between Evanne and the top of the stairs. "I know you've got a troublesome ticker, but it's not that far."

"Eat a bowl of dicks without sauce," she countered.

"You're overusing that one," Hitch warned. "You need a better rejoinder. Perhaps, 'May a diseased yak taking a liking to your sister'."

"Do you have a sister?"

"Maybe." The spectre sounded evasive.

"And thus you set me up for a rejoinder without impact." Evanne dusted off her hands, squared her shoulders, took another step up, then stopped. She was on the verge of asking Hitch where he thought the dead had got to, but... "Hullo. What's that noise?" It was a kind of rhythmic *clanking*, a hissing note keeping the beat alongside.

Sight of Day appeared at her side like he'd always been there, casual and relaxed, but his hand gripped her elbow. Evanne turned to take in his Handspeak. It was sharp, precise, and quicker than she was used to following. *{That is the sound of us needing to run, fast.}*

"Which way?"

His golden eyes narrowed. *{I'm not sure it will matter.}*

"Because my heart will give out?"

{Because hearts don't matter in this race. But we should try anyway. I will see if I can find a path.} Then he was off, Feybrind-quick, tail giving a final lash.

"He's not wrong," Hitch said. "I think I remember—"

"You need to run," Tarragon said, *right* in Evanne's ear as the fairy landed with a buffet of warm, cinnamon-scented air on Evanne's shoulder. "I know things are confusing for Bigs, but this is one of those times you should listen to your creations."

"Creations?" Evanne blinked. "I'm—"

"I know, I know. You're part Vehement Systems. And right now, you're going to find out what *else* they made. It wasn't fairies and cats!" She jumped for sky, buzzing after Sight of Day, trailing hot air and glimmer.

Barret trudged past Evanne. "They're not wrong."

"You're not running!"

"I don't want to die tired." The matriarch paused, scratching an armpit. "You should hustle, though."

"I don't under...*whatthefuckisthat?*" Evanne's voice climbed to a higher octave than she thought possible as her hand pointed like a compass finding true north, arm snapping out like it had a will of its own. Her brain tried a few things on for size. *Like a wagon with legs* didn't seem right, because wagons weren't three stories off the ground, and didn't have legs either. *It's a horse-drawn carriage* didn't work either, because while it looked a little carriage-like, there were zero horses in the air above her.

"It's an Artifice!" The Raven Queen sprinted past Evanne, Heser the Cheg following slightly after, carrying a massive hammer he'd scared up, but held low as if he didn't want to try his luck against the Artifice.

"Eh." Barret spat. "Ready to run?"

Ah, that's where all the dead are. A legion of ghostly blue forms scudded about the feet of the machine, faces full of terror. Some tried to clamber up the smooth sides of the Artifice. Others tried to pull those ones back to earth. A few had made it to the top of the machine, worrying at something outside of Evanne's sight. *Maybe trying to get in?* Her brain tried to work out what would stop a ghost from walking through walls, then another part of her mind gave that original piece a solid punch in the side of the face. *Move. Right. On it.*

Evanne set off at a dead sprint. *Fuck all this*, her brain said. *Fuck it from on high. Fuck it from below. Fuck it sideways, while we're at it.* Her legs hammered stone, and she lowered her head, bulling on. There was a Three-cursed machine walking the streets of Ravenswall. She'd heard the stories of Artifices, Uncle Day sitting by the fireside, hands whispering their tale, but she hadn't believed a word of it.

Not until now.

A ghostly woman stood ahead, mouth open as if she wanted to speak, but they never had anything to say to the living. The ghost pointed out a trail through the streets ahead. *Got you. That way.* Evanne ran harder, her breakfast wanting *out*, her heart wanting to explode. A dead child, the pavers visible through his bare feet, pointed around a corner. He was crying, or as close to it as the dead could get, and clutched at a spectral bear. The soft toy was singed, a reminder perhaps of how he'd died. Fire, rather than the blade, but dead all the same.

It didn't take her long to pass Heser the Cheg, then overtake the Raven Queen. Her heart slammed against her ribs, her stomach clenching, and she wanted to be sick, or stop for a breath, or both. Rounding a corner, she skidded to a halt, because right *there* was *another* Artifice. Where the last one was a carriage held three stories high, this was lower slung, two fangs on its snout, and something deep inside her whispered: *Beware. Fire and death.*

She coughed, a tiny noise that wanted to become a groan, because the way was blocked by the machine. Other streets were choked with wreckage made of bodies and rubble. Blood, smoke, and dust were the specials of the day. The Raven Queen rounded the corner behind her, then slid to a stop, lost her footing, and slid on her rump a pace or two.

Heser the Cheg caught up, hauling his ward to her feet. Evanne couldn't see Sight of Day, but a spectral barber, scissors still in hand, pointed to a door to Evanne's left. It was stout enough, still standing in its frame, the building above good stone. Evanne glimpsed red coals forming in the Artifice's fangs, turned, and charged for the door. She grabbed Morgan on the way, slinging the monarch over her shoulder as she went, because the queen was rooted to the spot like she could use that high-born chin to stop imminent death.

The queen gave a short scream, but Evanne didn't care. She lowered her other shoulder and hit the door with a *crash* of splintered wood. The *ping* of lock popped from jamb led her on. *Time for a breather.* A sound like frying bacon came from the street, a hissing that grew into a roar. She turned, and saw fire, *real* fire, mountains of it chewing at the doorway. It was almost solid, a wave of force that picked her up like a wooden toy and threw her after the lock.

Dust. Evanne coughed. The Raven Queen struggled, but not with much enthusiasm. Evanne's heart hammered fast one moment, then straggled like a lame duck the next. She *needed* to be sick, so she pushed Morgan aside and tossed her breakfast to the floor. One breath, two, then she wiped her mouth. *Up.*

The room near the door was on fire. The very stone wept molten rock. Evanne's eyes were dry, her throat parched. The bile on her lips dried in a heartbeat. Then: *Tarragon is out there.* She glanced at the queen, but Morgan wasn't doing much of anything useful. A quick scan of the room said, *You are in a spice warehouse.* Evanne hauled Morgan over her shoulder, then hustled her with Vhemin strength to a waist-high silo that smelled of burnt cardamon. She placed her charge in the lee, then squared up against the door.

"You are fucking nuts," Hitch said. "Do *not* go out there. There is an *Artifice* out there. They were weapons of the ancients. A single one could take a city. They can—"

Whatever an Artifice could do was lost as Evanne powered for the door. She covered lavender eyes with her arm, human skin feeling the heat more than the scales on her shoulders, then she was out in the street beyond. Evanne smelled burning hair, pawed at her head for a moment, then looked about for the fairy.

The ghostly barber looked at her in astonishment, then pointed at the spice warehouse behind her. The Artifice was there, right *there*, so she didn't butter this up with her usual finesse. "Fucker, where is the fairy?"

"Here," Heser the Cheg gasped. He lay beneath a piece of masonry. Blood mixed with dust to form a ruddy chalk. He held a tiny glimmer against his chest, arms clutched close.

The ghostly barber got in her grill again, so she waved him off. "Look. I don't have time. If you want to be useful, deal with that." She jabbed at the Artifice, trying to ignore it as it took a step closer, the street shaking. Remembered heat tickled her back as the spice warehouse's frontage made a slow journey into stone slurry.

Evanne huddled beside Heser. "Uncle?" She got her fingers under granite. "This will hurt." Then she heaved. Muscles bunching, Evanne strained with all her Half-Made strength. Teeth gritted; eyes closed. The Vhemin in her snarled, *growled*, heaved, but her weak human fingers trembled, slipping against the granite. The skin of her palm tore, but she didn't care because this was *Uncle Heser*, and this piece of rock was going to *move*.

Then, it did, all at once. Evanne stumbled back, eyes popping open.

Barret was there, the old matriarch lifting masonry like only a Vhemin could, all strength, making it look *easy*. They grunted the stone aside by raw brawn, then dropped it. Barret's arm was singed, blistered, the scales gone, flesh underneath weeping, and Evanne looked away. *She could do more than me, and she was crippled by pain. What kind of worthless monster am I?*

"Right," Evanne said. She wanted to wallow a little longer in misery, but it wasn't the time. She spun on her heel, facing the Artifice. The barber's spectre had made the top and was trying to get inside. The machine's fangs glowed a cherry red as it primed for another burst of heat. Evanne squinted, considered the timing of it, then hauled Heser the Cheg and his precious tiny burden upright.

Then she was running again, fucking *running*, because her heart didn't have enough to do. She stumbled like a drunk with Heser clutched awkwardly beside her, shouldering through the ruin of the spice warehouse's door. Heser yelled, and she smelled burnt meat, then they were inside. She bulled on, tossing him to the ground beside his queen. "Wait here."

Hitch pulled up in front of her. "Evanne! Don't go back out there! It's not—"

And she ploughed through him, grabbing a mason jar from a bench in passing. It was full of a saffron liquid, the fluid lazy like oil. Once more through the burning doorway, this time crouched low because the stone was giving up the will to live. Outside, Barret stood, one arm hanging, the other up, middle finger extended at the Artifice. The machine stared down at her, massive metal snout a bear's grisly visage facing an ant.

"Oi!" Evanne cocked her arm back and as the Artifice's snout turned to her, she let fly. The mason jar impacted the dark line of its eye, splashing rust-orange on it. It didn't stumble or sway, but it also didn't track her as she ran—*again!*—toward Barret.

A curl of smoke came from the machine's face, then the oil caught, fire curling from its skin. Evanne ignored it, because it was made of metal. She figured it for an angry skillet on legs now. She pushed Barret toward the doorway. "Move!"

And then they both moved, through the doorway, stumbling

together, the broken and the Half-Made, into the spice warehouse. The wall slouched to the ground behind them, and Evanne choked ashen dust.

Barret pulled her farther back into the gloom. "Not bad, kid."

Not bad? Evanne wiped her eyes. "Where is Uncle Day?"

Chapter Twenty-One

If Tarragon hadn't seen it, she wouldn't have believed it. One second, Evanne was standing strong and tall, those amazing arms bare, violet eyes fierce, and then ... she crumpled. The tiny spy knew how she felt; Tarragon had felt exactly that eight hundred years ago when she and Helio had been captured, all because Tarragon couldn't control her glimmer.

And then, almost eight hundred years later, Helio died. He died because they'd been trapped from the sun for too long, and everything broke because there were no more Builders, but mostly because Tarragon had let him down.

So, when she saw Evanne's face, that realisation that *she could've done something* but *hadn't*, the fairy wanted to hold her. That was impossible, because Evanne was a Big, just a really good looking one, and if Tarragon tried really hard, she might be able to wrap her arms around Evanne's wrist.

She buzzed, freeing herself from Heser the Cheg. The man might be a Big, and a human at that, but he'd grabbed her as the air turned to rock when a wall collapsed, and hid her against his chest, and tried not to scream when his leg broke. He smelled of sweat and strength, and she didn't think he had a ridiculous name anymore.

Tarragon headed toward Evanne, then flitted close and wrapped herself around the maybe-Vhemin's bicep. She put her face against the smooth scales there. Sure, she couldn't even hold Evanne's one arm in both of hers, but the maybe-Vhemin needed a hug, and this was the best Tarragon could do. She put a little glimmer in it. "It's okay."

"You don't know that," Evanne snapped. "There was ... a fire."

"I *do* know," Tarragon said. "I know because you saved everyone else. He wasn't there, Evanne. The Fey Bra... Feybrind don't die easy, and he is one of the best of their kind."

Evanne slumped a little, but Tarragon couldn't tell if it was relief or resignation. "What do I do now?"

Tarragon thought about that. There were a thousand trite answers. *Take some time*, that was a popular one, or, *Focus on your work*. But they came from another age, when machines toiled and Builders were everywhere. She let Evanne go, a sparkling of glimmerdust left against the maybe-Vhemin's scales, and hovered before her. "I think you do exactly what you've been doing."

"Getting people killed? Some plan that is—"

"Saving everyone," Tarragon urged. "You saved the queen first, then the rest of us. There was an Artifice. Still is, probably, and it might come in here, so we still need saving. Maybe you're not sure what's going on, or how to do it, but we can't tell. You're doing a really good job. You are saving *everyone*, no, don't show me teeth, I won't hear it. The cat is *fine*, Evanne. He's fine, and we're not, and you are the best person here for making us fine." She tried to keep her voice soft and her glow warm.

Evanne looked about, those wondrously luminescent lavender eyes wide as she took it in. The queen, out for the count. Heser the Cheg, so pale it felt like Tarragon could see daylight through him. Barret, old and tired, a state her monstrous kind never managed. All spent, used up, and Tarragon was too tiny to do anything about it. She didn't even have a sword!

The ghost was fine though, despite not having much of a face, arms, or legs. Hitch seeped over. "She is right, Evanne."

"You stay out of this ... wait. I'm right?" Tarragon blinked.

Hitch ignored her. "You are doing a better job than I managed. I died! And so ... it would be good if you could help the rest to live a little longer."

"How do I do that?" Evanne stood a little straighter.

"By being pig-headed and stubborn. It's how you usually roll."

Evanne bristled, then she laughed. "Thank you, Hitch."

"Don't thank me. Thank the fairy. She's the one who's telling home truths here." The ghost looked away. "You should do it soon, though. The Artifice will be back when the pilot works out you've got the queen of Or'sen. I suggest you run."

Evanne nodded, eyes growing distant for a moment. "Okay. Okay! We're going to do something about this whole survival thing."

Barret grumbled, getting to her feet. "More walking, huh?"

"No." Evanne grinned. "We ride in *style*."

THE PLAN WAS SIMPLE. THE PARTY HUSTLED THROUGH THE STREETS of Or'sen, looking for a carriage. Evanne said *we'll steal the royal chariot* and Heser the Cheg had just stared at her, but really hard, so she'd sighed and said, *okay, okay, but it's still going to be an epic chariot.*

Barret had Heser the Cheg slung over her shoulder. Evanne hauled Queen Morgan like a sack of grain. The ghost lurked behind and hunted in front, looking for ambushers as he sifted through solid walls at speed.

Tarragon flew high above, well clear of the roof line. She had a bead on a carriage, a pretty good one too by hick standards. It had gold paint and a roof, and only a little blood where the wagoner had met his demise. The team of four horses at the front looked ready to bolt, but the carriage was tangled in some wreckage, and wouldn't be getting far without Big intervention. She kept urging them on with flashes of glimmer.

The ghost returned from ahead and spoke with Evanne. Tarragon couldn't hear from up here what they spoke about, but Evanne beckoned her down. She flitted closer, hovering between the two.

Evanne adjusted Morgan's weight on her shoulder, not looking like the royal's weight bothered her much. "Say it again, Hitch."

"The carriage is fine, a bit of grunting and you'll—"

"Says the man who won't do the heavy lifting." Evanne shifted Morgan's weight for emphasis.

"Cophine save me." Hitch looked at the sky. "Actually, I'm not fussy which of the Three it is. Ikmae or Khiton would work."

Evanne growled. "On with the grunting."

"You'll get the horses free for sure." He sighed. "There is a small group of Feybrind and humans in a house nearby. If you make noise, I'm sure they'll hear. There are bodies, which means they probably did the killing."

"What if they need help?" Evanne frowned. "The carriage is big enough for a few more."

"Do you want to take that chance?" Hitch looked to Tarragon. "What would the spy corps advise?"

"Avoid unless we have solid intel," Tarragon said. "If we get the carriage free and clear, and they come after us and don't look homicidal, we can pick them up then. It gives us options."

"Fine." Evanne turned, lugging Morgan with her. "We'll be quiet."

Tarragon climbed the sky, then zipped ahead to make sure the coast was clear. The small party below made good time, arriving at the carriage without fuss. Tarragon kept overwatch while Evanne stuffed Morgan into the carriage. Barret looked to be about to add Heser to the baggage compartment, but the human waved her off.

Another session of heroics. Tarragon flew down, zipping between a whispered conversation between the two. She hissed, "What's going on? I ask because, you know, there's a lot of death going spare. We could catch it."

"I was saying," Heser wheezed, "horses don't like Vhemin. *I* need to free them."

"And *I* was saying he can't walk," Barret gritted. "So, that's about where we're at."

"No sweat." Tarragon beckoned Barret. "This way. No, not you, Heser the Cheg. We won't be a moment." She led the Vhemin into a small corner store. Tarragon entered through a small hole in the window. Inside were shelves stocked with tat and bric-a-brac, showing humans still managed to sell the most trite nonsense to each other regardless of their tech level. It was dark and didn't smell bad. A relief from the smoke outside, anyway.

The matriarch followed through by busting the door from its hinges as dust silted down. Smoke followed her in. "Classy," Tarragon said.

"Why are we here?" Barret shuffled inside, glanced about, then hefted a music box from a shelf. "We don't need oddments."

Tarragon flitted through a shelf, skimming about the deserted store. "Here." She flared a little brighter as she reached the back of the room. Wedged between a crate and the wall was a straw-headed broom. "It's not much of a crutch but it'll do."

"Nice." Barret grabbed the broom, then led the way back outside. The matriarch marched to Heser the Cheg's side, then eye-balled him critically. "You're not very tall."

"What's that supposed to mean?"

"It means you're not very tall." She put the head of the broom against the ground and kicked it near the end. The broom became a hand span shorter with a sharp *crack*. Barret handed the broom to the Queensguard. "Put the bristles under your armpit."

"I've used a crutch before." Heser hobbled to the horses on his makeshift crutch, then fussed with the wreckage-tangled traces. Barret moved to the other side, helping clear broken wood and stone while Evanne checked the wagoner's seat.

It was all going so well until the bad thing happened. Tarragon wasn't sure what exactly happened because she was eyes-front toward the house the maybe-enemy Feybrind were in. Perhaps the Vhemin got too close to the horses. Maybe they were tired of things being on fire, and it wasn't anyone's fault. But one moment everything was fine, the next one of the mares whinnied, tried to rear, then kicked. It wasn't a bad kick, slamming into a box of buckets. The box hit Barret with, well, the sound of a box of buckets, knocking the Vhemin to her ass on the ground.

The *noise* it made would've woken the dead on a sunny day, and Tarragon couldn't see a lot of sun. Two Feybrind burst from the doorway, followed by two humans dressed like Heser the Cheg. Tarragon did a quick once-over, noting the uniform and the colours, and thought, *Oh, this is bad, because the Queensguard are with the enemy and against their queen.*

The Feybrind pair ran like water in a stream, flowing around or over obstacles. Tarragon thought, *We're boned*, because the cats looked fresh enough and her team wasn't. *Wait. My team?* And then there was no more time for thinking, because a cat was on Evanne, green eyes deep and hungry like a drowning pool, and another went for Heser the Cheg, a half-smile worn under an agate gaze.

Tarragon put her head down and headed for Evanne, wings abuzz, but the Feybrind casually swatted her from the air with the flat of his slender blade, then stabbed Evanne once, twice, three times in the stomach. The girl clutched her middle, blood flowing as the Feybrind took a half step back, and Tarragon wanted to get in the way of that sword, she did, she *did*, but she was still flying backward, and oh the cats, they were so fast, and they weren't made for killing, and *why is this happening?*

Then, Barret. Anger made real, a mountain manufactured of rock and hate. She roared, barging past Tarragon, an entire whole Feybrind in her hands, the one who'd gone for Heser the Cheg. Barret threw her Feybrind at the green-eyed cat, then charged, just claws and shark teeth, snake eyes fixed like the predator they'd made her to be.

The green-eyed Feybrind darted aside his tumbling companion, then slipped aside Barret's charge and ran the monster through. Barret didn't slow, just eased on up that blade like it was a handrail but inside her, and got her hands around the cat's throat, and squeezed, and then squeezed harder.

Evanne had a hand up, babbling something like *stop* or *why*, or maybe that was Tarragon, but there wasn't time for questions. Tarragon landed feet first against a wall, then boosted off, straight for the agate-eyed Feybrind who'd found his feet, two half-blades coming to his hands. She had no sword, but she still had glimmer, so she turned up the heat as she flew, the air shimmering and sparking, right for the cat's head.

He dodged, not even having the common decency to make it look hard, sped past Evanne and her tears and pain, right for Barret. And during all this, the Queensguard with the enemy Feybrind had only just cleared the doorway, because human Bigs were frightfully slow compared to their creations.

The cat Barret held thrashed and coiled, tail lashing, fangs bared, but the matriarch had a monster's strength. The cat tried sawing with the sword, but Barret didn't seem to *notice*, just bearing her prey to the ground, implacable as the hungry tide. She wasn't paying attention to the other Feybrind, and Tarragon could see how this would end, those twin half-blades buried into the monster's skull.

Then Heser the Cheg was there. He swung at the agate-eyed Feybrind with his crutch, overbalanced, then put his broken leg down. Tarragon felt sick for him, heard his pain buried under a war cry as he took one, two, three, *four* slices from those half-blades. Heser swung his crutch, which splintered against the Feybrind's head with a *crack*, then put his back to Barret's, tiny human teeth bared as best he could.

There was another *crack*, and the cat Barret held twitched before going limp, neck broken. She stood, pulling the sword through her stomach free, red wet splattering the ground. Her eyes narrowed as the remaining Feybrind lurched in, and Heser tried a Barret, getting his body in the way, and he managed it.

Just not well enough.

Two blades went through his gut, the Feybrind driving the crippled man back and into Barret. Tarragon couldn't see where the blades entered the matriarch, but she dropped like a puppet with strings cut. The fairy snarled, because that was *her* monster, and put her all into glimmer. She burned through the air, and this time the Feybrind didn't get away. She couldn't see when she hit the Feybrind, the air on fire before her face, like she flew through solid flame, then she punched out the other side of his smoking body to fall against the worn cobbles of Ravenswall's streets.

She lay, stunned, exhausted, glimmer spent, wings limp, but watched the Feybrind topple to the ground beside her. His agate eyes found hers, a hand reached toward her in supplication. She reached for him, but then he died, the animus in him leaving just like the smoke curling from the fairy-sized hole in his chest.

Tarragon wanted to cry, just like Evanne, but there wasn't enough left in her. And still, the human Queensguard came. She could see how their speed didn't matter, their creations always doing the fighting and the dying. Two men, axes in hands, expressions hard as they came to finish off Heser the Cheg, Evanne, and Barret.

There was a *thwip-thwip*, and both men toppled face-first on the ground.

Silence.

Tarragon lifted her head, trying to find the new threat. From atop a low-slung building to the north came another Feybrind, golden eyes everywhere, tail lashing. He walked to them, bow in hand, not pausing to retrieve the arrows he'd fired into the Queensguard. *Sight of Day.* The cat went to Evanne, crouching before her.

His fur soft hand found Evanne's face. Checked her bleeding stomach, and came away red, making his Handspeak bloody. *{We must go.}*

"Barret," she sobbed. "Barret."

The cat nodded, then walked to the Heser-meets-Barret shish kabab. Frowning, he yanked the blades free, ignored Heser's hoarse cry, hauled the Queensguard up, then leaned him against a fallen crate. He bent to Barret, rolling the matriarch over. Tarragon could see Barret's snake eyes full of fear. "I can't feel my legs."

{That's because your spine is severed.} Sight of Day looked away for a moment. *{We must get you to the carriage.}*

"Leave me. I'm just dead meat."

He half-smiled. *{I tell you what. Let's have a fight to decide the outcome. One on one, no weapons. If I win, you get in the carriage. If you win, we leave you here.}*

"I ... I'm crippled! I can't win!"

{Carriage it is, then.} The cat hauled Barret upright, the Vhemin groaning, a long, drawn-out sound that almost ended in a sob. He put her into the carriage, then went to Heser. *{I need you to get in the carriage too.}*

"What of her?" The Queensguard looked to Evanne. "Or the fairy? She saved us at the end." He pointed to Tarragon, who still couldn't stand.

{One problem at a time.} Sight of Day swept to Tarragon, lifted her in

gentle hands, then handed her to Heser. The man still smelled of safety and strength, and Tarragon needed that, because she'd just killed a cat. She hiccupped.

Sight of Day went to Evanne. *{I need you with me in the wagoner's seat. I know you're hurt, but I can't look, shoot, and drive at the same time. I would not ask this, cub, but I know you are built of the strength of this world. Can you help me?}*

"You mean, can I stop bleeding?" Evanne wiped her nose with her forearm.

{That would also be useful.}

Evanne got to her feet and onto the wagon with Sight of Day's help. Heser staggered Tarragon over to the wagon and got inside, shutting the door and the misery outside away. She hiccupped again as the wagon moved. It was slow at first, then picked up speed as it wound through Ravenswall's streets. Tarragon didn't want to look outside. She didn't want to see more dead cats, because it would remind her that she had killed one herself.

What happened to this world? She shivered, glimmer gone. *What happened to me?*

Chapter Twenty-Two

The carriage didn't so much rock as roll. Evanne wasn't feeling her level best, because someone had shoved three hand spans of steel through her in multiple places. She felt each place, the warm seeping under her jerkin, and the cold gripping her core as life leaked out. The city was broken, ruined, its people murdered, its queen lost. Fire and ash lay between shattered buildings and ruined tenements. Old brick showed rough and raw where it lay broken. Red smeared the streets they rode on.

"Stop being melodramatic." Hitch rode behind her atop the carriage's roof, looking like the jouncing journey bothered him not at all.

"I haven't started being melodramatic," Evanne wheezed.

Sight of Day gave her a sideways glance, then looked at the—to him, anyway—empty air behind her. He spoke one-handed, other gripping the reins. *{You are bleeding emotively.}*

"How do you even ... never mind," she said. "Look out. Eleven o'clock, on the roof."

The cat nodded, then made the carriage weave more. An arrow whizzed past from the human sniper she'd spotted, the impact lost in the sound of wheels on cobbles.

Evanne eased a hand under her jerkin, hissing with pain as she touched a still-bleeding rent in her flesh. *If I was a real Vhemin, this would've stopped by now.* She thought of Barret below, better suited to the job of warrior in every way. But Barret couldn't walk, and Heser the Cheg wouldn't be up for a lot longer than her Half-Made body. She fossicked about by their feet, fetching Sight of Day's bow. She nocked an arrow.

{Please, don't hurt yourself.}

"I don't plan to." She hissed as her blood-slicked fingers lost their grip on the bowstring, the string snapping against her forearm. "That didn't count." She felt light-headed, almost giddy. *It's the blood loss. I'm probably going to die.*

"You won't die," Hitch promised. "It's not your turn. There. The teahouse window."

"I see him." Evanne spotted the Feybrind archer on her right, drew the bow, and loosed. *I'm a terrible shot.*

"You missed." The ghost sounded vaguely surprised.

"I didn't mean to hit." The Feybrind ducked out of sight as they sped past. "I meant him to not shoot at us."

"Clever. Not just here to eat your lunch, are you?" The ghost walked past her, standing on the thin air above the surging horses. "Don't waste arrows. You have insufficient for all the Feybrind in the world."

Evanne growled, then pressed a fist to her side as she felt another seep of warm wet. She gritted her teeth, then glared at Sight of Day. "This is your fault."

The cat glanced at her, then back to the road. *{Is this the best time for a storm of emotion?}*

"A storm?" Her voice climbed about forty octaves in two words.

{And there it is.} The cat offered her a half-smile. *{I did not leave you, cub.}*

She loosed another arrow at a man who came out of a side street. She couldn't tell if he was friend or foe, but based on the markings in the ledger pretty much everyone was on the other team. "I know. But..." She trailed off.

{You feared I was dead.} He slowed the carriage as they approached a

chicane of rubble, then flicked the reins once through. *{There was a moment I was concerned about the same.}*

"I tried to keep up." She heard the pleading in her voice. "My heart. I'm too weak."

He tipped his head to the side for a moment, considering. *{There are many things I could call you. I offer you a counter proposal to weakness. I name you saviour.}*

"I almost got everyone killed!"

{And yet, somehow by the Three's mercy, they still breathe.}

"And I was already dead," Hitch said.

"Shut it, spectre," Evanne snapped. She faced Uncle Day again. "Where did you go?"

The Feybrind slowed the carriage again as they entered a narrow laneway. *{We approach the western gate. 'Ware.}*

"There's no one here." Evanne readied her bow anyway, feeling the orneriness inside her warring with the desire to stay living.

Sight of Day ignored her. *{I went ahead to scout the way. I found an alley that looked safe enough, but when I came back to find you, the walls crumbled. The Artifice, perhaps. Or shoddy human construction. They are not very good at building much of anything.}*

"We built you," Hitch snapped.

"He can't hear you," Evanne said. *And they built me. Mostly. Half-Made, ill-wrought. It fits.*

{It is a blessing for all of us.} Uncle Day half-smiled. *{I decided to go around the building and try from another angle. While I was trying to make my way back to you, I encountered a group of my kin. The People hunted humans and Vhemin with focus and commitment. Never have I seen its like.}* He let his hand fall to the reins for a moment. *{I spoke with them for a time, playing the dedicated disciple. They believe they are cleansing the world.}*

"Cleansing?" Evanne blinked. "Of what?"

{Of those who would do the People harm.} The cat's shoulders slumped. *{Pretty much everyone, I think. They seek ancient weapons. They have tame humans helping them. Their kind lust for power for its own sake, but the People want,}* his hands stilled for a moment, *{vengeance.}*

Evanne looked at her bow. Felt the perfect manufacture of it, the smoothness of the wood. How it was a hunter's weapon, not a warrior's. "But ... Feybrind don't make war."

{We make many things, and we make all of them well.} Sight of Day glanced to the sky. *{It will be dark soon. For the first time, I fear it. When the sun's light leaves, the evil in the hearts of all can flourish.}*

"That escalated quickly." Hitch sat cross-legged above the horses, drifting along as the mares walked. "Ask him what they want to gain."

Evanne stretched, feeling her wounds pull, but no longer with burning agony. "My poltergeist wants to know why."

{I don't know.} Sight of Day shrugged. *{I was discovered as a fraud before I could get more information. I managed to escape and stumbled upon you. All I had to do was follow the sounds of emotional outbursts.}*

"We were attacked!"

{There it is again.}

She gritted her teeth, then lowered her eyes. "Thank you, Uncle Day."

{You need never thank someone for doing what their heart needs.}

EVANNE'S EYES TOLD HER THERE WAS SOMETHING WRONG WITH THE ground outside the gates. Grass drifted on the wind, patterns stroked on fields of green, but here and there the field was clotted with black clumps that moved.

One clump surged, breaking shape and scattering to the sky, and the illusion was broken. *By the Three. Those are piles of crows feasting on the dead.*

No Feybrind or human stood guard outside the gates. Perhaps they had left, but Evanne thought the reason was more straightforward. *No one remains to fight them. They sack the city hoping to find the Raven Queen and liberate her head.*

She glanced at the carriage behind her. The occupants were silent, maybe dumbstruck by the field of dead about them, but also maybe comatose, bleeding out their last. *They hunted Queen Morgan, and I did their job for them.* Evanne remembered how she'd grabbed the slip of a woman as she charged inside the spice warehouse. *They are not built Vhemin strong.*

"Stop brooding," Hitch said.

"Will your weapon fix all this?" Evanne swept an arm to the rolling planes outside Ravenswall. "I came to a great city seeking wonders, but all we've found is a different flavour of destruction to that we left behind."

"Weapons don't fix things." Hitch sighed. "They might solve problems, but there's always a price."

"I'll pay it," Evanne snapped. "I've bled enough already. Lost..." She trailed off, thinking of her mother and father, and then her mind snared on the memory of Cleo. How the young woman drank with her, then killed Old Merle. "I've already paid. I've paid too much."

"Then the weapon will hold to you." Hitch glanced across the field. "They're coming."

Evanne saw the ghostly shapes drift free of bodies, wandering toward the carriage. She tugged Sight of Day's sleeve. "Can we drive faster?"

Golden eyes softened, and he flicked the reins. The horses picked up their pace.

"They only want peace," Hitch said, glancing at the dead behind them.

"Don't we all?"

"Yes, but you've got a bucket list you can work toward. Their lives are done, and tasks remain undone. It is a terrible burden."

"Aye? And what of your burden? Has your ailing memory broken out from behind the misty clouds of forgetfulness?" Evanne scanned the tree line ahead. "Look sharp. There could be ambushers ahead."

"We don't want to go that way." The spectre hunched. "We need to go south. The weapon lies," he pointed vaguely, "that way."

Evanne glanced southwest, then pointed it out for Sight of Day. "What's that way?"

{Death.}

"Sure, but everything's like that right now. Specifically?"

{The blasted plague lands lie that way. I came by this road once before, with

your father and mother. A sorcerer walked in our company. We had a daughter of the Three with us, and like you, she was wracked with doubt.}

"I'm not wracked with doubt. I'm going to..." Evanne frowned. "We're getting Hitch's weapon. Then we're going to shut down the mountains. The weapons of the ancients, all that."

{And vengeance.}

She glanced at the cat. "I wasn't making an exclusive list."

{This is where the doubt comes in. Who are you getting vengeance on?}

"Cleo?" Evanne heard the question in her voice.

{Are you hunting the organ grinder or the monkey?}

Evanne looked at the rolling fields and their grisly burden. "Cleo didn't do all this."

"Cleo wasn't even here. She's on the other side of the ocean." Hitch pointed behind them, past Ravenswall, and to the seas beyond. "We had a god's speed to get us here so quick. She will be a little late to the party."

"She's got a price to pay nonetheless." Evanne winced as she stretched, wounds pulling beneath her jerkin. "How long will Barret be, uh." She folded her hands in her lap. "How long will she ride in the carriage?"

"I'm a ghost, not a doctor."

{I'm an artisan, not a sawbones.}

"Neither of you are any help." Evanne scrubbed at her face. She smelled of smoke and burnt spice, blood and sweat, steel, and hate. *I want to go home. I want my parents. I need them.* "So. We need a sawbones?"

Sight of Day nodded. *{I have some healer's skill, but her wounds are severe. A human or Feybrind would be dead already. The beast within won't let her go, but I'm not sure if it's a mercy.}*

"The cat's right. But there's good news."

"Finally," Evanne growled. "What, pray tell, is this good news?"

"My weapon is at a hospital."

Evanne blinked. "What's a hospital?"

{I have no idea. It sounds important.}

Hitch glanced between them, as if expecting a better answer. "It's a place where the injured go. Or those expecting a baby. Or... Wait. A doctor—I mean, a sawbones—practices the medical arts."

"I'm not sure sawbones do that anymore," Evanne hazarded. "They're risky. Yando had a boil that wouldn't heal, so he—"

"Yes, this age is full of incompetence." Hitch sounded frustrated. "Back before the world broke—"

"When you were alive?"

"Yes," the ghost gritted. "Back when I sucked oxygen and—"

"What's oxygen?"

"Please." the ghost turned his head to the skies. "Khiton, all I ask next time is to kill me properly."

"Don't get angry with me," Evanne growled. "You're the one not making any sense."

The ghost looked down at the horses he stood over, silent as if he were counting to ten. "Okay. Pretend sawbones are good. Imagine— you're good at make believe, I know it!—they can fix anything. But to make it efficient they put them all in the same place at once. Rows and rows of them, in beds, and the sawbones walks between them."

Evanne thought about it. "So you can heal people faster?"

"Exactly."

She chewed on that. "Uh. This ... hospital?"

"That's it."

"This hospital is for healing those with hurts aplenty. Mending the body?"

"And the mind."

She stumbled over that. *How can a mind be hurt?* "Sure. What I mean to ask is, why is your weapon at a hospital?"

Hitch turned away. "I..." He trailed off.

"You don't remember?"

"I remember," he whispered. "But I don't want to."

Evanne felt the sorrow in him, a pain that lasted centuries. She looked at the dried blood on her hand. "You don't have to remember it alone."

"I don't want you to see," he pleaded. "It's—"

"Hush," Evanne said. "Show me."

Hitch's shoulders slumped, but he eased into her, the cold of the grave inside her, and then—

"I'm dying." Hitch felt the itch in his arm where the IV sat but didn't have the energy to scratch. It wouldn't make a difference. Hadn't, the thousand other times he'd worried it.

"You're a worthless sack of shit, is what you are." The man wore an officer's uniform, crisp lines, but that wasn't the remarkable thing in a place like this. It was the look on his face, disdain made pure, as if it was a thing you could wear like lipstick or rouge. "People like you sucked the life from our society. It's why we're losing! But you have a chance to do the right thing here."

Hitch knew the refrain. His spine was curved, his left foot ended in a worthless club, and his hands twitched uncontrollably. He'd been born on the edge of the war zone. Medtechs thought it was a sickness in the air that killed his mother, and it'd poisoned her womb before she'd been carted off for fertiliser. But she'd served, and Vehement Systems honoured their contracts. Healthcare, even if you couldn't ever be healthy.

He twitched a little more, rewinding that. "Do the right thing? I've got cancer. It's the bad kind, you get me?" His body was almost done, his nervous system shot along with everything else. His neck twitched savagely, and he bit his tongue. "I'm not getting out of this bed. Even if I could—"

"You'd cost us more resources we don't have. Doctors tending to you instead of the wounded. It disgusts me." The asshole looked out the windows at the beautiful rolling plains outside the hospital. Green and thriving, unlike those inside. "Lucky for you, what disgusts me isn't important. You've got just the right kind of sickness to be useful for once in your miserable life."

Hitch sagged, strength almost spent. "I want to be alone."

"And my daughter wants a pony. Neither of you are getting your heart's desire." The guy really had the whole 'I'm a motherfucker' down pat. "We have a weapon, Hitch. It's one of a kind. We stole it from them. And it needs a particular kind of fuel."

"The bodies of cripples?"

The asshole smiled, grim as a rainy dawn. "Exactly."

Hitch stared at him, trying to work out what kind of sick joke this was. No one came to the door. The doctors should've been crawling up the walls by now, because the machine to Hitch's left was having a full-blown beeping seizure. It was the kind of device that told a medtech how you were dying, as if that was important. Hitch just wanted to know when, because it might stop hurting then. He wheezed, "I've got a question."

"Shoot."

"What do I have to do to get you to leave?"

The asshole pursed his lips. "Help us. Use the weapon."

"Will it kill me?"

"Almost certainly."

Hitch stared out the window for a few moments. "I'm in."

THE TRICK WASN'T CURING THE CANCER. NOT ONLY WAS IT IMPOSSIBLE, IT *was the opposite of what they needed.*

The asshole wanted to make Hitch's cancer worse. He explained as they wheeled Hitch from the hospital, tubes, beeping machine, and wide-eyed stares all along for the ride. "We don't know what Itikari are up to. The weapon uses the body as fuel. It's the kind of thing our Architectures were made for. They ... heal. Burn them up, and they'll keep right on running." He slammed fist into palm, teeth clenched like they could shear steel.

"But you put an Architecture inside one and they died."

A nod, but like they were discussing the certainty of rain tomorrow. "Itikari have nothing that regenerates. No, don't give me the dragon story. They only regenerate if they eat our guys." A grim satisfaction at that last, as if the enemy eating the home team was a worthy of respect. "Bad tech, you get me?"

"They can fly," Hitch said. "I saw one once."

"Of course they can fucking fly. The dragons rule the skies. Their Fey Branded rule the ground. But we've got the raw horsepower with the Architectures and the Artifices. And the boys in the lab—"

"Boys?" Hitch winced as the auto gurney hit a wall. "I'm sure we've got women scientists."

"Don't get funny with me."

"No problem." Hitch wanted to be strong enough to punch the asshole in the face. "I think even if I tried my best, with a whole team behind me, men and women scientists maybe, we'd find it impossible to locate your sense of humour anyway."

The asshole gave the tiniest hint of a smile. "You're disgusting, and that's the truth, but you've got a spark. If the weapon works, you and me might have a beer."

"If the cancer doesn't get me."

"I don't think you'll live long enough for that."

THEY PUT SOMETHING IN HIS BLOOD. IT BURNED LIKE FIRE, AND HE spent two days in agony. The skin fell from his twisted back and club leg, and he bled more than he thought a person could. He screamed until his voice gave out.

The asshole only visited once. It might've been the pain, but Hitch thought he looked ashamed. "This will pass."

It passed. Hitch didn't die. And when it was done, he stood straight. Leg fixed. Back fine. No more twitching. When the asshole came back on the third day, Hitch said, "That was some weapon."

"That's not the weapon. That's making it so you can get inside it."

EVANNE SHUDDERED, THEN THREW UP. "SO MUCH PAIN." HER cheeks were wet.

"I'm sorry." Hitch drifted free. "We should stop."

Sight of Day drew the carriage to a halt. {You were gone for a moment, and now you are white as a sheet. What ails you, cub?}

"The dead worry at my bones."

"Watch it," Hitch said. "I don't eat bones. I was a vegetarian."

{Perhaps the dead can leave you alone.}

"No," Evanne said. "I wish it too, but they won't. Not now, and not ever. Let's keep on."

The cat's golden eyes were sad, but he nodded, flicking the reins. *{As you say.}*

Evanne stared at Hitch, his ghostly form hovering above the ground to her left. "Is that what killed you?"

"I wish." He laughed. "That would've been easy."

"Show me," she urged. "I need to see."

IT WAS LATER, BECAUSE HITCH FELT STRONGER. HIS ONCE FRAIL BONES were firm, and his back didn't even remember being crooked. And he flew, just like the angels. He soared above the battlefield. Itikari had used their sky cannons already, and all that had been green was ash. The very rock burned, gases escaping as lava flowed.

But it was also indistinct. He couldn't remember the details. Just the anger, and the fear.

The weapon held him like a lover, soft but strong. His target was ahead: Cobalt. Friend. Confidant. Lover. Traitor. All those labels would do, and none. The weapon showed him where Cobalt could be hurt. There, in his chest, a beating heart. But that wouldn't be enough for an Architecture, and the weapon knew it. It highlighted Cobalt's head, the only way to be sure of killing monsters.

He is not a monster. He is mine. *Hitch pushed the weapon harder, but he was almost done. He'd given so much, and still the weapon needed more. Ever hungry, grinning like the darkness, wanting the stardust that made him human. The burning blood Vehement had given him was doing what it could, but the weapon wanted more than a man could offer.*

"Empathy core online," the weapon said. "Firing solution ready."

"No," Hitch breathed. "Not yet."

Cobalt stood beside the woman who could save them. Knight Champion Mireille was one of the Three's Wardens, armour gleaming red and orange as it reflected the fires of destruction. Her dragon Rulbenen stood nearby, roaring impotent fury. Mireille was unconscious, poisoned through treachery. She shouldn't be here. *She should be at the final battleground astride Rulbenen. Sword in hand, guiding the charge against the Precept. If she couldn't face the*

Precept, all would be lost. Even now, weakened by venom in her veins, the battle would be impossible.

But she would go anyway, and die regardless, because that's how she was made.

Cobalt waited for Hitch, his blade against Mireille's throat. Ready to kill her and doom them all to die under demon claws. All because Hitch wouldn't give the enemy the weapon.

"Empathy core online," *the weapon reminded him.*

No. Not this time. Mireille dies that way. This needs something else. *Hitch slowed as he approached Cobalt, then landed.* "Hello, lover."

"Don't call me that," Cobalt snapped. His snake eyes still seemed more golden than yellow.

Hitch wanted to take away the last week. Rewind time. Do it again. But there were no do-overs. Not even Cophine, Ikmae, and Khiton could do that. He felt the weight of their regard. A crippled orphan boy, unwanted by either side. They only wanted the weapon. "You can't have it."

"Then she dies."

//IF SHE DIES, YOUR AGONY WILL BE ETERNAL.//

"Yeah, but she'll still be dead. Don't toy with me. You're just a big iguana." Cobalt didn't bother looking at Rulbenen, blade never leaving Mireille's throat. "You, though. I expected better from you. They hate *you. Why do you stand by them?"*

"Because I love you," Hitch said. "And if I do what you want, you'll die. Everyone will. The world will end."

"A pretty notion," the monster growled. "Best I end her now." He tensed, blade ready to drive through Mireille's neck.

"Why do you stand by *them?" Hitch grasped for something to delay the inevitable.*

"Because they'll make me a real man. Not a monster. Not like this."

Hitch blinked. "But that doesn't matter to me."

"It matters to everyone else."

Hitch nodded, then nudged the weapon. It spat its metal, and Cobalt's arm splintered above the elbow, blade falling away from Mireille's neck. Cobalt roared, then jumped for Hitch.

HITCH STAGGERED FREE OF EVANNE. THE GHOST SHIMMERED, HIS body shuddering, then he snapped out. Evanne lurched upright, forgetting she was on a carriage, still in that half-remembered fight with Cobalt, blood trailing from what was left of his arm but murder in eyes that once looked with love.

She staggered from the wagoner's seat and fell on the grassy plain. *Pain in her mouth. Bright sky. Hard memories.* Evanne vomited, hands clawing sod, blood running down her face from where her teeth had bit through her lip.

Sight of Day was there. Fur soft hands on her shoulders. *{Cub?}*

"I'm okay." Her voice was hoarse like she'd screamed for an hour. The lie sat between them. "Really."

{You are not okay. You are hurt.}

"My lip will heal."

{That's not what I mean.}

"They were lovers!" she wailed.

He nodded, golden eyes heavy. *{That hurts the most.}*

Evanne tried standing, managing it on the second try. "We must get on. The ghosts will..." She trailed off. Behind them on the grassy plains the ghosts had stopped. Watching, waiting, or both. There, a man wearing a footman's livery. Beside him, a baker's girl. Another from the docks, cap in hand. On and on, the thousands of Ravenswall's dead, no longer following.

Then the footman knelt. So did the baker's girl, and the longshoreman. Like a ripple, the sorrowful dead bowed to Evanne. She could *see* their pain, but *felt* something else the dead had never shown her before.

Evanne felt their hope.

Chapter Twenty-Three

They'd hit desert verge today. Green gave unexpected ground to share space with brown, and while there were still trees Tarragon could smell dust, heat, and sand. There were no people. None that showed themselves, anyway. Just the people in the creaking carriage, a thing she'd have thought a relic of a forgotten time. *Except I'm the one who's been forgotten.*

They camped in a cute cottage near a burbling brook. No one had been here for some time, the roof having given up some years back. A hive of bees still did bee things with a low hum. Tarragon liked bees, so she spent some time playing with them on the wing.

Sight of Day had led them here. It was off the not-really-a-road, a thin meandering trail that was tired before it was born. Urging horse and carriage off the road into definitely-not-a-road took Feybrind skill and patience.

He looked about when they arrived, his golden eyes soft, and she knew he wasn't seeing this place. The cat was lost in a memory, when he'd been here before, with other people. Sight of Day seemed sad, but in Tarragon's view there was a lot of that going around. She put a book-mark in that chapter, because she was going to come back to it.

Evanne hadn't spoken much in the carriage ride, but Tarragon saw how she kept looking over her shoulder. The legion of spectres had dogged their steps a short way from Ravenswall. They hadn't kept up, but those luminous lavender eyes sought for them anyway. The stunning woman had drifted into the trees, perhaps seeking the water, or just some space to be alone.

Tarragon wanted to tell her, *It will be okay*, but she wasn't sure. The fairy hadn't seen the dead in such numbers, like, ever, and that wasn't the worst part of it. Where the cottage stood hadn't been on the edge of a desert when she'd last been here.

There hadn't been a desert *here*, last time she'd been above ground. The front that had been the Forsaken Lands was torched, sure, but the gods had made this world lush, and the Councils of each region husbanded their protectorate with verdant life despite the harm dealt to it. *I need intel.* The fairy went looking for anyone still up and about. Sight of Day was long gone, off hunting as night fell. Heser the Cheg slept beside the Raven Queen, close but not touching. The royal inbred was still unconscious.

Which left the monster. Tarragon flitted closer to Barret. "How are you feeling?"

Snake eyes watched her. Barret leaned against a tree, legs in front of her. If she was uncomfortable, she didn't show it. "Peachy, Sandwich. I can't walk. Hell, I can't shit right. How about you?"

"I'm good. Thanks for asking." Tarragon ignored Barret's sneer, landing on one of the Vhemin's legs. From the size of it, it should be *strong*, able to hold up mountains. But it felt lifeless beneath her tiny legs. "What's in the desert?"

"Sand."

"Good talk," the fairy said. "I'm trying to be prepared. There are few fighters left in our group now you're out. It's up to me—"

"Wait." Barret wiped an imaginary mirthful tear from her eye. "You're telling me you're going to protect us? I've had taller beers." Tarragon looked at her for a moment, her glimmer fading, and waited. The matriarch had the decency to look away. "Okay, I get you. I'm crippled because a cat got me, and you took care of the cat."

"I didn't want to."

That sat between them for a while. When Barret spoke, her gravelly voice held a hint of softer sand. "I know. They were on your side."

"I ... yes. No. I don't know." She scrubbed her face, wings fluttering. "They were never like that. *I* wasn't like that. What happened here?"

Barret watched her for a long time. "Same thing that always happens. Someone wanted something that wasn't theirs. Cranked out an army. Got up and took it. No one thought anything of it while the blood soaking the sands wasn't theirs. When the red matched what was in their veins they tried to stop it, but by then everything was fucked."

Tarragon heard a crack in the trees and sprang up, trailing flare. "I'll be right back."

Barret grunted, then almost too low to be heard said, "Be careful."

The fairy buzzed into the trees, pushing back darkness with her glimmer. *There.* A humanoid shape, hand raised to ward off the glare. *Evanne.* The maybe-Vhemin hissed, "Turn that down, will you?"

Tarragon lowered her glimmer, feeling the night cool around her, and landed on Evanne's still raised hand, swinging her legs over a finger. "Sorry." This close, the maybe-Vhemin's beauty couldn't be denied. Strong cheekbones. Lips that wouldn't quit. And those eyes. Evanne had said something, but Tarragon missed it. "What was that?"

"I said, 'How is everyone at camp'?"

"The humans are sleeping. The monster is grumpy."

"She's paralysed. She might not recover." Evanne looked away. "It's my fault."

"You're silly." Tarragon hiccupped a laugh at the absurdity of the statement. "No. It is the fault of a thousand people before you."

"I did nothing!" Evanne shook her off, so Tarragon hovered. "If I'd been—"

"A warrior? Trained with the blade or bow? Perhaps an evoker, able to conjure elemental fury, hmm?" Tarragon huffed. "If you'd been any of those things, maybe we could talk about your share of blame. But you are one person, and not an old one. You—"

"I'm sixteen!"

"Like I said." Tarragon drifted closer, and after a moment, Evanne held her hand up again. The fairy landed, hooking her legs over a finger again. "Your heart isn't the best, is it?"

Evanne looked away. "It's always been that way."

"Hmm." Tarragon looked about. "The ghost. He hasn't been here since the incident."

Evanne gave a small, fragile laugh. "'Incident'. I chucked my lunch on the grass and fell on my face. Some incident."

Tarragon thought about it, then swooped in and hugged Evanne's arm about the bicep. It was strong, built for this time, not the one Tarragon was from. The maybe-Vhemin's skin was cooler than a human's but not cold like the monsters of her father's race. *Say it. Sometimes it's okay to lie.* "It'll be okay."

Evanne stiffened, then sighed, and sank down with her back against a trunk, knees hunched close. It was quiet, the night insects becalmed by their presence. Tarragon drifted free, letting her go, then landed on an upraised knee. She sat cross-legged. The maybe-Vhemin looked up at the sky. "Thank you for the hug. I needed that."

"You're worried about Barret."

"I'm worried about everything," Evanne admitted. "Aunt Barret most of all, but I'm scared for Hitch. I know he's dead, and the worst has already come, but..."

"But he's your friend."

She nodded, rust locks falling over her face. "I worry for Uncle Day. He must make a choice each day as to whose side he's on. It cuts at him. I can see it, fairy! I can see the cords binding his heart. I can hardly bear it."

Tarragon let a little glimmer land on Evanne's knee, leaving a sparkle of glowing sand about her. "They were not made for war."

"Were any of us?" Evanne brushed her hair aside with an angry arm. "No, scratch that. Of course we were."

"Some more than others." Tarragon sighed. "I was made to Build, but I was bad at it."

"I wish I could've buried my parents." The maybe-Vhemin's voice took on an anguished tone. "They didn't want me. Not the Half-Made. Not, not," she gestured at her body, "*this*. But they were all I had."

Tarragon held still for a moment, her glow fading a little. "All parents love their children."

"Love, aye, plenty of that, but what of want? Love is a thing here," she hammered two fingers against her chest, "and we don't get to choose. But want? That's here." Evanne's fingers touched her forehead. "I know the Tricks inside people. The lies they tell to everyone, even themselves."

The fairy frowned. "If you say so. Doesn't seem likely though, does it?"

Evanne blinked. "What?"

"They bound the Three in chains of promise for you. Made a place where you could grow up safe. Fought a mountain. All that." She trailed fingers in her glimmerdust. "Seems they wanted you quite a lot."

"You don't know what you're talking about."

"Probably not," Tarragon agreed. "Bigs are confusing."

"Hmm." Evanne looked down, fingers lacing across her middle. "I worry about you, too."

"Because Bigs are confusing?"

"Because you're not from here." Evanne looked at Tarragon with those gorgeous eyes. *I could get lost here, just staring.* "You're small, in a world of terrifying things. There aren't many fairies left."

"I get scared," Tarragon said. "I get scared all the time. Except when I'm with you." This last came out in a jumble, one big long word: *exceptwhenI'mwithyou.* She wanted to take it back.

Evanne's lavender eyes narrowed. "Don't mock me."

"I'm not," Tarragon said. *Lame. Lame! I'm being lame.* "I, um. I wish we were the same size, that's all." *More lame!* She cringed, waiting for the doom hammer of rejection.

"I like you too, fairy." The maybe-Vhemin seemed to relax, giving Tarragon a sideways look. "Three help me, but I like you a lot. I wish..."

Tarragon fluttered. "Hmm?"

"It doesn't matter." Evanne unlaced her fingers. "Wishing won't make the impossible so. We don't live in a time of miracles. Ours is the hard road. A bridge between the wondrous past and a glorious future." She gave Tarragon a lopsided smile, and for a heartbeat Tarragon saw just how *young* she was. *Easy to forget, because she's solving all the problems.* "You said you Build things. Feel like Building us a future?"

Tarragon thought about that. "I don't know how."

"Neither do I."

"Okay." She lifted off, waiting as Evanne lumbered upright. "Does it start with dinner?"

Evanne laughed. "Of course. Let's see if Uncle Day's back."

THE CAT HAD RETURNED AND WAS ALREADY SKINNING AND GUTTING an anaemic-looking deer. Tarragon followed Evanne to Barret's side. The maybe-Vhemin squatted. "How you doing?"

The monster eyed Evanne, then glared at Tarragon. "Same as before. I'm fine." Her snake-eyes dared Tarragon to reveal the lie.

Tarragon drifted closer, landing in a stray drift of leaves with a soft *crunch.* "She's a monster. They're always fine. They're the ones who hide under the bed and terrify everyone else."

"Right." Barret gave a slow nod. Was that gratitude in her voice? "Missed my head. Only way to be sure."

Evanne's eyes were the soft, deep violet of a bed of lavender in bloom. Her hands moved to Barret's leather shirt. "Let me see."

The matriarch's eyes widened, and she batted Evanne aside. "Save your fussing for someone who needs it. Like the human. He's been worthless since day one." Even Tarragon could hear the lie in her words. *This monster thinks of the human as her clutch. Someone she fusses over, despite one's blood being warm and the other cold.*

Evanne let her hands fall, and as Barret relaxed, she lunged, tearing open Barret's jerkin. The twin wounds torn through the monster's undershirt still leaked a sullen red. "You're bleeding!"

"I'm fine!" Barret shouted. That seemed to cost her a lot, the old woman sagging. "Leave me be."

"You're a ... *real* Vhemin." Evanne pulled away, and Barret tugged her jerkin closed. "The wounds should've healed."

"You *should've* left well enough alone, but here we are."

Tarragon flew to Evanne's shoulder, trailing glimmer. "Barret, Evanne's right. Your wounds should be healed. I don't know much about monsters, but. Um." She looked away. "Sorry. Vhemin."

"Oh, we're monsters all right." This came with a bared, shark-toothed grin. "The darkness was made for us."

"You're dying." Evanne's voice was small. "You can't die."

"Not yet. Still got things to do." Barret shook her head, eyes hard. "People to kill."

Evanne stood, then stalked off. Tarragon gave Barret's leg a touch for all the monster couldn't feel it, then grabbed sky. She landed on Evanne, riding the maybe-Vhemin's shoulder, hanging onto rust locks. The fairy leaned close to her ear. "She'll be okay."

"She won't." Evanne made her way to the carriage. "Where is it? Oh. Here." She pulled her guitar from the interior. The case was battered, and a blood smear trailed down the side from the handle.

"What are we doing?" Tarragon peered at the case. "That won't help Barret."

"Yeah, it will." Evanne made her way back to the campfire. "Hitch's weapon is at a special place called a, a, hostibal."

"A what? Oh, a hospital."

"That's what I said." Evanne gave her glaring side-eye.

"Why is there a weapon at a hospital?"

"Buggered if I know." Evanne hunched down beside the fire, feet stretched to the heat. "But I know who does." She snapped open the clasps on the case, then pulled out the guitar. She rested her fingers against the strings.

Tarragon waited, but Evanne didn't do anything. "Okay. Why are we staring into the fire?"

"I don't know if this will work." Evanne ran a hand through her hair. "Who am I kidding? I'm half of nothing special twice over. I don't have any gifts. Not like..." She trailed off, glancing at Barret's slumped form in the gloom.

"Oh." Tarragon hopped from Evanne's shoulder to balance on the fret board. "That's totally wrong."

"You what?"

"I said, you're wrong. But, you know," she twirled, scattering motes of yellow and ochre, "maybe you could brood some more about it. See if that helps."

The maybe-Vhemin stared at her pretty hard, and Tarragon felt her chin jut. Evanne sighed. "Okay, fairy. You win. I'll play."

"And I'll dance." Tarragon waited.

Evanne's fingers dipped onto the strings, a teasing note coming forth, then she twisted a key, wincing. "It's had a hard couple of days. The notes are off."

"We all know how it feels." Tarragon patted the fretboard beneath her.

Evanne laughed, then strummed again. "Here we go."

The song she played wasn't the same one she'd played on the beach, nor the one that woke Tarragon from a stunned daze. This was soft, strings plucked, offering their song to the night. The music was tentative, shy almost, but Tarragon felt it lift her feet anyway. She twirled along the fretboard, a hand against Evanne's arm as she spun.

Sight of Day set aside his deer, golden eyes warm as they caught the firelight. He padded closer, then squatted, listening. A moment later, Heser the Cheg joined them at the fireside, the human's eyes wide with wonder, glistening with unshed tears.

In a time when gods bestowed their grace from high above,
Two souls intertwined, blessed by deities of love.
In ancient gardens where roses bloomed with grace,
Two hearts united in a sacred, hallowed place.

WITH WORDS AND OATHS, THEY MADE THEIR SOLEMN VOW,
To honour and to cherish, and forever avow.
Hand in hand, they'll navigate life's winding stream,
With blessings from above, as in a dream.

AS THE YEARS ROLL ON, LIKE SCROLLS OF ANCIENT LORE,
Their love will deepen, growing more and more.
Through life's journey, united by a divine start,
Blessed by Cophine's grace, never to part.

. . .

OH, THIS LOVE, A TALE AS OLD AS TIME,
  Ikmae's blessing, in each sweet design.
  In this bygone age where blessings take flight,
  Two hearts in love, beneath godly guiding Light.

AND AS THEY DANCE UNDER THE STARRY SKIES,
  Their love's story etched in the gods' watchful eyes.
  In this bygone age where invocations give their might,
  Two hearts in love, beneath Khiton's calming night.

A blue glimmer came from the wrecked cabin, but it wasn't Hitch. Two ghosts drifted through the wall of the hut. They walked hand in hand. The man was quite tall, solidly build, and the woman was shorter but still athletic. They didn't have the look of peasants. They were dressed like people from Tarragon's age, clean lines on their clothes, the cloth of finer weave than anything she'd seen made now. They held their peace at the fireside, sitting on a log, watching Evanne sing.

Perhaps a minute into Evanne's playing, Hitch drifted in from the woods. He sat on the log beside the other ghosts. His face was still blurred, hands and feet gone, but Tarragon could see from how he leaned forward that he yearned for the substance of the song.

"That is beautiful," Heser the Cheg croaked as Evanne's hands stilled, bringing the song to an end. He wiped an eye. "There is too much dust here."

{I have not heard that before.}

"It was their wedding song," Evanne said, pointing to the new ghosts.

Sight of Day looked to where she pointed, but of course he couldn't see the spectres. *{They must have loved each other very much.}*

"I think so." Evanne sighed, then turned to Hitch. "Where have you been?"

"Sulking," the ghost admitted. "I was enjoying it, too."

"Barret is dying." Evanne lifted Tarragon from the fretboard, putting the fairy back on her shoulder. "Can the hospital fix her?"

The male shade left his dead wife's side, stepping closer to Evanne. She stood to meet him, Tarragon almost losing her perch. Tarragon tried to back away as the ghost surged forward, but the spectre wasn't after her. He slipped into Evanne like a shadow returning home. Tarragon felt her stiffen, and the maybe-Vhemin's breathing stopped. The fairy tugged her hair. "Evanne?"

Evanne shuddered, then gasped, falling to her knees as the ghost slipped free. Tarragon took to wing but descended to follow Evanne to the loamy ground. *I'm fretting. Why am I fretting? More importantly, what do I do?* She wrung her hands, wondering if she should go in for a closer look, but Evanne threw out an arm. "I'm fine. I'm okay." She clambered to her feet. "For all that ghosts don't speak to the living, they sure have a lot to say."

{What did you see?} Sight of Day stood still as a forest pond, golden eyes concerned. *{What happened?}*

"I saw ... a battle." Evanne rubbed her face. "The sky was scorched, and the air was on fire. The heavens," she looked up at the still night sky, "were ablaze. Lances of light touched the ground. Where they hit, the earth wept molten rock. I saw Artifices striding across the land, while others flew. These two," she pointed to the ghosts, "ran. She was a, a, uh." Fingers scritched rust locks. "A battlefield sawbones. He, her aide-de-camp. Or, something like it."

"A surgeon. A nurse," Hitch murmured.

"They ran, but that's not the heart of it." Evanne hugged herself, so Tarragon brought her glimmer and its warmth closer, settling on her shoulder. Evanne raised a grateful finger to touch Tarragon's leg. "They ran *toward* the fire. Where the sky burned brightest, do you see? They made it to a patch of ground where the stones *burned.* There was nobody left to save, so they left. Came here."

{Why show you this?} Sight of Day glanced to Tarragon. *{What message do the dead bring?}*

"Haven't finished," Evanne said. "They came here. Built this cabin, but the air they'd breathed carried poison. It was in them already. They lived here maybe half a turn of the seasons." She glanced at the woman. "I think it was more than many got when the world died."

{So, the desert about this place of healing carries poisoned air. Wonderful.}

"We can't get sick," Evanne said. "We are Vhemin."

Sight of Day gave her a little side-eye. *{We?}*

"Um," she said. "Well, some of us don't get sick. Or we get over it better." Evanne looked at her guitar, then the ghostly pair. "I'm sorry you died."

"The hospital can fix Barret." Hitch stood. "It can fix anything, if it still works. It's lucky we have a Builder."

"Wait, what?" Tarragon blinked. "I failed my exams! I can't—"

"Then it's settled." Evanne put the guitar down. "Uncle Day, will you stay here and guard Barret?"

{No.} The cat stood. *{You need my help out on the sands. I will go with you.}*

It was Evanne's turn to give the cat a little side-eye. "Weren't you listening? The ghosts say the air is poisonous."

{There will be a way.} The Feybrind steepled his fingers for a moment. *{Perhaps we should discuss this in the morning. Eat. Sleep. Then make a plan where the one who is worthless in a fight doesn't go across a blasted monster-infested desert alone.}*

Evanne thought about that, then nodded. "You're right, of course."

{I ... am?} Sight of Day's tail *swish, swished. {I admit, that was easier than I thought.}*

"Let's eat," Evanne said. "I'm starving."

Tarragon waited on the path. She'd flitted out here after dinner, waiting as the firelight burned low. Sure enough, as the moon rose Evanne crept away from the hut, the ghostly Hitch shadowing her. She seemed surprised to see the fairy. She hissed, "What are you doing here?"

"I thought that was obvious." Tarragon fluttered from her tree perch to hover before Evanne. "You're running away from Sight of Day, Barret, Heser the Cheg, and the Raven Queen to go to the hospital in the plague lands. You're doing this because you don't want them to die. So, I'm going with you."

"You're not," Evanne bridled.

"Or I can wake everyone up." Tarragon examined a fingernail.

"You'll die too!"

"I'm from a race of reactor technicians. The 'poisoned air' is probably fallout, and it can't hurt me. It can hurt you quite a lot, but you'll get over it. No one else will. And, you'll need my help." Tarragon ignored, just for the moment, that she was worthless at Building anything. "What's it to be? Company, or a ruckus?"

Evanne glared, so Tarragon weathered the storm. Then the maybe-Vhemin sighed. "Okay, you can come."

Tarragon glimmered. "Great! Let's go. Certain death awaits."

Hitch gusted a sigh. "And then there were three."

"Yeah, but only two of us can do anything useful." Tarragon smiled. "We still have hands."

Hitch laughed. "You're all right, fairy."

Tarragon kept her smile up, unsure if it looked as fake as it felt. *I hope I don't bollocks this up like I did everything else.*

Chapter Twenty-Four

Who wants to go where the air burns? Me, that's who. Evanne trudged through the pre-dawn light. She tugged her cloak about bare arms. The fairy cruised on her shoulder, the tiny lamplight of her glimmer giving a warm glow against Evanne's neck. The plague lands she'd heard so much about were boring so far. It didn't smell of much. Nothing poisonous assailed her. Just ... dirt, and a lot of it.

"Who wants to go where the air burns?" The fairy tugged at her hair. "I'm just asking what everyone's thinking."

"Hitch wasn't thinking that. Neither was I," Evanne lied.

"I was," the ghost said. "I don't think the air will be burning anymore, but it won't be a fun time. There won't be a picnic. No unicorns or rainbows."

"Unicorns aren't real," Evanne snapped.

"Uh." Tarragon whispered *right* in her ear. "They kind of—"

"Anyway," Evanne shook her head, because Tarragon whispering in her ear tickled, "we've got a job to do. Aunt Barret is dying. We need what this 'hospital' has."

"Hmm," Hitch said. "It might not be that simple."

"You're right." Evanne stamped on, sands giving beneath her feet. "'Simple' would be waiting for her to die."

"I didn't mean it like that," Hitch said. "Besides, being dead isn't so bad. Apart from being stuck with you for eternity."

"Hah." Evanne looked away though, because she'd only known Hitch for sixteen years. She would die like normal people did, and didn't want her ghost lingering on to curse some other poor fool. She'd do her best, and if it wasn't enough, she'd do it harder. *It's the Vhemin way.*

The desert wasn't a picnic either. As Hitch prophesied, Evanne saw no unicorns, nor rainbows. She'd walked for hours, leaving the scrub land and hills behind. The sparse, brown grass struggling to grow between rocks and gravel gave way to sand. An ocean of it, stretching as far as her half-human, half-Vhemin eyes could see. It made no difference which part of her did the seeing; the human part of her saw shadowy dunes, and the Vhemin side saw cool blues and blacks. *Nothing lives here. Nothing wants to live here.*

Why am I here, then?

"Where are we going?" Tarragon huddled into the crook of her neck, pulling Evanne's hair about her like a shawl, sharing her tiny heat. The warmth was a welcome balm for Evanne's sluggish half blood, because it *was* cold out here. "I mean, long walks on the sand are fine if there's a beach, but I don't see an ocean."

"That way." Evanne pointed south. "I ... remember ... where to go. From the ghost." She shivered, remembering the blasted land, the once-warm sky full of death. The dead, legions of them, bodies scattered as weapons to rival the power of the gods ravaged the earth.

"Then south it is," Hitch said. "Best pick up your feet. It'll get hot soon, and that'll suck for those of you with a pulse."

'HOT' DIDN'T DO THE HEAT ANY SORT OF JUSTICE. THE SUN WAS A weight, like carrying an anvil made of fire. She felt it pressing on her.

Hitch didn't seem to care, but Tarragon wilted. The fairy's wings drooped, and she looked like she wanted to die.

"Chin up," Evanne said. "It's only another two days' walk."

"Two *days?*" the fairy wailed.

"And you're not doing any of the walking," Hitch said. "You might be riding coach, but at least you've got wheels."

Evanne thought about that for a few moments. *Nothing he said makes sense. As if he shone up an old phrase from when he drew breath.* "What did you just say?"

The ghost looked away, uncertain, his not-eyes turning to the east. "I said, we need to hustle. Look. Dust."

Evanne visored her eyes with a hand. Sure enough, dust crowded the horizon. "I don't know how I feel about that. On the good news front, there's too much for it to be a war band."

"Who said anything about a war band?" Hitch looked between her and the cloud. "My tone of voice would be different if ravening hordes were coming for us. Or, coming for *you*, because no one cares about the already dead."

"Nice," Tarragon said, her voice a dry whisper. "I'm going to die serenaded by a sarcastic ghost. This isn't what I signed up for."

"On the bad news side," Evanne gritted, "*because* there's too much of it to be a war band, it's got to be a desert storm. We had those back, uh." Her voice gave out for a moment. "Home."

Silence dogged her heels for another ten metres before Hitch stepped into the gap. "Imshir had desert storms, it's true, but this looks like some next-level shit."

"Do you have anything positive to say?" the fairy asked.

"The storm will be a break from the sun," Hitch offered.

Evanne patted herself down. Belt knife, check. Canteen plus a spare, check-*ish*, because while the fairy didn't drink much and Evanne less than a human, that first canteen felt a little light. Cloak, check. *I can huddle under that.* A few hunks of deer meat, good enough for the walk. Guitar, checkity-check. It felt odd having the instrument strung over her shoulder, naked outside its case, but that would have been an extra burden on the sands. *I should have left it behind, but...*

But I couldn't bear to be without it. Uncle Day had given it to her, and she'd betrayed his trust by leaving him at the edge of the desert. He would be beside himself about now, but anchored to the hut in the forest as sure as if he wore chains of steel.

She shook herself. *Enough moping. Leave that to the ghost.* "We need to make shelter."

"Don't you mean, find?" Tarragon struggled to her feet, leaning out from Evanne's shoulder, using a lock of hair like a rope.

"No finding shelter here," she said. "It's a desert."

"I'll go look." The fairy looked at the sky without much enthusiasm. "I mean, I could. If you want."

Evanne shook her head. "Save your strength. We'll need it before the night's through."

"Night?" Hitch gave her a glance. "It's barely past noon."

"That storm will last plenty long enough. Come, now." She stalked on, feet sinking to the ankles, the sand trying to steal her strength. But she was Vhemin, and her people were made of stone.

THE STORM HOWLED LIKE A TORTURED PRISONER. IT HAMMERED against Evanne, the sound of grit trying to find its way in a hurricane's lament. She sat cross-legged, hunched over, Tarragon huddled on her calves. Evanne had her cloak tight about them.

"Are we going to die?" Tarragon's voice was almost lost in the storm, her glimmer faded.

"Stop asking that." Evanne ran a finger along the fairy's wilted wings, her voice gentle. "It'll be okay."

"I'm the one who's supposed to lie to you." Tarragon rolled over. "I'm over eight hundred years old. You'd think I'd have learned to not get myself into situations like this."

"Spend a lot of time in deserts?"

"Not so much." Tarragon sat upright. "Is the ghost coming back soon?"

Evanne ... *listened* for him. She could feel Hitch out there somewhere, the spectre hunting southward, the tie that linked them thin but strong. "I don't think so. He'll be gone until morning."

"Hmph." Tarragon faced her, tiny face looking up at Evanne's no-doubt-huge-to-her one. "I think we're the only people in the world. Just you and me, here, under this blanket."

"Cloak."

"Whatever."

Evanne nodded. The fairy was exquisite, her face all high cheekbones and emerald eyes. The glow under her skin was like gold made into light, a solid thing that kept the fear of dying away. "Have you ever wanted to be bigger?" The words were out before Evanne's brain had fully engaged, and she wanted to take them back.

"Eww. No." Tarragon shuddered. "Bigs are so clumsy! You walk into things and fall over a lot."

"Uh, no? We don't." Evanne raised an eyebrow. "We're full of poise and grace."

"I've seen you fall on your face at least twice."

"We were being chased by killer machines, the dead, and Feybrind. I think that gives me a pass."

"Did you see *me* fall on my face?" Tarragon's glitter landed on Evanne's legs.

It felt like warm breath, like what talking to Cleo was like. *Should* have been like, but wouldn't be like ever again. "Hmm." Evanne thought about it. There was the time the fairy had bored through a Feybrind, leaving a smoking corpse and her laying on cobblestones without that glorious glow, but it seemed churlish to mention something like that. "I'm sure you'll fall over before the quest is done."

"We're on a quest, then?"

"Yes."

"Good." Tarragon sighed. "Just weeks back I wanted you dead because you were the enemy. Now..." She trailed off.

Evanne waited for a moment. "Now ... what?"

"Nothing." The fairy smiled, glimmering more. "How long will this storm last, anyway?"

The wind howled louder in response, but Evanne didn't mind. She and Tarragon were cocooned in a bubble of fairy light. *Everything seems possible.* Her insides relaxed, and she bowed her head, waiting for the weather to pass.

Silence woke Evanne.

The weight of sand pressed on her back, shoulders, and neck, but it wasn't so bad. Tarragon slept curled in the crook of Evanne's leg, a gentle glimmer rising and falling with the fairy's tiny breathing.

"Hey," Evanne said. "Time to wake up."

"Hmm? Why?" Tarragon stretched, a tiny fist covering a mighty-enough yawn.

"Storm's passed." Evanne got a hand beneath her by worming it into her cape. She felt the sand piled outside give a little. She grunted, surging upright.

Dawn's light almost blinded her. The dunes around her were different, valleys where dunes were, and dunes rising from previous slumps in the landscape. Yet still *feeling* the same as yesterday: featureless, barren, lifeless. She helped Tarragon to her shoulder, uncapped her canteen, and poured a tiny share into the lid.

The fairy slurped the offered bounty. "It tastes like ass made of metal."

"Yet it is life-giving ass." Evanne tipped the canteen into her mouth but didn't drink too much. It had to last. The hospital might have supplies, and it might not. Best not tempt the Three's twisted sense of irony. She took the lid from the fairy, recapped her canteen, and shivered. The water borrowed from the desert night's freezing memory. "It is also *cold* ass."

Tarragon glimmered, warmth coming from her like the mid-morning sun. "Does that help?"

"Mmm." *She is so warm. I wonder what fairies would be like if they were our size.* Evanne set off, fairy tangled in her hair. *I wonder what* Tarragon *would be like.* Evanne thought of those emerald eyes and amazing cheekbones, and mused on what her lips would taste like.

"Copper baron for your thoughts?"

"You what now?" Evanne jerked away from the fantasy.

"That's the base currency, right? Barons, regals, sovereigns, and solars, yes?"

Evanne nodded. "Aye. Although I've yet to see a solar."

"Handled plenty of sovereigns?"

"A few," Evanne admitted. "Best not ask how."

The fairy giggled. "We'll make a spy of you yet."

"I think I prefer to play." Evanne patted her guitar. "These—"

The sand in front of her erupted. Granules got in her eyes, and she threw a hand out, glimpsing a horror of teeth and leathery skin. Tarragon shrieked in her ear, which caused Evanne to shy to the right. This probably saved her life, because the teeth came down on her shoulder rather than face.

Right atop Tarragon. Evanne felt teeth savage her flesh, a hundred sharp needles, then in a spray of blood, the creature left.

The sand surged, then was still. Evanne blinked, rubbing her eyes to clear them. Hot wet scalded down her chest, but she didn't care about that. "Tarragon!"

Silence.

Evanne spun. *There.* The sand shifted as if something flowed under the surface. She charged, belt knife in her hand, and jumped. The sand bucked beneath her, and a scaled, clawed horror burst forth. Evanne stabbed it in its let's-call-it-a-face. Her knife skidded off scaled hide, and she felt it curl as if to burrow again.

Oh, no you don't. Evanne grabbed the creature about the neck with her free arm. It rolled, trying to throw her off. Blood and sand sprayed into the air as they tumbled down a dune. Evanne stabbed again, blind, desperate because *oh gods it's got Tarragon, it's got her*, and there was no one else, no Uncle Day, not even Hitch, just her and the knife, and it was a tiny slip of steel, nothing like what she needed, but it was all she had, and she struck, rolling, seeing sky and sand.

Her arm was heavy, sickly heart already stuttering, and the wound in her shoulder was weakening her, but she wasn't going to give up, not this time, not here, not because of human feebleness because she was fucking *Vhemin*, and wouldn't let the fairy be taken, not her Tarragon, and her knife skidded once, twice, and then ... *lodged*. The monster bucked, shuddered, then stilled.

Evanne rolled free, wrenching her miserable blade. Gore showered as she pulled it free. The creature she'd killed was like a dog, maybe, if dogs had leather skin, claws, and a maw of horror. Its armoured hide was tough. *How to get in? She'll suffocate!* Evanne grabbed the thing's jaw's wrenching them wide, then—*don't think about it don't think*—rammed her arm down its gullet. Meat squelched, and she felt the still-warm flesh around her arm.

Something warmer than the rest touched her fingers, and she opened her hand. *Please let that be tiny arms.* Evanne grabbed hold of hopefully-Tarragon and pulled. With a *schlick-pop!* the fairy burst free. Tarragon was covered in a grey-green slime, and struggled to wipe her face clean.

"Hold on." Evanne shook the fairy, and slime splattered sand. She put the tiny woman in the flat of her other hand. "Are you okay?"

Tarragon gave her a bleary stare, then coughed. "No. Put me down."

"Why? What can I do?"

"Put me down, for a start." Tarragon's wings fluttered, spraying sludge.

Evanne put her on the ground, and the fairy took a staggering step, then flared. There was a sizzling sound as the whatever-it-was coating her smoked and burned. Tarragon burned so bright Evanne shielded her eyes with a hand.

The light faded, and the fairy stumbled, laying her tiny length on the ground face-first.

Evanne picked her up, putting her on her palm. "Why'd you do that?"

"I was just dipped in acid," she said. "I didn't want to dissolve after you'd gone to the trouble of saving me."

"Acid?" Evanne tried the word on for size. "What's that?"

"It's..." Tarragon fluttered, then sagged. "It's in your stomach. It dissolves stuff."

"Like, makes it melt?" Evanne looked at her hand. "Will my arm fall off?"

Tarragon shook her weary, tiny head. "You are made of stronger stuff than that. At least, half of you is." She tried for a smile. "The other half is made of spite, so I think you'll be fine."

"Watch it." Evanne squatted, rubbing her arm with sand to clean it. *Best be sure.* "Anyway. You know what this means?"

"No."

"It means you, too, fell over. Score one for the Bigs."

Tarragon snorted, then winced. "Don't make me laugh."

Evanne eyed the creature's corpse. "What do you think that is?"

"No idea. We didn't have those back in my day."

"Hmm." Evanne stalked to the corpse, then kicked it with her foot. "What do you suppose it tastes like?"

Chapter Twenty-Five

I will never know what it tastes like. There's not enough seasoning in the world to make me try it. Tarragon sat atop Evanne's shoulder as the maybe-Vhemin trudged through sand. Evanne chewed on raw meat she'd hacked from the corpse of the whatever-it-was. They had no wood for a fire, and no time to dry it, but the young woman hadn't commented on that. She'd sniffed the meat, shrugged, and chewed.

She is half-Vhemin, and also half-feral. Tarragon checked the sun's position. It was getting close to midday. *I like feral.*

They headed toward what looked like a cloud bank, except unlike clouds, this didn't move. The sun above them was relentless, and Tarragon enjoyed the shade of Evanne's rust locks. *I don't know how she keeps going. She says she's Vhemin, but the skin of her arms, hands, and face is human enough. There. She's getting sunburned.* For all that Evanne might be cast of the brittle clay of humanity, she walked like her father's people. Shoulders, unbowed. Chin up. Grinning when the devil came to call.

Itikari said they made us better than *them.* Tarragon gave a tiny sigh. *I don't think they told the truth. We're different, for sure, but they thrive in places that kill the best Itikari has to offer.*

There was sand everywhere. Tarragon didn't like it. She tugged her shift. Her ancient-made clothing wouldn't wear out, but despite being hydrophobic, anti-staining, and built of nano spun microfibres, this world had managed to press smudges into the fabric. *Just like it's done to me. I'm dirty right to the inside. It's a wonder I've any glimmer left.*

"Shouldn't be long." Evanne spat out a piece of gristle.

Tarragon started. "Sorry?"

"To the hospital." The maybe-Vhemin pointed. "It should be right under that cloud."

"That's not a cloud." Hitch appeared before them. Evanne didn't jump, walking right through the spectre. "Wait up!"

"We're going there, Hitch. We're going there to get a," and Tarragon heard the pause as she remembered the unfamiliar word, "doctor. We will save Barret. And get your weapon. Then we'll host a fuck-up party for Cleo. That's the plan." Evanne glared at the ghost.

"I'm on board with the plan." The ghost drifted backward, better to look at the living. "The problem is the specifics."

"The cloud?" Tarragon pointed. "It doesn't look like a cloud."

"It's a cloud, but it's something else too." Hitch hunched. "It's a last defence against Vhemin. The monsters..." He paused, glancing to Evanne. "Sorry. Uh."

"Keep digging." Evanne's voice was sickly sweet. "You're in a hole. Why not make it deeper?"

"You might strike oil," Tarragon offered. "I'm up for seeing where this goes."

Hitch sighed. "Fair enough. This is an Itikari hospital. Vehement Systems struck from the sky. Their Artifices could fly, like the dragons."

"I saw it." Evanne tossed her head. "I lived it."

"Vehement tried to storm the hospital. They—"

"Wait." Tarragon fluttered. "Vehement went for a, a *hospital?*"

"They were ... motivated," Hitch said. "I was there. They wanted what I had. I don't want to talk about that part. What's worth discussing is the cloud, which is a freezing storm."

Evanne slowed, then stopped. "Freezing?" She rubbed her arms unconsciously.

"Architectures were their main fighting force. Cold blooded. Very efficient. You need less food for cold-blooded creatures, see?" Hitch shrugged. "Or, same food, and you can make them bigger and stronger. But you suck in temperate climates."

"Temperate?" Evanne blinked. "What does that mean?"

"He means places where it's sometimes nice, but sometimes rains ice." Tarragon clambered up Evanne's hair, perching atop her head for a better look at the cloud. "That storm's been going for eight hundred years?"

"I guess," Hitch agreed. "There's nothing alive outside the hospital. Inside, I couldn't see guardians, but there are sleeping tigers."

"What's that supposed to mean?" Evanne stormed up to Hitch. "Speak plainly, man. I don't want mythic bullshit. I want to know what's inside!"

Hitch took a step back. "I meant what I said—"

"Forget it." Evanne faced the storm. "It doesn't matter, does it? We need to get in. Whatever's there, well, we'll deal with that when we find it. If it's friendly, fine, and if it's not," she tossed the remains of her whatever-it-was meat to the sand, "we'll have dessert."

TARRAGON WAS COLD. HER BREATH FROSTED BEFORE HER FACE IN tiny puffs. The maybe-Vhemin hugged herself, shawl close. They approached the verge of the storm. It was a wall of ice and sleet raining from the sky, torn about by hurricane winds. Tarragon saw the line in the sand where the storm started. It was precise, as if someone had drawn it with a compass. On one side, muddy sand. On the other, a nightmare-fuelled freezing hellscape.

The hellscape rose in a mighty circular pillar as far as Tarragon could see. *I can't imagine how much energy it's taken to keep a wall of ice swirling from ground to space for eight hundred years.*

They stood twenty metres back from the storm wall. Despite the distance, it was *loud*. Near the verge of the wall were bones. There, a bleached arm sticking up, hand frozen in a wave. Beside it, a cracked but still grinning skull. Tarragon couldn't see the ribcage of whoever it was. On and on they went, an eddy of bones circling the storm.

Why are the bones outside *the Stormwall?*

Tarragon felt Evanne shiver. She caught a glance from Hitch. For all the ghost had no face, he conveyed a power of meaning with a tilt of his head and the set of his shoulders. The glance said, *It's your turn.*

"So," Tarragon said from her perch on Evanne's shoulder. "What do we do when you die?"

Evanne glanced at her. "What do you mean?"

"Well, you're half-Vhemin, which means you're half cold-blooded. A normal person walking in there would turn into a corpsicle in about five minutes. I give you two and a half, best case." She *hmm'd.* "So, when you die, what do we do? Take a note to someone? You're a bard, so ... any last, epic words? That kind of thing?"

"I'm not going to die," Evanne said. "It's just a storm."

"It's a storm made by Itikari sorcerers," Hitch said. "They cursed this land with a thousand years of ice. There's nothing 'just' about it."

"You need a plan," Tarragon said. "It better be a good one, too."

"If it helps, the Stormwall is only about five hundred metres. Then you're through. Blue skies." Hitch hunched. "Five hundred metres is—"

"I can make it," Evanne growled.

"You can barely jog a hundred," Hitch countered. "You are not going to ... Three's mercy, what's *that?*"

Evanne whirled, almost dislodging Tarragon. The sand surged behind them. Humps coursed in their direction. Tarragon never got a glimpse of what the thing that ate her looked like as it approached, but if she was a gambler—*which I'm not, because I'm good at math*—these would be them. There were what, ten of them? *Evanne barely took one of them, and she's already injured.*

The maybe-Vhemin didn't get the memo on that tiny matter. She flung her arms out, teeth bared. "Come on, you fuckers!"

"No. Do not come on!" Tarragon tugged her hair. "Into the storm!"

"We'll die." Evanne seemed surprised at her suggestion.

"See the bones? These things have herded people right here. It's a killing zone. If we stay, we're lunch. I don't want to be lunch!" *Ignore the fact I can fly away at any minute. I don't want* her *to be lunch.* "Just ... *run!*"

Tarragon imagined the conflict going on in Evanne's head. The whole *Vhemin don't run* side of things, or the *maybe it'll be a quicker death out here* from her human half. Difficult to tell which part was in charge, and both those arguments said to stay stuck fast. *We're so boned.*

Evanne spun, sand scudding under her feet, and she bulled into the Stormwall. Tarragon held on, squinting as they approached the ice, feeling even here the force of it, heard the ice *cracking* and *crunching*, and then—

"THIS WAY!" HITCH SCREAMED. THE FADED BLUE OF THE SPECTRE was barely visible before them.

Tarragon couldn't see the end of Evanne's outstretched arm. Ice rime grew down the maybe-Vhemin's limbs. Tarragon felt herself frosting over.

She tried to yell *Hurry!* into Evanne's ear but didn't know if the maybe-Vhemin heard her. She couldn't hear herself. A chunk of ice the size of a child's fist hit her, and she was flung free.

White and black. Snow and ice.

Tarragon tumbled in the storm.

A ROAR. ABOVE THE FAIRY, JAWS WIDE, ANOTHER OF THOSE SAND things.

It wasn't having a great day. Even though Tarragon was pummelled from a hundred places with ice, the whatever-it-was looked to have it worse. *Maybe it's cold-blooded too.* It looked like it was having second thoughts about taking a bite, then it *flumped* into the snow, twitched, and was still.

"Come on!" She heard Hitch from her right.

"I'm not leaving her!" Evanne's shout, the storm teasing her normal growl to reedy thinness.

"You will die."

"Hitch! Help me find her, or Three save me, all of us will die here."

Blue above. The ghost stood before her. "I hope you're worth it."

Through the storm, a darker shape. *Evanne.* She felt the young woman's hand about her, but it was cold.

Oh. She's going to die.

IT'S ONLY BEEN A COUPLE MINUTES, AND SHE'S STOPPED SHIVERING. *That's bad.*

Tarragon clambered over Evanne's shoulder. The maybe-Vhemin put one foot in front of the other, sinking now into snow rather than sand.

Another one of the sand monsters lumbered at them, just a shadow surging out of the storm. It took a staggering lurch toward Evanne. The maybe-Vhemin gave a sloppy sidestep and swung a brutal-looking uppercut that hit nothing but air and ice.

Both monster and girl toppled, the crippling grip of snow about them. Tarragon tumbled from Evanne's shoulder but clung to her hair so's to not get swept away again.

The beauty of Evanne's violet eyes were lost in the howling gale. Tarragon leaned against her face. "Evanne!"

Hitch crouched beside them. "Get her up. It's not much farther."

"How can I do that?" Tarragon wailed. "I'm so *small*. I'm not good for anything!"

The spectre managed a withering glance, surprising since he had no features, let alone eyes to roll. "Aren't you made of fire?"

"Only a little bit."

"Better make it count, then."

Tarragon leaned into Evanne's ear. "Honey? Get up. *Please* get up."

And then she glimmered. She started low and slow, but it wasn't enough. The maybe-Vhemin didn't stir. Tarragon clambered beneath her outstretched arm, cosying beside her ribcage. The snow about her melted, but there was plenty more coming from the sky.

"More," Hitch urged. "More!"

Tarragon gritted her teeth, and *flared*. Like the stars, and like the sun itself. Like summer skies and Cophine's smile. Warm-baked bread, a hot soup on a cold day. Warm blood, not cold.

And then she was done. Empty, and it was dark, and they were alone.

TARRAGON FELT MOVEMENT. SHE OPENED A SLEEPY EYE.

Evanne, tall and strong, but rust locks bedraggled with ice melt. Skin cut in a hundred places from ice shards. The spectre, ghosting at her side. Blue sky above, and green grass below. The maybe-Vhemin carried Tarragon in the crook of one arm.

"We're dead, aren't we?" Tarragon struggled to rise, but she was so weak.

"Hmm?" Evanne looked down on her. Her skin was paler than it should be, her lavender eyes were soft. "No, fairy. We're not dead. We're through the Stormwall." She turned so Tarragon could see.

Behind them, the Stormwall raged ever on. A perfect hurricane of ice ringing an oasis of calm. Evanne kept turning, showing Tarragon green, calf-high grass. A butterfly nipped between tall flower heads. And there, in the centre of the Stormwall, a white building. Big and low, it was a couple klicks wide. The front was smooth stone, a single wide door hanging on broken hinges.

But what drew the eye was the spire. A single rod of polished metal reached for the Three's thrones above. Tarragon craned her neck, looking higher. The spire rose with the Stormwall's oasis, a sliver of metal reaching for the stars. Lightning crackled in the heavens, touched the spire, and danced down its length.

The front of the building shuddered, glowed, and then subsided. Watching, perhaps, or merely waiting? Hard to know.

"The hospital," Tarragon breathed.

"Aye." Evanne winced, holding Tarragon out from her body a little..

Tarragon saw the cost of salvation. The maybe-Vhemin's leather jerkin was burned through, the scaly hide beneath charred and blasted. She bit her lip. "Oh no. No! I didn't mean—"

"It's all right, fairy." Evanne passed Tarragon to her other arm. "It'll heal. We just need to take it easy until—"

A low, deep growl came from across the field. It sounded from within the hospital. Tarragon looked at Hitch. "What was that?"

"I tried to tell you earlier." The spectre sighed. "Tigers."

Chapter Twenty-Six

I'm *so tired*. Being cold sapped Evanne's strength like being encased
in a granite blanket. Unforgiving. Rough. And the weight of it
stayed with her even though the sun was shining, warm grass
about her legs.

I'm also sore. The burn on her side hadn't started to itch yet, but it
would. The strong part of her, made of teeth and spite, would heal it as
it did all things. She'd get over it. But Evanne needed *time*, and maybe
some food, and if it wasn't *too* much trouble, a moment to sleep.

"You shouldn't go inside." Hitch moved to stand in front of her,
arm out. Despite having no hands, she imagined he had a palm out,
trying to make the universal symbol for *hold up*. "The guardians are ...
fierce."

The growl came from within the hospital again. Evanne bared her
teeth, trying to scare up some courage. *All right then. Come get some.* She
squared her shoulders, and stormed right through the spectre's not-
hand, arm, and body. The chill of the grave wasn't anything compared
to what she'd just been through. *Or maybe I'm getting used to it.*

As she approached the hospital, the roar of the Stormwall faded
with distance. The grass whispered against her legs. *This oasis lives
hidden from all. I could live here, if there was anything to eat.* Closer, she

could see the building was made of a uniform, slightly yellow material. It looked like stone, but perfectly cut, better than anything she'd seen. The shadowy interior wasn't hostile, but a cool balm from a hot sun. *This feels like it was a nice place, once.*

She strode up the steps leading to the broken door, then slowed. An ancient, bleached skeleton lay, hand outstretched in supplication. Legs toward the door. Hand toward the light. "Hmm. It looks like it was running from something."

"Tigers," Hitch suggested.

Tarragon hopped from the crook of Evanne's arm, fluttering weakly to the smooth stone floor. She walked to the ancient corpse, touching it with a finger. It slumped into dust. She took a startled backward step. "Nothing's disturbed it in hundreds of years. We're the first here."

"So?" Hitch hovered at the hospital entrance.

"So, these tigers don't come out here. Or, they're imaginary. Which makes more sense, because what would they eat for hundreds of years?"

"Their own spite?" Hitch suggested. "You *heard* one growl, right?"

"Enough," Evanne growled. "I can handle a tiger." *I hope.* She walked to the entrance, shoulder to shoulder with Hitch. Tarragon hurried to stand beside her left ankle, a wan little glimmer touching the inside with gold. It coloured the interior like a watercolour sunrise, reminding Evanne she had friends with her. *In, child of human and monster. I don't fear the dark. The dark fears me.*

She gripped the neck of her guitar and stepped over the entrance. Then paused, listening.

Nothing. No gates of doom slamming shut on her. No screams from the abyss. And... "Where are they?"

Tarragon wandered in her wake. "Where are who? The tigers? Like I said, I don't think they exist."

"I mean the Ghosts," Evanne said. "This was a place of the ancients. Many died. But none wait for me."

"Give them time," Hitch suggested. "They might be shy. Or they don't want to bank on someone who's about to get eaten."

The entranceway was surprisingly clear of dust and detritus. Mysterious shapes mouldered into dust about a wide room. Evanne spied desiccated leather weeping between tarnished metal frames. A long, low table wandered from the east wall, crooked a leg southward, and disappeared under a slump of broken ceiling. There were two remaining exits. One against the eastern wall, big doors with glass portholes set in them, and another opposite. The western exit doorway was like the entranceway: ruined, and open to all.

A growl came from that way.

"Of course!" Evanne glared at the shitty, useless doorway. "Why would the monster come from a place we could create a barricade? Well, fuck it. Fuck it all! I'm going to—"

The tiger stalked from the ruined doorway. In Evanne's mind, a tiger was a large cat, perhaps the size of a miniature pony, equipped with fangs, claws, and a bad attitude. This creature took her imagination out back and shut it in a box. This fucker was *huge*. It stood as tall as the largest horse she'd seen, slinking low through a doorway made for humans. The tiger had eyes of pure gold, hard like metal, hot like the sun. Where she imagined tigers to be banded yellow, this was striped black and grey. Runes of fire red walked a line from its length to tail. It opened its mouth, roaring, and Evanne saw fangs the length of her forearm.

Tarragon took a step forward, gave a tired glimmer, spat a spark, and fluttered. "We're boned. *Hic.*"

"I told you so," Hitch said, perhaps less helpfully than the situation called for.

Evanne put her guitar on the ground, then fingered the hilt of her knife. She didn't draw it. *It's just doing its job. Maybe we can go through the other door.* Evanne held her palms out. "Nice kitty." She gave a suggestive nod toward the porthole door. "We're going the other way."

The tiger crouched, bunched, and charged.

The human part of Evanne wanted to scream, but the monster in her was tired, sore, and oh so *over* it. She bared her teeth. *I need to make it stop. I'm going to make it stop.* She charged right back, worthless heart shuddering in her chest. The tiger roared, and she roared right back. The beast tried to rear, but it collided with the ceiling. Ancient dust rained down, and as the monster came to Evanne's height, golden eyes screwed shut, she wound up, and punched it in the face. She put all her orneriness into the hit, rage-powered scream first, knuckles right behind.

The tiger stumbled back as if unprepared for the fight, which was surprising, but Evanne was past stopping. She swung again with her other hand, yelling at the beast. She took a powerful swipe to the side, and felt leather and Vhemin scale give, but the pain was sweet, it was ecstasy, and she grinned through the blood, hitting again, and once more for luck.

The tiger fled.

Evanne panted, chest heaving, then tottered. "I need to sit down." So, she did. Blood pattered against old stone. The floor drank it up, dry and thirsty, then gleamed like Tarragon. Big squares lit, giving up a faded yellow glow, lining a path to the porthole doors.

"That way," Hitch suggested.

"Why?" Evanne felt faint. "I don't want to fight another tiger."

"The hospital knows what you need. It tasted your blood and wants to help." The ghost sighed. "At least, I hope that's what it means. This place is Itikari. They have no love for Vhemin."

I FEEL BETTER THAN I SHOULD. I JUST KICKED A GIANT TIGER'S ASS! Evanne staggered through the porthole doors, which banged wide like those in a giant-sized saloon. She trailed blood and curses, guitar in hand once more. Tarragon zipped through the doors, a flash of glimmer passing Evanne's face as she sped into the darkened room beyond.

And my, what a room. Evanne paused on the entrance, doing her best slack jawed impression. The room was massive, and almost completely dark. Her Vhemin eyes picked out blues and blacks in the old cold stone, but her human vision was shown wonders by Tarragon's light.

The fairy's golden glow pushed back the night. The room was windowless, the ceiling high above. It seemed higher than what she'd seen of the building outside allowing for, and she wondered how the ancients managed that particular trick.

Tarragon's glimmer showed massive sunken rectangular depressions in the floor. These were twenty metres long and ten wide, easy as you please, and set along the room's length and width. Evanne figured there might be a hundred of these pits in the room.

The floor beneath her glowed its lacklustre yellow, setting a path beneath her feet into the gloom. She followed, the *drip, drip* of her life's blood a reminder she was bleeding out. *I wonder whether the monster in me will let me die.* She felt jubilant after her run-in with the tiger though and didn't feel like she was going to die after such an epic victory.

The feebly lit path stopped by a pit, the yellow turning a sullen red before it plodded on, one tile at a time. Evanne stood beside the empty pit it paused at. Tarragon flitted down, illuminating what looked like a perfectly cut rectangular cuboid depression in the stone. The walls were smooth. A decrepit ladder led its crooked way to the bottom.

Nothing else.

"What the hell?" Evanne said. "It wants me to get into an empty hole?"

"Doubtful," Hitch murmured from her elbow. "It moved on. Maybe it's not supposed to be empty. This place is very old, Evanne. It's older than me."

"Maybe it's got some maturity, then." She lurched back to the path, stagger-stepping on the yellow, glowing tiles. Tarragon darted ahead, the fairy's glimmer getting stronger. Her light still couldn't do much about the ceiling. It was dark to both Evanne's Vhemin and human vision.

The path repeated its trick of stopping at a pit, flushing amber, and continuing on. Evanne felt her strength ebbing as they continued on. "Oh well. At least I won a fight before I died."

"What?" Hitch snorted. "Hardly."

"I just punched a tiger and it ran away," Evanne said. "I won!"

"There's no way you beat one of those things." Hitch shook his head. "I don't know what to tell you, but it's twice your size—"

"Thirty times my size."

"Maybe five times your size, with a finger on the scale." The ghost sighed. "It was made by ancients to guard the sick. No disrespect, but I think it would view you as a snack."

"Because I'm only half Vhemin?" Evanne felt the growl in her voice.

"Because you're the size of a miniature poodle by comparison."

Evanne thought about that. "What's a poodle?"

"Ikmae's sometime cock," Hitch muttered. "The point here is it's designed to beat battalions of invaders. People with weapons that turn the air to living flame. Necromancers. Enchanters. Evokers, Vehmin, and even the odd stray dog. The chances of you landing three hits and, and..." He wound down.

"And?"

"And I'm glad you're alive," he whispered. "I'm really glad."

I don't know whether to shout or laugh. Evanne felt the truth of his words, no Trick in there at all. "Thanks."

"Anyway, it'd be boring without you. Who'd set off all the traps in here?"

"Wait. There are traps?"

"Hurry up." Hitch pointed. "The path hasn't moved on."

He was right. Ahead, the yellow path halted beside a pit, and hadn't turned red. It pulsed gold at her, insistent. She padded up, eyeing the pit suspiciously, because this wasn't empty. Her Vhemin sight showed a warm material filling it. Tarragon zipped to hover above. The fairy dimpled in delight. "It's a pool!"

Evanne *drip, dripped* her way to the water's edge. Pool it was, filled to the brim with warm liquid. She crouched, dipping her hand in. Her human skin agreed with her Vhemin eyes: this was warm, deliciously so. *It's not water, though. Water's not this ... thick.* Tarragon's glimmer touched the bottom, ladder and all. "So." Evanne stood. "What the hell?"

"Get in," Hitch suggested. "I would, but I'm dead already."

Evanne gave him some side-eye. "You want to turn around?"

"Oh, for pity's sake." But the spectre turned, shoulders in an angry slouch.

Setting her guitar down with care, Evanne pulled her jerkin free from her side with a hiss of pain. The blood had started to clot, leather sticking to Vhemin scaled skin. She growled, yanked, and dropped the ratty jerkin to the floor. She put her belt on the floor, then stepped out of her breeches. The air wasn't warm or cold, as if someone had imagined comfort for those disrobing here. Evanne dipped a toe in the pool, then used the ladder to lower herself in.

The liquid closed about her. The feeling was delicious. Like the taste of honey, but on her skin. The feel of summer rain. And the way she felt when Tarragon glanced at her when she thought Evanne wasn't looking. She shivered in delight. "This is *wonderful!*"

The liquid about her tiger-rent side coloured red as blood diluted the water. Then, curiously, the red swirled, then flowed back into Evanne. Her skin itched, not just where she'd been hit, but her shoulder where the sand monster bit her, and on her feet where they blistered. Evanne laughed. "It's a healing pool. The ancients made such wonders. How did they fall?"

Tarragon landed at the pool's edge, splashing her legs in the water. "The same way we all do. Stupidity."

"Hmm." Evanne splashed, then turned a lazy circle. "I'm going to soak in here for *hours.*"

"And then what?" Tarragon glimmered, wings fluttering.

"I dunno." Evanne shored up beside her, folding her arms on the pool's edge. "Do you suppose there's anything to eat around here?"

Chapter Twenty-Seven

Tarragon thought Evanne's lavender eyes were pools you'd want to drown in, and the lines of her face begged a finger to trace down them. But seeing the young woman enter the pool was something else. *She is so strong.* The maybe-Vhemin had muscles aplenty, but not like her father's kind. Where most Vhemin were so musclebound as to be almost grotesque, Evanne looked like a dancer. Lean, but strong to cut like winter wind. No wasted space on her frame.

She was part skin, part scaled. Her face was human enough, as were her forearms and lower legs. Stomach, too, but her back, upper arms, and upper legs were borrowed from monsters. She turned in the water-like liquid like a natural swimmer, long limbs sure and strong.

By the Three, she's gorgeous. And then: *I'm glimmering like a child. I need to get a grip.*

"Food?" There was nothing further from Tarragon's mind. "You want me to find *food?*"

"I mean, sure." Evanne submerged herself, then came up, splashing. "You know how places like this work, right?"

Tarragon bit her lip. "Kinda."

Evanne coasted to a halt where Tarragon's legs dangled in the pool.

"This is an ancient place. You're ancient. I mean, uh. You don't look ... uh. What I mean is, you're as old as this place." The maybe-Vhemin winced. "Uh."

"I get you." Tarragon heard the frost in her tone. "I'm older than dirt."

"Fairy, you can access places she can't." Hitch crouched by the poolside. "Service ducts, right?"

"I didn't pass my exams." Tarragon looked at her knees. *I sound so lame.* "I wasn't allowed."

"That's the beautiful thing," Evanne said. "There's no one left to stop you." She offered a lopsided grin by way of apology.

Tarragon took it, shone it up, and gave a shy smile in return. "You know what? You're right." She stood, arched her back, and glanced about. "Should be that way." She pointed to the southern wall.

"Hitch, can you go with her?" Evanne rested her chin on her arms as she bobbed.

"The tiger will come back and eat you," the ghost said.

"First up, even if that happens, what are you going to do about it? You're only good for conversation, and sometimes not even that."

"Hah," Hitch said.

"Second, I beat the tiger." Evanne slicked her hair back. "I can beat it again."

"You didn't," Hitch said. "It ran away."

"Give me this," Evanne said. "Just this once."

"There's nothing to give." The ghost sighed, stood, and walked across the water to the other side of the pool. "Coming, fairy?"

I'VE NEVER BEEN IN A HOSPITAL. TARRAGON WAS FRONT LINE, A SPY who got secrets from people who didn't want to give them up. She was young when she got caught, then spent most of her life mouldering in a Vehement Systems lock-up, talking with the man whose life she'd managed to ruin, until he died.

Sure, sure, she knew the basics. Tunnels riddled Itikari establishments. Ducts where tiny people with clever hands and quick minds could go. Fairies found faults and fixed them. The tunnels were miniature. A cat could fit, perhaps a small dog, or a hunched fairy.

Tarragon hustled along one such tunnel. There were no cobwebs, because Itikari built homes where spiders weren't welcome. There was a film of dust on the floor, and no footprints in it.

All my people are dead. Tarragon stopped short. *All the Builders I've known are spare atoms on the wind.* Her glimmer faded.

"You okay in there?" The spectre called from below her. He'd walked through the locked door Tarragon couldn't pass, and wandered the corridor below her, on the watch for tigers or other fairy-hostile creatures.

"No," she said. "Everyone is dead."

Silence for two heartbeats she had but he didn't, then, "Yes." He didn't lie, tell her it was going to be okay, just *yes.* "They all died. You are possibly the last of your kind. I saw a few of you after Mireille banished the demons, but not many. Most were lost when Itikari fell. You are so small." He sounded sad.

"We punch above our weight," she countered.

"You do," Hitch conceded. "It is the very fight in you that made you die so fast. You wept for tyrants who were past caring, and raged against an enemy no one worried about anymore. You tried to Build, or clash against your foes, but it didn't matter."

"You don't sound like you're trying to be mean, but what you say doesn't feel good to hear." Tarragon sat in the tunnel, resting her head against the wall where his voice was loudest. She closed her eyes. "I don't understand you at all."

"It doesn't feel good to say. I need to ... remember." He paused so long she thought he'd gone away. "I was dead, you see? I died before Mireille, before the demon army's defeat, and before the world fell as the heavens broke the planet. Perhaps it was mercy, but I think sometimes bad things happen to good people."

"Bad things happen to everyone," Tarragon said. "Bad things are just bad."

"Sure."

"Are you here to help?" She opened her eyes, placing a hand on the tunnel wall. "Are you here to help Evanne?"

"I don't know." Hitch sounded sad again. "I think I'm here because I have to be. Something anchors me to this half-existence. I yearn to return to the stars, but I can't walk free. Not yet. There's still much to do."

"Are you here to hurt her?"

"Never," he spat. "I would sooner die..." He trailed off, then laughed. "Well, you know."

"Good enough." She stood, dusted herself off, and gave her wings an experimental flutter. "Let's find something to eat."

WHEN SHE FLUTTERED INTO THE CAFETERIA'S KITCHEN, TARRAGON'S heart sank. *Everything is broken!* The room's eternal stone was still more or less eternal, but cracks showed in every surface. The scarring of light lances marred the walls and benches, and what looked like fragments of bone lingered in piles of dust here and there.

"I feel like we missed the party." Hitch ghosted to her side. "I don't remember this. Not even a little part of it. I don't think I came through here."

"Your weapon could do this?" Tarragon flitted to a countertop. A pan rested on a cooking element, the contents long since turned to a matte residue.

"No. It's not a light lance." Hitch crouched by a person's remains. "This one was Vhemin. See? Shark teeth."

Tarragon ignored the sorry pile. "Where do we find food?"

"MREs." Hitch pointed deeper into the structure. "There should be an emergency collection inside somewhere."

"'Somewhere' sounds really vague." Tarragon shed more light on their surroundings. "I'm the one who needs to carry whatever we find."

"It shouldn't be far," the spectre said. "I feel like..." He sighed.

"Feel like you're being a pain in the ass?"

"I feel like I've been here before. Not here in this room, but here, in this ... moment. The weapon I carried left a lot of people's bodies separate from their souls."

"Grim reaper stuff, hey?" Tarragon glanced to the far end of the room. "At least the door's open. I don't like the ducts."

Hitch drifted toward it. "Then let's go. This place gives me the creeps, too."

THEY STOOD AT A SEALED DOOR. A CORRIDOR SEEMED TO LEAD THEM here, each of its branching passages blocked by roof cave-ins or piled high with equipment pressed into service as makeshift barricades. All was silent. No sign of the tiger, or anything else. *This isn't a hospital. It's a crypt.*

Tarragon wondered if destiny brought them here. *I don't have much truck with destiny. It didn't feel much like divine intention that left me in a cage for eight hundred years.* The door before her didn't care either way. It was big, the kind of thing you could ride three horses abreast through. Tarragon shook her head. *Horses abreast? I'm a Builder!* She groped for a forgotten analogy. *You could drive a truck through here..?*

The door itself was unlabelled. No handy markings said *Morgue* or *Medical Supplies* above the lintel. It was made of sullen grey metal and had a look that said *try me*. Tarragon didn't feel up to trying much of anything with it, because she was barely the size of a pint of beer.

The front of the door had been crudely painted. The paint was white, and much of it still stuck despite the passage of time. The paint was a circle, a splodged dot within. *Clearly some cretin thought to graffiti this with a makeshift eye.*

The panel outside looked like it would take a Big's hand, and then open wide. Tarragon glanced at her tiny fingers, then closed them into a fist. "Of *course* it's sealed. Of *course* it needs a Big! They never trusted us!"

"They did," Hitch argued. "They trusted you with everything. The machines that kept them alive, or that killed their enemies. The devices that powered their cities and skycraft. The World Engines and

Skyforges. All of it." He leaned against the door. "They trusted you more than they trusted themselves. This isn't supposed to stop you. It's stopping all the other Bigs from getting in."

"I'm supposed to go inside?" Tarragon blinked.

"I guess." He stood. "Do you want me to see what's beyond?"

"Sure."

The ghost stepped through the door, then slid back out a handful of seconds later. "It's an armoury."

Tarragon frowned. "Like, with guns? What's one of those doing in a hospital?"

"I don't think it was supposed to be an armoury. There are a few cots pushed aside." He looked away. "Bassinets, really."

"This was a ... this was where they had their *babies?*" Tarragon took wing, hovering before the panel for a closer look. "And they swapped out babies for *guns?*"

"I don't think they meant to." Hitch looked to the ceiling, but she got the feeling he looked to the stars above. "I think someone took their children away. I remember ... *something*. A weapon that stole breath from the young." He shivered. "The war made monsters of all people."

Tarragon looked up from fussing with the panel, rounding on the ghost. "No. *People* make monsters of people. We have a thing inside us, Hitch. It's ugly, and it's big. It does stupid things, like get our best friends captured, and then we wish we could just *die*, but they won't let us! They keep us alive, even though your friend is dead, they're just *gone*, and for hundreds of years you live on and on, wondering what the point is, until one day you see the sky, and you keep wondering, but this time you wonder if you've made amends, or just marked time, and then the world, it's harder than before, don't you see? It's a sword edge with more cracks, blunt so they need to force it in, and jagged so it hurts when it comes out."

"I didn't—"

"And you meet someone, and she's cute and all, but not for you, but you can't help what you want, and you're *still* wondering if you've done enough time to erase all the muddy water from within the jug of your soul, until you find the cats, and they're *wonderful* Hitch, they made them soft and wise, coats smelling of cinnamon, with big jewels for eyes. And you find them, you see, and you kill one of them, and the world will never be the same." She stopped, drifting down, and sagging against the wall, breath ragged. *Hic.*

He watched her with those not-eyes, that blurred not-face. "Ah."

"What's that *hic* mean?" she screamed. *Hic.*

"It means—" He cut off like someone had thrown a switch, ghostly body taut. "Oh, no."

Tarragon looked back down the corridor. "What?"

"Evanne," he hissed. "How can someone get in trouble having a *bath?*" And then he snapped out with a pop.

Tarragon gave a last glance at the door, then scrubbed the traitorous tears from her cheeks. *I don't know why I said any of that.* She jumped from the floor, urging herself to speed, but her glimmer was faded. *Or, I don't want to know why I said it.* She urged her tiny body faster. If Evanne was in trouble, maybe Tarragon could save her and valiantly die in the process.

Then I'll have paid my debt.

Chapter Twenty-Eight

T his pool is unbelievable. Evanne floated, eyes closed, bobbing like a Half-Made cork. She thought about the desert outside for a limping heartbeat or two, and the wall of ice that separated this hidden garden from blasted sand. *Whether it was made to keep people out or in, it's kept this precious piece of the ancient world safe for hundreds of years.*

Her side itched, but she ignored it. Itching was a part of healing, and she was used to it.

Aside from the tiger, this could be a haven from the things that want to kill everyone. They say the ancients broke the world, but this 'hospital' is proof they wanted us to live better lives. She tried that truth on a couple different ways until it fit better. *They didn't want to: they lived better lives. They had it all. Carriages that flew, dragons, and...*

And, of course, slaves. Her eyes snapped open as she thought of Uncle Day, and how he'd have been someone's pet—or worse—if he'd been alive eight hundred years ago.

The pool was still warm, but it felt cloying. She splashed toward the water's edge.

Her side itched again, then she felt a stabbing pain. She yelled, floundering in the water, sweeping her arm beneath the surface. The water was clear enough, still treacle-thick, but her Vhemin eyes saw something else in the orange warmth. Below the surface, an eddy of darker colour swirled about her, reaching tendrils toward her wound. Where the tiger marked her, the skin that was healing was open again, red seeping into the water.

The tendrils surged fingers of cold toward her, and she felt another stab, then something jerked her under.

She flailed, arms churning, then swung a sluggish punch at the dark swirl lurking in the warm. It ebbed back easily, because fighting in water was for suckers, and then sought her tiger gash again. *Fuck this!* Evanne swam toward the ladder, grabbed rungs, and pulled herself from the pool. She spun, eyeing the water, not-quite-Vhemin teeth bared.

Drip, drip. Red spattered the pool from her re-opened cut.

The water surged up, the horror thing in the pool rising toward her. Evanne screamed, back-pedalled, slipped, and fell on her rump. She hit her coccyx on the hard floor, felt her legs numb, and scrabbled awkwardly back.

The pool creature quested for her, blind face made of sluggish fluid seeking, *sniffing*. It was like a cresting wave frozen in motion, the tip of where surf would break a kind of snout. It curled, tasting the red splatters she'd left at the pool's edge, then tried to follow her.

Evanne crab-walked back, feeling coming back to her legs. She lurched upright, took a fighting stance, hands raised, and snarled.

The creature's 'feet' were rooted in the pool. Where water met stone, it couldn't follow. It surged about the lip where she'd left, water slopping over the side, but it was mired in its world, leaving her safe.

She eyed her things, and thought, *I can do without everything except the guitar, but hell with it. I don't want to give it the pleasure of a souvenir.* Evanne shivered a little as air whispered over her skin. It felt like the kiss of the grave. She lowered her arms, considering her guitar, clothes, and knife. "How do you even fight water, anyway?"

The water monster ignored her, continuing its circuit of the pool, seeking an exit, or the taste of her blood, hard to tell. Evanne turned to the pool behind her, gaze resting on the old metal ladder. She smiled, grabbed the metal, and yanked.

It complained, but came with her anyway. She held a weapon that wouldn't frighten a Vhemin babe, but she was trying to kill a creature made of fluid. Evanne faced the creature, waiting for it to complete another circuit of the pool. *Bait. I need bait.* She wiped a hand against her side, hissing as fingers touched flesh, then flicked bloody spatters into the water.

The effect was instant. The creature surged for where the blood hit water. Evanne yelled, bounding forward, and swung her makeshift weapon.

The rungs passed through its body, sectioning it neatly in three. They hit the ground with a wet splash. The headless creature swirled, and Evanne felt triumph.

For a moment, anyway.

Water trickled back into the pool, and after a second it started to rise again. Evanne glanced at the ladder, thought, *You know what? I don't need to kill it,* tossed it aside, and grabbed her things. She backed away, eyes never leaving that cooler liquid that rose from the warmer pool, and wondered, *Did the ancients make that thing? Or did it move in after they left?*

And then: *What's it been eating for eight hundred years?*

DRESSED, SHE CLUTCHED THE GUITAR IN ONE HAND, PADDING ON silent feet back the way she'd come. Evanne made it half-way back to the entrance, then thought of Uncle Day. The Feybrind would've given her a half smile and asked, *{Why are you going this way?}*

He'd be right, of course. Why *was* she going this way? There was a stray tiger out there.

It's because I beat the tiger, but the monster in the water won. Or near as counts. She frowned. *Would the tiger think I'd won? Are tigers monsters like me?*

I wish Hitch was here.

I wish Tarragon was here more.

A roar came from the direction she'd headed. The tiger, make no mistake, but this time it wasn't a hunter's cry. She felt the skin on her nape goosebump and clutched the guitar tighter. *The cat is in pain. Someone other than me is hitting the tiger*.

"That's *my* tiger," she growled. She thought of Uncle Day offering another half smile, a nod perhaps, and a hand out in an *after you* gesture. Evanne squared her shoulders and marched toward the noise.

Back in the entrance area, everything looked as it had. The doors the tiger had entered through were still busted, and no more footprints disturbed the dust. The tiger roared again, more panicked this time, and she broke into a run, following its tracks left in the detritus of time.

She passed through a big room full of ancient clutter. Maybe-chairs by maybe-tables. The ceiling crumbled in parts, but not a spectre in sight. An open door beckoned, and she followed. Barged into blackness. Vhemin eyes, fever bright. Heat prints leading the way, *there*. Evanne slowed, crouched. Listened.

Nothing.

Move.

She hurried on silent feet, limping, beating heart struggling on. Guitar clutched close, no real use for it, but she wasn't leaving it here. Evanne put a hand on the knife at her belt. *Still there. Good*. A corner, another crumble of rubble sprinkled on old stone. Evanne ducked through the cold blue of broken rock slabs. She let her fingers rasp as she passed. The edges were sharp enough.

Another room. This one, big like Mama's tournament arena. A dais at one end waited below windows high above. Light speared the room, her human vision whiting out, but the Vhemin in her saw those tracks leading on. Before the dais, a pit. She padded to the edge.

Below her, the floor had caved in. Rubble promised a difficult descent if you were crazy enough to try it. The stone dust was scuffed, showing where many feet had passed.

Many feet? She checked the heat path behind her. One set of tracks, tiger-like, dimming as a body's blood heat memory on ancient stone faded. Below, those tracks, but alongside a scrabbling of others. She took a step back, because the pit contained jagged fangs of stone that could end her life if she fell on them.

Evanne pursed her lips, considering. There was no blood below. The cat was probably dexterous enough to skate about the hazard below, but what followed the creature? Machines like the Artifices would leave no blood heat tracks, but she'd never heard of a human-sized Artifice. If the ancients made such a thing it wasn't great news.

A scuffing sound from behind her. Evanne whirled. There, right fucking *there*, stood an everliving horror. It might've been a person once, but time had rotted skin and flesh. Ghastly teeth leered from sloughing lips. Bright metal lay along parts of its skull, and its eyes glimmered with eldritch blue. It was dressed in muddy, torn clothes of an unfamiliar style, time fading any bright colours to browns and greys. An empty holster like Mama held her scattergun in sat at the creature's hip.

Why didn't I sense this? I know the dead. They usually seek my solace, but this didn't.

Silly questions for another time. The monster reached a sickly arm toward her. Evanne recoiled and stepped right back over yawning space.

Her heart lurched, then jumped. Skipped another beat. She remembered the fangs of rock below, and the scuff of footprints that said this undead horror had friends below. And then she fell.

Evanne lost her grip on the guitar. It bounced away with a hollow, banging discord of notes, spilling noise as it fell. She landed on her back, rock biting her arm, and hit the back of her head. Her skull bounced, and she rolled, still falling, a slab of ancient stone punching her in the face. She saw red and black, and tumbled, feeling stunned, her arms pinwheeling.

The monster above followed, tipping into the pit after her.

She lost sight of it as the darkness of the hole swallowed her. Her Vhemin eyes couldn't see a creature already dead, and her human eyes were worthless at the best of times. Night swallowed her as she landed flat on her back, breath knocked out of her.

She tried to breathe. *Please, Cophine. A breath, just one.* Nothing. Her diaphragm spasmed, and she sucked in more dust than air. She coughed, clutching for her knife, because that thing was down here with her, but her knife was gone.

I can't see. I can't fight. She wanted to wail.

Be still. Think. And she remembered Uncle Day, those golden eyes, that ready calm. If he were here—which he wasn't, because no cat lost its footing—he might ask her how she was getting out of this.

I can't, Uncle Day. I'm Vhemin, but I can't fight what I can't see.

And of course he'd nod, and say something like, *{You're* half *Vhemin. The human part of you is there too.}*

But humans were weak. Her heart was human, and it didn't do its job. The skin of her forearms burned in the sun. There was nothing that feeble half of her could do that the monstrous part couldn't do better. And she'd have said this to Uncle Day, and he'd have listened. Believed her. Helped her up, and saved the day.

Right?

No. He would have asked me what a human would do.

Evanne almost laughed, because a human would have *died.* Just fucking quit and bled out in the dark once that thing got teeth into it.

Right?

There are a lot of humans, though. There aren't many Vhemin, and almost no fairies or Feybrind.

She thought of Mama, that sword no one was better at using, and the Storm she called. Evanne swallowed. *Maybe humans don't quit. Maybe Vhemin got that from them.*

Her eyes hunted for stray light, the cold stone trying to steal her breath away. Evanne got a hand underneath her, the bright orange of her blood heat leaving marks where she touched. Slowly, oh so slowly, so *quietly*, she got up.

She'd fallen into a small nook. Broken stone had hidden her. Protected her, like Papa.

She saw why the monster hadn't killed her. It was smashed. She found its smeared remains impaled on rock. It wasn't dead, if a dead thing could die again, one arm still reaching for her, but spears of stone were through its chest and right leg. It wasn't going anywhere.

Evanne thought of whether she should finish it off. That's what the Vhemin would do.

The tiger roared again, echoes of its pain behind her.

She found her guitar and knife, then turned and ran toward it. The

Vhemin in her could come back later. But the human part had work to do.

WHERE IS HITCH? THE SPECTRE WAS NORMALLY ON HER HEELS. Truth: he never let her alone, except when he was in a huff. This didn't feel like one of those times. With a flash of guilt, she also thought, *I wonder if he is with Tarragon. I wonder if something happened to her.*

There was nothing to be done about it now, though. She'd fallen into a hole without an obvious way out. The living dead walked these halls, and alarmingly, they were dead people Evanne couldn't see, hear, or ... feel. *Steady on, Half-Made Girl. A living dead walked these halls. One. Not multitudes. Footprints aren't proof.* Evanne shivered. *It's not fear. The air is cooler down here. Right?* Perhaps whatever magic the ancients used to keep things comfortable died along with them. But it was more likely the Vhemin in her shivered in anticipation of another fight, and the human cowered in fear.

Might not be fear. Might be sensible caution in the face of the unknown. Evanne chewed on that thought as she padded through the gloom. *I can't see—those monsters do not glow with the blood heat of the living. My link to the dead gives me nothing here. And yet dead they are, but ... everliving.*

The tiger roared again, close now, and she rounded a corner to finally see it again. Above, a few cracks in the stone let fingers of light in. Those precious beams fell through dust, painting the scene below. The tiger was as she remembered. Grey and black stripes. Golden eyes. Tall as a big horse, but with fangs that no horse had. It was backed against a cracked wall and stood on a raised platform.

The platform had plinths spaced evenly enough about it, some solid metal, others rough fangs of glass, just broken shards hinting of what they might have been. The giant cat looked to have made a last stand of sorts, because the platform was surrounded by more of the undead.

Okay, it wasn't just one shambling horror. There are at least ten in here.

The good news was, none of the monsters had seen Evanne from her crouched position by a fallen piece of ceiling stone. The tiger hadn't either, and if she wanted, she could turn and leave. No one would blame her. Three's mercy, but no one would even know.

I would know.

She bared not-quite-Vhemin teeth, putting a hand on the stone to vault over. She didn't jump, because her other hand held nothing but a battered guitar. The knife at her belt was for cutting bread and cheese, and while she'd killed a creature of the sands with it, she was honest—with herself, at least—enough to admit that was mostly by accident.

Think.

A soft pop at her left shoulder almost made her scream, but she bit down on the noise as Hitch materialised beside her. "Hi."

"Hi?" Evanne felt her voice rising and clamped down on it. She hissed, "Where have you *been?*"

"Oh. You know. Around." He waved a not-hand in a vague and unsatisfactory manner. "Have you been keeping busy?"

She glared but kept her voice low. "I've been attacked by everliving monsters. The tiger's in trouble." To punctuate this, one of the dead creatures shambled before the tiger, lunging with an ancient spear. The rusty metal tip scored a red mark on the tiger's side. The giant cat roared, smashing the creature off the platform. It tumbled, bounced, and came to rest beside the spear.

The blow would have killed anyone, maybe even Barret. But after a handful of heartbeats, the monster twitched, then shambled upright, bent to fetch its spear, and faced the platform once more. Evanne caught a glimpse of that curious metal alongside a skull mostly devoid of hair or skin.

"So I see." Hitch sat atop her cover. "You can't kill them, you know. They're not really dead, and they're not really alive either."

"What are they?"

He looked over his shoulder at the fracas. "In the Great War, Vehement Systems were best known for making machines. Artifices are what you see most often in the marketing material, but toward the end they made all manner of other clockwork monsters. My least favourite were the Personates. Those were ... really something." He didn't sound like *something* was *anything good.* Evanne wondered what *marketing mate-*

rial was. "They could kill Tresward. That's what they were for, do you see? The weapon to kill our greatest hope."

"You're moping. The tiger is dying."

"Right, right." He straightened. "Vehement made machines, and dabbled in bioengineering. They made—"

"Biowhat?"

"They made you. Or, half of you." He hunched. "Itikari made ... creatures. It was their thing. Dragons, and Feybrind. Tigers." He jerked a thumb behind him to the growling horse-sized feline.

"Hurry this up," Evanne said. "The cat won't last forever."

He tilted his head. "You know, it might. Itikari ... built to last. But I get your point. They dabbled in machines toward the end, when all seemed lost. When the ... commodity of Vehement steamrolled the quality of Itikari. They had good soldiers, but not enough. And the Vhemin were a wellspring that kept giving. So, the challenge was how to make Itikari soldiers keep fighting. You know, after they'd died." He sighed. "This was the answer. The bodies keep going, you see? But there's nothing in them. A few memories. A clockwork keeps it all going, and they'll keep doing what they think they should until the end of time."

"Or until the clockwork winds down." Evanne glared at the everliving husks. "Do they have a name?"

"Would it matter?"

"It might. I have an idea." Her brows furrowed.

"Just the one? Careful, it might get scared, being so alone in that thick skull of yours."

Evanne ignored the spectre. "I need your help."

"Of course you do. You always—"

Evanne reached out to him. Really *reached*, deep inside him, and pulled her to him. All that Hitch was, his ghostly form, his past, present, and what he was meant to be. The spectre slipped into her, a second shadow, and she felt the chill rime her bones.

She held her guitar in both hands, fingers resting on the strings. Like before when she'd played on the beach, or when everyone fought Feybrind, she felt peace settle on her, a calm that lay on her like a cloak. Evanne closed her eyes, feeling her breath mist out, ice crystals on the air. *Tarragon isn't here. I can't do this for long. Not like last time. I'll freeze.*

Just one Trick then. A tiny one was all she had space for. She felt about for the monsters before her, and saw how the shadows of their souls were missing from their rotted bodies. *That's the way in.* She strummed, the ghost riding within her playing too, him a bridge to the land of shadows, and her to the world of light, both linked by the strum of her fingers.

This song was for children. She'd heard it herself often enough in Imshir. It was a clever rhyme to remind you of why you went home. *Cakes on the hearth. Woodsmoke and a mother's embrace. That's it. Make them remember. Make them ... feel, one last time. Like they were children.* Evanne pulled the song from her guitar. The ancient instrument loved her touch, and ... gave it back.

In a world of wonder, let's sing a song,
About a place where you truly belong.
Close your eyes and let's all go,
To a place where the warm fires glow.

CAKES ON THE HEARTH, WOODSMOKE IN THE AIR,
A mother's embrace, so loving and fair.
This is the rhyme that will guide you right,
To the comfort of home, in the soft, warm light.

WHEN THE DAY'S ADVENTURES HAVE ALL BEEN DONE,
And you're longing for home as the setting sun,
Remember these words, and you won't feel alone,
Cakes on the hearth, woodsmoke, and a mother's tone.

WHEN THE WORLD IS BIG, AND YOU'RE FEELING SMALL,
Just remember these words, you'll feel ten feet tall.
With cakes on the hearth, the sweetest embrace,
You'll always find your way back to that special place.

. . .

So sing this song whenever you roam,
   And it'll bring you right back to the warmth of home.
   Cakes on the hearth, and that sweet embrace,
   Will guide you back to that special place.

The guitar didn't give it back all at once, and not to everyone. A single monster, the one closest to her, turned its head as if listening, the spear in its hands lowering. *That's right. Remember who you were.* She let her fingers stop their stroll on the strings, the last note dying away, the music unafraid of the dark, just trying to find a new home. On the last note, she remembered for him. "I know who you are. Gabriel, I give you back your name."

Hitch drifted free with the last of the music, and he staggered. "What was that?"

"Confusion to our enemies," Evanne hissed. "Watch."

The monster who'd listened twitched, then turned about to his allies. He stumble-stepped to his comrades, but was surer than before, firmer of purpose. *I gave him back more than his name. I gave him back a piece of his soul.* Gabriel, everliving monster for eight hundred years, stabbed his nearest companion through the spine with his spear. The shambling corpse didn't pause as his former ally fell, moving to the next and sticking her through the skull.

"How'd you do that?" Hitch looked between the monster and Evanne.

"It's a Trick. You just have to know people." Evanne wanted to brush it off, but there was more to it. That road Hitch laid for her in spectral tones to the underworld was still there. She might never be free of it, but it let her know what she was. What she could do. See the dead, and all they'd ever been. And what they could do for her.

I'm a necromancer.

Evanne shook her head. *No. Not like the others. Half-Made in all things, even this.* She looked at her guitar. *I'm something different.*

The melee by the platform picked up speed. The creatures attacking the tiger turned, sensing disturbance, and converged on Gabriel. The monster looked like it flexed, chest out, but it could've been Evanne's imagination. His allies shambled toward him, but Gabriel didn't back down. The metal in his head told him to kill, but it no longer controlled who.

Evanne relaxed her grip on the guitar, raising her voice as she called to the tiger. "Come on! We haven't got all day."

The tiger bared fangs, and as a surprise to no one, didn't immediately follow. *Fair enough. I punched it in the face an hour back.* Evanne turned on her heel, looking for an exit. *There.* She jog-limped, best as her limping heart and banged up body could manage, for a set of doors set into the wall below an ancient banner.

In the next room there were boxes stacked atop each other. They still looked firm, crafted of an iridescent metal that showed no sign of tarnish. Plenty of them, as if someone had repurposed this place into a hasty storeroom. Evanne was about to stumble on, but Hitch pointed. "Take one of these."

"They look heavy."

"It's lucky you're so big and strong, then." Hitch drifted by a stack of crates, then another, before shoring up beside a smaller stack. "Here. One of these."

Evanne growled, but shucked her guitar on its sling behind her, and hefted a crate. *I was right. It's heavy.* She lumbered after the ghost, his blue luminescence welcome in this place of shadows. Hitch led her through corridor and down junction, past closed doors without pausing.

She slowed, noticing a door was chained through its handles. Evanne nudged it with her boot. "Why are these chained shut? What are they hiding from us?"

Hitch laughed. "That's not it. They're not hiding something from *us*." He laid a ghostly hand on the door. "Behind here are more Gabriels. Many, many more. Something went wrong, and this place died."

Evanne eyed him. "You know what it was, don't you?"

"Maybe," Hitch said, in a manner that caused Evanne to grit her teeth. "Come on. It's not far now."

"To what?" But she had to hurry as the spectre set off again.

A few more turns and doors barred their way ahead. Grimy

windows set in them leaked light from beyond. The ghost slipped through the doors. Evanne barged through, shoulder first, the tinkle of glass on stone her companion as the windows broke.

Light speared her eyes. It was harsh and wonderful. *Daylight.*

She put the crate down, taking a breath, and let her eyes adjust. They were outside, but on a rooftop. The view across the green field surrounding the hospital reminded her of home for no rational reason, because she'd come from a desert wasteland. Beyond the green, the wall of ice howled on, a border against the rest of the world. At this distance its cry was muted.

Evanne walked to the edge of the roof. "We're high up."

"We've got a ways to go." Hitch pointed above her. "The weapon is higher still."

Evanne turned, taking in the hospital rising above her, a guardian to protect them, or demon set to kill, impossible to know. She visored her face with a hand, craning her neck, looking at the metal spire stabbed into the heart of the heavens. "How high does it go?"

"All the way," Hitch said. "It goes to where there is no air or heat."

Evanne gave him a little side eye. "I don't understand. It looks heavy. How has something so tall balanced on such a small base?"

"The hospital isn't small."

"Oh aye, I couldn't lift it, and neither could you." She glanced up again. "But that spire is something else."

"The gods built it," Hitch said. "Or so they say. The gods can balance a sword on its point for a hundred years—"

"Mama showed me the trick of it," Evanne sniffed. "So this is ... balanced?"

"Hmm." Hitch sounded like he didn't know and was just making noise to cover it up.

Evanne turned her attention to the crate. "What's in that?"

"Something near and dear to your heart. Open it."

Evanne walked to the box, the sun's light leaving her as she stepped into the hospital's shadow. She shivered, then grabbed the box and dragged it into the warm. It took her a moment to work out how the fastenings functioned. Not like a buckle, but a clasp of some clever contrivance that made a happy *clunk* as she flicked it open.

The lid yawned wide with a slight creak. *Even the ancients couldn't keep everything perfect forever.* Inside a series of silvery packets nestled on a tray. Some were the size of her fist, others low and flat, and one looked suspiciously like a bowl. She removed the tray, finding another beneath it. She glared at the ghost. "What the hell is this?"

"Food."

"Hah ha."

"No. You tear the ... thing." He *grr'd.* "I wish I could show you."

"You mean you wish you had hands?"

He looked at where his forearms vanished into ethereal mist. "I had hands. Once."

"Whatever." Evanne lifted a package that had the heft and size of a Granny Smith apple. She worried the silvery material until, in a fit of pique, she got a piece between her teeth and pulled. It tore, but silently, no ripping of fabric or scream of metal. Within, riches: the scent of fresh-baked cake assaulted her nose. She held up her prize. "This is a muffin."

"It is."

"It's the size of a child's head." Evanne turned the muffin around. It looked fresh-baked, not spotted with fungus or shrivelled to dust. She nibbled, then closed her eyes in delight. "This tastes like... happiness."

Hitch leaned over her shoulder, and examined the silvery paper she'd dropped to the ground. "It's apple and cinnamon."

"It's fucking delicious."

"It's..." He trailed off, and she got the impression he smiled. "Happiness."

Evanne ate, small bites at first, then the Vhemin inside her took over and she ate like a feral. In moments, the muffin was gone. She licked her fingers, one by one. "Is there more?"

"The other packets are different. Some will contain chicken, or—"

"Meat?" Evanne leaned forward. "You have my attention. Which ones?"

A noise drew her attention. From the door they'd exited from, the pad of great feet. Evanne stood, belt knife in her hand. She held her precious guitar behind her, shielding it with her body. "Get back, Hitch."

"Why? I'm already dead."

She glared, and he drifted into her shadow. The doors slammed wide, and the grey-striped tiger burst out. It skidded to a halt when it saw her, golden eyes on her knife. It growled, low, deep, and Evanne felt the fear curl in her gut.

Fuck that. "You want a piece of this?" She pushed her chest out. "Come on, then!"

The tiger lowered its head, still growling, and backed away a pace. Hitch sighed. "Just once, I'd like to see you try the non-predictable route."

"You what now?"

"You don't have any friends. Well, there's me, but we're kind of stuck together, so that doesn't count. And there's Tarragon. But, you know." He paced. "Try being nice."

"It's a tiger!"

The tiger sidled away, moving to the edge of the building and glancing down. Hitch stared at her for a long moment. "What's your point?"

"They eat people."

"Have you seen this tiger," he jabbed a misshapen arm at the beast, "try to eat anyone?"

"Well, there was that *one time* it attacked me." Evanne felt herself relax, because the tiger hadn't actually tried to tear out her throat.

"We're talking about eating, not panicking in fear of its life."

"*It* was afraid?" She scoffed, then pointed at the tiger with her knife. "It's twice my size."

"We've had this conversation. It's probably five times your weight."

"Are you trying to make my point for me?"

The tiger paced the ledge, looking for all the world like it wanted to jump down. Evanne frowned. *Why is it trying to get away? It's just me up here.* She looked at her knife, then sighed, and put it away. Then she looked at the box of food. *Hitch said chicken. Tigers like chicken, don't they?*

She bent, rummaged, and began tearing silvery packets. *Soup.* She sniffed. *Potato and leek. A classic pairing, but not for a tiger.* She put that aside. *Here we go.* She found a tray inside one that contained what looked like chicken wrapped with bacon and cheese. *Do tigers eat bacon?* She almost laughed. *Everyone likes bacon.*

Evanne stood, holding the little tray before her, then walked halfway to the tiger. She put the tray on the ground, then stepped back. "Here you go." The tiger's head came up as it sniffed the air, then it padded to the tray. Two bites and gone. *Not even on my best day could I eat that fast.* "You must be hungry."

"This tiger has been ... frozen for eight hundred years. It is probably starving." Hitch glanced at his feet. "Literally."

Evanne looked at her box of food. There were plenty more where she'd found this, and maybe it *was* better to have friends. She rooted through the contents, sorting packets into *muffins and thus not good for tigers* and *probably made of an animal so good for tigers*. As she opened another packet, the rich smell of beef hitting her, she paused. "Where's Tarragon?"

Chapter Twenty-Nine

Tarragon was lost.

That asshole Hitch! She wanted to scream it, shout the words to the ancient ceiling, but Tarragon thought it quite likely there were things in here that would find fairies tasty. So, she buttoned it up, marking a special ledger in her mind with another IOU for the spectre.

She drifted from room to room, trying to keep her glimmer at a bare minimum. *My glow would work like a fishing lure for some of the denizens of the dark.* Her wings seemed to have come right, and so she was able to use flight rather than foot. Tarragon glared at the service tunnels above. *Hateful. Spiteful. Only a sadist would have built crawl spaces for those with wings.*

Her listless path led her through a ward with smaller beds. Not fairy small, but for little Bigs. Most of the beds were full of sad, dusty remains. A pile of larger action beckoned from the room's middle, so she fluttered closer. Her glimmer faded as she saw what lay there.

The brutish skull of a Vhemin monster identified a Big in the middle of it all. Shark teeth in a body structure of nightmares. The creature was in full shock armour and looked to have crumpled mid-fight. The centre of its skull had a hole bored through, which was the only sure way of killing their kind. The monster had dropped a rifle. The weapon was sheared in two, and scorch marks on its breastplate showed the fiery effect that'd had.

Two tiny, tiny skeletons were beside it. One was mostly mashed kibble, the other cleaved in half. Tarragon landed by her fallen siblings and fussed about their remains for a few moments. She straightened their limbs as best she could, putting some semblance of respect to their fallen grace. It was harder for the mashed one, and she guessed the Vhemin had done for that tiny warrior.

A glint drew her eye, and she almost shouted in triumph. *The hilt of a fairy-sized rapier!* It gleamed from its dusty shroud. She hopped closer and drew it forth. Crushing defeat: the sword was broken, a melted, rotted end showing this was the tool used to shear the Vhemin's rifle. Tarragon tossed it aside, a tiny *tink* sounding over-loud in this crypt of the lost.

She hugged herself, feeling a shiver despite her inner heat. *I don't like it here. I want Evanne.* But Evanne wasn't here. She was in danger, and the ghost had raced off, as if he—with his not-hands and not-body —could do anything about it. *Hitch wasn't in management. I can tell he doesn't have the head for it.*

There was nothing to be done here, so she took wing and flitted further into the gloom. An ancient control room held no prizes. *Maybe I could fix it.* She snorted as she settled beside an ancient glass slate, the magic within having seeped out by way of a crack even the blind could see. Tarragon touched the crack, remembering.

Hating herself.

"Helio!" Tarragon wailed, trying to keep up.

Helio Amberwing. Champion of the Tiny Corps. Hero of the hour. Devilishly handsome, not that it mattered to Tarragon, because she didn't like boys, and even if she did, Helio wouldn't like someone as plain as her. He had a hundred fairies pestering him for stories and laughter each night, and Tarragon —again, not liking boys—couldn't help but feel jealous of the attention he got.

She wasn't jealous of his sharp jawline and rakish stubble, but because he was good at something. Helio came from the same Mite Forge as her, the exact same batch. He probably even had the same starting serial number. But he'd passed his Builder exams, and she'd failed. He hadn't blown up the commander's skycar. He hadn't almost cut off his own wings while learning to fence.

Helio turned at her shout, a glitter of silver eyes hiding mischief in a bark-dark face. "Tarragon."

"You dropped this." She huffed, holding out his sword. It was the size of a Big's toothpick, and exquisitely made. Just holding it made Tarragon feel sick with envy, because Helio made it as part of his Builder exams, and it was perfect. Tiny gems studded the hilt, and she knew the edge was sharp enough to shave with. It wouldn't ever blunt, not until the end of days.

Helio took the sword, freeing it from a scabbard. He took an experimental swipe of the air, a moue of disappointment touching his lips. "It feels a bit heavy on the ass-end, doesn't it?"

She goggled. "No!"

"Oh?" He arched an eyebrow. "You know so much about steel? Aye, I'd bet you'd hold a hammer with the best Smiths of the Three's Wardens, nay?"

She huffed, feeling like her honey brown skin was about to be marred with a blush. "I... no! I mean I wouldn't presume to ... no!"

The moue turned into a lazy smile, and he tipped the sword about its hilt, perfectly balanced on his fingers. "Take it."

She put her hands behind her back. "Oh, I couldn't—"

"Tarragon Greyflight!" At the command in Helio's words, she couldn't help but stand to attention. Softer now: "Take the sword."

She reached out a tiny hand, feeling the hilt kiss her palm. The perfect weight of it, the majesty of promise in its quicksilver length. Tarragon gave it a swing, then frowned. "It feels fine to me."

"You're using it like a tennis racket. Use finesse."

She gritted her teeth. "I. Don't. Have. Any."

"You what now?" Helio blinked. "You're a fairy. We were born to dance."

"Haven't you been paying attention from your throne of praises?" It was all coming out now, the resentment and the jealousy, and she wanted to put her hand in front of her mouth to stop the words. But also, didn't. She jabbed a finger at him. "You're the best of our Mite Forge batch. The only one who passed anything! I failed, like, everything. That doesn't make me happy. We have a

Manifest, *Helio. A Manifest! Given by the Three, their word become our desire. The Manifest has, has,"* she waved the sword, and Helio took a cautionary backward step, *"instructions. How to build a Skyforge. What temperature a Build Engine runs best at. How to balance a mote of stardust in the fiery—"*

"Engines of creation. I know. I have the same Manifest."

"That's the point," she spat. *"You don't. You've got the only Manifest. I don't know how to use this,"* she waved the sword again, almost slicing a wingtip off, *"any more than I know how to fire up a Build Engine. We all failed, Helio! All of us. There were sixty-four in our clutch, and you're the only one who's good at anything."*

He frowned. She fumed. He frowned some more. *"And what would you do?"*

Tarragon blinked, wanting to be angry some more, but ... more curious at his question. *"I don't get you."*

"You have no instructions. No codes from the Three demanding anything. I'm riddled with them. I seek—"

"Oh, so it's a curse?" She glimmered, not the yellow glow of skysparkle, but the angry vermilion of destruction. *"Being so good at everything is a—"*

"How are you doing that?" Helio pointed to her. *"The red. I can't do the red."*

She bunched her fingers, taking a step forward, ready to give him a fist of fives. Tarragon felt the menace in her tone as her voice lowered. *"Are you trying to be funny?"*

"I'm trying to work out why we're different."

She screamed, swinging a tiny-yet-savage uppercut. Helio avoided it with ease, and for good measure took her sword away, tossing it with a tiny tinkle to the pavers beside them. She whirled, trying for a haymaker, and he touched her elbow gently as it safely missed his face. The tap was enough to overbalance her, and she tumbled into a tangle of wings and righteous anger. She hiccupped.

Helio didn't laugh. If anything, he looked concerned, which wasn't the expected expression for someone who'd almost had their block knocked off. *"If you promise not to try killing me for at least forty-five minutes, I promise to buy you a coffee."*

Tarragon felt the tears come, and even though she tried to stop them, that just made everything worse. *"I can't even get angry right."* Hic.

"I think you got the anger part down fine." Helio stroked his chin, gossamer wings shuffling. *"It's the follow-through that could use some work."*

"I will knock your teeth in."

"Maybe. If I do my job right."

"What's that supposed to—hic—mean?"

Helio offered her his hand. She glared, and stood without his help. He lowered his hand as if nothing were amiss. "You say I can do everything. Let's see if I can teach you."

"Oh, now the—hic—mighty master strides down from on high—"

"The mighty master is happy to be shouted at all day, but it's not making you better at anything. The Flight School wants to flunk you out." He tried that winning smile on for size. Despite herself, she had to admit it had a level of rakish charm she admired. "It's raining, and I'm offering umbrellas."

She squinted. "Hic. That's a piss-poor analogy."

He held a hand out, as if checking the weather. "Maybe. But it feels like it's raining harder every minute you don't have that coffee."

Tarragon glowered. I don't want to let him off that easy, but... But had Helio done anything wrong? They were different. He was perfect, which was highly annoying, and she was a flawed casting. Yet, here he was, unoffended by her outburst, and even offered coffee. "Just one thing."

"Coffee has conditions?"

"Everything has conditions. Everything! That's what..." She clamped down on the rest. "Hic. Yes. The coffee has conditions."

Helio crossed his arms, rakish charm shifting to rakish amusement. "I'm listening."

"I don't want to go out with you."

He blinked. "You what?"

"It's the condition. Everyone else wants to, and I'm not everyone else."

He laughed. "Tarragon. You know what? I think we're going to get along just fine."

TARRAGON STILL HAD HIS SWORD. IT'D BEEN MONTHS SINCE COFFEE. Coffee hadn't led to the bedroom, because Helio wasn't a dick. She'd expected him to be, but he seemed fine with keeping his perfection all to himself, or anyone who happened to throw themselves at his feet.

So, coffee led to training, and training led here, to the sparring hall. It was for Bigs, but empty of their lumbering forms. That was probably because it was three o'clock in the morning. Three moons watched through large windows. She could see Cophine easily, her summer luminance just what the doctor ordered if you were a fairy. Ikmae was sullen as per usual, and Khiton was all but invisible.

She could feel the god of night nonetheless. All who carried a blade in his service of war could, and she was no exception. Helio had left her with his blade, and she'd never left her nest without it. Breakfast? The sword. Lunch? Sword there too. Just coffee? Swords everywhere. The sword was a part of her now, and she wanted to show Khiton she was good for it.

Or any of the three. Cophine's summer smile would be enough.

"What do you think of the blade now?" Helio held a hand out, palm up, toward the weapon in her hand.

Tarragon gave it a swish. "It is heavy on the ass end."

Helio laughed. "But you like it, for all its flaws?"

Despite the silver bright twinkle in his eyes, she felt a hidden question. Tarragon couldn't understand what he was really asking. "I guess? It knows me, and I know it."

He nodded. "I understand the feeling well." Before she could ask what he meant, Helio drew his own blade. "Now. Show me."

She lunged, a flurry of wings driving her forward. He parried, but not easily. Months on this mat had turned her into a swordswoman. Tarragon would never command the Three's Light. Only Bigs could be Three's Wardens. But she studied their patterns. And she found she liked them.

Helio batted her blade aside, then lunged forward, point of his sword extended to her heart. Tarragon let hers kiss the edge of his, a tiny chime like wind bells, and stepped inside his guard. He smiled, so she stamped on his instep. Helio stumbled back, and she pursued in a whirl of steel.

Tarragon noticed Helio sweated. He never sweated. She pursued her advantage. His blade came at her throat, and she welcomed it, if only to get closer to him. Tarragon rewarded his advance with another kick to his instep, and got a backhand for her trouble. She spat golden blood. And kept at it.

He fell, and she swung for his groin. Helio buzzed back with emberfire grace, her blade biting the floor and naught else. Once, twice, and a third time she struck, and he parried each, but gracelessly. Helio took to the wing, and she followed, both trailing stardust. She hit his steel, and thunder roiled outside. He snuck inside her guard, so she kneed him in the groin. He was ready for that, taking the blow on his inside thigh, and in a second her sword was his again, and her without a weapon.

She gave a tiny scream, and head butted him, then swung for a savage cross. He dropped both blades, and touched her arm as it passed the same way he had all those months ago. Airborn, she spun like a dandelion seed puff in the wind. She fluttered, but he slid in close, bound her arm up around her own damn throat, and held her tight. "Hold. Tarragon! Three's mercy, hold."

Tarragon hic'd. "I had you. I had you!"

"Aye. The best with a blade I've seen outside the Three's Wardens. Yet here we are, me without a scratch and you with a bloody lip and about to be choked out with your own arm."

"I suck at unarmed combat."

"And yet." *He let her go, and they settled to the ground.*

She spat more gold. "And yet?"

"How would you like a job no one else wants? Full of danger. No recognition. Fighting, sure, but not fighting too, which will be harder."

Tarragon scowled, rubbing her arm. "You really yanked it that time."

"You were trying to eviscerate me."

"Only a little." *Tarragon turned the scowl to a frown.* "Is that what this is about? This midnight rendezvous—"

"It's three in the morning."

"This early morning rendezvous is to, what, to offer me a job?"

Helio gave her a devilish smile. "It's a little more than that." *He held out his hand.* "I need a partner."

She stared at his hand, but hard, like her eyes could melt it or something. Her voice felt very small. "Me? Hic. But I'm nobody. I can't do anything."

Helio didn't withdraw his hand this time. "You can do everything. You were made for this. Trust me."

Trust, aye? She thought about it, then cautiously, as if his palm would bite, took his hand in hers. "Partners?"

"Until the end." *He winked.* "Now let me tell you what you just signed up for."

Tarragon shuddered. She saw herself in the glass, a shadowy reflection less substantial than even the spectre Hitch. Her cheeks were gaunt, eyes haunted. *I don't look like a fairy. Not even the wings hide what I am.*

I'm a failure.

She placed her palm against the ancient panel, feeling the mark of time in the material. It'd been Built by someone like her, but with skills, a purpose, and probably friends. Even with those things it had failed. Lost to the decay of time, or the destructive potential of the Bigs.

A slight *toc* noise echoed in the darkness, startling her. Her fingers caught on the cracked glass, slicing a tiny nick in her index finger. She winced as beads of gold touched the ancient, dead panel. Tarragon sucked her finger, angry at herself. *I don't even know why I'm angry. I was angry* then, *but all that's past history. Gone these eight hundred years. Not even a relic's memory.*

"I'm not convincing anyone," she said to her reflection in the glass. Her reflection didn't deign to answer.

Tarragon cocked her head. That noise from the darkness wasn't *nothing*. It was *something*, or something's neighbour, so she should check it out. With a little luck, something would eat her, and she could stop feeling so mopey. With a little more luck, it'd be something to eat, because she was starving.

She took wing, flitting into the gloom. She didn't feel much like shining, so her glimmer was the barest murmur of light.

The fairy passed through a vaulted chamber with a cracked wall, masonry slumping inward, a glimmer of dust caught on fingers of sunlight. The chamber was scarred by light lances long ago, and the scattered remains of perhaps twenty people were here. She counted Feybrind among them, the cats' skulls unmistakable.

No fairies, though.

The end of the room held the Council's chamber. Every place like this had one. The chamber hadn't been breached. The old metal showed signs of scrapes and ballistics fire, but it hadn't given up. The Council would still be inside, if there was magic enough to spark their awareness.

She glanced up. *Remember Heaven's Gate. That Council almost killed me.*

To be fair, it almost killed a lot of other people too. Perhaps it was time to see what the hospital's Council would be like. Fair? Balanced?

She snorted. *Not likely.* It was better to think of them as ... *analytical*. They weighed the numbers. Saw the bigger picture. Did what was necessary, for those who couldn't, to save those they could.

Right?

Tarragon landed before the door. It may as well have been the height of a mountain for someone her size, the vast expanse of metal stretching even higher than a Big above her. She put the same hand she'd put on the panel against the metal. Listened. Leaned her head against it, and just *breathed*.

"Please," she said. "Please help me. I don't know what to do."

More golden blood trickled from her finger. It slicked the door under her palm, the tiniest of smudges, a hint of glimmer inside it. The old metal's dark skin was matte beside it, impervious, impassive. Just like the Council within.

They won't be there anymore. Eight hundred years is a long time for a Council.

The door under her fingers *toc'd* again, and she jumped as a seam opened before her. It split from floor to ceiling by perhaps the width of one of Evanne's rust-red hairs. Silence. Time passed, seconds creeping up on her.

Then, with a grumble, it slid wide. A gust of dusty air blew out, tugging Tarragon's hair, and she fluttered her wings to stay upright. Within, the darkness was complete. She glimmered a little brighter, pushing her golden light inside.

Old glass. A dais. The Council themselves, but silent forms in the gloom, none of the rainbow light she expected. "Hello?"

The dais glinted. *It's not a trick of the light. I'm the light here.* Tarragon hop-skipped inside, fluttering to the dais. "Do I get on, or what?" The Council remained impassive. "It's just that, uh. It's for Bigs. It's forbidden for the Kingdom."

To her left, a sullen orange glow kissed the night. It flashed, slow, but insistent. Ancient, but ... so was she, and she was still doing okay. The dais glinted again, then its surface brightened with ochre before turning the colour of the sky right after dawn. Clean and clear. Welcoming.

Tarragon looked at the door behind her. It'd only opened the width of a fairy's body. No Big could've got through. *No Big was meant to.* She sighed, then fluttered onto the dais. "Okay. Now what?"

The door behind her slammed closed with the crack of thunder as the Council woke before her.

Chapter Thirty

The rooftop below Evanne trembled. It was subtle at first but arrived right on the heels of her question. Asking *where's Tarragon* was too close, too damn *coincidental* to be unlinked to what was going on beneath her feet. "Think carefully, Hitch. Where was she last time you saw her?"

"I mean, I guess she was beside an armoury. But it was locked, so..." He trailed off.

She put her hands on hips. "Where was she, and what was she doing?"

The tiger padded forward, and she felt like giving it a glare, but the cat slinked past her and started nosing in the food bins. "Well." The ghost gave a delicate cough. "See, there's a Council on that same level. But they're dust and ashes. Gone for centuries now."

Evanne gave him a little side eye. "What's a Council? Tarragon said something about that at Heaven's Gate."

He pointed to the cat. "Don't let her eat that. It'll make her sick."

Evanne rescued a muffin-shaped package from the cat, then tore the wrapping from what smelled like the best steak she would ever have. Wistfully, she offered it to the cat. The tiger didn't even pause to chew, then licked Evanne's fingertips with a tongue that felt like a rasp. She gave the beast an absent-minded pat on the nose, ignoring the cat's widening eyes, and turned her glare up a notch as she faced Hitch. "Don't change the subject. Council. Who are they?"

"It's more of an it. Less of a who."

"More or less, I don't care. My friend is in there," she stabbed a finger at the hospital, stumbling only a little as the floor gave a solid shake, "and the building is shaking. It's shaking a lot! I don't think it's supposed to do that."

Hitch nodded. "The Council is a sort of, uh," he waved his arms, as if trying to find the words, "retirement village."

"I don't know what that is either."

"Imagine a place where, when you're too old to do stuff like you used to—"

"Like you?"

"Ouch. But let's say you can't swing a sword, or ride a horse. With me?"

"Vhemin can't ride horses." Evanne frowned, thinking hard. *I don't know anyone too old to swing a sword or...* "You mean a burial ground?"

"You're thinking along the right lines, but the ancients didn't *die* when they got old. They lived out their days in luxury. Or, if they were important enough, their essences were put in phylacteries. They would be everliving."

"Mama told me of the lich that lived in Heaven's Gate."

"The Council are not liches. They are, uh," Hitch sounded *frustrated*, like he didn't have the words for this, "no longer what they were. It's like when you bake a cake—"

"I don't bake."

The spectre gave a small growl. "Work with me a little. If someone else, talented, and with skill, baked a cake, they would take eggs, flour, butter, and so on. They would—"

"Like this muffin?" Evanne tore the seal on the treat she'd rescued from the cat and took a bite.

"Exactly so. The ingredients would go into the muffin, and no longer be individuals. They would be one thing, but with the wisdom of the group."

Evanne chewed, thinking of the mob that killed Old Merle. *Cleo. More mistakes.* She tossed her suddenly tasteless muffin over the rooftop. The tiger watched it go, as if it were a golden chalice of incredible value she was tossing into the ocean. "I've never met a wise group."

Hitch glanced at the Stormwall. "This is different. Say, do you think the ice is letting up?"

The spire above Evanne crackled. She glanced up in time to see spidery, brilliant legs of lightning stampede toward her from on high. She crouched involuntarily as the energy slammed into the spire's base above her. The hospital shook, and she almost lost her footing. The tiger leaned into her, and she put a grateful hand on the beast's coat. Evanne's fingers told her it was thicker than it looked, and not as coarse as she expected. She patted the beast. "Thanks."

"No problem."

Evanne screamed, back-pedalled, and stumbled away from the tiger. She staggered into the roof's ledge, hooked her foot, and with a sickening lurch, fell gracelessly over the side. Evanne saw Hitch's outstretched arm as she passed the spectre, had time to marvel at the wall of ice—*yes, it looks like it's thinning out*—and think about how, because she was about to fall on her head from high up, she might actually die this time. *Go for the head. Well, if I land on my skull, that'll be it.*

At least I met a talking tiger before I died.

She stopped falling with a jerk. Her belt hitched her hip as something held the leg of her pants. Evanne swung above the ground, feeling the kiss of a spring breeze before looking up at her feet. Hitch looked over the edge, his blue smudge of a face glowing brighter than she'd ever seen. She had no time for that, because her gaze landed on the tiger, which held the hem of her pants in its mouth. The beast didn't look troubled by her weight, as if hanging a person from those massive jaws was what it did before taking a morning piss.

"Hi," Evanne said. "Did you just talk?"

Hitch glanced at the tiger, then to her. "Did you somehow hit your head on the side?"

She touched the back of her skull. "Not that I remember."

"How do you think the tiger's going to talk with a mouthful of your pants?" Hitch sighed, putting his head in a not-hand. "And if you tried to make her, she might let you go."

"Good point." Evanne curled up, but carefully, because even though the tiger looked like it could do this all day, if someone yanked a piece of leather Evanne had in her mouth she might let go. As she got closer to those golden eyes, Evanne saw the cat wasn't glaring, or angry. It looked *amused*. She got her fingers over the edge, and with only a modest amount of swearing managed to make the safety of the ledge. The cat let her go, licking lips and backing away. "Thanks."

"*No problem.*"

Same words. "Is that all you can say?"

"*No. I can recite Shakespeare backward, too.*" The cat's lips moved almost like a person's. Her voice was on the edge of a growl, but definitely a woman's, but one with a hard pipe habit. "*What? Never seen a talking cat before?*"

"Uh." Evanne stood, straightened her pants, and ran a hand through rust locks. "No. The Feybrind don't talk."

"*They got hands. We got voices and good looks. What can you do?*" The cat padded away, nosing the food box again. "*I smell emu. I like emu.*"

Evanne glanced at Hitch, then back to the tiger. "What the hell is an emu?"

"*Lunch,*" the tiger offered. "*You should get your friend from the Council, though. Think about hurrying.*"

Evanne sighed. *This day is unusual.* "Why's that?"

"*They have awoken after a millennia of slumber. They need to eat, just like the rest of us.*"

Evanne frowned. "I'm not going to schlep food all over the place for everyone who asks!"

"*You miss my meaning. The Council eats souls.*"

EVANNE RAN. SHE PUSHED HERSELF HARDER THAN SHE HAD BEFORE, limping heart trying to drag her heels, breath ragged. She bounced off a wall, ducked under a broken beam, and barely noted the jagged kiss of broken stone as it scraped the scales on her back.

Hitch beckoned, not-arms urging her on. "This way!"

She wanted to scream *I'm coming as fast as I can!* Evanne wanted to puke. But Tarragon was going to *die*, after eight hundred years in a cage, and all because Evanne brought her here in what, some kind of *quest?* Seeking a fucking *weapon?* Probably didn't even work anymore. Probably was a waste of time.

Aunt Barret isn't healing. It's not the weapon that pulled me here. Not really.

She lowered her head, barging through a closed door. Ancient timber shattered, dust and fragments spilling about her feet. In the room were three undead warriors. Evanne spotted the exit across the room, inconveniently behind the three monsters. *No time for a song. No time for hope.* She ran for it.

A creature that might have been a woman groaned, reaching for her. Outstretched arms hung with rotted, stringy meat. Evanne didn't bother dodging. She got in nice and close, tried not to breathe the stench, and slammed the best haymaker she could give into the woman's face. It felt like punching a rotted melon. The monster's head gave with her swing, Evanne's fist disappearing into the murky depths of a skull gone soft with age.

Those hands didn't stop grasping, and now rotted teeth *clacked* before her face. Evanne flexed her fingers inside its skull, found something hard, and pulled. Whatever it was didn't come free easily, but Evanne wasn't here to fuck about. She took a rotted claw swipe to the face, ignored the four burning lines as ancient fingernails scratched her, and kneed the monster in the gut.

It had little effect except to make Evanne feel better, like she was *doing* something. She stamped on the woman's leg, feeling the knee *pop* free, and then wrenched her hand from its skull with a burst of blackish fluids. She held a curve of metal, not much longer than her fist was wide, writhing tendrils questing from one end. They looked like living hair, so very fine, and as they felt the air, turned blind noses toward Evanne.

The undead woman dropped like a discarded sock puppet. Evanne tossed the hunk of metal aside, then gagged as another one got a rotted arm about her throat. A half-forgotten lesson, in her mother's hall: *Place your foot forward. No, Evie! Other foot. That's right. Hip back, and twist.* Her father, his massive bulk sailing over her shoulder.

Evanne placed her foot, twisted her hip, and *heaved*. The monster went over her shoulder, taking her guitar with it. The creature and instrument both bounced, one with the sound of dropped lemons, the other with a *bonk* as the ancient wood took a hit.

Her heart pounded, limped, pounded again. She swayed, light-headed. Gritted her teeth as blackness swam. "No. No! I will *not* go down!" And then beat harder, urgent, anger in her chest. The third monster leered broken teeth, so she punched them out. It felt like hitting a lump of clumped rice, not much resistance at all. Its jaw popped free, but that didn't slow it. Evanne shouted, dropped her shoulder into its chest, and rose with a savage uppercut.

Its head popped clean from its neck, bouncing and rolling away. The body swayed but didn't fall. Evanne glared, pacing about to the back, and grabbed ancient fabric as she lifted the thing by its jacket.

The one she'd tossed to the floor started to rise, the motions soupy, imprecise, so she yelled at it, then swung the body she held as a floppy makeshift bludgeon. They both went down in a tangle of limb slurry. Evanne stalked in, stamping down once, twice, a third time, and *one more for fucking luck*, feeling rotted bone give.

"Come on!" Hitch urged. "This way."

"A moment." Evanne spat bile as her stomach roiled. She crouched, rooting about in the remains of skulls for another two curves of metal. Tossed them aside. Stood, then sighed. "Rest, now. Rest, like you never could." Then grabbed her guitar.

The tiger looked cautiously around the doorway. "*Is it clear?*"

"What kind of tiger are you, anyway?" Evanne swatted sweat-slick hair from her face, then ran after Hitch. Shouldered through another door. Found a corridor, black and empty. Her Vhemin eyes saw nothing hot, made of bloody meat. She staggered forward, then put some curry in her steps. *No resting. Tarragon!* And on she went.

Her breath burned in her throat. Her chest felt like it would explode. Hitch, ahead. "This way. Evanne, you must hurry."

"I know that." But her legs didn't. Wobbly, because she'd never used them like this before. Hot, and tired, because the Half-Made's heart wasn't good for running, could barely do a fast walk for long stretches. "Come on, feet."

The tiger was at her side. Blunt head, fur soft under her hand. The cat nosed her upright. *"You don't smell lazy. Stop acting like it."*

Evanne coughed, clutched the neck of her guitar, and staggered upright. Onward. *What does lazy even smell like?* She didn't have the breath to spare.

She passed a door on her left, a crude circle painted on with a dot in the middle. *Khiton's Eye, if Mazin really was the god.* She remembered the sea captain drawing the picture for her. What had the merchant said?

When you find the weapon, look for this mark.

"Here," she wheezed.

"No time," Hitch said. "Come on."

"The god said." Evanne gulped air. *Am I making excuses for not running?* "He said to look for an eye."

The spectre rounded on her, jabbing a not-finger at her face. "He was an ornery salt dog who rammed his ship into a dock because he lacked competence at the helm. Tarragon is that way," his arm swung down the corridor, "and she needs you *now*."

And Evanne was running again, a single last backward glance at the door, then she put her head down and charged. Hitch ghosted at her side the pair making better time than Evanne had in her life. She burst into a big room—*by the Three, this room is huge!*—before taking in the sea of ghosts clustered about a door at the far end.

The room was dark, no surprises there, the ghosts shed soft luminance. Evanne skidded to a halt. "So *many* of them."

Hitch slowed his roll. "It's perplexing, I'll admit."

The big door had a look that said *certain death waits within*, so Evanne headed right for it. The ghosts clotted before her, and she waved them aside. All wore attire that was strange, forgotten, like the pair at the cottage on the verge of the plague lands. Their gazes were fixed on the door, but none reached a spectral arm out or tried to get inside. They just ... stood there.

A lot of them.

Evanne made the door, still breathing like a racehorse after thirty laps, and hammered her fist on it. "Open up, you sack of pickled dicks!"

Hitch leaned against the door. "You could try asking nicely."

"The tiger said they eat souls." Evanne slammed her fist on the dull metal again. *BOOM. BOOM.* She glanced about. "Where is she, anyway?"

"Avoiding having her soul eaten, I'd bet."

Evanne growled, then tried to get her fingers in the door's seam. She broke the tip off a fingernail, hissed, and yanked out her belt knife. She jammed it in the seam, wiggling the blade about. "Give, you bitch!"

The metal *pinged*, a piece of metal lashing her cheekbone before spinning into the clustered ghosts. Evanne held her broken knife before her eyes, then tossed it aside. "Hitch! What's happening in there?"

The ghost made to seep through the door, but bounced off. "I can't get in. There's a ward."

Evanne hammered her fist on the door, then froze, eyes wide. "A ward? That's *perfect*."

Hitch glanced at her. "You what now?"

"Hush a moment, spectre. I'm thinking."

"First time for everything."

Evanne ignored him, glancing at the ghosts behind her. A ward meant the Council were trying to protect themselves against whatever they warded. Slim hope for certain, but she'd take the offered thread and be thankful. She felt her limping heart slow, slicked sweat from her brow, and rounded on the ghosts. "You guys want to ... that's not it. You *need* to get inside, don't you?"

First one set of eyes, a man who looked at her with lost eyes set above a white smock. Another man at his side shifted his gaze to meet Evanne's. A woman was next, her hair done in an impossibly fantastic style, looping curls of what might once have been copper and bronze twined high above her head. On and on, a ripple growing in urgency, as each of the dead faced Evanne.

None spoke. They never did. *But that's okay*.

Evanne faced the door and put her palm against it. "Help me." She closed her eyes, trying for the Trick of it. The feeling inside her, where her crippled heart lay. *Tarragon is going to die. Eaten by the already-dead*. She pushed her hand against the door, leaning into it, trying by main strength to make the dead *feel*. "Help me!"

"I'm here." Hitch whispered into her ear. "What do you need?"

"I need you, Hitch. I need it all." Evanne gritted her teeth. "I need your pain. What killed you, and what anchors you here. And I need it all at once."

"Oh," Hitch said. "Is that all?"

And he surged into her. On his heels, a hundred more, a legion of the damned, and Evanne felt them all. The hungry dead, yearning for the light and what lay beyond it. The woman with the hair? She'd died by a Vhemin's blade. Sharp and cruel, it entered under her arm and found her heart. The white-smocked man? He'd carried a babe to the door, and turned to ash as a weapon of fire took them both. He remembered his eyes boiling in air made of fire, his sight gone, but not his hearing, because the child screamed before the end. That child was at his side, all her dreams now made of ash.

They came on, ever on, so many, those who'd died in this place of safety. An older man, a leader in war as people of his time accounted things, touched her soul. *War here was forbidden*, he said. *And it came anyway*. A last stand for Itikari's people, against a terrible host.

Evanne heard screaming, and realised it was *her*. Her throat was raw, her lungs empty, her heart barren, but they weren't done yet. From outside, she felt the dead surge across the sands, and through the fading Stormwall. Their urgency brought them to her side, *into* her, to be a *part* of what she needed.

Between one breath, and the next, she had it. Clenched in her fist, arm trembling with the terrible horror of it. Evanne gasped but didn't let go her anger or pain. She opened her eyes.

There was no one about her. The dead were gone. Inside her, and in her clenched fingers.

Do you see? Hitch's voice. *Do you feel what it is to die? To leave all undone?*

Evanne touched her face. It was wet. Of course it was wet. No one could take what she'd seen and be unmoved. *And I don't want to be unmoved. I want to move mountains.* But she needed one more. "Hitch." Her tortured throat croaked his name. "What took you?"

Love, of course.

Evanne saw, just for a moment, the man who'd killed him. A Vhemin monster, self-loathing in eyes gone flat and hard. She screamed, turned away from that final blow that killed her friend, and slammed her fist into the door.

The legion within her rushed free. They shattered the Council's wards like they were naught but spiderwebs. The door shuddered wide. Ancient air smelling of rot and decay pooled by her feet. Within, Tarragon lay on a raised platform. Ancient, hulking stones lay beyond. They were corroded, pitted as if a thousand storms had washed against them, despite being inside and sheltered from the elements. Evanne walked inside, seeing into the core of them. Spirits, intertwined. Locked, eternally damned.

She felt her lips twist into a smile. "I *see* you, motherfuckers." Evanne reached out, hooked her fingers into the stuff that made them up, and ... *pulled.*

The people that made up the Council were as mixed as flour and sugar in cake, but she'd have them out anyway. Tarragon, wilted, her glimmer barely there: that was the sight she needed. Evanne yanked on the shadows within the stones, pulling one out, setting pieces of soul free on the air. It was grim, brutal work, but as she tore the spirit stuff of the Council aside, the legion within her slipped out in their ones and twos. Before long there were twenty, then a hundred in the tiny chamber.

They lurched toward the terrible stones and began to feed.

I'm almost done. Evanne staggered, her heart stopping for a moment. She almost fell, almost fucking *died*, but there was Hitch. Always, Hitch. "Come on, Half-Made. Get on. Get out. Job's not done."

"*I'm* done, Hitch." She was on her hands and knees, no idea how she'd got there.

"A quitter is it?" He sneered. "I'd have expected even the human half of you to be better."

Her heart pounded once, then surged, and she stood, fist clenched. "I will knock you the fuck out!"

"Good," he urged. "But do it after you're out."

Evanne stamped toward Tarragon, floor shaking with her anger. She swept the fairy up, clutching her close, and left the dead to their feast. There was enough there for their frenzy for a time yet.

Chapter Thirty-One

When the Council gave Tarragon their demands, it all seemed so simple. *Give us everything*, and she had. She wanted to be done with everything that was hard. Worrying about her past. What she'd done, and to whom. Where she might go, and the person she might hurt next.

Someone like Evanne.

So, she'd fallen like a leaf on their dais and surrendered. There were so *many* of them in there, and they promised a future free of pain. A togetherness where all could share the burden of what a solitary entity had done wrong. No longer would it be a single badly made Builder that shouldered the load.

In exchange? The hospital would awaken. The failing Stormwall would rise again. The lightning tower that sought power from the Three would sparkle anew. And the invaders trying to breach said Stormwall would perish as they passed, or be struck from the earth by the tower.

All for the simple, easy transaction of a fairy's life. Bought and paid for, something you wouldn't even get a tarnished copper baron for. It was an *answer*.

And then: Evanne.

She'd struck on the door. Tarragon knew as she faded that it was her. And she wanted to yell out that there wasn't any room in here, no place for such a wonderful person, not on the dais, and not with Tarragon in the Council. They wouldn't appreciate those lavender eyes.

The Council agreed, because they saw something in Evanne that made them fear. Frightened like children at their first thunderstorm, cowering as the heavens cracked open. And, just like the heavens, the door sealing Tarragon inside slammed wide, and the maybe-Vhemin stood on the boundary between *there* and *please don't come here*, green light a nimbus around one raised fist, anger in her eyes, and oh *my*, but so many dead at her heel.

She'd strode to Tarragon's side, and her feet cracked the stone as she walked. Snatching the fairy from the dais, she'd retreated, and now here they were, outside, without any dead, and the Council tatters on the wind, the hungry dead gone to wherever they went when they'd finally whispered their goodbyes.

"She's not saying anything," Evanne said. Tarragon had a perfect view of the underside of her chin, cradled as she was in the crook of the maybe-Vhemin's arm. "She's so light, Hitch. It's like there's nothing left."

The spectre's face filled Tarragon's vision. It was marked and pitted as always, no sign of the face he once wore. "Give her a shake. Seems to work with babies."

"You'd be a terrible parent." Evanne ran one of her huge fingers down the side of Tarragon's head. Stroking her hair. "You're okay. You're okay now."

"What," Tarragon croaked, pushing Evanne's finger aside, "did you do?"

Blank incomprehension. Wide, startled eyes, violet in a way a snake's never could be. "I got you out."

"I wanted to be there." Tarragon looked away, turning her face into Evanne's chest. "I wanted it to end. Don't you understand? It's the only way you'll be safe."

"Huh," Hitch said. "Maybe she got hit on the head."

Tarragon felt movement as Evanne sought her feet. The fairy felt strength there, the Three-damned *ease* the maybe-Vhemin did everything with. She had a prime view of the room now she was higher up. The Council's chamber door was cracked wide, one door fallen free. The stones encasing their souls were cracked, escaping smoke seeking safety higher up.

And, right there, was a tiger. Tarragon screamed, startled upright, struggled for flight, and found her wings didn't work as she left Evanne's arms. She fell, right toward the floor, and then halted with a sickening lurch as Evanne snared her. Tarragon writhed, arm jabbing toward the tiger. "Tiger! Tiger!"

"It's all right," Evanne said. "We've come to an accord."

"*She feeds me, and I don't eat you.*" The tiger sat on her haunches, and if a tiger could smirk, she was doing that too.

"More like," Evanne put Tarragon on her shoulder, "she doesn't get sassy or she gets another fist of fives." She made a fist for emphasis.

"*Oh, please.*" The tiger yawned, showing a frightening array of teeth. Tarragon thought she might be able to fly inside that maw and right the way down without touching the sides. "*We are so past that. If I wanted you dead, I'd simply kill you in your sleep.*"

"That's comforting," Hitch said. "I don't know what's worse. A horror guardian, or one that's too frightened to fight a person head-on."

"*To be fair, you outnumber me.*" The tiger sighed. "*You have a fairy and a ghost, too. The ghost I can manage, but fairies bite.*"

Tarragon peered out from beneath Evanne's hair. "I've never seen a talking tiger."

"Aye?" Evanne tried to glance her way. It made her shoulder a rocky ride, so Tarragon gave rust locks a warning yank. "I thought you were from, you know. Back then. Before. Ancients. Miracles. Days of yore, where wonders were the stock in trade of every street corner hawker."

"My Manifest is missing," Tarragon admitted. "It's why I was better as fuel for the Council."

"*My Manifest is also missing,*" the tiger said. "*I don't even have a name. I think there are important instructions I need. Who to eat, and when. Perhaps, also, who not to eat.*" She paused, looking to the ceiling in thought. "*But then who would want to stop a tiger eating? No one sensible.*"

"We can fix the name thing." Evanne waved the problem aside. "What's a Manifest?"

"Back up," Hitch said. "Before this conversation gets too far off track, what did the fairy say before?"

Tarragon gave it some thought. "I've never seen a talking tiger."

"Before."

"Tiger, tiger?"

"No. Back a bit more."

"I don't want to talk about that," Tarragon said. "I just wanted it to stop being ... me."

"No, not the self-sacrificing heroics part." Hitch paced on invisible legs. "Something about safety."

"Oh, that." Tarragon looked down, letting Evanne's rust locks hide her.

"Yes, that." Hitch crossed ethereal arms. "Safe from what, exactly?"

"I don't know who they are," Tarragon said. "They're in Artifices."

"*That's my cue. I'm out.*" The tiger stood.

"Wait," Evanne said. "This might be important."

"Artifices." Hitch glanced at the wall as if he could see through it. "There are no Artifices here."

"Right." Tarragon nodded. "They're outside the Stormwall. They're trying to get in. The Stormwall will die in a half hour, maybe. And then they'll be here."

Evanne glanced at the ghost. They both spoke at the same time. "*The weapon.*"

WHICH WAS HOW TARRAGON TRIED TO HOLD ON AS EVANNE slammed her way toward the whatever-the-weapon-was. They passed through a room with fallen undead nightmares, which looked like someone had taken a stretch goal on compacting skulls into paste, and then out through another door.

The tiger loped at their side. Or, above their side. The tiger's shoulders were higher than Evanne's head, and it didn't look like Evanne's feeble attempt at running was giving it much trouble. If anything, the big cat had a slightly amused look as the maybe-Vhemin lumbered along, huffing like a bellows and making walking look like a struggle.

Evanne paused at an intersection. She leaned hands on her knees, breathing hard, which made Tarragon swing free on a rust lock. The fairy dangled before Evanne's eye line. "You should stand up straight. It helps you breathe better."

Evanne went almost cross-eyed trying to stare her down. "I shouldn't be running in the first place. Running is—"

"*For prey,*" the tiger suggested.

The maybe-Vhemin glanced at the giant cat. "I was going with, 'for suckers,' but whatever works."

"*Prey are suckers.*"

"Necessary part of the food chain," Hitch countered. "Look, stop dicking about. We need to go up to the weapon."

"I thought it was only your older memories that faded, but it seems you're going senile *and you're already dead.*" Evanne straightened, so Tarragon alighted on her shoulder again. "The room with the painted eye was on this level."

"We don't need a room with an eye. We need a room with a weapon."

"Same thing, innit?" Evanne squared her shoulders and headed off.

"Umm," Tarragon said. "The eye?"

"Mazin," Evanne said. "Or, the god. He *might* have been one of the Three. I give it maybe three percent chance."

"He was Khiton," Tarragon said. "I would know the Lord of Endings anywhere."

"*Even with a corrupted Manifest?*"

Tarragon glared at the tiger. "How about Clawdia? That sounds like a nice name. Or maybe Pawla."

"*Maybe we should have left you back with the Council.*"

"You weren't even there." Tarragon leaned into Evanne's hair and lowered her voice. "Thank you for getting me."

"You're welcome." Evanne made it sound like Tarragon wasn't very welcome at all, because Evanne had bigger things on her mind. She stopped short as Hitch shored up in front of her. "What now?"

"I will *not* let you squander your life." The ghost sniffed. "The weapon to end all wars is *above* us. The weapon you're heading toward is naught but a gaudy trinket."

Evanne sighed, rubbing her face and closing her eyes. "Let's do the sums. The maybe-a-god said his weapon was the shit. Not shit, but *the* shit. He was very specific. *Your* weapon, on the other hand, didn't actually end a war, and you died using it."

"Those are trifling points," Hitch insisted. "My weapon is better."

"Do you even know what your weapon is?"

"Do you know what the gods' device is?"

The tiger eyed Tarragon. *"Do they do this often?"*

"Like you wouldn't believe." Tarragon tugged Evanne's hair and ignored the maybe-Vhemin's *ow*. "Whatever you do, do it fast. We've got fifteen minutes. Tops."

"Right. God weapon it is." Evanne held her hand out to the side. "Hitch, if you wouldn't mind?"

"I forbid it." The spectre didn't budge.

"Suit yourself." Evanne stamped through the ghost. Tarragon felt a momentary touch of the grave as a chill got inside her glimmer, then they were through.

The ghost sped in front of them. "You must get the weapon. It's the only way."

"You're not the boss of me." Evanne kept stamping on.

After a few more twists and turns they arrived at a big old door with a painted eye. The paint was still clinging stubbornly to the metal, being sheltered as it was inside the hospital. Tarragon frowned. "That's a storeroom."

"A what?" Evanne glanced at her, then went to work on trying to open it.

"Storeroom. You put stuff in there. Like brooms."

"Food?"

"Sometimes," Tarragon allowed.

"I'll help." The tiger nosed Evanne aside like she weighed nothing at all. She bunted the door, which shook. Dust silted from the ceiling, but the door didn't open.

"Don't bring the place down." Tarragon eyed the ceiling. "I don't think they made this place tiger proof."

"*Nowhere is tiger proof. Hold my calls for a moment.*" The tiger padded to the left and right of the door, indecisive, then slammed into the wall on the right. Nothing happened, so the tiger did it again, and once more for luck. The wall cracked, then broke open. Dust billowed. Tarragon sneezed. Evanne coughed. The tiger sounded smug. "*One tiger door. Don't say I don't do anything for you.*"

Evanne stood, but Tarragon was faster off her perch this time. She flared a little glimmerdust in her wake as she sped through the opening. She let her glow out, the storeroom's shadows giving up their mystery in favour of familiar shapes. Some brooms, check. Shelves with mysterious-yet-aged boxes, check. A few things that looked like they might be field ration cases, which would make everyone happy, because the tiger would eat those instead of, say, a spare fairy.

The wall opposite the door had a storm shutter closed against the outside world. Tarragon flitted to it. "Open."

The shutter grizzled its way up with the grating of stone on stone. Light fell inside to play with the dust and motes. The Stormwall lay at the edge of the verdant field outside, but to Tarragon's eye it didn't seem quite so ... *cold*.

A crash and a cough announced Evanne's arrival. Tarragon turned, hovering as she trailed sparkle. "I don't know if they keep weapons here. Not ... there's nothing here but food." To emphasise, Tarragon flitted to the ration crates.

Evanne moved carefully through the storeroom, eyes wide with wonder at the sealed secrets of the ancients. She trailed a hand over a shelf, and Tarragon wished for a moment she was a Big, and that hand trailed over her arm. *Focus, Tarragon Greyflight. Now is not the time for fantasies*. She wished Helio were here. *He* had a Manifest. *He* would've been able to help the maybe-Vhemin.

"What's this?"

Tarragon jerked from her brief reverie. Evanne crouched by a trunk that looked like it would hold a good-sized watermelon. It had letters on the outside, which the maybe-Vhemin traced with her finger. "What language is this? I know the letters, but not what they mean."

Tarragon sidled over, bringing her light closer to the trunk. "It's not a language. It's a name." She landed on the trunk. At her feet, the letters memorialised: *MIREILLE.*

Evanne sighed. "I ... I think I should remember that." She frowned. "Hitch knew her."

"Knight Champion Mireille." The spectre drifted through the door, coming to lean against a shelf. "She was a good friend."

"You know what's in here?"

"I've got no idea." He sighed. "But I think it *is* a gods weapon. Mireille spoke with the Three. She was their strong arm on this world."

"Why did she leave it here, then?" Evanne glanced at the trunk. "If it's a gift from them, why didn't she use it against the demon horde?"

"Once you've seen a demon horde, you'll know a single weapon makes little difference." Hitch glanced away. "It takes courage. Strength of heart. Things I didn't possess. But she did. And she burned them on the pyre of our salvation."

"You saw it?"

"I was already dead," he spat. "Because I lacked courage."

Evanne touched the trunk, her fingers by Tarragon's feet. "How do we get it open?"

"There." Tarragon pointed with a toe. "The clasp lifts, and then ... that's it." She flitted free as Evanne opened the trunk. Within was black velvet cloth, on which rested perhaps the strangest-looking scattergun Tarragon had seen. "Umm. What is it?"

Evanne lifted it free, then clasped what was clearly a grip. "I think it's a scattergun." She pointed it, squinting one eye as she mock-aimed. True enough, there was a barrel of sorts, but unlike a scattergun's elegant design, this had a large chamber before the trigger and beneath the barrel. "I think it's a *big* scattergun."

"What need does a Three's Warden have of a fancy scattergun?" Tarragon leaped into the air, hovering before Evanne's eye line. "They have the Storm. And ... stuff."

"Sway," Hitch offered.

"Aye, aye," Evanne snapped. "I know it. I know it all! I heard for hours at Mama's knee. Smithsteel to keep them safe. The Light, to guide their steps. Keep them ever young, and bring destruction to their foes. The Sway and Storm, paired together, to create warriors to bend the dark and break it." The maybe-Vhemin's voice rose, her cheeks flushing. "Twenty-one hundred patterns. Taught by masters all, in the vaulted keeps they hid within. Hid, as the world broke, and left, and, and..." She crumpled, big scattergun clattering to the floor beside her. Evanne's shoulders shook as she sobbed, great wracking cries. "They're gone! They left, and just when they were needed, they weren't here!"

Tarragon looked down at Evanne. At how rust-red hair hid her face, but not her pain. Hands tangled in locks, back hunched, and even without the Manifest, she knew. *She misses her mother, but there's something more.* She drifted low, landing before Evanne's sprawled legs. "I think you've not cried for her. You've kept it inside, and here it is."

"Who?" Evanne rubbed her face. "Mama? She didn't want me anyway. Prayed to the Three for deliverance. Got me instead. Half-Made. Ill-Wrought. Untempered, no Smithsteel here!" She slapped her chest over her heart, voice dropping to a hiss, snake eyes a hard, sickly violet. "No pretty daughter to mirror her good looks. Ugly made, and ugly shown. Hidden in the desert, far from those she once knew. No skill of my own. Bad with a blade, because my heart is weak as the forging that made me. Oh *aye*, I've Papa's strength," she sneered, but Tarragon thought at herself, "but not. He fought hundreds one night. Hundreds, and didn't bend. I can't fight *four*."

Tarragon nodded, feeling Evanne's misery, a weight that settled atop them both like a blanket made of trash, threads of bile. "That's not what's bothering you."

Evanne startled, eyes widening, and the maybe-Vhemin leaned back. "Oh? Pray, Sandwich, what heavier weight do I carry?"

Tarragon ignored the barb. "You're angry at yourself, because you didn't cry, and you should have. You should have done it a long time back, but always there wasn't time. Then it wasn't the *right* time. Then there was a lot going on! You hit a tiger."

"*Is there any lunch in there?*" The tiger peered in the hole she'd made in the wall.

"Now's not a good time," Tarragon advised, making a shooing

motion. "You've fought the dead. Bested a Council. Walked with shades, and stalked the Stormwall. But your parents clutch at your soul. Their fingers tear your heart, and you wonder what kind of heartless monster couldn't shed tears when it counted. And then, *hic*, everyone watched. Even if no one watched—*hic*—it felt like they were. And so you got mad." She held up a hand as Evanne was about to speak. "I don't even mind. I'm mad, too. I'm mad because I might be working with the enemy. All my friends are dead. Literally no one I knew is still alive, and I don't know why that's fair, because I'm worthless. I'm a Builder who can't Build. A warrior without a sword." She rubbed her face, finding it wet. "But I'll fly with you. I'll fly to the end, if you'll have me. Because I don't think you're the enemy." She hiccuped again. "Also, you're wrong."

"If you two have *quite* finished," Hitch leaned forward, "we have a ... situation."

Evanne snarled, looking up at him. "Really? *Now?*"

"Really. Now." The spectre pointed to the window. "The Stormwall is down."

Ah. I got the timing wrong. Just one more thing I'm not good at. Tarragon caught sky, flitting to the window. Sure enough, the Stormwall was just slushy rain, good only for damaging paper. Through the murk lurched an Artifice. This one was as old as the rest, but still shiny enough. The pilot's canopy was a gleam of black. Twin fangs jutted from under a body that stood three stories above the grass.

A second stepped from the murk, metal head nosing about like a sick parody of a giant hound.

The tower trembled, and thunder boomed. Arc light leaped from above them, a brilliant flare of lightning. It touched the first Artifice, a tendril of raw gods' power. It savaged the ancient machine for two seconds, then silence fell.

Tarragon had covered her eyes with a hand. Her vision was spotted, and she blinked to clear it. On the grass, the Artifice still stood. *Impossible! The defences should have destroyed it.*

"Was something supposed to happen?" Evanne looked at the Artifices, then to Tarragon. "I don't see—"

The struck artifice exploded, shards of ancient clockwork sent in all directions. A great roiling ball of fire flared skyward, seeking the Three's benediction. The shockwave hammered the hospital, and Tarragon would've been thrown against the back wall by the force of it, were it not for Evanne.

The maybe-Vhemin caught her in one strong hand. Teeth bared in challenge, eyes fixed on the scene outside. *She didn't even think about it. Just caught me, and saved me.*

Even after what I said.

The remaining Artifice turned its metal snout above them, and those twin fangs flared, ember red, golden, then brilliant white. Twin streams lanced above them, and the hospital shook. A rain of stone fell before the window.

Another Artifice joined the other, then another. Three ancient machines challenged the hospital, and no answering flare of lightning came.

"What's wrong with it?" Evanne pointed. "Shouldn't there be more lightning?"

"We killed the Council," Tarragon said. "Nothing's left to muster a defence. They probably took out a remaining sentient vestige, and—"

"A sentiwhat what?" Evanne blinked.

"A ghost trapped in a machine," Hitch murmured. "Damned, to be bound inside a metal cage. Free now." He sounded wistful.

"Ah." Evanne backed away from the window. "New plan." She relaxed her fingers from around Tarragon, and the fairy fluttered free.

"Which is?" The spectre lounged against the wall.

"*Lunch?*"

"Still not a good time," Tarragon said.

"We get the weapon we came here for." Evanne glared at the window. "We get the weapon and get out of here."

"You don't want to destroy the Artifices?" Hitch sounded surprised.

"I couldn't give a shit about them." Evanne scooped up Mireille's scattergun. "I need the weapon, and I need to get medicine for Aunt Barret. These ancient devices can carve each other to dust for all I care. I've eyes on the living." She headed for the hole in the wall, gently pushing the tiger's head aside before slipping out.

"*No lunch, then.*" The tiger sounded sad.

Tarragon flitted after her, almost colliding with the maybe-Vhemin in the corridor outside. Evanne's eyes looked luminous in the gloom. "Wait. Wrong about which part?"

"Huh?" Tarragon bit her lip. "What do you mean?"

"Back in there. I had a rant, you didn't get upset. It was touching. Ballads will be written. All that." She rolled her eyes. "But you said I was wrong. Wrong about which part?"

"*Hic.*" Tarragon gave a tiny smile. "You're not ugly. You're the most beautiful thing I've ever seen."

Chapter Thirty-Two

Evanne didn't want this, whatever *this* was. Not the Artifices. Nor the halls filled with spectres—admittedly, those seemed to have gone elsewhere since she set them loose on the Council. She didn't need to think about the everliving rotted husks that roamed the halls. No time at all for a cowardly tiger.

And she didn't want to feel the weight of someone thinking she was *beautiful*.

Sure, sure, as she panted and huffed her way through an ancient place for fixing the sick, which also appeared to be a place that killed people, it buoyed her steps. She felt her weak heart flutter, warmth inside where she'd always been too cold-blooded to feel anything.

But it felt wrong, like a two-headed ox. *Tarragon* was beautiful, with her high cheekbones and enchanting eyes. *Tarragon* had a voice that sounded delicate like Evanne imagined the beauties in ballads would have. The fairy glowed, her skin not just lustrous but luminescent. And she could *fly*. It didn't matter to Evanne that Tarragon was the size of a pint of ale. *I think she is wonderful.*

And so, she hunted for the Trick of it. The barb within, perhaps a rejoinder for being called Sandwich all those times. For being kept prisoner, almost drowned, put in harm's way, taken away from what she knew, and to a place that wanted nothing but fairies sacrificed to emperors long dead.

It's not fair. It's not fair! Evanne scrubbed at her face, breath ragged, and knew she should be focusing on Hitch. The blue glow of the spectre beckoned her on, his voice insistent, concerned for her, feeling for her, despite him being all those many years dead.

But I can't. I want to be beautiful too, even if it's only a lie. To accept the Trick? To discard? *Is it even a Trick? I should know.*

Evanne stopped, panting, and was knocked into a wall by the tiger. "*Sorry.*"

"Watch it," Evanne growled. But she didn't put her heart into it. The tiger was another misshapen thing, a relic from a time of wonders, but all the magic was gone. "We need to solve one thing."

"*Lunch?*"

"Your name," Evanne said. "I can call you 'tiger', but it feels generic. Out of place, for a heirloom of the ancients. A wonder," her hand went out to Tarragon, and she didn't remember *telling* it to, "of the old world. Something that deserves a title, and a purpose, as do we all. Hear me, tiger. We are all of us lost souls, bound together in common purpose—"

"*We all want lunch?*"

"A common purpose to overthrow the evil, create justice for the weak, and stand on this world that is *ours* as it is everyone else's." *There. That didn't sound half-bad.* "Also, we will find lunch. I'm hungry, too."

The tiger sat on her haunches. "*The weak are delicious.*"

"I'm not getting through." Evanne rubbed her face. "This felt easier inside my head. In that version, you nodded and agreed."

"I'm not a wonder," Tarragon said. "I'm—"

"Will you stop fucking about?" Hitch stepped from a wall. "They are getting out of the Artifice."

"Who?" Evanne straightened, sucking air.

"*Pakhet,*" the tiger said. "*My name is Pakhet.*"

"Cool story," Evanne said, turning away from the tiger. "*Who* is getting out of the Artifice?"

"*Pakhet is a good name,*" Pakhet urged. "*I chose it myself.*"

"Goddess of war?" Tarragon sniffed. "You can't even take a punch."

"*It also means*," the tiger stretched, bunching claws to *scritch* against the eternal floor, "*she who scratches.*"

"Three's mercy," Hitch breathed. "We're all going to die."

"You're already dead," Evanne said. "How can you die again?"

The spectre looked at the ceiling. "Can you send someone competent next time?"

Evanne glanced upward. "Who are you talking to?"

"No one. Not anymore. Not for a long time, I think." The ghost hitched his not-pants. "Shall we get on?"

"We shall." Evanne *hmm'd*. "Who is getting out of the Artifice?"

"Everyone, I think." Hitch sighed. "Everyone who ever mattered."

It was many stairs up. Evanne didn't like stairs. Never had; they seemed to be hard on everyone, but a special sort of torture for her, whose heart wasn't in the most basic of tasks. These stairs were well made, smooth, unbroken by time, an oddity in this place of broken dreams. They smelled dusty, but not rotted. Climbing them gave her time to think about what Hitch said. About whom he named, and what it meant.

Barret, he started with. *She looks bad*. He'd done her the courtesy of sparing her the details but not the impact. *Morgan and Heser the Cheg.*

They'd stared at each other, long and hard. Then he'd said, *And Cleo, of course.*

So, Evanne straightened her belt, slicked back grubby hair, and headed up. Toward the weapon, and its promise of salvation.

There was one name Hitch hadn't mentioned. *Sight of Day*. The Feybrind wasn't with the invaders. Cleo seemed to lead their band, the young woman issuing commands like a sergeant, if Hitch were to be believed. Barret was trussed like a hog, her wounds still grievous, but the enemy knew her kind. A feral Vhemin that just didn't have *time* for being hurt.

I want to be like her. Evanne paused for breath on the stairs. *I want to save her.*

This is very complicated.

Uncle Day's absence grated at her. If he wasn't there, did it mean he was dead, or had he escaped? And if he was alive, why had he stayed away when the rest were taken here? *I think he is dead. I think I killed another wonder by leaving in the night.*

So, Evanne climbed, a tiny penance for the sins she'd committed. *I can't think about it. I can't think about him. His golden eyes, his soft fur, his gentle ways. I can't think about how I made that stop.*

One step. Another. Boots scraping on old stone. The hiss of her breath through not-sharp-enough teeth.

"Here," Hitch murmured. He'd been softer-spoken since saying who was, and wasn't, with Cleo. *He knows who is precious to me. He, best of all.* "This door."

He'd shored up by a door on a landing. It was like other doors they'd passed, although this one was neighbours with a large pot. The pot held a still-living tree with large, round fruit. Evanne ignored the door for a moment, because going through there meant she would have to do something, and she didn't want to. *There's a lot going on.* She plucked a fruit. It was the size of a small child's head, with soft, golden skin. She rubbed it with her hand, feeling the smoothness of it. Sniffed. *Sweet.* She bit, and marvel of marvels, fruit of a tree eight hundred years old was still good, the flesh delicate. Juice dribbled down her chin. She rubbed it away on the back of her arm. "It tastes like honey pork."

Tarragon landed on her forearm, stalked to the fruit, and leaned forward, wings fluttering for balance, and took a tiny bite. "Melon."

Pakhet sidled up, swiping the tree, and tearing half of it away. She rooted through the branches, coming up chewing. *"Bison."*

"Yes, yes." Hitch sounded irritable. "It tastes of what you need it to be. All the body's wants in one globe. By all means, let's fuck about some more. Eat candy and daydream, while the enemy climbs ever higher. Soon enough, it won't matter anymore, because they'll be here and have the weapon."

"Don't be daft," Evanne slurped a mouthful of sweet salty. "They were klicks away. They have to get through," she waved her hand, "everything."

"The guardian tigers?" Hitch pointed his chin at Pakhet, who was batting a fruit across the landing. "Or the everliving dead, who you've punch-driven into somnolence?"

"Ah," Evanne said. "I don't think I got them all."

"You made all the stray ghosts leave," Tarragon said.

"Not helping," Evanne hissed. "Besides. They weren't here for us. They were here because evil people chained them here and they needed to leave."

The fairy landed on her shoulder, using ropes of hair for an anchor. "I'm not arguing. You did a good thing. The *right* thing. But they would have been good in a fight."

Evanne raised her eyebrow. "Ghosts can't fight. Hitch is barely competent with words, and if he swung a punch—"

"I'm just *fine* with words, thanks very much. They're," he pawed the air, and she imagined fingers reaching, "word-ish."

"My point," Evanne nodded. "So they can't do anything useful."

"You're not asking them right," Tarragon said. "You're the necro-mancer. Necromance!"

"I'm a bard. I hold no truck with the dead."

"*You sing and have a sweet voice with it. But that is learned, like walking or talking. The dead cluster about you. They bring you their cares and fears. The things they couldn't put down after lives were cut short.*" Pakhet yawned teeth the size of knives. "*You are a necromancer. I smell it on you. The wind whispers it. The sun knows it. Why don't you?*"

Evanne gave that some thought. "You all suck."

"The door," Hitch urged. "We must hurry."

"I said they'll be a while," Evanne countered.

From below, a sound like a scuffed step, old leather on older stone. Evanne froze, fruit halfway to her lips. Hitch held his hand up, and although he had no fingers left, she imagined him pressing his index finger to his lips. *Hush.* The spectre leaned over the side of the landing. "I think they're almost here."

Evanne gritted her teeth. She wanted to shout, but unlike Hitch, the living would hear her words. Handspeak, then. *{How do these things keep happening?}*

"It's because you're young," Hitch said. "You don't know shit, and don't listen."

{I know enough to still be alive.}

"Ha ha," he said. "Now, get inside."

Evanne felt about the door's handle for an obvious way of opening it. None appeared to present itself. The jamb was smooth, a slim seam about it. An ancient panel of metal was set in the door. On a whim, she put her hand against it.

The door *clicked*, and with a gasp of dust, cracked open. Evanne covered her mouth, trying not to cough, and shouldered her way inside. She made it five paces, Tarragon hanging onto her hair, the tiger on her heels, before, she stopped dead.

"Three's mercy," she whispered. "What happened here?"

"Let me show you," Hitch said, and slid into her. "I finally remember how I died."

Chapter Thirty-Three

Hitch blasted across the heavens. The weapon held him, kept him going even through his injury, just as it suckled on his life, water down a drain.

There was plenty more where that came from. The sickness they'd given him made it so.

//THERE.// Rulbenen led on tireless wings, the dragon angrier than Hitch had ever seen him. His midnight scales were marred from battle, but like all his kind, he didn't seem to care. *//THE VILLAIN IS INSIDE.//*

The weapon let Hitch know what the dragon saw. The hospital held its silver spire into the heavens, reaching for the Three's power. Within the lower levels, a vaulted room held a summoning chamber. A gateway to the demon realm.

"He means to sacrifice Mireille," Hitch breathed.

//IF YOU HADN'T...// The dragon glared as they flew, but his words died on an ember grin.

If I hadn't let Cobalt get away. "I know."

//YOU WERE NOT TO KNOW HE COULD USE THE POWER OF THE THREE.//

"I should've known he wouldn't try to box with me." Hitch had tried to take Cobalt one on one, but his lover had used a wand. A tiny sliver of twisted wood that glimmered with Light, and Hitch had frozen. To be fair, so had Rulbenen. The two had strained as Cobalt dragged unconscious Mireille away. They'd tracked him to the hospital, and its gate. "What if he does it again?"

//THEN WE FOLLOW AGAIN.// The dragon roared, flames scarring the heavens. *//AND AGAIN, UNTIL WE RUN OUT OF SKY, AND THE WORLD RUNS OUT OF TIME, THE SUN GROWS DARK, AND ALL HUMANS FADE. HE HAS MY MIREILLE.//*

He has something of mine, too. Hitch felt the ache in his chest, right where his heart was. Where he'd placed his trust, dared dream the impossible could be real. *Even in an age of wonders, we still face the impossible.*

The hospital approached faster than thought, an edifice of protection for those within. *If you wanted to run and stay safe, this would be the place.* It was Itikari, built to protect the sick and injured, and Rulbenen didn't *care.* The dragon accelerated, and Hitch's weapon struggled to keep pace with the creature's anger. At the last, Rulbenen spread his wings, flipping legs forward, claws out, and smashed through the side of the building.

Fragments of stone fell, silting like sand, but it was an error of perspective. *Those are huge rocks.* The spire above trembled, lightning crackled, and the heavens shuddered. The hospital sensed the attack, its Council confused, because dragons were on *their* side. They threw up defences, the restless in the morgue called upon, the Stormwall rising into place on Hitch's heels.

Within the breach, dragonfire flickered. Hitch saw blue-white lancelight, heard Rulbenen's roar, and more fire. *In there. Do something.* He spread his arms, braking as he entered, dust wash swirling.

Cobalt stood at one end of the room, an actinic lance in one arm. Hitch remembered the strength of those arms, how they'd held him at night. The other arm held Mireille as a shield. Behind the Vhemin was a Gate. Runes rimed the surface, glittering purple, the surface starting to collapse into a portal to the demon's plane.

The Vhemin's grip on the actinic lance was slicked with blood. His people were shamans, and opening the gate needed a blood sacrifice.

They'd been built to give blood, over and over, and Hitch had no doubt Cobalt could keep the Gate open for as long as needed. A single demon lord would be too much. A legion of the enemy would be their undoing.

That's not what he's going to do. When the demons get here, Mireille will be the sacrifice. A Three's Warden, a mighty gift of starlight tossed into the void, lost to us. That tiny cut on Cobalt's palm is naught but a taste.

The dragon bellowed, pacing in futile anger. *He can't kill Cobalt because he will hurt Mireille. Mireille will be taken into the demon realm. She is our last, great hope. The best Knight Champion, and about to be sacrificed.*

I must kill the man I love.

Cobalt's eyes widened as he saw Hitch, the actinic lance coming to bear on him. The rifle trembled, then swung back to Rulbenen. Hitch ran, the weapon pushing his steps, lifting him, and he landed before the dragon. "Cobalt! Stop!"

The Vhemin gave a shark-toothed grin. "The Gate opens. There is no stopping it." His voice caught, that gravelly growl snaring like a cripple's step. "Not anymore."

//HE HAS NO WAND.// The dragon sounded pleased. *//I FEEL A LESSON IS IN ORDER.//*

"Be still, lizard." Cobalt shook Mireille for emphasis. "There will be a lesson. About power, about who rules and what is right, but it's not you who'll be doing the teaching."

"Please," Hitch pleaded. "It doesn't need to be like this."

"It does," the Vhemin rumbled. "It has always been like this. You've never seen it. Felt it. *Lived* it."

Hitch looked for an escape, an angle, anything he could use. The Gate snapped like a sail, the wall behind Cobalt sagging into blackness. Runes flared purple. The weapon about Hitch trembled, and it spoke to him. "Material threat detected. Luminal breach must be aborted. Target acquired."

"No," Hitch said.

"Material threat—"

"I heard you!"

Cobalt tried for a grin, but it died. There was too much between them. "Not much time now, lover."

//HITCH!//

"I know!" He turned to the dragon, meaning to hold the beast back, and Cobalt fired. The actinic lance carved air, bright and angry. The weapon flared, the thaumaturge's magic suckling on Hitch's body, a shimmering shield of golden yellow curving between him and Cobalt. The drain after the flight was too much, and Hitch screamed.

Rulbenen made to push forward, but Hitch didn't move. He held a trembling hand up, feeling the weapon *feed*, his body giving what it could, and then what it couldn't.

He tried to hold back the weapon's response, but it was designed to fight when its pilot couldn't. Thaumaturgy held and was joined by evocation. The orbs at his waist detached, orbiting around him, then spat at Cobalt. Precise as a Fey Branded's arrow, all five went through the monster's arm. Blood sprayed, and Cobalt screamed.

Behind him, a demon's head appeared through the Gate. It wore a crown of bones, eyes of blood leaking rivers down its face. It put a foot on the floor, and the spire above shook, the boom of thunder arriving with the lightning. But the Council couldn't get their defences in here. Not to the gate, or the demon at their heart, and not in time.

Rulbenen roared flame, the demon holding a hand up under the torrent, and then it was in, smoke trailing from limbs so thin they looked like bones. It grinned as another tried to shoulder through the breach behind it.

The dragon can't beat them.

The weapon lurched, retrieving the orbs, and Hitch's heart stopped under the load. It shocked him, evocation shuddering through his chest, then drank more from his empty cup. Golden orbs spat through the air, peppering the first demon, the fifth shattering a piece of bone from its grisly crown.

It wouldn't be enough. Cobalt turned, ragged stump shedding blood, Mireille held like a doll. Hitch staggered forward, and his leg snapped. He screamed, but the weapon wouldn't let him quit. It knew what he wanted, and it urged him forward. His other leg was gone, nothing left, his hand outstretched.

It needs a sacrifice.

He gave a last surge, his sight failing. Hitch pushed his body. The armour whispered in his ear. Calm, and certain, in all the ways he wasn't. "I know what you need. I will see it done."

Hitch staggered into a sightless run, hitting a huge body—*Cobalt*. He shoved his lover backward, the Vhemin falling into the demon gate. The weapon *clicked*, and the Gate snapped shut. Hitch collapsed, face burning, and he tried to remove his helmet, but he had no fingers.

There's nothing left.

A shaft of agony speared his chest, piercing the weapon. It had nothing left to shield him, or itself.

It was enough. He was free.

Chapter Thirty-Four

Tarragon wasn't okay. Not at all. Point one: she had no sword. Point two: the maybe-Vhemin was like a pole-axed steer, except she hadn't toppled. Just *stood* there, dumbstruck, hand halfway up in a *no, wait* gesture, but the ghost was in her and they were having a moment.

She felt the flicker of jealousy and almost laughed at herself. *There's no time for that.*

Three: the tiger had gone. No clue where, it wasn't like there were a lot of places here that could hide a tiger the size of a Clydesdale, but there it was. Pakhet was as silent as she was cowardly, showing no interest in helping them out with a pack of invaders. *Perhaps she's found a giant ball of yarn.* Whatever, she wasn't here.

Speaking of *here*, the room was immense. It was bigger on the inside than the outside, which was a standard trick fairies of her time used to economise on real estate. The curious thing was it hadn't collapsed along with everything else in this Three-forsaken land. Some quirk of the Build kept it going strong enough to hold the walls and roof up.

There was rubble strewn across the ground, stretching from a massive hole in the wall that looked about the size you'd fly an Artifice through. Tarragon squinted, framing the breach with her hands. *Or a dragon. Could be a dragon.* It wasn't a regularly-sized hole, and it wasn't hard to imagine how a dragon's wings might've smashed *there* and *also there* to let one of the bigger beasts in. *It must have been a huge dragon.* She remembered their wings against the sky, their battle against Vehement Systems blazing a trail above as Fey Branded died below, and then she shivered, hugged herself, and focused on what else was here.

There will never be a time of such wonders again.

The far wall held a summoning ring. Tarragon knew what they were, and had a layfairy's view on how they worked, but didn't know the ritualist tricks that caused the circles to sink into another place, to extend a hand onto the realm of other, and pull whatever it found here. Purple runes still glittered around the Gate, evidence of a big sacrifice last time it was opened. That kind of magic didn't come in a bottle. It came from the heart, usually through loss of someone close enough you'd welcome your death instead. Although, the type that sacrificed their family to demons weren't usually big on hugs and cuddles.

Curious, and a waste of time. There are no summoners here, so it will remain quiet.

Still, it added to Tarragon's not-okayness, because the gate could be coaxed into life without too much effort, and if that happened, the shitstorm on the other side would walk over here and no fairy would be safe.

That accounted for the two largest things in the room, but a few smaller things drew Tarragon's eye. There was an old suit of armour on the ground, the body on its knees, back arched, the breastplate pierced by something that could've been a lance. The ground behind the body was patchy with an old brown stain and what could have been, in the right light, pieces of bone. She flitted over, glimmerdust trailing in her wake, to look at the armour. It wasn't anything she knew from the Builder recipes. Sure, she'd failed her exams, but she knew what they *looked* like.

The faceplate was still intact, a shiny curve of reflective material that she could see herself in, stretched in funhouse proportions. She hovered close, eyes widening as she saw her reflection. *Worn thin. Hollow eyes, despite my glow. My wings don't have their lustre.* She glanced at

Evanne. *Will she want someone so tired? She is full of life. She is what I wish I was like.*

Tarragon made a face, and her reflection made it right back. That done, she flew to the rear of the suit. The back of the armour held a thing that looked like a slim metal backpack. Ruined by the piercing, of course, so it wouldn't work. Old-style lettering glittered. *ITIKARI STARLIGHT DRIVE.*

She pursed her lips. *I've never heard of an Itikari Starlight Drive so small.* Something experimental? Was *this* the stupid weapon Hitch kept on about?

If it was, they were super boned, because it was broken. Helio could have fixed it, but Helio was dust and memory, all his Build knowledge lost to time. Tarragon couldn't fix a ruler, so: *This is outside my area of expertise.*

I know swords. That's my thing.

Of course, no one had left a handy sword laying about. She hovered above the helmet, looking for a way in. There was a cunning array of clasps and fastenings a Big couldn't have managed with their clumsy fingers, but she didn't even need any tools for this one. She cozied up to the back of the helmet, reached her arm into a socket, found the mounting turnkey, and turned it. Nothing happened.

I see my mistake. There were a couple other sockets, so she fussed with those two, and was rewarded with a *hiss* followed by a *click.*

The helmet snapped open at the back, then rolled down the arched figure to land on the floor. It exposed a skull, but there was something wrong with it. Tarragon had seen a skull or two back in her day, and they didn't look like this! The back of this person's head was ... *chewed,* as if by acid.

She buzzed around the front to get a good look at the occupant's face. Tarragon expected a grinning death's head, eyeless sockets gazing at her, but she got slightly less than that. The person in this armour looked melted, the bones of their face softened up before time laid fingers on them. No teeth, for a start. The mouth had eroded unto the nose, the eyes after that. She tipped her head sideways trying to imagine what this Big must have looked like before whatever got into his armour melted him alive.

No face. No eyes, or nose. Lips, gone, and no teeth to smile with.

It was a human Big, no mistake. The Vhemin were a horror show of mixed ancestry, and the Feybrind looked like the cats they were. This was just a big ol' melted monkey.

She huffed, because it was a mystery that would have to keep until they survived the invaders' swarm. Tarragon didn't know how many there were, or whether they had swords, perhaps even a tiny one she could steal.

I hope Evanne wakes up before they get here. She's the one with the Big fists.

Pakhet would do in a pinch. The cat had all the courage of luke-warm tea, but you couldn't tell that by looking at her. She was larger than a horse, and those big teeth would make a person pause. *Except, not Evanne. She didn't pause.*

Is she stupid or brave?

Tarragon flew to the Gate, flitting a circuit about the ring. It was wide enough to drive a cart through, if demons had wagons they wanted to bring to this world. The rock face was smooth, and as cool as you'd hope. No signs of life, aside from the residual glow of the runes. A quick blood sacrifice would set it running again, but you'd need a Big for that. A fairy didn't have enough joules to get it excited enough.

Besides, the magic to open Gates had been lost. It wasn't well understood in Tarragon's time. Hedge wizards and mock witches thought they had answers enough, but it was the Vhemin who cracked it. She felt a mocking smile touch her lips. *Their one 'gift' to the rest of us. "Here's a doorway to a world of terror. You're welcome."*

It didn't fit right. She couldn't imagine Aunt Barret thinking like that. *Did something change the Vhemin? Did eight hundred years make them stronger, or weaker?*

A ragged wheeze drew her about in a spray of glitter. Evanne stumbled, hand over heart, face stretched with pain. "Hitch."

"He's not here," Tarragon said. "I thought he was with you."

"He's not with me," she said. "Not..." Evanne trailed off as she took in the armour. The maybe-Vhemin walked about the fallen form, and Tarragon saw her eyes take it in. The pierced chest plate was most obvious, but curiously Evanne didn't pause at the important *Itikari*

Starlight Drive, if she even noticed it. Her steps slowed as she reached the front of the form, and then she crouched. She reached a hand out to touch the melted skull before her. "Oh, Hitch. I see you. I *see* you."

"Wait, what?" Tarragon flitted to her, perching on Evanne's shoulder. "*This* is... was... Hitch?"

Evanne gave a sad nod. "He has no face. No hands neither. Help me with this." Together, they worked a gauntlet off the form. Sure enough, the body's arms ended in chewed nubs, no hands inside the suit. "What would do this to a man? He was in such pain before he died, but he couldn't see. *I* couldn't see what killed him."

"Does it matter?" The voice was mocking, the tone commanding. Tarragon looked up, past Hitch's body, to the doorway. There, flanked by many Bigs, was Cleo. "Dead is dead."

Chapter Thirty-Five

Evanne pressed a hand to her chest, struggling to breathe. She felt like she hadn't sucked air in hours... or was it centuries? She tried to forget Hitch, to step away from what he'd shown her, and what the sad corpse in the room meant.

It wasn't working. Her heart was *his*, pierced by a demon's anger, and for all they called her necromancer, she was struggling with the shackles of death like one new to it. *As if I don't know all its forms. I've seen the drowned, the burned, the crushed. The betrayed, the forgotten, the forsaken.*

Mama. Papa. I haven't forgotten you. I promise.

"Oh?" She could imagine Vertiline's raised eyebrow, a not-quite-smile at her mother's lips. *"You forgot not just us, but what I taught you as well."*

What was that first lesson? Was it that silly thing about—

A tide of memory surged over her.

"Evanne, how will you fight if you can't breathe?" Vertiline stood, arms crossed, face calm, as Evanne stumbled through the first of Cophine's patterns. She'd held her breath, concentrating on making her shoddy footwork suck a little less, and now her mouth was gaping like a landed flounder.

Not a good teacher then, and perhaps not now, Vertiline was still the master of all the Three's patterns. She tried to help a forgetful, wilful, *weak* girl through what she knew, and Evanne didn't have the wit to listen. But she remembered that first lesson. *Breathe. Just ... breathe.*

With a ragged gasp and cry, she tore air from the world, sucked it in, and then coughed.

The past moments filtered back in. Some fucker did something, right? Evanne whirled. There, right fucking *there*, Cleo stood, one hand on hip, the other holding a fancy device that Tarragon could surely name. One of the ancients' light weapons, perhaps. She was flanked by a host of misfits. Evanne glanced over humans, a couple Vhemin, and five Feybrind, but she had eyes only for three.

Aunt Barret. Uncle Heser. And the Raven Queen.

The journey had not been kind to any of them. Barret slumped in the arms of her captors, useless legs dangling like meat on hooks beneath her. But her eyes. *Oh my. She is so angry.* Heser the Cheg was standing, but bloody, battered, his face showing an ungentle time. Heser's right arm dangling limp, crooked, swollen at the wrist. *Broken.* But he still struggled in the grip of a Feybrind pair, as if he held the Vhemin's immunity to pain.

But Morgan: there was a picture. She stood, every inch a queen, the shackles at hands and feet and bruised, swollen left eye worn like jewels of state. Lips, bloody and cut. But chin up, that one remaining eye glaring, hard, a burning coal of spite.

Cleo saw how Evanne ignored her and wrestled her attention back. "The journey has been ... difficult."

"Go fuck yourself." Evanne glanced around, trying to see one she hoped snuck here, but couldn't see Uncle Day. Barret caught her eye, the tiniest shake of the head. Evanne knew the Trick of it, how it didn't mean *lost and fallen* but rather *don't ask, because they don't know about him.* Sight of Day wasn't here, but he hadn't been killed in Barret's sight.

"You were never good at your lessons. Handed all, on a platter. Given reach to the Light of the Three themselves, but you tossed it aside for a set of broken strings and a wilful manner." Cleo's mocking smile dimmed, her face turning darker. She lashed out, hair licking her face, and landed a punch into Barret's head.

The matriarch took it, nowhere else to go really, spat a tooth, and said, "You punch like a child." Cleo spun, kicking Barret in the gut, but the old woman didn't even flinch. "I can't feel anything below my tits, you useless cunt."

"But you remember," Cleo seethed. "What if we cut off your toes while you watch? They say it's worse than the pain."

"I doubt it," Barret growled. "I think pain is worse than the thought of losing a few toes I'll grow back anyway. Plenty more where they came from. Your miserable mewling kind might care more. Try the Queensguard. Although your work on his arm didn't slow him much. Might have more balls than I thought."

Morgan's chin lifted a little higher, the tiniest quirk of her lips showing she liked how this conversation was going. The Raven Queen said nothing, and Evanne sensed a Trick of a sort there. *Say nothing until you must. Let the enemy do the hard work for you.*

Cleo looked like she wanted a little more action but gathered calm like most people broke kindling. Piece by piece, with angry jerks. "Plenty of time for that later. Evanne." Her voice was honeydew sweet. "I find myself in need of your assistance."

"Why would I do anything for you?" Evanne heard the incredulity in her words.

"Beside me having hostages against your parole?" Cleo pursed lips Evanne once wanted to taste. "I don't think you know how this works." She gestured, and her people manhandled Evanne's family further into the room. "We serve a man who was once kind, but the world has broken like so many others. A few join our quest. Mostly Feybrind, those so abused by the rest they can stand it no more. The odd Vhemin, their strength welcome enough, but their loyalty always questionable."

One of the Vhemin growled. "Watch it."

"Like I said." Cleo shrugged. "Humans aplenty. Those of us who've seen what the relics of the ancients in the wrong hands will do. We are putting an end to it. Tearing down the powers, righting the wrongs—"

"What wrongs have you seen?" Evanne frowned as she tried to face everyone at once, wanting no one at her back. *Well, try the breach.* She paced backward to the hole Rulbenen had smashed into the chamber. *Unless they have a collection of very good climbers, no one will come this way.* "You lived in peace with us. Imshir was your home! You were loved, had parents, a *family*—"

"I had a lie." Cleo glared, but Evanne sensed it wasn't at her, but the world in general. "Those you knew as my parents were part of our band. All lost someone. My real kin died in the battle of Ravenswall. I was but a babe, born poor, but loved for the briefest moment. I was swept aboard a refugee ship bound for Tebrani. Then there was a dragon, a Knight, the legion of demons, and Imshir died. I was lucky enough to find a new calling. A group who will stop it all." A sneer, as she walked the room, scribing an arc toward the gate.

"Oh aye, led by a wizard of power in a tower of gold no doubt." Evanne gave a mock bow. "You kowtow to those above still, and bring down those who are good. Merle did naught to you but—"

"But be your friend," Cleo hissed. "You're an abomination. A cast-off memory, a mistake of a bygone time. But you can give me one thing." Her band had drawn closer to the Gate.

Evanne snorted. She reached for the Trick that Barret might have used. "If you were freezing, I wouldn't give you the steam off my shit to warm your hands." *Good enough.*

Cleo didn't reply, perhaps because her head was so far up her ass she didn't hear it. She strode—more of a flounce, really—past Evanne's eye line, making the purple-runed wall. "You don't need to give a shit." Ah, she *had* heard. "You just need to keep breathing a few more moments. After that, you can stop."

That doesn't sound good. Evanne looked about for an option, some way to deal with Cleo and her band, but Barret—always the strong one, stronger ever than Evanne—was dragged between two massive brutes. Heser the Cheg looked like he wanted to start the party but lacked a good bard, and here was Evanne without a tuned guitar. Morgan looked like all she could start was a war of words, and they were beyond diplomacy or bargains.

Sight of Day. Where are you? Evanne sucked air through not-quite-sharp-enough teeth. *I left him. I left them all, and didn't even find a cure for Barret.*

Cleo stopped at the runed gate, beckoning without looking. Evanne was surprised when a human sucker-punched Heser the Cheg in the side of the head, knocking the man prone, then grabbed the Raven Queen and dragged her forward. Morgan hissed and spat like a cat, but she wasn't war trained. It was like watching the wind argue with a mountain. The man threw Morgan to the floor near the gate.

Cleo bent, tipping Morgan's chin toward her. "All your power, and yet you sit at the feet of the rabble."

"You call yourself that. Not me." Morgan's chin lifted further of its own accord. "You wear the cloak well enough, though."

Cleo let her hand fall from Morgan's chin, then faced Evanne. "What I want from you is to stand right there, and do nothing." She paced around Morgan, nodded, then let her weapon dangle by its sling as she rummaged in the satchel at her hip. A few moments' effort produced a small brush and a glass jar of an oily black liquid. She held these aloft for a moment, then smiled. "The world will be undone by the stroke of a brush."

"What's in the jar?" Evanne wondered if it was some horror creature, like the ooze that lived in the pools below. She Tricked her voice into being firm. "If you think to torture us—"

"No need for that." Cleo uncapped the jar. "This is paint."

Evanne blinked. "You what?"

"Exactly." Cleo walked around the Raven Queen, dipping the brush into the might-be-just-paint and scribing on the ground. Evanne couldn't see what she scribed on the floor. "This is the work of but a moment, but learning the knowledge was as difficult as learning the Tresward's patterns. Alas, I couldn't master them. The Light doesn't answer my call, but I'm a fair swordswoman despite that. These runes need someone of true power, and although I know the letters like my own face, I have no power. No majesty, no kingdom, no sorcery." She completed her circuit of Morgan, stood, and beamed. "That's why you're here. Both of you."

Morgan snorted, somehow looking loftily from Cleo's feet. *A neat Trick I will have to master.* The Raven Queen said, "And what, prithee, does paint in a circle around me do?"

"You're a ritualist." Cleo smirked. "Oh, aye, I know you've no skill in nature magic. You've lived too long with stone walls about you, the muddy feet of too many people damping your power. But then, you died. You died, and passed the veil into the other place. And once through, you were forever marked in the canvas of the heavens as dead. Risen, true, and living once more, not a horror to stagger and shamble about the world. But dead all the same."

Evanne felt a gnawing unease in her gut. "She lives like any of us."

"Not like any of us. Not like any but one other, and he is on the other side of that gate." Cleo patted the wall. "The Holomancer Meriwether du Reeves lives again by the Sway of his forever love. He is, sadly, beyond my reach. Lucky me: High Justiciar Eleni, in all her wisdom," these words dripping with sarcasm, "raised the Queen of Or'sen from her eternal rest. And now, with a necromancer—"

"People keep saying that," Evanne said. "I'm not a necromancer. I'm a bard. I play songs."

"You are vile filth," Cleo said. "But you do play pleasingly enough." This felt grudging, like Cleo was trying to say mud pie was delectable. "It's not your gift with strings I need. You command the dead, Evanne. Not well, but I don't need you to call on them. Magic is a process, powered by a gift. The process is the markings on the floor, with the ritualist at the centre. It matters not whose hand draws the runes. Morgan is untrained, her power the barest wisp. But a necromancer can command the dead beyond all feats of a mortal shell. I need you as an ... amplifier."

Evanne thought about that, and then locked eyes with Morgan. True enough, they had no kind words to say to each other, but that look shared common purpose: *whatever this is must not come to pass.* So,

Evanne turned to the hole in the wall, steeled herself, and made to jump.

Tarragon punched her in the side of the face. She'd forgotten the fairy was there, all warmth and gentle light aside, but that teeny fist didn't feel gentle. It felt bony, and it felt like Tarragon had put a lot of hip into it. "Don't!" The fairy hissed. "Not that way, Evanne. Never that way."

"I'll walk it off," Evanne lied. "I'm Vhemin."

"You are not Vhemin. You are half of nothing and an ounce of meritless worthlessness." Cleo laughed. "And now, it is too late."

Evanne rubbed her face where Tarragon hit her, wincing, and glanced at Cleo. "Too late for what? Your gate is still closed."

Morgan stiffened, then collapsed in the runed circle about her. Her back arched, mouth wide in a silent scream. With the crack of ancient, breaking stone, the gate to the demon world glowed a disc of brilliant mauve, then sagged into a circle of purest black. Evanne felt it too, like she was trying to tug o' war with a horse, and the horse was dragging her to her death. She stumbled, shaken, feeling sick, her weak heart stutter-thumping, skipping a beat, then struggling on. She wanted to scream, but her diaphragm was locked rigid.

Wind stirred the chamber. It smelled of rot, the foetid stench that rolled off marshland in summer. Or perhaps the miasma of a room of rotted corpses. Evanne sagged further, hand outstretched to Morgan, but the Raven Queen didn't see her. Eyes wide, only the whites showing, and that endless, silent scream a rictus on her face.

Cleo raised her arm. A glimmer shone in that inky blank space between worlds. A sparkle, like fairy light, getting brighter. Something was drawing closer, glimmering in the black between worlds. It tumbled closer. Evanne tried to walk to Cleo, to do *something*, but the will was gone from her, everything she was now powering Morgan to create an abomination.

Sparkling like a star, the object spat out of the gate, straight into Cleo's outstretched hand. The woman held it aloft, face alive with glee. A sword, glittering skymetal blade glowing as if fresh from the forge.

Requiem, sword of Knight Champion Geneve—the blade that killed a demon lord—had returned home.

Chapter Thirty-Six

This is bad.

Tarragon perched on Evanne's shoulder. It wasn't how the maybe-Vhemin stiffened when the sword arrived from the demon realm, or how she sort of stopped breathing. It was because that sword belonged to someone on the other side of that gate, and they no longer had it.

How will they fight demons without their blade?

She couldn't Build for shit. As a spy, Tarragon was pretty passable. But as a swordsfairy? Unparalleled. Helio said so, and he had the Build knowledge of the entire clutch of fairies in their pod. *I've seen a lot of swords, and that one is a masterpiece. The wielder of it must be magnificent.*

A lot of things happened at once.

One monster holding Barret roared, charging the slip of a woman who held the skymetal blade. The Vhemin was all rage and bared shark teeth. He shoulder-barged the very surprised apparently-not-leader of their group, and the sword sparkled as it tumbled free.

Evanne broke into a ragged stumble toward the fallen blade, but she may as well have been klicks away and would never make it before the Vhemin. Her lurching take-off was so sudden Tarragon almost lost her perch, but this wasn't her first rodeo. The fairy rode the bucking bronco like a pro.

Heser the Cheg appeared out of *actually* nowhere, wrestling the other monster holding Barret. The man looked berserk, mouth flecked with spittle, face red like the setting sun. He slugged the Vhemin with an uppercut that made Tarragon wince. Shark teeth flew, and the monster staggered back. On a normal day Tarragon would've marvelled that a mere *human* could hit a Vhemin so hard, but maybe his ward in the circle of spite had something to do with it.

I need to do something. Everyone else is getting heroic things done and all I'm doing is holding hair.

Tarragon needed a sword, but there weren't any handy. Not sized for a fairy, anyway. *If I could hold that sword for a moment... maybe it'd be worth being a Big for.*

The Vhemin who'd slammed Cleo reached the fallen blade, holding it aloft with a victory cry. Everyone froze as the skymetal blade gleamed. It didn't catch the light or any of that poetic nonsense. It *was* light, the blade glowing with it.

It is a magic sword. I have never seen one before.

What a time to be alive.

Thunder rolled, then—defying the laws of physics, because light moved faster than sound most other days—a brilliant pillar of lightning smashed through the wall, making another hole not as big as the probably-dragon-made aperture. The lightning connected to the sword, and just like that, the Vhemin holding it turned into a collection of glowing motes, and the sword clattered to the floor.

Tarragon wanted a few moments to process that, because it felt like Cleo had held the blade for longer and not been turned into ash and water vapour, yet there it was: one for the home team, and no one needed to lift a finger.

Evanne was gaining speed, so Tarragon yanked her ear, causing the maybe-Vhemin's head to turn, and the woman lost her balance and sprawled her length on the ground with a squawk. Tarragon fluttered free, trying for the sword, even though she didn't have a hope of lifting it. She could burn someone to a cinder before she dropped, and from how Evanne seemed to deeply dislike Cleo, Tarragon thought she knew who it should be.

Chance would be a fine thing: Cleo reached the blade first, holding it aloft, a move that was by now well overused. Tarragon put a little curry into her flight, dropped her shoulder, and let her sparkle flare. She burned for Cleo, and with the practised ease of someone who knew their way about a sword, the woman swatted the burning fairy from the air, using the blade like a bat.

Tarragon tumbled, trailing emberfire and smoke, stunned, to plop on the ground back near Evanne.

Heser looked about to start some more shit, which was when the Vhemin he'd dropped turned out to be only stunned—*I knew it! What a bad time to be right*—and slugged the human in the side of the head. Tarragon would've winced if she had the fine motor skills as Heser sagged like a sack of lost cares on the ground.

The Vhemin roared, "You've got to go for the head!" which seemed dumb because that's what Heser had done. Then he twitched three times before blood leaked from his lips, then his head popped like a gourd. His body fell, trailing a Barret, the Vhemin matriarch having pulled herself up his back by way of a pair of knives before ramming one through her enemy's skull.

Cleo made for Barret, sword aloft, as Evanne regained her feet. Barret seemed fine with this, pulling herself along the ground with surprising speed for someone without their legs. Cleo swung low, and Tarragon had to admit the woman was excellent with a blade. No Tresward, sure, the Light didn't walk with her, but with that sword, who cared? Barret rolled, again showing impressive motivation, as Evanne staggered forward, lip split, but no eyes for Tarragon. The fairy saw the fear, naked, vulnerable, as her aunt fought as her kind were made to.

To die, and keep dying, while others lived.

Barret grabbed Cleo's leg, piercing the woman's foot to the floor with a dagger. Evanne screamed, "*No!*" Cleo screamed too, pain and anger, swung, and just like that, Barret died, head separated from her shoulders to bounce in red, wet splats across the floor.

Tarragon got to her knees as Evanne made Cleo, and it looked for a moment like she might do the other woman some harm, but Cleo slid her blade through the air and with a sickening *shink* ran the maybe-Vhemin through the gut.

Evanne keened, falling to the ground, and Cleo removed the blade from her foot. Evanne threw up, spat bile, and said, "You've got to go for the—"

"I don't care," Cleo said, and ran Evanne through again, but this time through the heart, that skymetal blade glimmering with Light, and just for a moment, the entire world went quiet. The moment held for those who still had a heartbeat for one, two, three hard kicks of a tiny fairy's ticker, all still, all silent. Then it shuddered back into motion.

Kicking Evanne's body free, Cleo stalked toward Tarragon. The blade she held smoked, Evanne's blood gone in a blink, and she pointed the tip at the fairy. "Your turn."

Chapter Thirty-Seven

"Evanne."

The voice came from what felt like a long way away. She was having the nicest dream, where she lay on clouds of the softest wool, perhaps the kind of thing the ancients knew how to make. There was nothing in the dream but those clouds, a sense of floating on the softest surface, a lake of endless white until the end of time.

"Evanne, stop being a dick."

I know that voice. Still, the clouds were nice enough, and her chest didn't hurt any more. *Was there something I forgot to do? Did I leave the fire burning in the hearth?* Evanne stirred, a little listless energy creeping into her previous bonelessness, but fought against it. The clouds were *damn* fine, and she'd be happy here forever.

"You need to get up and get back into the fight." Hands on her arms, a shake, and after a moment, a ringing slap across her face.

She startled upright, eyes snapping open, fist cocked back, ready to slug... whoever *this* motherfucker was. "Give me one reason."

"To punch me?"

"I've got that already." She didn't lower her cocked arm, but relaxed a modest amount as she looked past the stranger with the familiar voice. Yes, they were in a place where the floor seemed to be made of white mist, if mist could be both warm and soft. And the floor did go on as far as she could see, despite there being something wrong with her eyes, because both her Vhemin vision and human were the same, if that made any sense to anyone. *It makes no sense to me.* "Where's Tarragon?"

The stranger eased back, hand dropping from her arm, but he remained crouched by her side. "The move to the other side can be difficult. Strange, and often—"

"Other side?"

"Often you don't remember, and when you go back the other way, you leave things here. You've just arrived. Rough ride. Try not to think about it too much."

"Remember what?" Evanne surged upright, glaring at the stranger, wishing she could place his voice. He looked nice enough if you were into that sort of thing, which she wasn't, but he had a jaw that she imagined drew enough glances, a short beard, and hair cropped close to his skull. Darker skin than she expected. *Why do I expect anything? I don't know him at all.* Strong arms, muscled, used to doing hard work, perhaps for harder men. "Who *are* you?"

"You know me. You've always known me. It'll be better if you remember yourself. It was for me, the first time." He looked sad, but also resigned, as if he could see a runaway cart about to flatten her but didn't have his hands on the reins.

Evanne rolled her eyes. *Fuck this.* She glanced around, seeking the fairy, but Tarragon wasn't here. Not nestled in her hair, fingers about a rust lock, soft whispers in Evanne's ear. Not anywhere at all. "How do I get out of here?"

"That will happen all by itself. You're not supposed to be here, you see. A ... mistake, of sorts. There was a promise. Do you remember that? Gods don't make promises lightly, because of what they have to do. So ... part of you is easy to kill. It's what brought you here. The other part is..." He trailed off. "You'll need to remember their promise, before this is over. You'll need to get around it, somehow, or you can't save the world."

She glared, then picked a direction and started walking. More of an angry stomp, if she was honest. There had to be a way up, or down, or out. Some way to get from here, back to Tarragon, and—

And what? Evanne pulled up short. *What was I doing?*

"That's right," the stranger said. "That look on your face? I remember feeling that."

"I will knock you the fuck out," Evanne warned. "Let me think."

"That would be the absolute first time you've done that successfully."

Evanne goggled. Strong jaw. Nice eyes, short hair, good strong arms, and *hands*. That's what had thrown her off, that and the fact he had a face. "*HITCH?*"

Hitch gave a small bow. "Lance Corporal Eric Hitcherson." His smile faded, drying up like rain on the desert. "Please don't tell me that, when we meet again. I won't remember what it means. Not when I'm not," he raised a palm toward the not-a-ceiling, "here."

"But..." Evanne closed her mouth, then wound back up. "You've got hands. *Feet!* And a face!"

"And you know how I died." Hitch gave an encouraging nod.

"I remember," she agreed, but it was only half there. "You ... flew?"

"Like the Three themselves," Hitch said. "But the weapon takes everything. At the end, I pushed the demon back. It cost me everything."

"No." Evanne's hair lashed as she shook her head, angry. "You pushed Cobalt back. You shielded Rulbenen so he could take Mireille to the final fight. And you threw your lover into the demon realm, and saved us all."

"And it ate me alive." Hitch nodded.

"Wait." Evanne scowled. "That was *the* weapon? The thing you wanted to put me in? Are you a huge asshole?"

He laughed. "It needs someone who's very sick, or very healthy. It ... suckles at your marrow."

"Someone healthy ... like a Vhemin?"

He sighed. "That's what Cobalt thought, or perhaps that's the secret he wanted me to steal." Hitch paced. "But if you put a Vhemin inside it, you get nothing but pulped Vhemin out the other side.

Itikari do not give up their power so easily." He offered her a tiny smile. "Someone very sick, or very healthy, but *human*. Itikari were human, Evie. They kept it all for themselves. They needed a human to put in the armour who could survive the price. I wasn't ... sick enough. They needed someone the world had never seen before, until you."

"Not Vhemin." Evanne looked at her hands, the human skin on them, and to where it became the scales of her father's kind. "Not ... all the way."

"Someone who's human enough," he agreed. "What we all want to be, when the chips land, and we make our accounting to the Three."

"But I'm Vhemin."

"Hmm." He gave a crooked smile. "Try picking up the sword. Actually, don't. It's smarter than the armour."

"What sword?"

He ignored the question. "Soon, the part of you that's Vhemin enough will pick you up, dust you off, and send you back into the world. There is a room of hate waiting for you, and Cleo won't make—"

"Who?"

"She won't make the same mistake again. Right now, in this moment, she is about to kill the person you care most about in the whole world. The person, and I don't understand this because I don't think you're remotely likeable—"

"Die in a fire."

"The person who cares about you most in the world, too." He frowned. "Almost. There are two others."

"When did you start drinking from the cup of mystic bullshit?"

"The same time you died," he snapped. "You got careless. You got lazy, and now people are dead."

The words hit her like the slap he'd given her before, and she took a step back. "Hitch—"

"Don't 'Hitch' me. This is serious, Evanne. This is the most serious thing that has ever happened. The gods are trapped, because of their promise. The demons want back in. The conniving scum Cleo has Requiem, and that means Geneve and Meriwether do *not* have it, if they still live. I haven't seen them here yet, so it's possible." He looked away. "I'm sorry. I waited eight hundred years for you. For who you are, and what you mean. Someone who can use the weapon, and save the world."

Evanne opened her mouth, closed it, and tried again. "But ... I'm sixteen."

"Do you want a medal?" He started pacing again, stopped, and started counting on his fingers. "You have broken into a place sealed against the world since the war."

"That was mostly Tarragon."

"You saved Morgan and Heser."

"But lost Merle."

"And Sight of Day."

"Did I?"

"You play the songs of old," he leaned into it, "and I feel it. I, who have been dust for eight. Hundred. Years!" He scrubbed fingers against his short hair. "You saved the souls of the people here. Felled a Council. And don't forget Gabriel. You gave him back his name."

"Umm," she said.

"No, really," Hitch said. "Don't forget Gabriel. You'll need an assist, and that worthless tiger isn't who you're looking for. You need friends, even if they're dead."

"I don't understand." Her voice felt small.

"You will." He walked to her.

"I ... I'm tired, Hitch." She looked away. "I don't think I can do it. I'm not a real Vhemin."

He laughed. "You think that's what makes you strong?" Hitch cupped her chin in a hand. "There is a saying from ... when I'm from. Fall down seven times, get up eight."

Evanne did the sums. "So they get up one more time? Why?"

"You'll work it out." He let his hand fall. "And even if you don't, just remember one thing."

"What's that?"

He took her hands in his. Smooth skin, strong fingers. He leaned in, kissing her forehead. "You are a child of this world. You deserve your place in it. And you are loved."

The universe shuddered, dug its claws in her, and *wrenched*. She screamed, the pain blooming in her chest, the unexpected agony of it, and she remembered the burning heat, that icefire as Requiem cut her crippled heart in two, her lifeblood leaving, the floor beneath her, and then.

Black.

Chapter Thirty-Eight

"**D**on't. Please." Tarragon backed away, the giant, glowing tip of Requiem just a few mils from her nose. Above, the long length of the blade, all exquisite sharpness, and not a hint of Evanne's blood on its forge-hot length. The hilt, held by a human hand, and above, on the human herself, a smug, gloating smile.

"And why not?" Cleo kept perfect pace with Tarragon's back-pedalling. "You're just as much to blame. Your kind made the things that brought us low. Ancient wonders, but all used to lift the already strong and bring down the forever weak. You. Killed. My. Parents!"

This last was hissed through clenched teeth. Tarragon hiccupped. "But." *Hic.* "You didn't know them."

Bad move. *I'm not good with words. Not like ... Evanne.* Tarragon wanted to wince, or sob, but she had to scurry away as Cleo gave a cry of rage, swinging Requiem, but cutting nothing but air. Glimmerdust sparkled in her wake, but only the barest hint because she was exhausted after her one shot at taking out the creature before her.

She glanced back at the remainder of Cleo's band. No more Vhemin, but five Feybrind stood by the doorway, no apparent concern about them. *In my best day I could take one. Not two, and certainly not five.*

Tarragon felt a chill. The air had so much death in it, it permeated even her shroud of glowlight. She *hic'd*, trying for more room between her and the woman with the magic sword. If she could get outside, maybe fly away ... but she felt so weak. *I don't feel like a monster who destroyed her parents. I feel like someone who's about to die.*

Maybe it was for the best. She wasn't good at anything. Not really. Not much use for tiny spies, now the war was done. And even if she had a sword, one made just for her, there was no way she could fight the glowing, shining length of a godsforged skymetal blade.

So, she stopped. Cleo stopped swinging for a moment, smile widening. "That's right. Let it come."

"I don't want to die," Tarragon admitted. "But I want to die tired least of all."

Cleo's smile turned to a sneer, then to a snarl, the woman pulling her blade back and up, one giant swing for so tiny a foe. Then she made an odd sound, a kind of *hurk*, her whole body going rigid. Requiem fell from her hand, going tip-first into the hard stone floor, smouldering as rock melted. Cleo scrabbled, arms wild, then she convulsed. It looked like she wanted to scream, but blood came from her mouth, a trickle, then a torrent, rich and foamy.

Tarragon remembered what it sounded like when Bigs used a lobster cracker. A kind of extended, grinding *crunch*. That's the noise that came from Cleo. With a shower of gore, her ribcage opened, gore spraying like a fountain. Tarragon shut her eyes and looked away, splatters landing both around and—*ew*—on her.

She wiped her face, needing to see, just for one Three-damned second. Where Cleo stood, there was someone else. Strong shoulders, a dancer's supple limbs. But such anger, too. Rust locks covered in blood, lavender snake eyes harder than the runes on the demon gate. Sharp teeth bared, fingers curled into claws as she let Cleo's ripped body fall.

Evanne stood, chest heaving, rent in her jerkin showing where Requiem had entered, but ... here she was. Tarragon wanted to hug her, but she needed to know *why* more. "How?"

Evanne shook gore from her hands. "Go for the fucking *head*."

The Feybrind at the door looked like this was their moment to shine, all lowered stances and lashing tails. Then one was yanked backward through the doorway, silent, but gone. The others turned to observe the new threat.

Shambling through the door, a risen dead. An unholy monster, leering through rotted lips. Tarragon thought, *Now we're screwed*, but Evanne laughed. The maybe-Vhemin put hands on hips and said, "Cats, meet Gabriel. He remembers who he is, now."

Tarragon turned to Evanne. "Really. How?"

The maybe-Vhemin bent and held her hand out. Tarragon hopped on and took her perch on Evanne's shoulder. So quietly not even a Feybrind might hear, Evanne said, "Tricks are like that. Just enough truth, and a lot of belief."

Enough truth. Tarragon bit her lip because she understood what she could do. Launching herself into the air, she brought out her glimmer. Bright and strong, but not warm. She didn't have enough left for heat.

The Feybrind looked at Tarragon, then at the undead monster. Torn, between which was the greater threat.

With a roar like a T-Rex, Pakhet pounced onto the ground. Nothing said *let's get the fuck out of here* like a tiger the size of a Clydesdale. The giant cat didn't lunge at the Feybrind, she just stood ground between Feybrind and Evanne, showing a lot of teeth.

And ... a lot of belief.

Evanne picked up the fallen blade. Tarragon wanted to scream *no!* because it killed a Vhemin just moments ago, but there wasn't time. The maybe-Vhemin held the blade in both hands, stance wide, smile wider. Thunder rolled, and an arcing, shimmering bolt of energy blew another hole in the wall as it connected the heavens to Requiem.

Evanne took it, tendrils of current falling down her body and snaking across the floor. The sword glimmered with sky fire. And she didn't die.

The Feybrind fled.

After a handful of heartbeats, Evanne dropped the sword, and collapsed. Tarragon flew to her. "Are you okay?"

"I just held a storm," Evanne said. "I'm not even a little okay. My whole body is on fire, and," she held up palms already blistering, "burned. But I'll live. Probably."

"So... that was a Trick too?"

The maybe-Vhemin nodded, weary. "I can't use the sword, fairy. It *will* kill me. Just ... slower than if I was a real Vhemin." She sounded bitter. "Only *real* humans can hold it."

There were a lot of things Tarragon wanted to say. To do. She landed on Evanne's knee. "You died."

"It wasn't fun." Evanne rubbed the rent in her jerkin, hand coming away bloody. "I can't recommend it."

Pakhet padded closer. "*What do we do about the zombie?*"

"Nothing." Evanne patted the cat, then used a fistful of fur to pull herself to her feet. "Where were you?"

"*About,*" the cat said in a vague and unconvincing way.

"Whatever," Evanne said.

Tarragon hovered before the maybe-Vhemin. She was tired, but Evanne looked worse. "You need to rest."

"I'll be fine." Even Tarragon heard the failed Trick of her words. "There's something I need to do."

Chapter Thirty-Nine

The walk to Barret's body was only ten metres. It felt like it took a year to get there. Her head had rolled some distance apart, and Evanne sniff-snorted when she saw her aunt's angry expression frozen for all time.

She dragged Barret closer to the breached wall, placing her severed head on the body. The sun was warm here, and a faint breeze tugged Evanne's rust locks. She closed her eyes for a moment. "I'm sorry, Aunt Barret. I'm sorry I left you to be captured. I should have been there, and then this wouldn't have happened." She wiped her nose with the back of her arm, then rubbed her eyes.

"The Itikari," Hitch said, and she almost jumped out of her skin. "Umm."

"Where have you been?"

"Nowhere. I can't really remember."

"You said you can't bring it here with you. What you were, before."

"I did?" His not face and missing hands seemed as they always had. "I don't remember that either."

"It's okay." She wanted to tell him what they'd talked of, or who he was, but he'd said not to, so she kept her peace. "What about the Itikari?"

"They had a ceremony, for their fallen heroes. They leave the body like this. They called it a sky burial." Hitch sighed. "It's probably just a story."

"It's not a very good one." Evanne paced toward Hitch's remains. She removed the rest of the armour, setting the pieces aside carefully. It was a gift he'd wanted to give her, and she'd honour it. "I have a better idea." Carefully, gently, she gathered the dusty remains of her oldest friend to her. It took less time than it should, because there was so little left. Tarragon kept her distance with Pakhet, the two talking in hushed tones. The fairy's glimmer seemed to be returning, and that alone warmed Evanne's heart some.

She brought Hitch's remains to Barret and laid them beside each other in the sun. A Vhemin matriarch, strong in life, and Eric Hitcherson, just as strong, despite how sick he was. Then she found Requiem, the fallen blade still glowing, lodged point-first in the floor, and wrapped the hilt with a strip of leather she tore from her jerkin.

Evanne carried the blade to Barret, then held it above the matriarch's body. "Be free. Rise, to share the rest of time with the Three." She laid the blade across Barret's chest, hilt on Hitch's, and scurried back.

Thunder, predictable here where it was nowhere else, rolled. Lightning slammed into Requiem as the Three denied their Light to the Vhemin. Barret and Hitch were turned to glowing motes. The breeze stirred them, carried them up, and offered them to the sky.

"Thank you," Hitch said. "That felt ... good."

"I'm not done."

SHE FOUND A SMALL FLASK AMONGST THE FALLEN VHEMIN BRUTE'S equipment. It was earthenware, stoppered with cork, and sloshed invitingly. A quick rummage brought up a cup. She poured herself a generous measure, then went and squatted a few paces back from Cleo's remains.

"That's not tea," Hitch said.

"It's hard tea," Evanne said. "It's the best kind."

She sat, and sipped, while Cleo's body cooled. Evanne wanted to feel *right*, or at least right*eous*, but her heart stirred painfully instead. She rubbed her chest, hand no longer coming away sticky, the seam in her ribcage healing enough to stop her leaking everywhere.

Cleo's remains looked miserable to Evanne's human eyes. Sad, and broken, a fallen puppet with no master. *I did that.* But her Vhemin eyes told a harder kind of truth, no hiding behind a Trick for this one. Cleo's body cooled, falling from the rich, warm temperatures of the living to the cold of the flagstones beneath her.

I did that too.

Someone's life, gone, all because Evanne didn't do the right thing back at that little cabin in the woods. Or perhaps farther back, when she shared rice wine with Cleo, hoping to steal a kiss. Or was it farther still, when a girl joined Imshir's clan, and Evanne hadn't seen the Trick that hid the orphan's past?

I did all of that.

"She died," Hitch said.

"That's not true though, is it?" Evanne sipped more 'tea', feeling the scrape of liquor in her throat.

"To be fair," the ghost squatted beside her, "you died too."

"I got better." Evanne put her empty cup on the ground. "I need to *be* better, Hitch. I need to—"

"What, swing a blade like the Tresward? Carry arms into battle?"

"No. I'm not that." She pulled her torn jerkin closer about her. "I'm a liar. Sometimes a thief. But I can sing, and make people listen to the heart of the song. I need to do that."

"You already are."

"Then I need to do it better," she snapped. "Because otherwise this," she threw her hand out toward what was once a woman with hopes and dreams, "will be my legacy. I won't have it, do you hear me?"

"I hear you." He stood by her side. "What's next?"

"Just one more thing."

MORGAN STILL LAY IN THE SUMMONING CIRCLE. SHE WAS OUT COLD, and Evanne thought she knew what that felt like. *Close to death. I can see the shadows gather about her. Well, not today. No one else, not even her.*

She found her guitar. It had seen better days, but the strings sang sweet enough after she tuned them a smidgeon. She carried Sight of Day's gift to Morgan's side, scrubbed the paint marks on the floor into smudges with her foot, then began to play.

The song she plucked was one that she'd heard somewhere. She didn't know where, but as she looked up, there was Gabriel. The ghoul stood, body slack but eyes attentive, just far enough away she could tell he meant no harm. Evanne felt the song under her fingers get stronger, the music seeping into the rock at her feet, into the undead horror the ancients had made of a fine soldier, into the unconscious Heser the Cheg, and finally into Morgan.

IN THE DARKEST OF NIGHTS, WHEN ALL SEEMS LOST,
> *A flicker of hope, no matter the cost.*
> *It's a spark in our hearts, a guiding light,*
> *A force that can conquer the blackest of nights.*

THIS SONG'S FOR THE LOST, THE WEARY, AND THE THREAD,
> *A melody of hope, to raise the dead.*
> *With courage and faith, we'll break through the chains,*
> *And let this hope bring life to what remains.*

IN THE SHADOWS WE'LL FIND THE STRENGTH TO STAND TALL,
> *Though the world may crumble, we won't let it fall.*
> *With each note we sing, with each word we pray,*
> *We'll chase all the doubts and the fears away.*

SO LET'S SING IT LOUD, LET THE WORLD HEAR OUR CALL,
> *With hope as our anchor, we won't lose it all.*

In unity we'll rise, with the strength to withstand,
For the power of hope can heal every land.

THE RAVEN QUEEN TWITCHED, THEN STARTLED UPRIGHT, ALERT ALL at once. Heser sprang up too, hands clutching for a blade he didn't have. He looked to Gabriel, not understanding, and made to engage.

"Hold," Evanne said. "He means no harm. He's lost, just like you."

"I'm not lost," Uncle Heser said.

Queen Morgan stood, then carefully stepped from the circle while Evanne played. She moved to Heser and touched his jaw with one cool finger. "Oh, Heser. You are more lost than even I."

Heser trembled, then took his Queen into his arms. They held each other, and so Evanne looked away. Her eyes found the burning need of Gabriel's. Fingers still stroking the strings, she looked him up and down. "You can go."

"*Heeeeeellp. Yyyou.*" The words were sloppy, like his lips.

"You've done enough," Evanne said.

"Hold, now." Hitch moved to stand between them. "Mighty handy in a fight, a man who's already dead."

"He's done enough fighting," Evanne said, and let the notes drop. With it, Gabriel fell, his soul stepping free of the ancients' chains on his person, and she watched as he glimmered heavenward.

"You are a good person," Hitch said.

"I'm a terrible person." Evanne rubbed her eyes. "Let's be away."

Chapter Forty

Tarragon watched Evanne drift about the room, listless as any of the ghosts that dogged her heels over the past weeks. *Except, she has no release. She's tethered here, to her memories, her pain, and can't let go.*

I don't know what to do.

Evanne always seemed to have a plan. Thought became action, and *bam*, the problem got solved. Take here: demon gate, closed. Everliving horrors, put to rest. The evil henchperson of a diabolical cult, put to death.

Henchperson.

"Umm," Tarragon said to no-one in particular. "If Cleo was a henchperson, who's the head of the cult?"

Hitch put his head in his invisible hand. "Can we have just the afternoon without a to-do list? I get there are high and mighty terrors roaming the land, but," and he gestured at Evanne, still listless, not listening, not *caring*, "perhaps we could have a small break."

"Coming here was your idea," Tarragon muttered.

"*If you are talking to the spectre, most of them have terrible ideas,*" Pakhet said.

Heser the Cheg stormed through the doorway, his Raven Queen on his heels. Since their heartfelt embrace they'd been separate, as if the moment hadn't happened. He held a massive harness, she an assortment of boxes that looked like they might hold lunch.

Pakhet eyed the harness. "*What are you planning to do with that?*"

Heser stopped cold, looked at the harness, then at the cat. "Put it on you, of course."

The cat bared fangs. "*I'd like to see you try.*"

Heser dropped his load, pulled back his sleeves, and rolled his hands into fists. "If it's got to be that way—"

"Hush," Morgan said, whispering past him, a trailing finger on his arm for the barest moment of time. "Noble cat, most here are people of action. You are not."

"*I deeply resent the accuracy of that comment.*"

"You do, however, have one small ability that is useful. You can vanish," Morgan snapped her fingers, "into thin air."

"*You've taken a hit to the head.*"

"I have, but not the sort you mean." Morgan pointed to the summoning circle. "I lay there, unable to move, eyes fixed on the horizon. And then, wonder of wonders, you stepped out of nothing. A neat trick. What were you made to be, I wonder?" She crossed her arms. "It is of no moment. What you were put here for is to be a good and gracious companion. One who will walk with us to the ends of the earth."

Pakhet, who had puffed up some at the *good-and-gracious* comment, bridled. "*Here, now. What end? Which earth?*"

"The best part about it is you'll get food and cuddles. All cats like cuddles." Morgan padded to the cat, rubbing Pakhet's ruff with delicate fingers. The tiger looked like she wanted to lean into it but was fighting the urge. "In return, you will be a valiant steed, to strike terror in the hearts of our foes. And then," she dropped her hand, and Pakhet almost stumbled forward, "you will vanish, safe from all harm."

Pakhet lowered her muzzle, staring the Raven Queen right in the eye. "*I am not a beast of burden.*"

"But you're so big and strong."

The cat lifted her chin. "*I am, true.*" A sneeze, from which Morgan ducked her head, hand up. "*All right. If I do this, who's horsie do I get to be? Yours?*"

Morgan gave a sad smile. "One day, perhaps. When I've earned it." Her eyes went past the grey-striped tiger to Evanne, who brooded by the gash in the wall. "I'm sure you'll work it out."

"I have an idea," Tarragon blurted.

All eyes but Evanne's turned to her. Heser blinked. "Are you going to share it?"

"We came here with the right concept." Tarragon glimmered. "Get the weapon, and use it to save, uh," and she glanced to the charred mark where Barret gave up her essence to the Three, "people. But the weapon turned out to be broken, because some people," she glared at Hitch, "can't remember the useful things."

"If only we had a Builder," Hitch murmured.

"But we do. Me." She put a tiny hand against her heart. "All we need is a Manifest. And with that, I can repair the weapon."

Pakhet sniffed. "*Where would we find such a thing? My Manifest was corrupted. Nothing remains here.*"

"Right." Tarragon fluttered her agreement. "And Evanne broke the Council."

"There." Evanne's voice was husky, cracked like the sand beyond the green below. Her arm pointed into the plaguelands. "Where all men die. That's where we'll find it."

"Kinda." Tarragon hedged. "It's a bit more north." She flitted to Evanne's shoulder, then hovered by her arm, and gave it a small push. "That way."

Evanne squinted down her arm. "It is all the same. Sand, and death. What's so special about that patch of sand and death?"

"It's what's past the sand. I hope, anyway. That way is where I was born. Me, and my clutch. Helio." She bit her lip. "A great city. It was made by Builders, for Builders. The Kingdom will still be alive there."

"A fairy kingdom?" Morgan's voice held no sarcasm. "I would see such a thing, before I die again."

Evanne's lavender snake eyes found hers. "You know this to be true?"

"No," Tarragon admitted. "But I'm pretty sure. Even if it's a ruin, there will be tools. Books. Things I can use, to study. To, um." *Hic.* "I want to be better."

Evanne watched her, then nodded. "Then we will be better together." She stretched, as if waking from a dream. "I will take Hitch's weapon to the fairy kingdom. I've assumed much and taken more." She sighed. "I thank you for your help. Uncle Heser, I, I," she looked to where Barret had been. "I wish we could say goodbye."

"Goodbye?" Heser the Cheg seemed surprised. "Why would we do that?"

Evanne blinked. "Because you will take the Raven Queen back to Ravenswall and—"

"The Raven Queen decides her own fate." Morgan raised an arch eyebrow. "Ravenswall needs more than me to make it whole. It needs help. An army, which I no longer command." Her eyes darted to Hitch's broken armour. "Or a weapon enough to convince the stubborn. I will go with you, Evanne. You can wake the dead. I must learn of your power, and of my own." She pulled her gown about her shoulders, but her voice grew small. "I owe you that much."

"I'm in," agreed Heser the Cheg. "There is a cult that ended a," he choked, then tried again, "friend most dear to me. We argued each day, and as I lay down to sleep, I yearned for the next day's repeat. Barret is someone I will not forget. Nor leave unavenged." He glowered. "I need a drink."

"*This place sucks,*" Pakhet admitted. "*I would like to leave.*"

Evanne sighed, as if all the tension in her found an escape. "Thank you, all."

"Also," Heser the Cheg said, "we need a Vhemin to pilot the Artifice. It will not answer to human hands. You're," he frowned as if uncomfortable with the words, "Vhemin enough."

"Aye," Evanne said, voice bitter. "And only as I stood among the dead, did I learn I might be human enough, too."

Tarragon flitted to her shoulder, nestled in rust locks, and whispered into her friend's ear. "It's not so bad. Bigs had all the best stuff."

Evanne snorted. "True enough."

The fairy leaned against Evanne's head. "When should we go?"

"A day of rest, then we'll be off." Evanne squared her shoulders. "I want no more of this place."

"The desert will take the hospital without the Stormwall to protect it," Hitch said.

"It's welcome to it." Evanne turned from her view, striding toward the door. "Let us gather what we need. We've a kingdom to save."

Epilogue

Black. *Why is it always black?*

She made to get up, then realised she couldn't. Her one good arm was trapped, and she couldn't see what had it. Couldn't feel it either, which was probably a blessing.

Let the black come back.

"You good?" His voice echoed, as if they were in a stone chamber.

"Love." She laughed. "I'm far from good."

"The arm?" He grunted. "Looks bad."

"I've been worse." She didn't tell him how her insides hurt, or how hard it was to breathe.

It was his turn to laugh. "Aye, that you have. You want me to get that rock off you?"

"If it wouldn't trouble you too much." She tried to keep her voice light, because he would worry, and the pain would come whether he worried or not.

His footsteps shuffled closer. He grunted, and the weight lifted from her arm. The pain came as she knew it would, a savage rush into her lower arm, hand, and fingers, but she bit her lip. *And old friend, pain. We've seen much, you and I. Let us be about it, then*. She tried to flex her fingers, but they were aching, unresponsive, and stubborn. Much like the rest of her.

"Mind your head." He helped her up, scaled hand at the back of her head. "The ceiling came in. Ancients couldn't build for shit."

She let him lead her about, ducking as he guided, then standing straight when he let her. The air was cool, no longer smelling of fire. She stretched as he stood by her. *That feels good*. "What do you see?"

"Rock. More rock."

"Is there a way out?" She kept her voice calm, as if asking of the weather over Imshir.

"Might be. Might be certain doom, too."

"I see you are cheery as always." She bowed her head, leaning into him. Smelling him, where the animal met the man. "Lead on, monster."

HE OFFERED HER BRACKISH WATER FROM A CANTEEN. IT TASTED OF age and metal. "Where'd you find this?"

"Around," he said. "Had to beat some kind of undead horror back into its grave to get it."

"Stop complaining. At least you can see."

"So can you, if you want." He took the canteen back. "It's just a hand. Bit fucked up, sure, but just a hand."

"I don't want to see," she admitted. "What if I've lost the Light?"

"The Three are huge dicks, I'll agree. But twice in a lifetime? Seems unfair." A *huff* as he leaned against the wall. "Maybe you shouldn't have bargained with them."

"She's our little girl, creature, and I will not have her be the pawn in some heavenly game of—"

"Aye, aye, unclench your asshole and take a moment." He didn't sound bothered. He never sounded bothered over that regular background level of orneriness. "You can see, and you can fix your hand. All you've got to do is try."

"I'm no good with the Sway."

"See anyone else here with any kind of happy clappy magic? No? Well, either get used to being led around, or sort yourself out."

She wanted to shout at him, to beg, to not be in this position. She didn't want to know if the Light left her again. *But, he's right.* She reached tentative metal fingers to broken flesh ones, shying away at the last. *Perhaps a little light, first.* She drew her blade, feeling as it stuck coming free of the scabbard. Bent in the cave-in, perhaps. *No matter.* //LIGHT.//

Just that one word hurt her throat, the sound made of razors, but it did the job. She felt the tug, the flow, and then her sword bloomed into a soft gold-white. She blinked, even this meagre glow harsh on eyes that had stared at the dark for answers.

Don't look at your hand. Not yet. She glanced about. They were in a bare room, the ceiling in one corner slumped in, a shoal of scree puddled beneath it. She glimpsed bedrock beyond, the mountain's flesh and bones no longer covered by skin of ancient manufacture.

I must see. She let her eyes drift to her hand. The palm looked mauled, her ring and index finger bent at an unwholesome angle, but it didn't seem irreparable. The fingers looked dislocated rather than broken.

"Let me see." He took her wrist in his big hands. "See? It's fine."

"The fingers will need splinting, and a sawbones to set them right —" She screamed as he yanked them straight, the *pop* and *click* as knuckles realigned. She swayed with the pain, wanting to punch him, but he held her until it passed, then held her a little longer.

"No sawbones around here," he explained. "Now you can stop worrying. We've got bigger issues."

IT TOOK LITTLE TIME TO GET THE HANG OF HER SWORD'S GAMMY

weight. If they needed to fight something down here, she didn't want to be without a blade.

"Stop waving it about like a baby's rattle," he suggested. "It's a sword. Stick the sharp bit into your enemy until they stop being angry at you."

She raised an eyebrow. "*You* coach *me* on the use of steel?"

"Just be thankful you're fresh out of glass blades. Steel might be uglier, but it's got its uses."

She gave him a wry smile. "Are we talking steel, or something else?"

He looked away. "This way."

"Up ahead. The rock is cooler." His Vhemin's eyes saw things her light couldn't show. He squared his shoulders, staring at where the corridor reached a wide door. It looked like the one she'd entered by. "Might take some doing to get it open."

She took three perfect steps, swung her blade, and Light flashed. The door turned to exploding rubble, blasting fragments into the air beyond. A warm breeze touched her face, carrying the taint of wood smoke.

"Or, we could do it that way." He muscled forward, hefting a slab of stone aside, then stepped beyond.

She followed. "Oh, it's good to see the sky." It was a cloudless night, but smoke pillared the heavens from countless fires. They stood on the side of Heaven's Gate, or what was left of it. Rivers of magma flowed into the valley below, and Imshir burned. The sea met molten rock near where the harbour used to be, great spumes of steam frothing into the air.

He helped her over a hunk of stone. "What now?"

"We seek the Three. There will be an accounting. They promised."

He laughed. "Maybe we can do that tomorrow. I meant today."

She scanned the valley. "The school still stands. Partially, at least."

"So, we get the Tresward."

"They are no Knights." She frowned. "Not yet."

"They're as good as we're going to get. Then what?"

"She's our little girl, monster. She's ours, and they took her. We will have her, and then have our accounting."

He nodded, slow and steady. "If it's to be an accounting, I can help with that."

"But, tomorrow." She felt her tone was grudging, so softened it. "Tonight, we see what remains. It's our turn to help those who've been our family for these past many years."

"Aye." He growled. "Come, wife."

"To the end, husband."

THE END.

THE BATTLE FOR THE PAST IS OVER. BUT the war for the future has begun.

Evanne left Heaven's Gate behind, but its echoes still chase her.

Across the sea, a kingdom crumbles. An old enemy stirs. And deep within the shattered ruins of a once-great city, a secret lies buried—one that could change everything.

Evanne's path is no longer hers alone. The song of the past calls her forward, but the melody has shifted. The next verse belongs to another.

Turn the page to begin *Heartsong*.

Because the story isn't over. **It's only just beginning.**

https://www.books2read.com/HeartsongFantasyAdventure

HEARTSONG
A DARK FANTASY ADVENTURE

The Rising Sun

It wasn't the bee that investigated his ear, or the gentle whisper of wind against his nose. Despite the deep reach the People had into the world, it wasn't the grass beneath him, nor the rock beneath the rich, loamy soil. The burbling of the brook didn't wake him, nor the rain squall that came and went in the night, or perhaps the night before. Or the one before that.

It wasn't hunger, or fear. Anger didn't make his heart beat hard, urgent, reminding him of tasks left undone. Much to his eternal chagrin, it wasn't love either. He'd known it, felt it trickle through his fingers no matter how he held on. Lost it, to time, or to the blade, or to the world that tried to mill all like him into a more pliable meal.

It was the call of the sky. It was the rising sun that woke him.

He knew he'd slept for days. *How many? Does it matter?* He flicked an ear, waved the bee away, and stretched. His tail *swish, swished,* disturbing the grass beneath him. The bee became agitated, and he focused on it. *It is very fuzzy.* Brown and black stripes, cautious in its bumbling way. He held his hand up, and it landed on his palm. He wanted to say, *See? We are not so different. Both are furred. You are lighter and darker than me, and it makes no difference. The dawn came for both of us, like she always does.*

But he couldn't, because the People were voiceless. A hive of industrious servants made for a time before this one, when humans were more monstrous.

Or, perhaps humans are as they've always been. He scratched his ear, worrying a burr from his fur, then rose. The bee alighted from his hand, trundling off to do whatever busyness the morning demanded. A quick pat down told him he had no weapons, not even the sliver of metal he'd made to keep him safe when a sharp wit or fast legs could do no more.

I'm at the bottom of a ravine. There was a trickle of water that wound beside his feet, too modest to be called a stream. The grass here was rugged, as much of this world had to be. Soft enough bedding compared to the stone it struggled through, but he'd have kinks aplenty. *I am far too old for this.* He scanned the side of the ravine, marking the telltale scuffs where stone and shale gave way on his descent. *I came down here the fast way, not the easy way.*

He scampered up the ravine wall because he had to find something. Or someone. *It's a someone. Definitely a someone.* Atop the ravine, he could see just how far down it was. It's a wonder he hadn't broken his neck. Who put him there? A small stain of dried blood marked the edge, and he bent, touched it, and sniffed his fingers. *Vhemin. Ancient enemy, but ... not this one. This one was a friend. Odd, that a friend would throw me to my death.*

The sun touched his face, reminding him he had business to be about.

The shale near the ravine's edge gave way to earth, then to trees that agreed to be a sparse forest. He followed the tracks laid by the one who'd thrown him. Weird, because there were no footprints, just scuffed dirt and rock, like something had been dragged. *Something like me! They dragged me.* No, that wasn't it, or at least not all of it. He felt his tail lash and grabbed it. It trembled in his grip, but he held it until it stilled. *There. No need for that.*

What if we were both dragged? It made a certain kind of sense, being the only answer that fit the facts. A dragger taking a draggee on a journey would take a lot of strength and a level of orneriness the People didn't possess. So, definitely Vhemin.

I know one of their kind. A brother, a friend, a strong stone wall at my back. But he wasn't here. He ... fell? That didn't seem quite right, but it would do for now. This one who'd dragged him had history with his brother. They'd known each other before the Knight with the hair like platinum metal had stolen his brother's heart.

No, he stole hers. That is the way it happened, I'm sure of it.

When he found the camp, he was surprised only at how ruined it was. Bedding, torn. Their metal cookware was bent, the wooden spoons broken. Even the small hut that stood for hundreds of years was smashed down, the bees who'd nested inside scattered on the wind.

The sun urged him on. He thought it said, *You've no time for that. You've got to find what you've forgotten.*

So, he picked through the camp. A bent knife lay beside a huge footprint. He puzzled over it, then looked up, following other prints through the smashed trees. *A machine did this.* His eyes rested on a small bedroll tucked out of the way. Unused, forgotten.

He hurried to it, lifting the bedroll. He smelled it and remembered.

Rust locks. A crooked smile, sharp teeth, but kind words behind them. A heart that wasn't strong enough, and that's why he'd given her a guitar—so she could make music instead of war.

Evanne. I remember you.

With her name and face came a rush of other memories, rattled free from the fog of his stubborn skull. How she'd tricked him—him! —by leaving him on watch and skiving off. How he'd heard the Artifices coming for them, and how Barret had said, *Well, I guess you'll have to get her after the rest of us are dead,* and knocked him out.

He had no memories after that because the matriarch had thrown him into a ravine. He couldn't imagine how she'd made the decision to die, just as she'd made the decision to save him. He, furred, not scaled. He, who'd lost a child, and couldn't be relied on to save another.

Sight of Day looked at the sun, then brought his hands between them. He pressed them together in supplication. {*Don't ask this of me. I'm not made well enough.*}

The sun watched him. He felt it, a burning glare that made a mockery of his Handspeak. And one more memory came, the key to the lock inside him. The sun gave him back his name.

Roars Like the Singing Sun.

Ah. Well, if you're going to be like that, I'd better get to work.

Chapter One

The lands breathed a story of loss and betrayal. A city, vanished. A people, murdered. War between those who had, and those who wanted.

"I'm not buying any of it," Evanne said. "You're telling me there's a mystical fairy fortress that someone buried under a pile of rock and water?"

"All know the tale." Heser the Cheg didn't face her, casting his glance out over a long, narrow valley. Below sat a small township that struggled with airs of grandeur: a crenelated keep stood amid the squalor of ramshackle wooden buildings in a lean workman's district. The workman's district would smell; that heady aroma abetted only marginally by the river that flowed freely into the Burroughs, and somewhat more sluggishly out, laden with all manner of vileness that promised a bad time for anyone foolish enough to try bathing in it. Drinking it was out of the question. "It is famous in Ravenswall. M'lady's father tried to make amends and found naught but misery and hardship."

"It's true." Morgan sat cross-legged, apart, her back to Heser the Cheg, but still *quite* close. Her spine was straight as a mast, chin high, the slightest hint of grey about her raven locks. *That's new*, Evanne thought. *I wonder if being used as a bonfire to heat the fires of a demon gate takes it out of you?* "My father heard the drums of war and looked to broker peace. By the time he made it here, there was little left but ashes."

"Was it ashes or hardship?" Tarragon fluttered to land on Evanne's shoulder. Evanne lent her a warm smile, leaning her cheek against the fairy, who leaned right back, if but for a moment. "Or ashy hardship? Hard ashes?" She glimmered. "Can ashes be hard?"

Heser the Cheg sighed as if the world were suddenly a hundred times as heavy, and he was the one doing all the lifting. "The tale involves love and loss." Did he look at Morgan for a moment? "The fairies held themselves aloft—"

"That's because we have wings," Tarragon purred.

"A flying city," Morgan murmured. "It was no standard keep. A relic of a bygone age, kept high by their magics. The city soared in the clouds but didn't move. It stayed up there," she pointed to the north and west, "never descending to where people suffered. It was said riches stayed with them, a magnificence of wonder. Ovens that made cakes without the need for chefs, or even flour. The weather... it was always spring, even when sleet coated the ground below. I heard tell that dragons once roosted there, but there were none by the time I was a little girl." She chewed a lock of raven-black hair, as if forgetting she was the queen of Or'sen.

"Let me guess." Evanne joined Heser the Cheg on his small hillock outlook, visoring her eyes to stare into the valley. "They didn't share their toys, and so a mighty force embarked upon a quest to take back the forgotten riches of a bygone age. Share, and share alike! There would be plenty for all, if only the fairies didn't control it."

"Are you telling this story, or am I?" Heser the Cheg gave her a little side eye. Evanne admitted it looked good on him, because his eyes didn't so much crinkle as crease at the edges.

"Morgan said—"

"My lady can say as she pleases," the big man rumbled.

Evanne snorted. "If you say so."

The side-eye turned to a glare, but Morgan tinkled a laugh. "She's right, Heser the Cheg. I rule no kingdom. Not anymore." She stood, the length of her gown teased by the breeze to flutter eastward. "Where's that useless cat?"

"*Here.*" Pakhet sat behind Evanne, tail curled about her forepaws as if she'd been there for hours. A small buck, neck at an unwholesome angle, lay before her. The grey-striped tiger looked pleased with herself, and if cats could smile, this one grinned ear to ear. "*I brought breakfast. What have you done to earn your keep, hmm?*" She leaned down, her sheer size the kind of thing that would stop the heart.

Morgan bunched fists onto hips and glared at the cat. "You call that breakfast? The way you eat, it's barely a snack."

"How does she do that?" Tarragon whispered into Evanne's ear. "You know. When she's done something wrong, she makes it someone else's fault?"

"Leadership," Evanne hazarded. "I'm more interested in how a cat the size of a Clydesdale snuck up on us without anyone noticing."

"*It is because you're blind, stupid, and possibly incompetent,*" Pakhet rumbled, her grin not dimming a mote.

"At least I've got fingers." Evanne turned from the cat to stare into the valley again. "So, down there are a mess of people who felled a flying city? And we want, what, directions?"

"We want to know what really happened." Heser the Cheg held up a hand. "Aye, quit your sniping. I know I said all know that tale. But it doesn't mean that's what happened, just what's remembered. The town below holds a secret or two. Near as we know, the city fell with the old world. Perhaps the people's names in the story changed so it could keep pace with time. Mist descended on the facts and there's no knowing the truth of things. If Queen Morgan's father found no trace of the city, it likely fell..." He trailed off, looking at Tarragon. The fairy's wings wilted further with each word. "It is but a story. I mean to say, I'm sure there are fairies left."

"The story *was* true, to a point. There was a city. I've been there! It was around here *somewhere*. You can't just lose a city! If nothing else, the town below may also hold a map." Tarragon turned away from Heser the Cheg, and clambered up Evanne's hair, perching atop her head. "I want to know where they think the entrance to my home is."

"Because you don't remember," Evanne said.

"I remember, sort of," Tarragon countered. "The thing is, I remember the city flying. If it's no longer flying, things will be quite different. The kinds of inbreds who'd crash someone's home into the ground probably have a map."

"They might know why there's a lake there now too." Evanne pulled out her knife. "I guess it's breakfast then a bit of old-fashioned spying, no?"

EVANNE PULLED UP HER HOOD. IT WAS A NICE HOOD, ATTACHED TO A cloak she'd liberated before leaving the strange temple that was supposed to heal people, but hurt them instead. The deep grey material was soft, as if it was made of pressed angel's wings, and warm as anything she'd owned, but a third the weight. It didn't get dirty, and water beaded right off it.

For all that, it didn't seem to draw the eye. She'd been concerned people might want to take it from her, but when she wore it, eyes slid right past her. The seam about the collar had runes stitched into it she didn't recognise, but Tarragon didn't either. The fairy had huffed something about *exams* and fluttered off in a disconsolate way only those of very small stature could manage.

The runes didn't glow, itch, or call to her soul. They did *something*, and that was good enough for a Vhemin going into human lands. Her face wasn't scaled like her father's, but her teeth and eyes set her apart enough for the obvious mistake to be made.

It's not a mistake. I am Vhemin!

Except, of course, she wasn't. She was half one thing, half another, and those two parts didn't quite make a whole. *At least my heart works right now.* Evanne rubbed the ribbon of scar above it, remembering how Requiem had slid through her ribcage. Remembering the hand that held the magic blade, and the eyes above that gave nothing but hate.

So: a cloak of shadows, a light step, and no fucking about.

A merchant on the road had called this place Wandermere. He'd argued with Heser the Cheg about who ruled, and both left dissatisfied, although the merchant had a bloody nose to boot. The Raven, as Evanne liked to think of her, hadn't even blinked when the merchant said Queen Morgan's reign had ended, but her Queensguard pursued the conversation to its natural conclusion.

A light drizzle started, affecting Evanne and her cloak not at all. Tarragon hid beneath it too, her warmth by Evanne's cheek, peering out while bunching the fabric about her head to stay dry. "I think the weather is worse."

Evanne snorted. "How can it be worse than the plaguelands? That was a killing desert only the foolish enter and only the strong leave. The sun hit like ten hammers, the heat stealing any lick of moisture from your body, and—"

"Not that, silly." Tarragon huddled into her hair. "Across the whole, um, world."

"I don't follow." Evanne found a line leading through Wandermere's gates. Ahead, a bored trio of guards played dice in the lee of a small hut, while a pair of their fellows inspected wagons and collected 'tithes'. "I don't like the look of those guards."

Tarragon stood a little taller. "Is it the sloping chins? Oh, I see: that man doesn't have all his teeth."

Evanne gave her cloak a companionable enough tug, jostling the fairy. "Back to the weather, sprite."

"Oh. Um." Tarragon sighed. "Since I came back. Like, eight hundred years ago the weather was fine almost all the time. The Three nudged the clouds over crops as much as was needed. Now it seems so ... accidental."

"It's just rain."

"It's *wet*."

"That it is." Evanne touched the handle of her scattergun, Fusillade. The weapon she'd looted from the temple didn't come with a name, so she'd given it one. It hung from a sling at her shoulder to just below her hip. Easy enough to grab if the situation called for action or bluster. A knife as long as her forearm lay in a sheath on the other side. She'd found it among the dead in the temple. The blade wasn't bright like her mother's Smithsteel armour. It was dull, the colour of the skies that delivered drizzle on her now, but even after eight hundred years it held an edge that only glass could beat.

Her guitar lay across her back, oiled canvas covering it, although like the cloak, Uncle Day's present didn't seem to mind the weather. It was banged up plenty by her adventures, but still sang a sweet enough tune.

By any account, she'd left the temple with riches. A scattergun that fired more than two shots without reloading, a cloak of shadows, and an eversharp blade. Hitch's armour, though? That was broken. She'd left the suit back at their camp above the town, because every time Evanne even looked at it, Tarragon got huffy again, said *exams*, and fled. *But I didn't leave with Cleo.*

"That's enough of that." Tarragon pulled her hair.

"Ow. Enough of what?"

"You're thinking about something bad," Tarragon said. "You're thinking about the things you didn't do, or someone you didn't do it for."

"True enough. You seem to know me better than most." Evanne tried for a little bravado, but it didn't land right. "I'm ... I'm happy you're here."

"Me too. I mean, I'm happy *you're* here. Um." The fairy glimmered for a moment. "How are we getting into the town?"

"Simple." Evanne let a breezy grin touch her lips. "We're going to walk right in."

THE ROAD THAT LED THROUGH WANDERMERE'S WESTERN GATE RAN atop a bridge, making it difficult to sidle off this close. A guard shack, and by association the resident guards, was stationed at the end of the bridge. The shack was the usual affair. It sported a roof in dire need of repair, shutters against frames with no glass, a rickety balcony to keep near zero sun or rain off, and a bell. From the bell hung a weathered rope still firmly attached to the knocker. Such a device promised reinforcements if Evanne cocked this up. Beneath the bridge ran the sludgy remains of the river that looped outside then through the township. From up here it didn't smell too bad, although the breeze holding hands with the rain did a little heavy lifting on that front. The river gave Evanne something to go on in case Plan A didn't work out, but it was far enough below she knew going down the fast way would hurt.

She approached a guard who wore a bored expression like most people wore pants. He was a little bent in the spine, and was draped in too-large chain armour, sporting a too-small sword. She fished about for just the right Trick. *I need a slight smile, but no teeth, at least not yet. Don't appear lazy, yet let my hair fall forward—yes, like that. Shoulders are too straight, slouch a little, everyone here does. Now I look just like anyone else, and since I'm wearing this boss cloak from ancient times, they won't even notice me.*

Trick in mind, she made to walk right past the guard, who was having exactly none of it. Despite his mismatched armour and ancient hand-me-down weapon, he swivelled to Evanne, then blinked. He adjusted his helmet, ensuring the visor wasn't in his eyes, shook himself, then placed a hand on her shoulder, firmer than would be considered companionable, and said, "Oi."

Evanne stopped and gave him a little side-eye. "Do I look like your daughter?"

"You what now?" The guard squinted, his brow furrowed as if he couldn't quite see her right. His brain tried valiantly for the right excuse, and despite the drizzle, came up with, "Damn sun in my eyes."

Evanne glanced heavenward, the steady drizzle still present, the expanse of clouds not breaking even a hands breadth horizon to horizon, then looked at the guard again. "Your daughter. Do I look like her?"

"Not especially."

"Then take your fucking hand off me," she hissed. "Right now."

"Here now," he dropped his hand, "just doing my job. Say. Don't I know you?"

"I've never heard that pickup line before." She gave him the up-and-down. "Besides, you're too old, and entirely too grody."

"It's not a…" He trailed off, rubbed his eyes, squinted harder, blinked, then grimaced. "Wait here." He ambled to his companion, a woman in her mid-forties. She looked bored, not just with her job, but with life. She was in the middle of shaking down a merchant for a few barons, but he dragged her away from that lucrative pursuit, back to Evanne. "Look at her."

The female guard looked past Evanne, then back to her companion. "Look at who?"

"Her!" The guard stabbed a finger at Evanne. "Right there. Plain as day, except—"

"Except it's raining," Evanne said. "Day's not clear at all, is it?" She glanced at the merchant, who was high-tailing it through the gate as fast as a man could with a donkey-drawn wagon.

"There's no one there." The guardswoman turned to the three lounging by the shack, bawling, "Captain! Yuro's been in your stash again."

"Have not," Yuro said. "Not today, leastwise."

One of the three playing dice made a great show of standing up, arched his back, adjusted his sword belt, then his pants, scratched an armpit, and trudged over, still carrying a battered tin cup. Attired like the rest in shit armour, with a shit weapon, he wore a cloak of rank as if it was a mighty benediction from the Three. His eyes slid over Evanne, back, then away. "What is it? Can't you see I'm busy?"

The guardswoman said, "Yuro's losing his grip."

"I'm not. It's just, this woman here—"

"What woman?" asked the captain. "I don't see..." He trailed off, glancing into his cup, and muttered, "Might be a bit strong this time."

Yuro rallied. "Here, this young woman tried to get past me—"

"I walked," Evanne said. "If I'd been *trying* to get past you, you'd never have seen me."

"She's different," he said. "Can't quite see her. But can't not look at her now neither."

"I can see why you're stationed here," Evanne said. "This post is the most miserable in the city, no? Wandermere's refuse toils its way downriver, sliding beneath your perch. You've nought but lice-ridden merchants to shake down for a spot of coin. Hard times, no mistake." She sidled next to Yuro companionably close. Evanne hummed a small tune, just a few bars, but the temperature dropped just as she knew it would. "You did something wrong," here she switched to song, her breath frosting the air, "and now you're stuck here." As she sang, her voice captured the attention of the captain and the guardswoman, even if their eyes struggled to see her.

FOLLOW THE WHISPERS, HEED THE CALL,
   Under this enchanting sky, stand tall.
   Trust the guidance, let your heart unfold,
   In the dance of destiny, do as you're told.

THE ANCIENT WOODS, THEY BECKON AND SWAY,
   In the melody of wonder, let yourself obey.
   With open eyes and a heart that's bold,
   In the tapestry of dreams, do as you're told.

"STUCK HERE," YURO REPEATED.

Evanne kept the song in her voice. "All you need do is repent."

"Repent," agreed the guardswoman.

"And let me pass," she crooned as she stepped behind the captain.

"Let you ... fuck that!" The captain rounded on her, grabbed Evanne by the collar, and hauled her close. His breath smelled of sweet wine, which wasn't too bad, but it caused her hood to fall away. His eyes cleared as if the sun had come out. "Yuro, I think we've got ourselves a thief."

"Bard," Evanne corrected.

"A what now?"

"Singer of songs. Teller of tales. A master of—" She cut off as he gave her a shake. "I don't steal things. People give them to me instead."

"What's wrong with your eyes?" He peered at her. "You sick?"

"There's nothing wrong with my eyes," she gritted. "What's wrong with your face?"

He loosened his grip a fraction, touching his face. "There's nothing ... oh, I see. You tried for a clever rejoinder."

"It was pretty good under the circumstances," Evanne said.

"Should I do something?" Tarragon fluttered free. The captain gave a small scream, pushed Evanne away, drew his sword, got tangled in his cloak, stumbled, and fell.

As he dropped, the guardswoman drew steel, as did Yuro. The two guards remaining by at the shack sprang into action, one hefting a pike, the other a stout club banded in iron. The one with the pike rang a bell against the shack, *clang clang clang*, while glaring at Evanne, who in turn glared at Tarragon. "Yes. Stop helping!"

"He fell down by himself," Tarragon said. "I didn't do a thing. It's like he's never seen a fairy before." She settled into a hover, crossed her arms, and gave a tiny *humph*.

"Sorcery!" the captain shrilled. "A sinner."

Evanne closed her eyes and rubbed her brow. She started with, "If I was a sorcerer," then stopped as Yuro tackled her from the side. She went down in a clatter of scattergun, guitar, and knife, the air going out of her in a *ugh*.

"Should I help now?" Tarragon fluttered, perhaps a shade anxiously.

"*Maybe* I *should help*," said Pakhet. The cat lounged against the guard shack, which creaked in protest due to the grey-striped's huge size.

Three things happened.

First, Wandermere's reinforcements arrived through the gate. These were a seedy-looking group of malcontents but held weapons that would let the sticky red out well enough. They approached at speed, with enthusiasm, a giant Vhemin at their head.

Second, the crowd waiting for entrance panicked, some running back down the road, but most running toward the malcontents masquerading as guards. There was a lot of screaming, yelling, braying of donkeys, and whinnying of panicked horses, all of which Evanne suspected had never seen a tiger larger than them. The one ray of sunshine in the confusion of livestock was a barking dog that looked like it was having the time of its life. The crowd pumped through the gate, a tide that brooked no argument, sweeping the malcontents and their Vhemin leader back inside Wandermere.

Third, the captain, Yuro, the guardswoman, and their two helpers made as one and vaulted the bridge's railing and into the murk below.

It might have been the captain who screamed as he fell; Evanne was never sure on that detail.

She stood, brushed herself off, and looked at Pakhet. "Really?"

"*You looked like you could use a hand.*"

"You don't have hands."

"*That's right, play on my deepest insecurities. Way to go, hero.*" The cat's tail lashed, and she stood, rubbing against the shack, which collapsed. "*Should we go into the city?*"

Evanne grunted, waited for Tarragon to land, pulled her hood up, and faced the gates. "I guess so."

"I *was* helping," the fairy muttered.

"I know, love." Evanne adjusted her guitar, then followed the final trickle of screamers through Wandermere's gates. "See? Just like I said. We'll walk right in."

INSIDE THE TOWN LIVED UP TO THE PROMISE OF THE SLUGGISH RIVER outside. It smelled bad, a mixture of rotted cabbage and old sweat. The houses were in various states of repair, but none shone with new paint, and Evanne couldn't see any signs of repair or renovation. Everything was slumping into miserable disrepair. No dogs wagged their tails. Cats arched and hissed, but in Evanne's experience that could just be cats. Not many creatures liked the Vhemin in her.

"This isn't what I expected a human town to be like." Tarragon huddled into Evanne's cowl as the misting drizzle threatened to turn back into rain. "I thought there would be more Bigs. I mean ... humans."

True enough, there were not many humans out and about. Evanne didn't find the raw number interesting, but rather their demeanour. "They all look so downbeat."

Hitch drifted through a house to slouch along beside them. He shoved not-hands into pockets. "What did I miss?"

"Nothing." Evanne gave her shoulder a shrug to keep Tarragon from interrupting. "Straight in. No problems at all. Scouting report?"

"Report? Hah." The spectre seemed distracted. "This town isn't a good place to be. Word on the street is there's a moderately bad man in charge of everything."

"Isn't there always? Explains the downtrodden air." A woman holding a broom with hardly any bristles left did a double-take as Evanne strode by, then bustled back inside a house and slammed the door shut. "And the unwelcoming visage."

Tarragon glimmered, shedding a little warmth into Evanne's collar. "I know I'm out of touch. I was in prison for eight hundred years. But don't towns these days have, I guess, shops? Malls? Arcades?"

"There's a market." Hitch pointed to the east. "It's closed."

"What's an arcade?" Evanne frowned. "You know what? Never mind. It'll be something I won't understand, leaving me more confused, or something I will, and then I'll want it even though I can't have it."

"And so it goes," Hitch agreed. "The moderately bad man in charge of everything is called Grind."

"Hold up a minute." Tarragon peered around Evanne's cowl at the ghost. "Why 'moderately bad'?"

"Doesn't eat babies. Kept the biggest tavern open. Overthrew the last dictator. Usual stuff." Hitch glanced skyward. "I don't miss rain at all."

"But he's still bad?"

"Of course. He made himself a dictator. Well, a robber baron, perhaps. He raids the countryside, ever since they put fire and sword to the neighbouring town up north. Place called Hollyhead. Used to trade with Wandermere, before they burned Hollyhead to the waterline."

Evanne glanced around. "Where is this biggest tavern?"

"Follow me." Hitch picked a slightly less dingy alley than most, guiding them south and east. "Hollyhead was a fishing village. It held—"

"Fishing?" Tarragon stepped free of Evanne's cowl, hanging on with one hand while she leaned out to peer at Hitch. "First we hear my city was crashed into a lake. There's no lake there! The fairy kingdom drifted above a plain, without water for klicks. Now it's a big enough lake to sport a fishing village?"

Hitch raised not-hands in mock defence. "People hereabouts talk of a fishing village. Eight hundred years is a long time. Could have rained a lot."

"Don't be a dick," the fairy advised. "While it suits you, it's not nice."

"So there's a ... *big* lake now. The fairy kingdom no longer flies the skies. Why not, and where it's gone, are what we're trying to find. Perhaps this Grind will know more?" Evanne crossed her arms under the cloak, shivering a little. "Grind sounds like a Vhemin name. I don't know much about how cities in Or'sen work but I thought humans ruled humans, and Vhemin ruled Vhemin here, just like everywhere else. Wandermere is a human settlement."

"Might be why everyone hereabouts is puckered at both ends." Hitch beckoned. "It's just around this corner."

True enough, rounding the corner let them out onto a wide road. It had cobbles, but they looked in a less-than-average state of repair. The road held very little in the way of traffic. People hunched, hurrying about their business. A lone donkey stood in the drizzle, looking less happy than Tarragon. No horses. No excitement.

Just the tavern.

It was big, the size of two ordinary taverns put together. A wide, welcoming gate immediately to the right of the inn proper led to a stables but Evanne couldn't see an ostler. Nor were horses in attendance: the stables held naught but a few clumps of rotting straw. The inn itself could use a lick of paint but was otherwise in decent condition by Wandermere's standards. Shutters were closed against the cool of the north, but a glimmer of warm orange light played around the sills. The main double doors of the inn were closed, perhaps to ward against the chill, but had a well-worn pair of handles that beckoned Evanne's touch. She sighed. "It's been a long time since I had a cup of chilled rice wine."

"Two things." Hitch stood before her. "First, you're working. Keep your head clear. Second, it's going to continue to be a long time, because they serve nothing but ale here."

"Hmm." What Hitch said wasn't useful, so she ignored everything about it. "Have you seen this Grind? Is he a tough guy?"

"No clue." Hitch shrugged. "People talk as if he's there in the room, but..." He trailed off. "I can't hear him."

"Wards." Evanne spat. "Maybe he's a shaman."

"Or he's got one on retainer." Tarragon left the safety of Evanne's hood, breathing deep. "This place stinks."

"It's a human town. They all stink." Hitch looked at his feet. "Okay, here's the thing. If they think you've got a spectre with you, they might start some shit. I'd like to try something new."

Evanne gave him a sideways glance. "You don't normally ask my permission when you're about to do something stupid. Why start now?"

"Because I need your help."

"Oh, great!" Tarragon giggled. "You're enabling Evanne to lose IQ points. I can't wait to hear about this."

Hitch looked like he glared at her, but it was hard to tell, what with his face not really being there anymore. He gritted, "It's a good idea."

"Cool," Evanne said. "Let's hear it."

"And it *should* work."

"I said let's... wait a minute. What do you mean, should?" Evanne amped up her eyebrow game.

Hitch leaned closer and told her. As he spoke, she nodded, then smiled, then grinned. "I love this idea."

"This is a terrible idea," Tarragon said. "It's the worst idea he's had, and he's had some super bad ones."

"We're doing it." Evanne squared her shoulders, then marched to the inn. She let her fingers rest on the cool metal doorhandles, then pushed the doors wide and strode inside.

SMOKE. PORK FAT. FRIED POTATOES. ALE. SWEAT. THE SOFT ROAR OF many voices. The clatter of cutlery, and the pop of logs on a fire. The tavern interior was one big common room, with a set of stairs leading up to the north, and a door to the east leading to the yard. Tables were arrayed in a rough semblance of order within, and enough people sat there to make it look busy.

A serving girl a shade older than Evanne carried mugs on a tray. A kitchen glowed cheerily from behind her. A bartender, thick with muscle sagging to fat with age, gave her a jaundiced stare. By the enormous hearth sat a Vhemin of giant proportions. He had the look of a man who'd seen his fair share of combat, but a prosperous waistline suggested he'd spent time on the bench since then. His chair was more throne than functional furniture, with what might have been a baby dragon's skull mounted to the wall above it. At least, it looked like a dragon's skull; Evanne hadn't met a dragon before, so it could have been a horror creature native to Or'sen.

I don't remember seeing a fat Vhemin before. Evanne took it all in. *So many people. I haven't seen this many all at once since...* The smile fell from her face. *Since Imshir died.*

"Keep moving," Tarragon hissed. "Everyone is looking at us."

"That drunk guy over there isn't." Hitch pointed. "It's possible he's drowning in his wine."

Evanne gave herself a mental kick and reached for a Trick. *Make it look like you meant it.* "Which one of you assholes is Grind?"

The hubbub faded away. Someone out back in the kitchen dropped crockery, which crashed over loud in the relative silence. A cat *rowl'd*. More silence, then a deep, rumbling voice came from the fat Vhemin. "Who's asking?"

She reached for another Trick, putting on a lazy smile as fat as his paunch. "Evanne. You may have heard of me."

"Seriously?" Hitch glanced between them. "You're playing that game?"

"What game?" Tarragon's voice was smaller than usual. She huddled in Evanne's cowl.

"And what would Grind, ruler of Wandermere, conqueror of Hollyhead, and slayer of dragons know of a sixteen-year-old named Evanne?" The Vhemin stood.

Evanne faced him head on. There was some distance between them. She had time. "Ah. So you *have* heard of me."

He paused. "Come again?"

"Well, you know my age. Stands to reason." She crossed her arms, tapping her chin. "One thing doesn't stack up, though." She pointed to the skull. "You killed that?"

She could see him trying to resist the pull of looking, but the rest of the tavern followed her finger, and with the force of the retreating tide it pulled his gaze around. Grind's shoulders hunched, and he turned back to her. "I did."

He knows he's being played. Excellent. "That skull is barely larger than a horse's. Are you in the habit of slaying infants?" Evanne waited a handful of seconds, just until he looked ready to retort, then laughed. "I'm kidding! Even a baby dragon is harder to kill than, well, a baby chicken." She buffed her fingers, then examined them. "But that's not why I'm here."

Wait him out. The monster waddled a few steps closer. "And why are you here?"

Got you. "Because it's my birthday. And you're going to give me a present."

"It's your birthday?" Tarragon glowed. "You should have said."

"Didn't you have a birthday last year?" Hitch seemed surprised.

"Just like every year," Evanne murmured out the side of her mouth. To Grind, she beamed. "And what you're going to give me is a story. And, because I'm fair, I will give you a story in return." Grind was close enough for her to make out subtle details. His snake's eyes were ordinary yellow, but his shark's teeth were crooked on the left side of his jaw, speaking of a terrible injury he was tough enough to walk away from. He was well, if not cleanly, dressed, sporting a stained waistcoat above a pearl-buttoned shirt. While his waist was big enough for two regular Vhemin, so were his shoulders. He might have given Armitage a run for his money.

Don't think of Papa. Not now.

The monster had a sword belted to his hip. The hilt was exquisite, suggesting a marvel of Feybrind-forged steel within. He rested a meaty paw on it. "And if I'm not in a giving mood?"

She eyed him up and down. "What if I give you my story first, and you tell me one if it's worthy of the tale?"

"Are you a bard?"

"I knew you'd heard of me." She whirled, heading toward the hearth, leaving his wide-eyed gape in her wake. The hearth was warmer than she'd like, her half-Vhemin blood not as sluggish in the wintry north as his pure cold-blooded red. She righted an overturned stool, pushed her cloak out behind her, and sat. The guitar found her hands as if by magic, and she strummed the strings.

If the inn had been quiet before, it mimicked the grave now.

"I see him." Hitch pointed. "There. In the nook by the stairs."

Evanne let her eyes wander the room, eventually landing on a cloaked shape huddled in the step's lee. A man much shorter than most, with a cloak far dirtier and worn than her own, face hidden within a cowl. She raised her voice. "Come, sir. Don't hide from good song and fine wine. Join us in the fire's warmth."

Grind blinked. "Here. You don't give orders in my house."

Evanne's fingers plucked the strings, and she turned her violet eyes on him. Those eyes that were so Vhemin, yet so different than anything he'd seen before. The notes from her guitar entwined in her fingers. "But Grind, my lovely. It's my birthday. And you want to please me on my birthday."

"I do," he admitted, sounding surprised.

"It is settled." She stilled the strings. "Come out and enjoy the hospitality of the house."

The hunched figure came from the shadows, a shuffle-step at a time. He was shorter than she'd first thought, standing no taller than a child, but gnarled like an old tree, and broad enough. As the light touched his face, she saw he'd been burned as if marked by the Three's lightning yet lived to tell the tale.

"Merciful Three," Tarragon whispered. "What's that?"

"An accident of birth." Hitch's voice carried the certainty of experience, and Evanne remembered the vision of his past he'd shared with her. "A thing most can't tolerate."

The man *was* Vhemin. Broad, yes, but stunted and twisted. Evanne couldn't imagine the tribe that had birthed him letting him live. It wasn't the Vhemin way, not if Papa's tales were to be believed. The monsters were strong, and anyone in the clan that wasn't mighty was food wasted. And maybe he'd been cast out or put on a pyre. The burns Evanne could see were a horror.

Wait a minute. Vhemin ... heal. Just what is he?

A moment later: *He's like me. Different.*

She didn't let her fingers leave the strings, or the smile walk off her face. "A drink, then?"

The gnarled monster spoke with a voice that was half-gravel, half-lisp. "I want nothing from you or the leech that feasts on your soul. Aye, spectre, I mean you." He raised a hand, pointing a crooked finger at Hitch. "You would take until there is nothing left."

Hitch looked at his own chest, then behind him, then back to the little Vhemin. "You're talking to me?"

"Aye."

"And you can see me? Well, *obviously* you can see me. How remarkable." Hitch clasped invisible hands. "Are you a shaman?"

"I am your ending," the little goblin promised.

"You are too short to even be a start," Tarragon glittered. "And it's Evanne's birthday. There should be no fighting on a birthday."

"Come, now," the Vhemin husked. "There should be no lies between us. You've come here to fight, and fight hard."

"I don't know about that." Evanne hunched over her guitar. "For a hard fight, there'd need to be hard men. All I see is the ruinous cast-offs of a tribe that forgot its way. See? A warlord who's let himself go to seed, and a man too short to reach the top shelf."

Tarragon winced. Hitch sucked in not-air. Evanne touched the strings again, feeling the temperature drop. And despite that, the warlord Grind stuttered into motion, rallying against the hold her music put on him. He opened his mouth, closed it, frowned, belched, then said, "What?"

Evanne stood, kicking her chair back. Tarragon fluttered into the hearth behind her, wreathing herself in the flames, while Hitch stepped *into* Evanne. She drew her hood close, plucking a bass string. "Hear me, Grind. Hear me, failure of your tribe. Hear me, and fear me, for I will remind you of what a chieftain *is*."

· · ·

In the hush of twilight's breath, I weave my song,
  To chill the air, to make it cold and strong.
  With words and melody, the frost I'll bind,
  A spellsong cast, an icy chill combined.

Zephyrs still, the world holds its breath,
  Whispers on the wind, a touch of death.
  With every note, I call upon the freeze,
  To make the air an icy, biting breeze.

With the chill of the north, the frost's embrace,
  I command the air, a frozen space.
  From tundra's heart to mountain's crest,
  I bring the cold, a wintry test.

As the notes fade, the spell is done,
  The air grows cold, the battle's won.
  With Frostwind's touch, I have my way,
  A world in ice, until the break of day.

The fire at her back roared, blasting flames tinged the colour of verdigris into the chimney, then guttering out with a snap. Evanne's breath frosted from her lips, curling free like cigarillo smoke. The bass crept through the tables, her fingers teasing the string, coaxing it, making all who heard remember all they had left undone. The fields, fallow. The hunt, deer still on the hoof. Thatched roofs that let in the weather, and hearts that let in traitorous thoughts. Through it, Hitch's power, *her* power, and the ever-present cold that grew from her, the floor glittering with hoarfrost.

Grind's eyes widened, and he reached for the Feybrind-forged weapon. It flew from its scabbard, and a pretty thing it was too, the blade glittering like it captured all the stars above in the edge of its smile. In a human's hand it might have been called a greatsword, but in Grind's huge paw it was merely adequate. He took a step toward her, foot crunching on ice crystals, then another.

Then he stopped, the colour draining from his face. Unlike Evanne, he was all the way Vhemin. Stronger, and faster. Maybe meaner, too, although she wouldn't admit that even over liquor. But he was also cold-blooded, his snake-eyes holding onto all that came before him and slithered. And without the fire, the great hearth's heat now held within Tarragon's tiny body, the room was cold.

The first of the inn's people came at Evanne from the side, and Hitch held her hand through all the moves. She stepped from a blow she didn't see, the ghost's eyes where hers weren't, and he made her body crouch, spin, and curl a leg behind her attackers. Her attacker gave a surprised yell, cut short as she stood half-way through his tumble, shoulder in his gut, and upended him face-first into the stool behind her. Teeth clattered to the wooden floor. Evanne's fingers coaxed the strings, the music's tempo moving higher, the pitch evening, but still urgent, still judging those here for the things they hadn't done.

WHISPERS IN THE DARKNESS, VOICES FROM THE PAST,
Unfinished dreams and promises that couldn't last.
With words and melody, I'll demand all,
The echoes of your past, your failures all.

REGRETS LIKE SHADOWS, LURKING IN THE NIGHT,
Mistakes and missteps, casting their blight.
A mirror to your soul, reflecting all you've missed,
The chances left behind, the opportunities dismissed.

ECHOES, ECHOES, HAUNTING STILL,
All you've left undone, your will to fulfil.
Echoes, echoes, a solemn tide,

A reminder of the moments when you let life slide.

SHE BARED NOT-QUITE-SHARK-TEETH. "YOU LEFT HOLLYHEAD TO die, people of Wandermere. They were your friends, your allies, and now they moulder beneath a frigid lake."

Then she stepped to the left as a chair sailed toward her. It clattered to splinters as it hit the wall behind her, showing evidence of manufacture that was most definitely not Feybrind. She stormed from the hearth, a muse leaving her stage, bringing music to the people who needed it the most. Evanne kicked a man in the groin when he made the mistake of swinging at her with a tankard, then kicked his woman in the groin for good measure as she tried to get involved.

Hitch touched her heart, her soul, and she shivered with the power of it. Her breath left her, ice crystals shimmering like Tarragon's glitter. She marched toward Grind, ducked a swung club, and raised an elbow into the jaw of her attacker without slowing her roll. Four meters. Her cloak cracked with ice, tiny shards dropping in her wake, because the grave was the coldest thing there was. A woman charged her, chair held high, and Evanne stepped back, foot out, tripping her and sending her into a gaggle of labourers. Three meters, and Grind's snake-eyes held desperation. Evanne held the guitar in fingers so cold they were blue. She couldn't feel the instrument anymore, but her heart knew it, *loved* it, and the strings hadn't moved. They were where she needed them to be.

The inn was *alive* around her. Her music touched the guilty, and the innocent fought for her. Some could see her, but the cloak hid her from others. All could hear her.

Two meters and she swung the guitar free of her shoulders. Another step. She grinned like firelight, ready to knock this clown back to the plaguelands.

"Enough." Gravel and lisp, followed by a flash of purple iridescence. Evanne blinked away stars, then stumbled as Hitch was knocked from her, the spectre shrieking as he flew from the inn, cast aside. She screamed, dropping to one knee, which was lucky because Grind had worked up the motivation to swing that fancy blade at her neck. The blow was slow and crude with the cold, cutting nothing but air, but it was best not to take pride in that since she was currently on her knees before him.

"Hitch?" Her teeth chattered in a spasm so hard Evanne thought they might break.

Tarragon flittered close, warmth falling from the fairy like summer rain. "He's gone. You've got to *move*."

Fuck that. Evanne rose, fended off Grind's backswing with a shove, and stepped clear. The little goblin fucker stood in a ring of purple light, a stick of charred wood rescued from the hearth in one hand, runes he'd scribed with coal into the floor glimmering with a light that reminded her of the demon gate. *A shaman for sure.* She gritted her teeth to stop them chattering, feeling the cold in her bones now, and snarled. "You trouble powers that are not to be disturbed."

The grotty little man sneered. "Spoken like one who is blind in the land of the sighted."

Buy time. Where is Hitch? "Hang about. Aren't you the sighted in this metaphor? Because a shaman's got *gifts*, man. But there aren't many of you. I think it should be a sighted person in the land of the blind, right?"

The little Vhemin frowned, the muscles of his face pulling his scarred visage. "What?"

"I think you might be wanting something like, 'spoken like someone who is awesome in the land of the less awesome'." She tried for a glittering smile, feeling the rime on her face crack.

"Listen, fuckwitch," the little man snarled. "*I'm* the one with the power here. Me! You're just a, a," he spluttered, "*musician*."

"Oh, my poor summer child." Evanne took another step back from Grind, who still had the look of a man spoiling for a fight despite being blue edge to edge. She hefted her guitar. "With this, I can change the world."

The shaman peered at her, as if seeing an unusual insect for the first time. "And with this," he stamped the floor with a boot, and by inference the circle he stood within, "I can summon those who will end it."

Ah, one of those. Evanne took another step back. "My Uncle Day said something once when I asked him why there were no sorcerers among the People. Vhemin have shaman, the consorts of demons. Humans have all the powers under the stars. They command fire and lightning and can draw hope from a dead man's chest. Thaumaturgists cause the world to tip on the head of a pin, and ritualists can bend what should be into what is. Feybrind have none of those things. Do you know what he said?"

The little horror pursed his lips. "I'll bite. What?"

"He said," and she used Handspeak, her motions clear enough if not as beautiful as Uncle Day's, {We like the world as it is. Who are we to put our will upon it?}

The grode chortled. "Spoken like hunted, not hunter."

Evanne felt the anger pull at her. "You know what? I think it's time we end this." She roared, grabbing the guitar by the neck, and swinging it like a bat at Grind, who'd taken that moment to lumber forward in a frigid approximation of a charge. The instrument *clanged* against his face, making him lose his grip on that beautiful sword. The Feybrind weapon clattered to the frozen floor. In the little space left by his wide-eyed stagger, she drew Fusillade, cloak billowing wide. The weapon sang as her hand found the grip, and she pointed it at the shaman. He shrieked, hands moving through the air, and wind curled around Evanne's feet. Evanne pulled Fusillade's trigger, ignoring the worry of its diminishing ammunition count, because if this heretic summoned demons here, they were *proper* fucked.

The weapon roared. Purple flared about the circle the little Vhemin stood in, the scattergun's round flaring into boiling metal. As if on cue, a hole into darkness gaped beside the summoning circle. And that's when Grind punched Evanne in the side of the head.

It was her turn to stagger, weapon falling from her nerveless fingers. It hit the ground, bounced, landed on its grip, and roared again. The scattergun's shot hit the dragon skull above the throne, which splintered into about a million pieces, revealing it was made of cheap plaster. One of the million pieces pinged into the ceiling, ricocheted off, and came down right onto the shaman's head, showing he'd made a protective wall rather than a sphere. This threw off his concentration for a moment, but the really exciting part was how it made him teeter like a child's top losing spin.

The shaman took a step, then another, hand to his forehead, blood trickling free. He screamed, "I will kill you," and then a horrible, clawed arm reached from the demon gate and grabbed him, because he'd stepped outside his summoning circle.

He didn't have time to scream.

The purple runes snapped out, the gate shut with a slam, and Evanne spun, decking Grind with a fist of fives so epic his ancestors would have felt it from the place beyond. The massive Vhemin slammed to the floor, causing tankards to jostle.

She panted into the silence. "Anyone else want some?"

TARRAGON HUSTLED ACROSS THE BAR TOP, LEAVING A TRAIL OF glitterdust in her wake. To and fro, back and forth, her frown growing with each stretch of the two metre stretch of polished oak. Evanne waited her out from her perch on a stool, the comatose Grind splayed on a chair next to her, a thin line of drool trailing from his open mouth to the bar. *A Trick I learned long ago is silence can do the best talking.* Evanne swirled the ale she'd ... appropriated, which wasn't half bad, and nibbled what tasted like three-day-old bread, which was pretty bad. The kitchen was out of anything that wasn't spoiled, apart from the ale, bread, and oats. *And I don't want to cook oats.*

Tarragon made her way back down the bar, step-step-step, wings aflutter, then when she reached Evanne's position at the midway point, rounded on her. The fairy shook a furious fist at Evanne. "That wasn't the plan!"

Evanne took another sip. "It kinda was."

"Wasn't!"

"The plan, if you'll remember, was to use Hitch to—"

"And look how well that turned out." Tarragon crossed her arms and glared.

Evanne raised an eyebrow. "It worked pretty well until it didn't. Then we improvised."

"You hit a man with your guitar."

"Like I said, it worked pretty well."

"Then you shot someone else. Accidentally."

"Also worked pretty well." Evanne swirled ale. "What's the problem, Tarragon? No, don't stamp a tiny foot at me and get angrier. We planned to come in here. Release the spell we thought Grind," she elbowed the brute, "was under. Free the town and be recognised as heroes. And, yay, here we are. Heroes all, the town freed, and the villain dead." She pursed her lips. "I hope he's dead. Where he went, I can't see living being much fun."

Tarragon looked about to stamp her foot anyway, then fluttered her wings, glowing a hot orange. "You've killed half the bar—"

"Truth, but they mostly killed themselves."

"And you don't even know if this imbecile" she threw an arm out toward Grind's head, showering him with sparkle, "knows anything. He could be the villain. And don't get me started on Hitch. The spectre was borderline useless. He lasted all of thirty seconds before he was cast aside, and—"

"I admit, that was odd." Evanne chewed the inside of her cheek. "I don't know how it happened."

"Spectral dissonance generation of the subatomic layer of reality." Tarragon sighed. "It's a subset of quantum entanglement and leads to the banishment of entities incorrectly bound to this plane. Don't you know anything?"

Evanne thought that through, trying to find any words she understood. "Huh?"

"And to think *I'm* the one who failed her exams." The fairy blew a stray strand of hair from her face, which was entirely too fetching. Evanne felt herself blush and looked away. "We had a thing for it. A wossit."

"You don't remember?"

"I don't remember." The fairy looked like she wanted to shriek but was running low on fucks. "I don't think I ever knew. I know it's possible. I can almost feel how it's done, but..." She trailed off.

Evanne leaned back, rolling a shoulder. Something had snared it in the ruckus, and it would take a while to sort itself. *Think, Half-Made. She isn't angry. Tarragon's scared, and that's worse.* "You're mad because you thought I was going to die."

"You were going to die!"

"And you said we shouldn't do this."

"I totally advised against it." Tarragon crossed her arms, slumping. "No one listens to me."

"I listened." Evanne gusted a sigh. "I listened all the way. I just thought this," she gestured behind her to the destroyed inn, "would be cooler."

"And you'd get to be a hero."

"That, too." Evanne fetched her guitar from its rest against the bar. She turned a peg, plucked a string, then winced at the off-key note it made. "Ballads don't write themselves."

"That guitar's not going to be much good if you keep hitting people with it."

"Now you're a musician?" Evanne turned the instrument over. "Come to think of it, there's no instrument I've ever touched that would bear the strain I've put on this. The belly is sound. Fretboard without mark or bend." She sighted down it anyway. "It's just the strings."

"The strings were made by your people, not mine." Tarragon turned away.

"What's that supposed to mean?" Evanne bridled. "Is this a Vhemin thing?"

The fairy cringed, turning about, hands out. "No, love. Not that. I meant ... I meant where, or *when* I came from, we made things to last. Sometimes we were successful. Like with the guitar. Sometimes less so, like with the Skyforges. These days, all those wonders and the knack to making them are lost. It's all just ... *stuff*, now."

Evanne relaxed a shade. "I get you. We suck."

Tarragon gazed up at her. "As an aggregate? Everyone sucks. But *you* don't. Not really." She looked away. "I was so worried, Evanne. I was worried until I felt sick. That snotty little man tried to open a demon gate. There is nothing good on the other side, and lots of bad things. You can't..." She kicked the bar top.

"I can't defeat a demon lord?"

"No one can."

"I think someone can." Evanne thought of Mama's stories of the Tresward, and a red-haired Champion who left them to fight the demons on their own plane. Of her Holomancer lover, and the dragon they both called friend. Then she thought of Vertiline's story of how the other people left in Imshir all died in a final fight that left the city sundered. Stories told with the certainty of a lived experience, no fables to be found. *I do not think Geneve is alive. It is impossible to think it might be true, and yet we recovered her still-glowing sword.* She hedged. "Maybe."

"We tried and tried and failed. The world died. We lost a war we didn't know we were fighting." Tarragon slammed a tiny fist into her palm. "I was taught to hate people like you." She gave a nervous laugh. "Now we just need him," she nodded to Grind, "to wake, and then we can work out what's going on."

"We also need to find Hitch."

"Do we?" Tarragon fluttered her lashes. "Really?"

"Really, fairy." Evanne stood, slugged back the rest of her ale, and faced the ruined inn. "Man, we really destroyed this place. Not bad for a birthday party."

"Is it actually your birthday?"

"Actually is." Evanne hitched her belt. "I'm sixteen. Or was last week."

"Sixteen and one week is a very pivotal age." Tarragon landed on Evanne's shoulder, voice grave. "So many things happen between this week and next, you will think it a lifetime."

Evanne laughed. "Let's see if we can find the ghost."

"You could try calling him." Tarragon clambered into the folds of Evanne's hood that nestled about her neck. "You are a necromancer."

"Bard."

"Potato, potato."

Evanne sighed. *Worth a crack.* She closed her eyes, trying to feel where Hitch was. *I know you, Lance Corporal Eric Hitcherson. I know your real face, and the colour of your eyes. I know where the rest of you remains, while a shadow of you is here. Come to me.*

"What on earth are you doing?" At Hitch's voice, Evanne's eyes snapped open. There the spectre was, arms crossed, leaning forward as if to inspect Evanne as a circus curio.

"I was, uh." Evanne gave up. "Never mind. We need to get this asshole," she jerked a thumb at Grind, "talking."

"Excellent," Hitch said. "I love talking."

Evanne stood, hands on hips, surveying her handiwork. Grind was tethered to a chair, and that was the iffiest part of the whole opera. The man was a monster, huge in every way, and like as not to wake in a monstrous mood. She imagined rage, straining muscles, splintered wood, and a punch to the face.

I like my face well enough. He hits like a runaway cart. Let's avoid that.

So, she triple-checked his bonds. Stout rope from the stable, designed to hold a heavy load pulled by proud equines. The chair was from a guest room upstairs. It had the look of Feybrind manufacture, the wood smooth, oiled, and harder than iron. She could make out no nails in its construction, which was a mark of the People. *Good enough.*

They'd cleared out space around the man. By 'they', Evanne did all the work, being of both appropriate size *and* tangible, qualities that Tarragon and Hitch lacked, respectively. Tarragon supervised, claiming knowledge of knots—*'I'm a spy. Tying people up's what spies do'*—and Hitch muttered to himself while pacing. Evanne kept Grind's chair separate from anything he could shuffle toward as leverage or weapon. *Also good enough.*

The bucket was an inspired choice. Evanne found it in the stables, and it took a lot of swearing to get it in here, what with the icy sluice she'd filled it with. The cold here was bitter, the drizzle outside turned hard like diamond sleet, but it meant the bucket was filled with a fun surprise.

Her guitar leaned against a chair. The axe sang sweet enough now after she'd spent some time teasing the strings. She brushed back rust locks. "I think we're good."

"We're not good," Tarragon said. "But we're possibly not terrible."

"I think we're terrible." Hitch sighed, the air chilling a degree or two. "But we need to know what happened."

"Light the fire." Evanne waited as Tarragon sped into the laid hearth. The marvel of her glimmer made Evanne blush, because the fairy was so damn beautiful it hurt to look at sometimes. The little sprite ducked into the wood, hunching with fists clenched. She dimmed for a moment, then flared. The fire burst alight with a *woosh*, which Grind would appreciate after his surprise. Evanne threw back her cloak, bent her knees—*Uncle Day said to treat my back like glass, because it won't last forever*—and hefted the bucket. It felt cold even through the banded wood, but that was the point. She tipped it over Grind in one swift motion, stepping back to avoid the runoff.

The monster awoke with a scream, snake eyes wide and panicked. "Murder!"

Evanne leaned close, eyeballed him, then strode to her chair. She sat, picking up her guitar. "Good morning, sleepyhead. Did you have a nice rest?"

"Everything hurts," the monster growled. He tried to stand, noticed his bonds, and bared shark teeth. "This your doing?"

"Seems likely," Evanne admitted. "I would like to sing a song. It's my birthday, after all."

"No," Grind said. "No more music. Please. The last was..." He looked away.

"Stirring?" Tarragon hovered before the Vhemin.

The creature flexed in a valiant struggle against the rope, then sagged as much as his ropes would allow. "I've no skill with words. But what I felt wasn't good. I ... I *did* things. Do you see what I mean?"

The fairy fluttered back, her voice uncertain. "We'll ask the questions here."

"It's okay." Evanne stroked the strings, the guitar taking a moment to weep into the silence. "The question is good enough. Grind, you stand ... well, sit, really ... accused of treachery."

"War is not treachery." The monster lifted his chin.

"You waged no war," Hitch spat.

Evanne glanced at the spectre. "He can't hear you." She faced Grind. "My companion claims you brought ruin on those who sought only peace and trade."

"I said nothing of the sort," Hitch said.

"Your companion?" Grind blinked.

Evanne leaned forward. "I am Evanne the Half-Made. I stand between two worlds. My father was Vhemin, my mother human."

"Impossible," the monster growled.

"And yet." Evanne tickled the strings again. "My companions are the queen of a broken land, a guardsman in love with one he cannot touch, a soldier who fell while the world was yet whole, and," she glanced at Tarragon, "a fairy who's heart is purer than gold. I came here—"

"*Don't forget the tiger,*" Pakhet said from her massive puddle of cat by the fire. "*The tiger is the best part.*"

Grind screamed, flexed, broke the chair, spun, and ran, eyes never leaving Pakhet. He made it seven rushed steps before he went face-first into the wall, the impact making a noise like a drum. The wall shook, the ceiling shed dust, and the Vhemin slammed back onto the floor, out cold.

Evanne sighed, putting down the guitar. "We need to work on your entrances."

"*I've been here the whole time.*"

"It's hard to misplace a giant cat," Hitch said.

"She was *not* there the whole time," Tarragon said. "I was just in the fire. I didn't see her."

"That's because she is invisible sometimes." Evanne stood, faced Pakhet, and put her hands on hips. "Right?"

Pakhet raised her nose from where it nestled against a grey-striped tail. "*Close enough.*"

Evanne ran a hand through her hair, straightened her cloak, and flexed her back. "Come on, cat. You're helping me fill this damn bucket."

EVANNE DECIDED IT WAS BEST TO ROLL SOLO. PAKHET WOULD terrify Grind. Hitch would provide unwelcome commentary. Tarragon would flutter, which was fetching and equally distracting. So, Evanne husbanded them all away. The tiger was outside, ensuring no interruptions from thirsty townsfolk. The fairy and the spectre argued upstairs. It left Evanne and a comatose Grind, and a newly filled bucket of ice water, in the inn's common room. *Let's try again.*

Evanne tossed water on Grind, the monster jerking awake again. He blinked, wiped his eyes, then looked at his unbound hands, then to Evanne, and then convulsed as he tried to look everywhere at once for a giant tiger.

"Hush, now," Evanne said. "The bad kitty isn't here anymore."

"That thing is *real?*"

"*She* is real. She eats a lot, too." Evanne examined her nails, then looked back to Grind. "You're probably wondering why you're still alive."

"I am?"

"You are. And by association, you're wondering why you remain unbound, hands ready to choke the life from me." She leaned forward, arching her neck. "Go on. I dare you. I *double* dare you."

Grind glanced behind her, then to his hands, which had curled reflexively. With visible effort, he relaxed. "I don't think so."

She patted him on the cheek. "Good man. Now, about my birthday present."

"Your what now?"

"Birthday. Present." Evanne grabbed a chair, spun the back toward Grind, and straddled it. "See, I've saved you and yours from a painful life of deceit. You'll get an opportunity to make amends. You can save your souls. And all you've got to do is tell me what happened to Hollyhead."

The monster sighed. "I could wait, you know."

"Sure you could. Make sure the cat isn't here, then murder me from behind."

He seemed surprised. "You've thought this through. I admire that." He gave her a speculative up-and-down as if seeing her for the first time. "You and I could—"

"Ew," Evanne said. "Gross."

"I didn't—"

"Sure you did. You're old enough to be my grandfather, and you're too..." She trailed off.

"Awesome?"

"Male." Evanne favoured him with a smile anyway. "Don't look so downcast. It's a numbers game, Grind, and today you didn't roll the right number. Keep at it." She let the smile fall. "Let's stay focused, shall we? Hollyhead."

"We killed everyone," he growled. "That's what you want to hear, isn't it?"

"No. I knew that part." She pointed to the wall, and by inference the direction where the Raven and Heser the Cheg should be. "My crew—"

"The same crew that has a queen and a runty guard?"

"You remembered!" She beamed. "I thought we'd hit you too hard."

"Hit meself," he admitted. "Ran into the wall. I've never seen a cat like that."

"No one has, not for eight hundred years." She snapped her fingers in front of his face. "Hollyhead."

"Seemed a good idea at the time. Head over. Break some skulls, the Vhemin way. And we did. Murder. Pillage." He tugged an ear. "Got most of 'em, I think. A few stragglers we left to rebuild. Mistake, though."

"Don't tell me your flexible moral compass pointed you to a new true north." Evanne could see she'd lost him. "What happened next?"

"What do you mean, what happened?" He glared. "We killed—"

"The part where you realised it was wrong." Evanne kept her voice low, calm, a little husk in it. A Trick she knew would calm him, keep his anger low, banked for another day. "Where you realised you'd been tricked."

"How'd you know about that?" He glanced away, as if ashamed. "Grit said—"

"Grit was the goblin?"

Grind nodded. "Grit said there'd be riches."

"Grit lied." Evanne crossed her arms over the chair back. "Grit wanted souls for his magic. And you were the sucker to deliver. Oh, aye, I know the story. Vhemin don't get what's deserved." She slapped her chest. "I'm half Vhemin, and I see it well enough."

He gave her a baleful glare. "What's the other half? Camel?"

Evanne put her chin on her arms. "Human. It's the part, I think, that lets me talk to the dead, to sing songs that wake the world, and holds me back from killing people like you."

"But you killed Grit."

"What's it to you?" She sighed. "I didn't kill him. Tried to, and that's the truth, but his own summoning took him away." Evanne stood, parking the stool to the side. "Well, good day to you."

"Uh." He stood, but nice and slow. "That's it?"

"That's it." She nodded. "You told me what I needed to know. Hollyhead died because a bitter man wanted souls to make himself big."

"Wasn't his fault." Grind grabbed the hem of his stylish-yet-stained waistcoat, twisting it. "He was born different."

"So was I," Evanne said. "Taken me a long, winding road to get to the point where I realised it was a strength. A *power*, Grind. When people see my eyes or my teeth or get a look at my skin—don't get any ideas—all they see is something that's not enough of one thing to stop being another. They don't hear the songs I sing, right up until I make them. I started on this road after revenge. Now I'm here to fix the world." She brushed her cloak down. "Now you get to choose."

"Choose?"

"Choose," she nodded. "Grit held you in thrall. A magic that twisted your soul. Oh, aye, I know you were twisted enough to start with. Had to be something there to work with. But you didn't do it all yourself. And I broke that hold. Gave you back yourself. Now you get to choose what to do with the rest of your life."

He frowned, brows furrowing in more thought than he'd ever tried before. "What should I do?"

Evanne shrugged. "Up to you, innit? You get to walk out that door, greet the citizens of Wandermere as an equal, help 'em rebuild, and teach them not to fear. Or you get to stay here," she pointed above his faux throne, "with your make-believe kingdom, the hate gnawing at your gut, the bitterness twisting you. You learned might is the Vhemin way, but you can learn a new truth too." She turned to go.

"Wait." He touched her shoulder, and when she whirled, hand going to Fusillade, he held his hands up in surrender. "Maybe I could travel with you."

She eyed him up and down, then shook her head, but sadly. "Not this time. Your path is different to mine."

"Yeah? Why's that?"

Evanne strode to the inn door, barging it open, then looked over her shoulder. "Because your path lets you live. Mine ends in blood and terror." And that's how she left him, astonishment on his face, hands empty, relaxed by his side. No anger in his heart, just hope.

It's all anyone needs.

A Kingdom Falls.

A SONG RISES.

Evanne never wanted a throne. She never wanted to be a symbol. But war doesn't wait for permission.

Across the sea, the Feybrind are tearing themselves apart, their ancient pacts unraveling in blood and betrayal. Some would see Evanne as their savior. **Others would see her dead.** As rival factions rise, she's caught in the storm—**torn between the weight of her heritage and the cost of survival.**

Evanne's journey is far from over. The echoes of Heaven's Gate still haunt her steps, and across the sea, **a kingdom crumbles, an old enemy stirs, and a long-buried secret is about to be unearthed.**

The melody has shifted. **A new verse begins.**

Grab *Heartsong* now!

https://www.books2read.com/HeartsongFantasyAdventure

Because not all wars are fought with steel. Some are won in fire, others in deception and shadow. **But the best are fought with the song of the heart.**

About the Author

Richard Parry worked as a senior marketing manager in one of the world's top tech companies. It sounds cool, but it wasn't all cocaine parties. He lives in Wellington with the love of his life, Rae. They have two cats, Harry and Friday, who chase birds. The birds, who have the power of flight, don't seem to mind.

WAIT. DON'T GO!

Thanks for reading my book. If you enjoyed it, let's keep the party going:

📖 Join *Roll for Narrative* for reviews, storytelling breakdowns, and writing misadventures:

https://rollfornarrative.parrydox.com

✉ Lurk, judge, or say hi:

https://www.parrydox.com

P.S. An angel still gets its wings for every five-star review, but I'm told they're on backorder.

🅰 amazon.com/author/richard.parry

Ⓖ goodreads.com/richard_parry

BB bookbub.com/authors/richard-parry-6ffc3911-9f2c-43ef-8ab4-13dc-cd7f5874

▶ youtube.com/@parrydigm

🦋 bsky.app/profile/parrydox.com

in linkedin.com/in/therealrichardparry

Also by Richard Parry

DAWN'S WARDEN

The Three Faces of Fate

The Undefeated Throne

The Fury of the Betrayed

THE SPLINTERED LAND

Tomb of the Six

Blade of Glass

The Storm Within

Requiem's Justice

The Copper Bard

Heartsong

The Hymn of All

THE EZEROC WARS

The Ezeroc Wars universe is big (and growing!). Get the reading guide here: https://www.parrydox.com/ezeroc-wars-reading-guide/

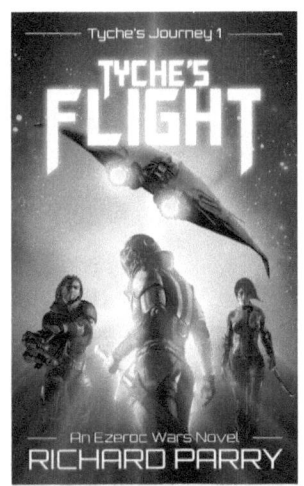

The Empire's Rogues: Volume 1

FUTURE FORFEIT

Not sure where to start? Get the reading guide here: https://www.parrydox.com/future-forfeit-reading-guide/

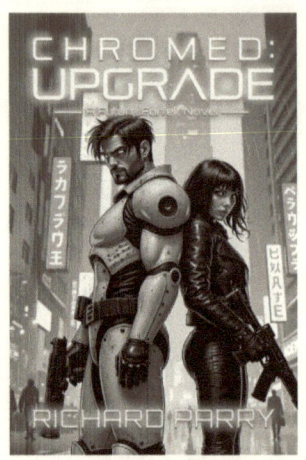

Chromed: Upgrade

Chromed: Rogue

Chromed: Restore

City Stories

Chromed: Consensus

Chromed: Delilah

Chromed: Meltdown

NIGHT'S CHAMPION